SILVER VALLEY UNIVERSITY

Secrets Revealed

ALISHA WILLIAMS

I'd like to dedicate this book to every sexual assault survivor. You are brave, you are strong, and I believe you. This book is for every person who didn't feel like they would be heard and was unable to get the justice they deserved. This book comes from a very personal part of my heart, and I feel your pain. You're not alone.

Author's Note

Please be advised. This is a reverse harem/why choose romance, meaning the heroine of this story does not have to pick between her love interests.

This book contains explicitly described sexual content and the excessive use of swear words. This is a dark-themed book and contains a lot of things that may trigger some readers. It is not for the faint of heart, so please read the trigger warnings before you dive in.

Please note that the court scenes in this book are not completely accurate and have been written as is for the flow of the story.

Trigger Warnings

This book contains survivors retelling their sexual assault stories in slight detail. This book, as well as this series, plays a big part around that tragic incident.
There is also a small amount of bullying that takes place. Please go into this book with an open mind. You have been warned.

Playlist

Come and Get Your Love by Redbone
Candy by Doja Cat
Smile by Avril Lavigne
Don't Stop The Music by Rihanna
Champagne and Sunshine by PLVTINUM and Tarro
Dip It Low by Christina Milian
Don't Dream It's Over by Crowded House

Chapter One

ELLIE

UNDERWATER. I feel like I'm underwater. There are voices chattering around me, but they all sound muffled. I can't make out who is saying what. My body feels heavy, like something below me has latched onto my foot and is slowly dragging me to the bottom of the ocean.

I try to focus. I can vaguely hear my name, but it sounds like it's far off into the distance, being swept away by the wind.

I'm in shock; I've gathered that much. My brain is shutting down, trying to block out everything that's just happened.

Why am I trying so hard to remember? I feel like it's not something I want to do. Maybe I'll stay here in the bliss of my own mind. It's quiet in here, nothing hurts.

Someone is holding me, but I don't know whom. Time has no meaning right now. I could have been standing here for hours or merely minutes, I can't tell you.

"Ellie." This voice sounds the strongest through the fog of my mind. I know that voice, I crave it.

My heart starts to pick up pace as my mind slowly registers who's calling for me. The others don't matter, only him.

"Ellie, baby, can you hear me?" Theo's voice is louder now,

clear as day. I take in a deep breath as if I'm finally able to get my head above water.

Reality crashes into me far too fast for my brain and body to comprehend. My arms shoot out, gripping onto Theo's with a grasp so strong, I must be digging my nails into his skin. But the look of pure fear on his face tells me he couldn't care less about that right now.

I've gone from numb to frantic in a matter of seconds, and I'm not sure how to process all this.

Everything comes flooding back. Sex with Chase, Tim cornering me in the backyard, all the sick and fucked up confessions.

A sob rips from my throat, partly because of everything that just happened, and partly because he admitted it. He said the words, that he raped me. A part of me all these years had wondered if it was my fault. Did I lead him on somehow? Did I give him signals that told him I wanted him as more than a friend? Did I really have too much to drink and somehow asked for it?

No, none of that is true. What happened is he drugged me, then raped me, and he just admitted it all.

This night is all too much for me to process. I feel like I'm spiraling out of control.

"Theo." His name comes out as a desperate plea as I throw myself into his arms.

His strong arms hold me tight to his body while I wrap my arms around him. My hands gather the fabric of his shirt as I cling to him like he's my saving grace. Because he is. Don't ask me to explain how I know this, but my soul just does. In this moment, I know he will save me from myself, from the memories of my past, and keep me from drowning like I almost did moments before.

"What happened?!" he demands of someone behind me, his voice filled with fury as he holds me closer. The pressure feels comforting, like a heavy security blanket.

Someone answers him, but I'm not paying attention. I put all my focus on my man, burying my face into his chest as I cry and breathe in his scent.

A name breaks through someone's maniacal ramblings. I think it's Val who's talking.

Brody. His name echoes around in my skull so loud, it's almost deafening.

Flashes of his fists pounding into the flesh of my attacker, like some dark avenging angel, appear in my mind. A wrath I've never seen him have before in all the years I've known him as he got lost in the violence of the act.

Other familiar faces make their way behind my eyes. Rain, Chase, and Jax. All with the look of shock, devastation, and anguish. They know now, they know everything; they heard it with their own ears right from the devil's mouth.

I'm not sure if I should be relieved that I don't have to say the words myself, ultimately reliving the worst night of my life, or afraid because that's one big secret I've been keeping that's now out in the world for everyone to hear.

They know. The people who once meant the whole world to me now know the truth of the night they misunderstood so gravely.

I can't worry about that right now. All that matters is him, Theo, and being surrounded by his love, his warmth, and his support. Everything else can wait.

Wait...if Theo is here, who's watching Lilly?

"Talk to me," Theo's voice demands desperately.

My lips try to form the words. "Lilly," I gasp.

"She's fine. She's at home with my mom, sweet girl," he reassures me.

Good, she's safe.

My eyes feel heavy and my cries slow as my knees buckle beneath me.

Your body and mind have a breaking point, no matter how strong you are or how hard you fight. And this is mine. I hear my name one last time before everything goes silent, the inky black of my mind swallowing me up entirely.

Chapter Two

THEO

VAL IS TOO hysterical right now so I'm not able to understand much of anything she's saying. Getting frustrated on top of being worried sick about my girlfriend who is passed out in my arms, I look to one of Ellie's other friends in hope that I can get some answers.

"Can you please tell me what you know?" I ask Tabitha as I try to stay calm.

Her eyes are red from crying, but she seems to be the most calm out of the three.

"Well—" she starts to answer but gets cut off by someone.

"Is she okay?" Chase asks, his eyes wild with fear as he storms into the backyard followed by Rain. "We got hauled out to the front yard to talk to the police. They're still talking to Jax. Fucking assholes, taking me away from my girl."

His words have me holding Ellie tighter to my chest. "Just because you two had a moment doesn't make her *your* girl. You may not have done the worst of the bullshit she had to endure, but you were a bystander. It's gonna take a hell of a lot more than some sweet words and orgasms before you have the right to call her that," I growl.

5

He narrows his eyes. "You know about that? It's only been a few hours."

"Here's something you need to know before anything else happens. Ellie tells me *everything*. Especially if it's something that could affect our relationship. We are very open and have amazing communication with each other. Now, can someone please, for *fuck's sake*, tell me why my girlfriend was out of her damn mind with grief?!"

I'm trying to keep it together, I really am, but seeing Ellie so broken is breaking me inside. I need to know what happened so I can help her in the best way possible. I can't if I don't know what's going on, and I don't want to force her to talk about anything she's not comfortable with.

"What's going on is that sack of vile shit Brody just pummeled with his fists like a meat tenderizer admitted some really fucked up stuff and was planning on doing it again." Chase is fuming and, by the way Rain is staring at Ellie with tears streaming down her face, I can tell they now know what really happened the night of their graduation.

"He was here?" I seethe. How fucking dare that fucking piece of shit come near my girl again.

"We didn't know," Rain says, her voice cracking. "We didn't know he did that to her."

Narrowing my eyes, I glare at her with so much anger. "Of course you didn't because you jumped to conclusions. You believed that dick of a best friend over the love of your life and assumed she betrayed you. But it was *you* who betrayed *her*. She needed you, your love, your support, and your fucking strength. Instead, she got left in that room with those sick fucks. God knows if they did more to her while she was passed out!" I spit.

Rain starts to cry harder while Chase's anger dies down, replaced with devastation.

"Let me hold her, please," Chase begs.

"No." I take a step back. "I need to get her home."

"Let us come with you?" he asks.

I can't. Lilly is at my place, but Ellie's apartment is a full on dead giveaway that a child is living there. I know Ellie is going to tell them about her soon, but they can't find out like this.

"When she wakes up, I'll talk to her. I'm assuming because of Brody's reaction, she knows you're all aware of enough about what happened? It's not my story, not my trauma. This conversation is done until she can talk to you herself."

"Fine," Chase says, running his hands over his face. "That fucker is lucky the cops came because the moment Brody was done with him, I was gonna take my turn." His anger starts to bubble up again. "Good thing we have the whole thing on tape."

That gets my attention. "You have *what* on tape?"

"Tim's confession. All of it. His admission to what happened that night, and his plans to do it again."

"Email it to me," I quickly say, ideas forming in my mind.

"What? Why?" he asks, his brows furrowing in confusion.

"Because, with that video, if Ellie chooses to press charges for this, as well as what happened in the past, then that video could be enough to put him behind bars. It's worth consulting a lawyer if Ellie decides to."

"He deserves death, not jail!" Chase barks, raising his voice. "And I'd really like to be the one to do the honors."

My eyes scan the backyard for any cops. "Watch what you say," I warn. "The cops are still on the property, and unless you want to land yourself in jail right alongside your friend, I'd keep my mouth shut."

Ellie stirs in my arms, still asleep, but she lets out a whimper as she grabs my shirt that breaks my heart.

Tears prick my eyes as I think about all the crap my girl had to deal with tonight. "I need to get her home. This night has been too much for her. When she wakes up and is in the right mindset, I'll talk to her and see where she stands with you all. Don't call and bug her. Give her time and space. This is a big deal, and it's something she's had to live with for a long time."

"I wish she would've told us... Even if it was only when she came back here," Chase says, his eyes fixed on Ellie.

"She was, she was gonna tell you everything. But you all descended on her like a pack of hungry wolves before she even had a chance. That's something you're all gonna have to make up for."

"We will," Rain sniffs. "I plan on doing everything in my power to make it up to her. I wish she knew how much I love her." She looks so broken. Part of me feels bad, but also, she deserves this. They all deserve to feel a little pain. Nothing will even compare to what Ellie's been through.

"I know you and Ellie are together, and you're not going anywhere..." Chase starts.

"Damn right I'm not," I growl.

"But I have her back now too. I'm okay with sharing. It's never been an issue, and I'm not letting her get away again. I will show her why she should give me another chance. I will spend every day loving her, caring for her, and proving it to her. But I'm not going anywhere either." Fuck, he's stubborn.

"You will do what Ellie is comfortable with. If she chooses not to give you another chance after all, you will respect that, or we will have a problem," I warn him.

He nods, then takes a few steps closer. He looks down at Ellie, who lets out a sleepy whimper. "I love you, Ellie Belly." He leans down and places a lingering kiss to her forehead before moving to stand next to Rain, pulling his crying best friend into his arms.

"I'll update you ladies on how she's doing, okay?" I tell the girls. They all nod, and I take off through the house with my heart and soul in my arms.

You're almost home, Theo. Get her tucked in, make sure she's okay, then you can take a moment to break. Then, you're going to suck it up and be strong for your woman because she's the one this is happening to.

"Sir?" A police officer stops next to the car as I'm buckling Ellie into the front seat. He looks at her with a skeptical look.

"She's not drunk. She just went through a really rough night. I'm her boyfriend," I reassure him.

"Did she happen to see anything regarding the fight?" he asks.

"It's complicated, but I'll have her call you to answer any questions you might have for her when she's up for it," I tell him.

"Thank you. Please see to it that you do." He nods as he says, "Have a safe night," and gives me his card before heading back to his car.

The whole car ride home, I'm shaking, biting the inside of my cheek as I hold back all the anger coursing through my body. I want to go to whatever hospital they brought that fucker to and finish what Brody started. But I can't because she needs me, and that would be selfish.

My knuckles are ghostly white as I grip the steering wheel so hard, I'm surprised it doesn't break.

She doesn't wake in the car or as I carry her up to her apartment. When we get to our floor, I see my apartment door open. My mom sticks her head out, her face morphing into concern as she sees Ellie in my arms. Saying nothing, I shake my head, letting her know that we can't have that discussion right now.

She follows me silently to Ellie's door, taking the keys from my hands. She unlocks it and before I enter, she places her hand on my arm. "I love you, Theo," she says, her face sullen. "I hope she's okay."

"She will be. I just hope someday she can go a week without life treating her so unfairly," I say, my voice sounding so defeated.

"You're doing amazing. She's lucky to have you."

"I'm the lucky one, Mom," I insist.

She looks down at Ellie and smiles. "That you are."

I get Ellie into her bed, careful not to jostle her too much. I don't take her clothes off because we have not yet discussed if that's something she's comfortable with me doing. I do, however, take off her shoes and tuck her into bed.

When I know she's safe and won't wake up, I head into the kitchen. My body is heavy and my mind is a jumbled web of thoughts and feelings.

I was here while she was at that party having to face her attacker alone. That thought sends a sinking feeling to the pit of my stomach.

He was planning to do it again? If he ended up following through with that plan, I'd be in jail right now on a murder charge. Hell, if it wasn't for the two little ones who own parts of my heart, sleeping just down the hall, I'd be grabbing my keys and going on a witch hunt right now.

But I can't. I have too much to lose, and I'm just so fucking grateful that he didn't hurt her again.

And as much as I hate Brody for everything he's done to Ellie the past few months, I'm glad he was there to stop the sick fucker's plans.

The only thing keeping me from my breaking right alongside her is knowing that Tim didn't succeed.

Checking my phone, I see that Chase sent me the video proof of Tim's admission. I immediately download it, saving it onto my phone. My finger hovers over the play button for a moment before I click the screen off, making it go black. Tossing my phone onto the countertop, I take my glasses off and put them down before letting out an exhausted sigh as I scrub my eyes with the heels of my hands.

So many emotions are running through my mind and my brain is just fried right now.

Moving over to the cupboard, I grab a glass before searching above the fridge to grab a bottle of vodka.

Cracking open the new bottle, I pour myself a shot and take a drink of it straight. I wince as the liquid burns. It tastes like shit.

I'm done with my first glass when someone knocks on the door, snapping me out of my daydream state. I look at the empty glass, then the bottle beside me, and shake my head. I can't be getting drunk, not at a time like this. I wouldn't be helping anyone in that state.

Putting the cup in the sink and the bottle away, I answer the front door.

"Hello, son," my dad greets me when I open the door.

"Dad," I say, stepping back to let him in.

"Your mother wanted me to check on you. Lilly had a nightmare so she and Toby are reading her a book to help her go back to sleep."

"Is she okay?" I hate the idea of Lilly being upset.

"Oh, she's fine," he says, waving his hand dismissively. "Something about losing her special stuffed dog. But she stopped crying when she realized it was all a dream, and the dog was in her arms."

I let out a sigh of relief. "Good." I nod, moving to take a seat on the couch.

"How are you doing?" Dad asks as he sits next to me.

"Worried. Stressed. Angry."

"There's been a lot of drama in her life the past few months. I don't mean to step on anyone's toes, but are you sure it's worth all this? Being with her, I mean. She's a wonderful lady, and I haven't seen you this happy in years, but when will you guys just get to live your lives?"

His words just piss me off more. I love my dad, but he's not as involved in my life as my mom. "Is it worth it? Is having the most beautiful, strong, caring, and loving woman I could ever ask for, *worth* it? Is a woman who would give up everything to make sure her daughter has everything she needs, *worth* it? I'm gonna say this once. She is worth every single moment of it." I'm getting worked up, the alcohol making my brain a little fuzzy.

"I know, but—"

"No!" I almost shout. "No buts. Ellie is my world, right alongside Toby. She and Lilly both are. They are my family. This isn't my pain, my past, or my trauma, but it does belong to the woman who owns every inch of me. I will stand by her side and support her in everything she does, in everything that happens in her life. All of this is out of her control. What kind of man would I be to leave the love of my life because the universe keeps shitting on her?"

"Okay, okay," my dad says, raising his hands in a defensive manner.

"No, it's not okay. Would you leave Mom if a ton of horrible things were happening to her that she had no hand in?"

He shakes his head. "Never."

"Exactly. Mom is your everything, and Ellie is mine."

"Alright. I understand. I'm sorry I said anything."

I feel bad for snapping at him, but I don't want anyone thinking, for even a moment, that I would *ever* up and leave Ellie because this is too tough.

We sit and talk about what's going on in his life, and how the restaurant is doing while steering the conversation to a pleasant topic.

When he leaves, I lock up, shut all the lights off, and head to Ellie's room. She's whimpering in her sleep, and my heart breaks for her. I wish I could take away her pain. If I could, I would in a heartbeat. After stripping down to my boxers, I climb into bed next to Ellie and pull her into my arms, holding her close to my body. Her whimpers stop, and she lets out the smallest sigh as she snuggles into me.

Ellie is worth it, and always will be.

Chapter Three

ELLIE

I WAKE up to the smell of fried eggs teasing my nose, and my belly rumbles in approval. Stretching out the night kinks, I lie in bed, waiting for my mind and body to wake up a little bit more.

Come and Get Your Love by Redbone plays in the kitchen, and I smile knowing it's one of Theo's favorite songs. He's so sweet to be making me breakfast.

But the smile slips from my lips as my mind slowly starts to piece everything together. How did I get home? When did I see Theo last night?

With my brows furrowed, I concentrate on the last thing I can remember from last night. My cheeks heat as I remember what Chase and I did.

The things he said and the song he sang had my mind a mess. But then I remembered, I called Theo and told him everything. He didn't seem mad because I did what he asked, I told him right away if anything happened between Chase and I.

Then I remember going back out to the party and dancing with my friends.

My eyes widen and my stomach drops as I recall the person who started dancing with me. I thought it was Chase at first, but I was oh, so very *wrong*.

My head starts to pound as I remember everything including Brody attacking Tim. My heart does this little weird flutter at the fact that Brody defended me. He was outraged by the things Tim said he wanted to do and kept it from happening.

But the feeling is short-lived because where was he the first time? When it was actually happening to me, he did nothing, believed the worst, and left me there like I was insignificant.

My belly rumbles again, and as much as the events of last night sicken me, it doesn't take away my need for Theo's cooking.

Stepping into the kitchen, my smile finds its way back onto my lips as I watch my sexy man dance around the island in nothing but his boxers and an apron. "Morning," I call out.

Theo spins around, a pan in one hand and a spatula in the other. He looks taken by surprise, but quickly gives me a sweet smile. "Good morning, sweetheart."

He puts everything down and turns off the stove before pulling me into his arms, placing a soft sweet kiss on my lips. "How are you feeling?" His eyes search my face as concern laces his.

"Tired, but I think it's more emotional than physical. I'm also hungry for your amazing cooking," I say, eyeing up the plate of bacon and eggs.

He lets out a husky chuckle that sends a tingle over my skin. "Anything you want, my love. I made it all for you." He kisses the top of my head before grabbing two plates and bringing them over to the table. He puts them down and takes a seat.

"I thought you said you made it *all* for me," I tease, getting a raised brow and a half grin from him.

"There are pancakes over there if you're still hungry." He nods his head behind me.

"I think this may be enough. My eyes are bigger than my gut, but I think this time, I'll be eating everything on my plate." I pick up a piece of bacon and take a bite, moaning as the flavor hits my tongue, and my eyes roll back slightly.

"Sweet girl, you're not playing fair," Theo growls, making my eyes flutter open to look at him.

"How so?" I ask.

"You can't make noises like that. It makes me wanna throw you over my shoulder, take you to that couch, and fuck you until you're screaming my name." His eyes are glazed with lust like he would rather eat *me* than the food before him.

Just to be a little brat, I lean back and look under the table. He wasn't lying. His cock is hard and tented in his boxers. Suddenly, I'm craving something more than just bacon and eggs.

"Love." His voice is a warning, but it sends a thrill through me.

"Sorry," I say, straightening up again as I take a bite of my eggs.

"No, you're not," he says, sounding amused.

A massive grin takes over my face. "No, I'm not."

He rolls his eyes, but his smile is almost as big as mine.

"Thank you," I say. I feel bad for ruining this moment, but it needs to be said. "For coming to get me and bringing me home last night."

His face softens. "You know I'm always here for you, right?" I nod as he continues, "Do you want to talk about it?"

Do I? Keeping my feelings bottled up and away from him doesn't help anyone. And Theo is always so understanding and easy to talk to.

"First, I wanna apologize about Chase. It kind of just... happened. I didn't plan it." I bite my lip, waiting for him to respond.

"You have nothing to be sorry for. It's your body. You have the right to do whatever you want with it and with whomever you want. You did as I asked and told me about it; you didn't lie or keep secrets. You haven't lied about how you feel about him, and you know where I stand. Everything else is in your court. If you choose to take this further with him and give him a chance to prove he's worthy of you, then I'm okay with that. I love you, Ellie, and I just want you to be happy."

My eyes prick with tears because I will never not be surprised at how amazing this man is. And I can tell he means it too; he's not just telling me what he thinks I want to hear.

"I want you to be happy too, Theo. This isn't *just* about me. You're in this relationship too."

"I know." He takes my hand in this, rubbing his thumb on the top. "And I am happy. Toby, you, and Lilly make me the happiest I've ever been. If we add more people to our lives, it doesn't take away what we already have, and what we've built."

"You're amazing, you know that?" I remind him.

"And so are you. If you don't mind me asking, what comes next?" he asks.

That's a wonderful question, isn't it? *What* does *come next?*

"Well, first, I need to talk to Rain and the guys about what they now know. I'd like to hear their thoughts. Then I need to find out how they've reacted to all of that, and see when it's a good time to bring up Lilly. I know I have to tell them. There's no more putting that off. I just don't know how they will respond."

"I'll be there with you if you need someone at your side," he offers.

"Thank you, but I think until all this is out in the open, it would be best if I talked to them myself. I just need a few days. School is starting back up, and my mind is a jumbled mess right now."

"Of course, love. You take all the time that you need. But maybe let the girls know you're okay? They've been blowing up my phone. Val is being the drama queen she always is, and is convinced you're dead because I won't tell her the truth." He grins, making me snort out a laugh.

"Sounds like Val." I shake my head.

"Let me know if I'm overstepping, but I wanted to let you know something that could help you put Tim behind bars," Theo says, making my smile fall yet again. Today is turning out to be a fucking emotional rollercoaster. *And I'd like to get off now.*

"Theo, I told you. As much as I would love to see that sick man behind bars, there's no evidence to prove he raped me. And just because Rain and the guys heard him admit it, it's still their word against his." Just thinking about Tim makes me want to take a shower and get this gross feeling off of me.

"That's the thing though, we have proof now," he says, a hopeful look forming on his handsome face.

My heart skips a beat. "What do you mean?"

"They recorded the whole thing. I'm not sure why they were recording in the first place, but they happened to get everything on tape, including Tim confessing what he did on graduation night." Theo's face fills with rage. "And what he was planning on doing again last night."

"They did?" My voice is no more than a disbelieving whisper.

"Yes, baby, and I have the video saved. If you choose to press charges, I think there is enough to put him behind bars where he belongs."

Looking away, I stare out the window, my eyes fixated on the little robin sitting on the windowsill as I take in this new information. This could work; this could help my case. But do I want to put myself through a whole legal case? I'd have to relive that night. I'd have to talk, out loud, to a judge and jury, telling them about the night that broke my soul.

But if I don't, can I live with myself if he goes out into the world and rapes another girl? I didn't speak up back then, and the idea of him doing what he did to other women all these years makes me sick to my stomach. I'm no longer hungry for the food in front of me.

Pushing my plate of food away, I look to Theo. "Alright. I'll contact my dad and see if he knows any good lawyers. I'm not sure how I'm going to pay for one, but I know I won't be able to live with myself if I don't at least try."

"I'll help out any way I can," he says, pulling my chair over to him before hauling me onto his lap. I snuggle into him, feeling safe and protected as always. He kisses the top of my head, and we stay like this for a little while before I get up to shower. After I'm done, I call the girls, assuring them that I'm fine, or at least, I will be. I call Cooper next to tell him the same thing.

There is one text message from Chase that says, *I love you, Ellie Belly, and I'm here when you're ready. We all are.* And that's all he or the others have said to me.

But at least this time, it's something positive and not a hateful, soul-crushing voicemail from Brody.

"Mama!" Lilly's sweet, little voice cheers when she sees me as she enters from the front door.

"Lillypad," I almost sob, not realizing how much I needed my little girl until this very moment. Scooping her up, I hug her tight to my body as her little arms wrap around my neck.

"Missed you, Mama," she says, placing a wet kiss on my cheek.

"I missed you too, bug." I pepper kisses all over her little face, and she starts to giggle, filling my heart with so much love.

"Mama crying?" she asks, her hands rubbing the falling tears on my face. "Mama sad?"

"No." I shake my head. "I'm happy because I have my baby girl home."

It's hard to stay mad, to be sad, or to think about anything bad in the world when I have the light of my life with me. Lilly is the reason I keep on going every day, the reason I strive to do better, and to give her the best life she deserves.

Everything else can wait for tomorrow or the next day. Right now, I'm going to enjoy the rest of my weekend with my family, watch movies, and just feel the love of these three humans who own a big part of my heart.

Chapter Four

BRODY

"MR. CREED, you're free to go," one of the officers says as he takes out his keys from his pocket and unlocks the cell door.

I sit there for a moment, wondering how I'm able to leave when bail was five grand. Jax came last night to try to convince me to let him put up the bail, or go to my dad and get the money, but I told him no. I didn't want help getting out of here and I didn't want my dad getting involved. I have the money to pay myself, but apparently, they don't let inmates do that. Something about too many repeat offenders using this place as a hotel bullshit.

Honestly though, spending the weekend here was probably a good idea because if I got out, I would have gone straight to the hospital, found that scumbag, and finished what I started.

The broken look in Jax's eyes right before he left the precinct hurt like a punch to the gut. On top of seeing the fear in Ellie's eyes as Tim told her what he had planned for her that night, and knowing that he's already done it to her. It was like someone had shoved their hand into my chest, ripped my heart out, and crushed it before my eyes, turning it to dust.

"Brody Creed, your bail has been dismissed, get your ass up and out of my station," the officer repeats himself, sounding annoyed. Taking one last look at the drunk homeless man who's been my cellmate this past weekend, I get up and follow the officer out.

The downside of spending the night here was the hard bench, listening to other people bitch and complain, and the homeless man that smelled like piss and shit. It's sad, really, and makes me happy for everything I have, like a house to live in and food to eat.

"Who paid for it?" I ask, standing at the front counter as another officer hands me a bag with everything I had on me when they arrested me.

"Paid what?" the officer asks.

"My bail," I say, cocking a brow.

"That would be me." A voice I know all too well for my liking comes from behind me, making my blood start to boil in an instant. She's the last person I want to see right now. Hell, she's the last person I'd ever want to see.

"What the fuck are you doing here?" I ask, done with this whole conversation before it's even started.

"That's no way to talk to your mom," she huffs, crossing her arms, and making her boobs push up so that they're practically falling out of her dress.

"How many times do I have to tell you? You might have given birth to me, but you're no mother of mine." I turn away from her, grabbing the bag of my items, slipping my phone and wallet into my jeans pocket, before turning back to her. "Also, shouldn't you be in the back, locked up with all the other prostitutes?" I ask, looking her up and down. She may be in a thousand dollar dress right now, but she wears it like a street walker.

Her eyes widen as she lets out an exasperated gasp. "You ungrateful little punk!" she sneers. "I got them to waive your bail and this is how you thank me, by insulting me?!"

"Maggie, sweetheart, is everything okay here?" a tall man with salt-and-pepper hair in a suit with a police badge that reads *Police Commissioner* asks as he wraps his arm around my mother's shoulders.

I let out a humorless laugh. "Well, this makes so much sense."

I look up at the cop, knowing what I'm about to say could land me back in that cell, but I say it anyway because I'm over this bullshit. "Hi, I'm the son of the married woman you're fucking. Thanks for letting me out of that shithole you call a holding cell, but I can assure you, whatever she had to do to get me out was all wasted. Well, I'm sure you enjoyed it just as well, but I'll be paying the bail money." I look at my mother giving her a disgusted look. "I don't want anything from you, and I don't need you coming back later telling me I owe you for this. How about you do Dad a favor and divorce him so you can at least be your whorish self as a single woman."

My mother starts to curse me out, but I ignore it. "I'll be back with the cash soon. When's my court date?"

The woman looks at the hot mess behind me as the commissioner attempts to calm my mother down. "Umm..." she says looking back at me, then over at the computer. "March 5th."

"Awesome, almost two months away," I mutter to myself. At least it's enough time for my lawyer to build some kind of case against the fucker. He may have money to try and get this swept under the rug, and he may win with my case, but I'm going to make it known why I did what I did. I hope Ellie decides to press charges and use that video to get his ass. We've just given her a golden ticket, and she better use it. She would be foolish not to.

Paying the bail myself after some negotiating, considering I'm no longer an inmate, I leave my mother behind as I leave the station. I don't want to go home right now because then I'd have to face Jax and the others. I'm not ready to talk about what we found out. I'm not ready for them to rip me a new asshole because I'm the reason why all of this happened.

I left Ellie in that room to be raped. *I* told the others she was a cheating whore, and *I* spent years reminding them of that. I'm a fucking piece of shit.

They spent years being in pain because they thought the love of their lives betrayed them in one of the worst ways, and this whole time she was actually raped; *fucking raped.*

Just thinking about it has me ready to break into a fit of rage and destroy anything in my path. It's all I'm good for, right? I fucking ruin everything I touch.

She's better off without me. They all are.

But they don't deserve to be without her anymore. I will do everything I can to help them win her back. For them to prove to her that they are worth a second chance because none of this was their fault, only mine. I'm the one who was too fucked up and damaged by the bitch at the station to realize that not every woman is like her.

I should have trusted that Ellie loved us enough to never do what my first thought was. I should have looked closer.

The more I think about it, that look in her eyes that I was so dead set on being a desperate need for him, was really fear. Pure terror. I saw what I wanted to see and not the truth for what it was.

Fuck!

I stop at the trash can on the street and puke up everything from the past few days, unable to keep anything in as my mind plays out all the things he probably did to her. How petrified she was at that moment.

And the pure, utter betrayal she felt when I turned all of her lovers against her.

We should have been there for her, holding her, caring for her, making everything okay, but we weren't. Because of me, she had to deal with this all alone.

I failed her, and I failed the others. All the pain from the past few years, I deserved it, but they didn't. I will make this right for them if it's the last thing I do.

I've been mindlessly walking for a while now. It was noon when I got released, but when I check my phone now, it says five pm.

Looking around, I see a corner store, liquor store, a tattoo shop, and a laundromat. I've never been to this part of Spring Meadows before. When we come here, it's normally for the club, to eat, or for the mall.

Needing something to eat, I check to see if there are any cars coming before crossing the street to the corner store. The little bell on the door dings as I enter. A song I've never heard before is playing, and as I look around, I can see there's not much to this place.

Browsing the few aisles here, I grab a bag of chips, a bottle of water, and a sandwich from the cooler. I pray that I don't get sick from eating this. When I decide that there is nothing else I want, I bring everything to the front.

"Hi," the cashier says.

"Hi," I grunt, not bothering to look at her as I place everything on top of the counter.

"I haven't seen you around here before." Her voice sounds flirty, and when I look up, I can see interest in her eyes as she looks me over. She's not bad to look at. Long black hair and bright blue eyes. But she's not Ellie. And, because of that, I have no interest in her in the way I'm sure she's hoping for.

"Because I'm not from around here," I say, placing a twenty on the counter.

She sees my bandaged hand. "What happened there?"

"Someone touched something that was mine. I don't like people touching my things, so now he's in the hospital with a broken face," I say casually, giving her a smile with no life in it.

I thought it might scare her from continuing to flirt, but the look in her eyes only seems to intensify. Awesome, another girl who loves a bad boy.

"Actually, can I get a pack of Marlboros too?" I ask, tossing down another twenty. I'm not a smoker, but if there was a day to start, I think today is that day.

17

"Sure. Can I see some ID please?" she asks, grabbing the pack from the back wall.

Grabbing my wallet out of my pocket, I open it to show her my ID. She looks it over and her eyes widen.

"You're Brody Creed?" she asks with a hint of awe in her voice. Fuck's sake.

"Yeah, that's what my ID says," I sigh, just wanting to grab my shit and leave.

"My friends and I went to your last football game. You guys did amazing. Of course you won too; you always do." That's a lie. We lose sometimes, but it's rare.

"Thanks, can I just get my change? I gotta get going," I say, putting my wallet away.

"Of course," she says and grabs a bag.

I tap my foot in irritation as she takes her time putting everything in the fucking bag while staring at me like I'm some kind of superstar.

"Here you go," she says, handing me the bag. *Finally.* "Hopefully, I'll see you soon."

I just give her a nod, grabbing the bag from her with more force than is needed, and get the hell out of there.

My stomach rumbles, demanding I give it something, so I reach in the bag and grab the sandwich and the receipt by mistake. Just as I'm about to put it back into the bag, I see writing on the back of it.

What the hell?

There's a phone number and under it says, 'Call me if you're looking for some fun. I'm down for ANYTHING.'

"Desperate isn't attractive," I grumble as I crumple the receipt and toss it in the trash. Looking back toward the store, I can see that she saw me toss away her number through the window. She pouts, looking offended, but I just flip her off because I've had a shitty fucking weekend, and the last thing I need is some chick trying to get into my pants.

I sit on the curb, eating my sandwich as I replay what Tim

said over and over. How he was bragging about raping Ellie and how he planned on doing the same thing again, knowing she had no one who would come looking for her just like before. No one to help her.

Maybe my mom was right. I'm nothing, useless, and I only fuck up people's lives.

Looking at the bottle of water in the bag, I know that just water isn't going to be enough; I need something stronger.

Getting up, I dust off my shorts before going next door to the liquor store. I head right for the whiskey and grab a bottle of trusty old Jack Daniel's.

After I pay, I start to walk down the street when I turn the corner and find a dingy motel. Knowing I don't want to go back to the apartment to deal with all the bullshit, I head over to see if they have any vacancies.

"Can I get a room for one?" I ask the creepy man at the front desk.

"Sure can. You want that on card or cash?" he grins at me.

"Card."

"Got yourself a pretty lady you wanna play around with for the night? I bet you do. All the young men find themselves here at some point."

"No," I growl. "I want to take this bottle, drink it until I pass the fuck out, and forget about all the bullshit going on in my life. So, if you don't mind, just ring me up and give me the room key."

He gives me a sour look as he takes my card. Then he presses a few keys on the keyboard before handing me back my card and a room key.

"Room sixteen. Enjoy," he says blandly.

Shaking my head, I take the things and head back outside to find the room. As I walk down the row of doors, I hear TVs blasting, people shouting, and as I reach my room, I find I'm next to the people who are having daytime sex and screaming like they are in a porno. *Just fucking great.*

Entering the room, I already regret it. The place looks like something out of the sixties. The tacky wallpaper is peeling in the corner, there are stains on the carpet, and the place smells musty. Checking the bedsheets, I'm surprised to find them clean and the bed well-made. Good, because there's no way I'm sleeping on nasty bedding.

Tossing the bag on the bed, I go to the bathroom, surprised, yet again, when I see clean towels sitting on the worn-down counter.

"Fuck it," I sigh, turning on the shower and stripping down. I wash myself quickly before throwing my dirty clothes back on. It's not much, but at least my body and hair are clean.

Grabbing the bottle of Jack, I head out the side door to my room and realize I'm right by the beach. I go back into my room then grab my key, phone, and wallet before heading down to the water.

For the next few hours, I sit on the sand and drink, remembering every shitty thing that has happened in my life.

Then my mind drifts to *her*. Ellie was my first love, still is. She was the first and only girlfriend I've ever had. She chose me to lose her virginity to. I remember being so fucking happy that I got the honor to not only have her be my first, but to be hers as well.

"I didn't deserve her!" I shout to the seagull who's picking at a dead fish a few feet away from me. "It should have been Jax or Chase." My words are a slur.

The bird squawks back at me in agreement.

"Glad to see we're on the same page." I nod, taking a swig from the bottle, only to be disappointed when I find it's empty. "Nothing good happens to me," I growl, tossing the bottle and almost hitting the bird. "Sorry, little dude." He flaps his wings with a few squawks before diving back into the nasty fish.

"But I love her." I sigh, falling back into the sand. "I love her so much it hurts. I wish I was good enough for her. I wish I was the man she needed me to be."

I stare up at the stars and remember that night that changed everything for the better between us.

We had a picnic in the meadow close to my house. I packed a bunch of her favorite foods, and we just sat and talked for hours. My face and stomach hurt from smiling and laughing so much.

We started to make out and one thing led to another. It was amazing, a little awkward at first, but it was perfect. And the fact that I actually made her cum was a huge boost to my ego.

"You know what?" I ask, sitting up and finding the bird still there. "I should show her how much she means to me. Even if I don't get to have her, she should still know."

Another bird swoops down and starts to peck at the fish, making Gully—that's his name, by the way—pissed. They start to scream at each other as the new dude tries to steal my little buddy's supper.

"Hey, fuck face!" I shout at the bird. "Fuck off." Getting up, I kick sand to scare him off, but they both end up flying away. "Well, now who do I talk to?" I grumble.

Turning around, I see a big neon sign that says, 'Skull and Bones Tattoo'.

"Bingo!" My face lights up, and I run toward the store, almost tripping over the sand a few times.

"What are you doing back?" the girl from before snarks.

"None of your fucking business," I sing-song back to her as I go over to the ATM. It has a pretty big limit, but I know the tattoo costs more than that, and I'll probably have to bribe them because I'm kind of drunk. So I take out as much as I can on a few of my cards. Once all the money is in my hand, I clutch onto it and head out of the store, snorting out a laugh at how the girl's eyes are bugging out of her head, clearly seeing all the cash.

I jog next door just as the shop's lights start to go out. "Hello!" I shout, banging on the window until someone opens the door.

"We're closed," a man dripping in ink says, unlocking the door.

"I need a tattoo, please. It's urgent," I say, my voice firm.

"What's so urgent about getting a tattoo at ten pm?" he asks, cocking a brow.

"Look, man, I fucked up with the love of my life. I'll never get her back, but I need to show her how much she means to me."

"You smell like you've been drinking. I can't tattoo you anyways."

"Thought you might say that." I grin, then shove the giant wad of money in his face. "Would ten grand change your mind?"

He stares at it for a few seconds like he's weighing the pros and cons. Then he lets out a defeated sigh and looks behind me, making sure no one is around, before opening the door wider.

"Fucking rich kids," he mutters. "Alright, what did you have in mind?"

Chapter Five

JAX

TURNING THE ENGINE OFF, I look out the window at the little rundown motel. It took everything in me not to come running here last night to take care of Brody. He called me, drunk out of his mind, rambling nonsense. All I managed to understand was that he was in a motel. So, at least he was safe.

I haven't had a moment to think since the night of the party, to process and understand what happened. When Brody got arrested, I had to talk to the cops for a while. And by the time I was done, Theo had already left with Ellie.

Chase's energy that night was like a pent up bull, and I don't think I've ever seen Rain cry like she did. The broken look on her face was the most emotion she's shown in a really long time. She's gotten good at brushing things off and hiding her pain. That is, until Ellie came back and forced her feelings to the surface. But she channeled all her hurt into anger so she could use it against Ellie. All over something we royally fucked up on.

Ellie was raped. She didn't cheat on us, and she didn't betray us. She was a helpless victim, and we were fucking monsters who accused her of the worst, all while she was living in hell from what happened to her.

She wasn't lying on that bed sleeping after a good fuck when we stormed into that room. She was drugged and passed out after being raped.

I've cried, knowing I failed the love of my life so fucking bad. The anger within me is so intense, it's like nothing I've ever felt before.

I lost years with her and I've spent years hating a girl I had no reason to. Spent years trying to push her out of my mind and move on with a life that should have included her.

I regret it all. I regret pushing her into the back of my mind, convincing myself I didn't need her in my life, that I didn't want her anymore. I'd never really hated her because I told myself she didn't matter enough to hate. All lies. I've never stopped loving her, and it's become more and more clear over the past few months.

But Ellie isn't the only one who owns my heart now. The man who's probably drunk out of his mind, hating himself in one of these rooms, owns the other half.

I want to be with Ellie, but I don't deserve her; I know that much. None of us do because we didn't trust in her love back then, so why would we think we deserve it now?

When I heard Tim admit what he did, something inside me broke. *We* allowed that. We cared more about the party-goers and having fun with the team than our girl. We left her open for sick fuckers to take advantage of her.

And Brody, fuck, I love him, but a part of me hates him right now too. He left her there. He saw it happening, and his mind jumped to the worst. All because his fucked up brain has him convinced all women are like his mom. I can't believe he would think Ellie of all people was anything like that bitch.

A part of me resents him for being so fucking convinced that she was cheating on us without any actual proof. And I hate myself for listening to him, for not seeing everything for what it really was.

Ellie has always been quiet, shy, and kept to herself with other people. But with us, she was bright and vibrant. She smiled and loved life. She never held back on being her true self with us. She trusted us completely with her mind, body, and heart. And we took that and crushed her.

Then she comes back years later, just wanting to get back to the life that was stolen from her, only to have the people who should have protected her, who turned their backs on her, make her life a living hell again. Reminding her every day how we betrayed her and continued to do so.

My mind has so many conflicting thoughts. I want to take care of my man like I always do, but I also think he needs to grow the fuck up and get his life together. 'Cause one of these days, his insecurities are gonna cause him to lose *everything*. Because I won't let him sway me anymore when it comes to life changing choices. From now on, I get all the facts before making any drastic moves.

Right now, I need to get Brody in this car, bring him home, and talk to the others on what we're going to do about Ellie.

We already stopped hating her before we found out what really happened—*not that we had any grounds to hate her in the first place*. We've been falling back in love with her all over again. Only, we never really fell *out* of love. We were getting to know the new Ellie from afar. The smart, confident, strong-willed woman who didn't put up with any of our crap. Who held her head high and took the bullshit in stride, never letting it take her down.

She's amazing, and it's such a fucking turn on.

I want her back. But first, we need to talk to her. We need to see where her mind is and go from there.

Sighing, I unbuckle my seatbelt and open the door. When I walk into the motel, an older woman smiles a toothless grin at me. I wave, trying not to stare.

"Hi."

"Hi, deary, what can I help you with?"

"My friend, Brody Creed, is staying in one of the rooms. I was wondering if you could tell me which one?"

"Oh, I don't think I can do that. We keep our guests' information confidential."

"Fuck me harder!" a voice from the next room screams. My eyes widen, and I raise a brow at the woman.

"We've got some interesting people staying here," she says, smiling like it's completely normal. From the looks of this place, it probably is.

"Look, he called me last night drunk. I haven't heard from him in hours and I'm really worried. He could be hurt or even worse, in that room as we speak. You wouldn't want to be the reason why he's dead and alone, would you?"

Okay, I'm laying it on pretty thick, but I need to get Brody and go home. His phone must have died because while he was drunk rambling to me, his call cut out. I tried ringing him back, but it went straight to voicemail.

Her eyes go wide with panic. "Of course not!" she screeches, then turns around and grabs a key off the hook. She spins back and hesitantly hands me the key. "You never got this from me, got it?"

"Got it." I wink, giving her a flirty grin just for fun. She smiles, a blush taking over her cheeks. This is so unlike me, but it got me the key and her off my back.

'Room sixteen' is what the key tag says. I walk down the row of doors until I get to the end. Putting my ear to the door, I try to hear if he's awake but there's no sound on the other end.

Unlocking the door, I slowly open it to find Brody laying on top of the bed. He's on his belly in only his boxers. The blankets are bunched at the bottom of the bed, and as my eyes look him over, they stop on a large bandage around his bicep.

Did he get hurt?

Needing to know if he's okay, I close the door and lock it behind me.

"Brody." My voice sounds so loud in the quiet room. I give his shoulder a little shake. "Brody."

"What?" he groans into the pillow. "Go away."

"Can't do that. Time to get up, get dressed, and come home."

"Jax?" he murmurs, rolling over onto his back so that he's facing me. He opens his eyes, then squints at me. "When did you get here? How did you know where to find me?"

"Just got here. And, before the call from last night cut out, I used the tracking app." We all have an app on our phone that helps us keep track of each other. We never had a reason to use it before, but thought it was a good idea to have in case something happens to one of us. Guess it finally came in handy.

"I called you?" he asks, his brows furrowing as he tries to remember.

"Yup. You rambled on about nothing for a while, then the call cut out." I shrug.

"My phone," he mutters. "Where the fuck is it?" He moves to sit up, cursing as he clutches his head. "Fuck, my head is pounding."

"Drinking a bottle of Jack all by yourself is known to do that," I reprimand.

"How do you know it was Jack?" he asks, glaring at me.

"Because I know what you drink, and you mentioned it. It's one of the only things I could make out while you were rambling."

"Whatever," he scoffs, throwing his legs over the bed and getting off as he searches for his phone. "Found it." He checks it, curses, and tosses it onto the bed. "Dead."

"Like I said," I deadpan.

"Don't be a smart ass with me!" he growls. "I didn't ask you to come here."

"No, you didn't. But I'm stupid, and I always come to clean up after your messes," I say, getting off the bed and into his face. "I love you, Brody, but you need help. I'm done with all of this. You have a drinking problem, and you need to get it under control."

"I do not," he seethes, jutting out his chin and trying to argue with me like a stubborn child.

I let out a humorless laugh and shake my head. "Keep telling yourself that. But I'm done taking care of your ass."

"I never asked you to in the first place," he says, bending over to grab a pair of pants on the floor.

"No, but what did you expect me to do? Just leave the man I love drowning in his own waste? It kills me, Brody; it kills me to see you like that. Every time I find you out of your mind drunk, a part of me breaks. I get it, watching your dad like that, it does something to the brain. Your mom's a bitch, your dad's a drunk, but you need to be better!"

"My dad is stuck with a gold digging whore. You would drink too!"

"But you're not. When will you see that? You never were. You have me!" I yell, tapping my chest. "And you had Ellie. She saw the real you, just like I do. But you've slowly changed over the years, letting your family issues become your own. You're not your parents, but at this point, you're not much better either. I love you so fucking much, Brody, and I'd do a lot for you. But I made the mistake of listening to you once because you let your family's trauma warp your mind, turning you into someone you're not. I already lost one half of my heart, I won't see the other half drink himself into an early grave!" I shout. "Now, get fucking dressed and in the damn car. We have a ton to unpack, and it involves all of us."

He looks pissed, like he wants to tell me off, but he doesn't. He just stands there, chest heaving and his hands clenched at his side.

"It's time to try to salvage what we can with what you destroyed."

With that, I turn around and leave the room, leaving him standing there with his pants half done up.

I return to the front desk and give the key back before heading out.

I'm shaking when I get to the car. Gripping the steering wheel, I take a few deep breaths. I've never talked to him like that, never spoken up like that. At least, not since we started seeing each other as more than just friends.

When my mom died, he was my rock; he kept me from drifting away. There were times I thought of ending it all. I didn't have my mom, my dad wasn't the same at the time, and I had lost the only girl I ever loved. But he made me want to stay. He gave me a reason.

I've put up with so much because I thought I owed it to him. Yes, I took care of him when he was at his lowest, but he did the same thing for me, only in a different way.

I've been so blind for so long. Even back when he was just the self-appointed leader of our group, I followed him. We all did. But look where that got us.

I'm not giving up on him, and when he admits he needs help, I'll stand by him. But I can no longer stand by and watch his self-destructive behavior.

Standing in the background, and even sometimes contributing, while Brody and Rain fucked with Ellie, making her life hell, left a disgusting feeling behind every time. I hate myself more and more everyday.

I should've said something. I should have stopped them. But I didn't, and I have to own up to that. I can't change the past, but I will do whatever I can to make sure the future is better.

A minute later, Brody comes out of the room that he's been staying in. He looks rough. His brown hair is a wild mess, his clothes all ruffled.

He goes into the main office for a moment, then comes back out to the car. He says nothing as he gets in the passenger seat and buckles up. He hisses as he twists his body, then looks down at his arm. "What the fuck?" he asks.

"I was gonna ask you the same thing. Did you hurt yourself?"

"Not that I can remember," he says, cautiously touching the bandage. Only when I look closer do I notice that it's not just any bandage; it's what tattoo shops use.

"Did you get a tattoo?" I question him, completely in shock.

"No," he says, his brows pinching in confusion. "Did I?" His responses are irritating the fuck out of me. *How can he be so calm about this?*

"Look and see," I demand. Fuck, if he pulls that back and there's a tattoo, that's going to go right up to the top of the dumbest shit he's done while drunk, and he's done *a lot*.

He picks at the tape, grimacing as he pulls it off, peeling away the bandage.

"What the..."

My eyes go wide as I take in the tattoo. It's a large piece. The whole top half of his left arm is a night sky, giving it an almost galaxy-style look. Only, the tiny stars in the sky spell out 'Ellie'.

A laugh bubbles up, slipping past my lips. I can't help it. I burst out into laughter, a full belly laugh. Of course he would get a drunk tattoo of her name. I'm honestly surprised it took him this long.

"Don't fucking laugh at me. This isn't funny!" he snaps.

"But it kind of is. The name of the girl you've been tormenting for months is now on your arm," I gasp.

"No, the only girl I've ever loved is now on my arm. But she shouldn't be. Fuck! Who the hell tattoos a drunk person?"

"Check your bank app." I bite my lip, holding back laughter, as I hand him my phone to check.

He snatches it out of my hand, grumbling as he types in his information. "Fuck!" he roars.

"What?" He shows me his transactions. There's over fifteen thousand dollars gone. One to the police station, and a few different ones from the ATM. "That's a lot," I whistle.

"Ten grand for a fucking tattoo! For fuck's sake!" He lets out a harsh sigh, closing his eyes as he places his head against the headrest.

"Karma, man. Fucking karma." I shake my head, pulling out of the lot. I don't feel bad that he's out that much money. And I'm loving the tattoo of Ellie. I think it's fucking perfect. The fact that he's going to have that on him for the rest of his life is icing on the cake.

Brody bitched under his breath the whole way home about the tattoo. I'm not sure what he's so pissed about. He did it to himself and the tattoo actually looks really cool. Whoever did it broke some rules, but they are a pretty damn good artist.

"Good thing ball is over because this is gonna take forever to heal," Brody says, slamming the door shut.

"At least it's not summer time, so you can still cover it up for a while. You know, until you're ready to show the world that you got a big ass tattoo for the girl you love. The same one you spent months making her life hell." I smirk as we head toward our apartment building.

"If I haven't told you yet today, fuck you," he grumbles back.

We stop at the front door to the building, and I turn to him. "If you stop being a royal dick, then *maybe* I'll be the one fucking you." I grin.

He steps closer, saying, "Baby, I don't get topped." He has, but it's not often. I know he likes it, but he just loves to be the one in control while we're in the bedroom, and I love letting him.

"For now." My grin widens as I open the door. We walk to the elevator and let the people off before we take their place.

"What's that supposed to mean?" he asks as I press the button to our floor.

I look over at him. "You saw how much Ellie loved seeing us together when she caught us. Don't you think it would be fun to do that, but with her or at least with her in the room? I'm sure, at some point, she would want to see me fuck you in the ass."

He glares at me. "Not gonna happen," he scoffs. "I'm gonna do everything I can to get you and the others your second chance with Ellie. Hell, Chase almost has his, but me, I'm not gonna get one. I don't deserve her, and I don't wanna allow myself to think for a moment that I could have her."

He's being a stubborn ass. He has a lot to make up for, and I do mean a lot, but maybe, the more time he spends around Ellie, under better circumstances, he will see her for who she is and realize he can't live without her; just like the rest of us.

But I'm not going to pressure her about forgiving him. He needs to work that out for himself. I'm going to work on getting myself on her good side. I'll show her how much I've fucked up, regret it, and that she's still my whole world, even if I spent years convincing myself she wasn't. I did a good job of fooling myself though, and I really had myself believing it was true. But it was all an act, and I'm done trying to push my feelings aside.

"Whatever you say." I shake my head as the doors open.

"About fucking time," Chase snaps as soon as we walk through the apartment door.

"Not so damn loud," Brody groans, holding his head.

"Fuck you, I don't give a shit if you're hung over. Our world just got turned upside fucking down and you skip out? Fuck you!"

"We just found out the woman we love was raped!" Brody shouts back, stepping into Chase's personal space. "What did you expect me to do? Just come home and go on with life like nothing happened? I almost killed the fucker for what he did, and if you guys didn't pull me off of him, I would have," he growls.

"And what, go to prison for murder?" Chase retorts.

"Would have been worth it," Brody confirms.

"You know, for someone who has been nothing but a bully to her for the past few months, you sure have changed your tune *real* damn fast." Chase laughs, shaking his head. "You're the one who pitted us all against her over something that never happened! You told us she cheated on us, you told us she was a fucking whore!"

Chase roars. "But she was raped, Brody. She was lying there in that bed after they did sick and fucked up things to her, and the first thing your 'mommy-issues'-mind came up with was that she cheated!"

"I'm not the only one to blame!" he yells back. "You all took my word for it. You didn't have to. You have your own minds; you could have questioned it, but you didn't! So don't put all the blame on me."

"And we all have to live with how fucking stupid we were for believing you. A lot happened that night and we were all drinking. We didn't have time to process everything with a clear head. And when we did, you kept saying she was a whore, she cheated, she betrayed us. But you know what?! I always had my doubts," Chase throws back at him.

"Then why didn't you go after her then? Why didn't you go and get the truth?" Brody fires back.

"He did," Rain says, stepping into the living room from Chase's room. "A few days later, Chase came to me. He said that something wasn't right. That there was no way Ellie could have cheated on us. That our love meant too much to her for her to do something like that. I told him he was only fooling himself because I was too heartbroken, believing the same thing you did. He went to her house to get answers, but the place was empty; she had moved away with her mom and dad."

Chase picks up where Rain stopped in their explanation. "I went to message her on social media, but all her accounts were deactivated. Her number was disconnected too. All I knew was that she moved across the country. I should have flown there to talk to her, to search the whole fucking city to find her."

"Let's just sit down and talk, okay? This is a big deal and us screaming at each other isn't going to do anything," Rain reasons, moving into the living room and sitting on the couch.

She looks rough. Her hair is in a messy bun, she's wearing Chase's clothes, and there're dark circles under her eyes. She's spent the past few days crying, and I don't blame her. I've been the same way. Any time I think about what really happened to her, I feel like puking.

We all move to sit in the living room with her. "So, what do we do?" Chase asks.

"I don't know. I think we should try talking to her first, see what her thoughts are on all of this," Rain says, snuggling into the blanket on the couch.

"Do you think she even wants to talk to us?" I ask.

"She had been talking to me before we found out the truth. I don't see why she wouldn't now that we know."

"She's never going to forgive me," Rain says in a quiet voice, tearing up again. "I was such a bitch to her. I let other people treat her like trash." Tears start to fall. "God, I'm a fucking monster."

"You didn't know," Chase consoles her, pulling her into his side.

"You didn't either and you stayed out of it. You didn't call her nasty names and have the whole school turn on her."

"No, but I didn't do anything to stop it. I'm just as bad."

"But she's talking to you; she's letting you back in. Hell, you slept with her the other night. If anyone is gonna be forgiven, it'll be you."

"You what?" Brody's voice is low and dangerous. Right now is not the best time for him to find out about that.

Oh boy, here we go. Just when I thought we could get somewhere with this conversation, everything blows up again.

Chapter Six
CHASE

ALRIGHT, *so we're doing this now, I see. Thanks, Rain.*

"Yeah, Ellie and I slept together the night of the party. And you know what? I'm not sorry. It was fucking amazing, and it's going to happen again. You wanna know why? Because while you guys just stopped being assholes to her, I've been working my ass off to win back her trust. I've been talking to her, spending time with her, and getting to know her again."

"Stalking her, you mean," Rain says, a small smile forming on her lips. It's the first one I've seen in days. I hate seeing my best friend hurt, but the pain isn't anywhere near what Ellie has felt, so I don't feel all too bad.

"You say 'stalking,' I say loving really, really passionately... from a distance." I grin down at her.

Brody looks pissed, but he says something that takes me by surprise. "Good."

"Wait, what?" I ask, my brows furrowing. Good? No yelling? No kicking my ass, just...good? Did he drink away his personality or something?

"I said good." He leans back into the chair. "You're right. All of this is my fault; I won't even try to deny it. You lost years with the woman who owns our hearts because of me. If she's willing to give you another chance, go for it. You all deserve to be happy. So, good, you're getting close to her again. You never should have been apart in the first place."

"Oh...well, good. I thought you would go all King Kong or some shit."

"If it was before the weekend, yeah, I probably would have. But now..." He shakes his head. "Now, everything has changed. Do I like that you've been with her? No. I'm jealous as fuck and not afraid to admit it, but I don't deserve her like that, no matter how much I want her."

"So, what do we do now?" Rain asks.

"Find her, talk to her," Jax says. "She deserves to tell her truth, and have us sit and listen."

"Guys." Rain's voice is a broken whisper. "We left her there. She was raped while we were downstairs getting drunk. And we just left her there with her rapist."

No one says anything, letting the reality of that sink in. I want to scream. I want to rage. I want to puke. But most of all, I just want to hold my Ellie Belly and tell her everything will be okay. But the damage is done, and now we need to figure out what happens next.

The rest of the day, we hang out around the apartment. No one really says anything after our conversation. We watch movies and order in. But I can't concentrate on anything. I keep staring at her contact name, wanting to message her. She hasn't texted back after the one I sent her that night, but I don't blame her.

I just hope Theo is taking good care of her. Seeing her in his arms like that, so small and fragile, it broke me. I wanted to rip her from his arms and hold her in mine. But the reality is, at least for now, she is his. We lost that right a long time ago. And as much as I hate to admit it, I'm kinda thankful for Theo. He's been there for her when we weren't these past few months. He held her together while the others tried to tear her down. He's been the man we didn't have the balls to be.

But that's all changing as of right now. I don't care what anyone thinks. I love that woman with everything I am. I will continue to gain her trust back, to win her heart again. And I will never in my life doubt her again.

I know I probably don't deserve her, none of us do. But does that mean I won't try? Fuck no, because I need my girl. She's like air for me.

"Chase," Rain says, cuddling into me. She's sleeping over again, not wanting to go back to her place and be alone.

"Yeah?"

"I miss her. I miss her being between us like this."

"Me too." I kiss the top of her head. "But we'll have that again. I know it."

"How do you know? She's never going to forgive me after everything I did. I don't deserve it."

"What you did to her was fucked up," I start.

She snorts a laugh. "Thanks."

"Am I wrong?" I ask, cocking a brow as I look down at her.

"No," she mutters.

"But you thought she was someone she wasn't. Was it wrong? Yes, but I can understand why you did it. I mean, you were pretty harsh, but I get it. You didn't know what happened. And from the time I've spent with her, she's still the same Ellie we had back then. Only now, she's stronger. She's smarter in more ways than we can dream of. She's sweet, funny, and sassy. But she loves hard, and I know she still loves you. I've seen how she looks at you. It's just gonna take a little longer for you."

"I'll spend the rest of my life waiting for her, proving myself to her," she promises.

"I know, and so will I."

"It hurts, Chase. Every time I close my eyes, all I can think about is what he did to her." She starts to cry into my chest and I hold her as a tear slips from my own eye.

"I know," I say again.

We don't talk again, falling asleep some time later.

When we wake up, we go to school like normal and I spend the whole day looking for her. I go out of my way to try and find her.

"She left for her next class already," Cooper says as I watch the door of one of her classes.

"Damn it, I missed her again," I sigh.

Cooper chuckles. "You're not gonna let up, are you?"

"Never," I growl.

"Down, boy. I assumed as much. Look, Ellie is my best friend and I want to see her happy. Personally, I think you all should fuck off and leave her to be happy with Theo. But I know that's not gonna happen."

"Fuck no," I agree.

"Right." He rolls his eyes. "But look, don't push her too hard. She has a lot going on. And if you force her to make important decisions before she's really ready, you could lose her for good."

"You knew?" I ask. "You knew what really happened to her that night?"

"Yeah," he says, his face turning grim. "She told me."

"How come you got to know and we didn't?" I huff.

"Because, her *friends* and I have been there for her from the moment we met. We didn't believe the bullshit you all were spewing. We thought for ourselves, making our own judgments based on who she was and how she treated us. She felt like she could trust us, so she told us. We believed her from the start. Something none of you did."

"Yeah, yeah, don't fucking remind me," I grumble.

"Look, if she chooses to give you another chance, I'll be a

good friend and support her decision, but if you hurt her again, I will end you," he tells me, completely serious.

"You don't have to worry about that. I never want to cause her pain in any way again," I say. "Thanks, by the way."

"For what?"

"For being there for her. For holding her up while the others tried to bring her down. For being a good guy," I explain

"I'll always stand by her side. She's my best friend, and she's been by mine."

"And sorry about the nose," I apologize while tapping mine.

"Yeah, sorry about yours," he snorts.

"What? I think I look good with a nose ring," I say, playing with the hoop.

"Sure." He shakes his head. "I gotta get to class. See you later."

"Bye."

She's not in the cafe for lunch. I watch her empty table the whole time.

"How do we talk to her if we can't find her?" Brody grumbles.

"I've tried texting and calling. It says she's seen the messages, so she knows what we want," I inform them.

"Maybe we're pushing her? Maybe she's not ready," Rain says.

"She can't avoid us forever." Brody takes out his phone and shoots a text to someone. A moment later, there's a ding and he gets a response. "She's just been seen by the staff parking lot."

"Why is she there, and how the hell do you know?" I ask.

"I don't know. Her boy-toy is a teacher. Maybe she's with him. And I have contacts all over this school. Comes in handy when you're looking to track someone down," he says like it's nothing.

"Creepy much?" Rain asks.

"It works," he snaps back.

"Whatever." She rolls her eyes.

"I have my bike, so I'll grab that and you guys take the car. Meet me in the parking lot. Let me talk to her first. If we all go at her at once, she might feel overwhelmed."

"Fine, let's go," Brody huffs.

The others go to Brody's car, and I head over to my bike.

Slipping my helmet on, I start up the engine and take off toward the staff parking lot. I get there before the others, but I don't get off my bike yet, leaving it idle for a moment while I look around to see if I can spot Ellie.

When I finally do, I see her over by the daycare. That's weird, she's talking to Miss Macy. Ellie's face slips into horrified panic as she starts to frantically search for something.

I'm about to shut off the bike and go see if I can help when I see her looking toward the main road. "Lilly!" Ellie screams the most heart wrenching sound I've ever heard as I see a man in a red car grab something and toss it into his car.

Ellie starts running toward the car, screaming, "Lilly!" over and over again. I'm not sure why Ellie is here, or how she knows Lilly, but I know there's no way in hell I'm letting that man get away with that little girl.

Shoving my helmet back on, I turn the bike around and gun it out of the parking lot. The car takes off, speeding full force down the street.

My heart breaks as I pass Ellie who falls to her knees sobbing. But this little girl needs me right now. Everything else can wait.

My head is ringing, my heart is pounding, and my body is filling with so much adrenaline. Lilly's little face flashes before my eyes, her cute laugh echoing in my mind. I have no fucking clue how this is happening right now, but I won't let him take her.

We speed down the road and right out of Silver Valley,

heading toward Spring Meadows. Fuck, fuck, fuck! There's a turn off at some point that leads to the main highway. If he takes it, I may not be able to keep up with him.

The road is clear with only us on it, so I take the chance and move into the other lane so that we are side by side. Moving the bike as close as I can without causing an accident, I bang on the window.

"PULL OVER!" I shout over the engine. He looks up at me, fear in his eyes before stomping on the gas and speeding up the car. "Fuck," I hiss, giving my bike a little more gas to match his speed.

Seeing the turn off ahead, I stay where I am, keeping him from turning. I let out a sigh of relief when we pass it.

I feel helpless. There's nothing I can do at this point but follow. If I try to ram into him from behind, I can hurt not only myself, but Lilly too.

A few painfully long minutes later, we enter Spring Meadows, and I curse when I see how busy the streets are, which forces me back behind him. It's after school and a lot of kids are coming home for the day. It's terrible fucking timing.

"Shit, shit, shit." I try to think. If he makes it through to the other side of town, I could lose him. There are so many back roads and different directions he can take. I need to cut him off now before it's too late.

I know the Spring Meadows roads pretty well. I often come out here to just go for a ride, so when I see an opening to turn off into a back alley, I take it.

Speeding down the back alley, I turn right at the end, taking the back road and bypassing all the traffic. It's a risky move, but if I'm right, it should lead me right in front of him.

Taking this road all the way to the end, I take another right, and my stomach drops as I see a delivery truck taking up most of the back alley.

"Damn it!" I roar, eyeing up the small space between the truck and the wall of the building next to it. "Fuck it," I say to myself.

I'd rather risk hurting myself and the bike than letting that bastard get away with that little girl.

With my eyes set between the gap, I gun it. It's a tight fit, my bike scrapes against the truck and brick wall on each side. It's going to cost me a pretty penny to fix, but I couldn't care less.

I make it through and out of the alley. Quickly, I look to my right and see the red car hasn't passed me yet. "Fuck yes!" I whoop. One side of the road is still busy, the construction making it slower for them to pass, but it works out in my favor. I see an opening, and pass into the lane he's in. I could kiss the gods right now because I make it just in time to cut him off. He slams on the brakes, hitting me and making me fall onto the hood of the car. I grunt, the force of the hit is a little painful, but I don't feel it much. Too much adrenaline is coursing through my veins at the moment. Rolling off the hood, I toss my helmet and go to his door. I rip the car door open, and waste no time in making my fist acquainted with his punk-ass face.

"You think it's okay to kidnap a little girl?" I roar, punching him. "Not today, you sick fucker." I keep punching him until he's passed out.

"Ace!" Lilly cries from the back seat. My gaze flies to hers. Her eyes are red and face stained with tears.

"Lilly," I breathe, letting go of the waste of space and moving to open the door. "It's okay, sweetie. You're okay now. I got you." She cries harder and I pull her out of the car and into my arms. I hold her tight, her little arms wrapping around my neck.

With my eyes closed, I stand there with her, thanking anyone who will listen that I was able to save her. That she's safe now. I'm not sure why, and I still would have done this if it was any other kid, but this one, I know I'd do anything for her.

Sirens blare in the distance, the sound growing louder and louder as they get closer.

"Lilly!" someone screams, and I spin around to see Ellie getting out of a car with Theo following behind her.

"Mama!" Lilly screams back as she turns in my arms to see Ellie racing toward us.

"Oh, baby girl," Ellie sobs as she pulls the little girl out of my arms and into hers. She holds Lilly tightly as they both cry.

Theo wraps his arms around the two of them, holding them for a moment before looking over to the ambulance. "Let's go get her looked over, okay? Let the cops deal with this," Theo says, trying to usher them away.

Ellie nods as I just stand there shell-shocked. She turns to me and "Thank you," is all she says, but the amount of sincerity behind it has my heart clenching.

They head over to get Lilly checked over while I'm frozen in place, my mind trying to process everything that just happened.

"Did she just call her *mama*?" I ask myself in shock. *Yes, I think she just did.*

I hear footsteps behind me and I just know it's Rain and the guys. They all move to stand next to me, but I don't look over, my eyes are fixated on the sight before me.

Is this really happening right now?

Chapter Seven

JAX

"CHASE!" I call out as Brody, Rain, and I get out of the car. He turns around, a dazed look on his face. "What the hell just happened?" I ask him.

"Ummm." I look over to the ambulance, then to the car where the EMTs are taking a man out of the front seat. He's unconscious and his face is a bloody mess. "I stopped him from kidnapping a kid," he tells us like he's unsure if that's what actually happened.

"Wait, what?!" Rain asks, her eyes going wide. "What kid?"

Chase just blinks at her. *Did he get hurt?*

"Are you alright?" I ask.

"Ahh, yeah, just a little bruised. I had to cut him off and went up on the hood of the car a bit. Bike's totaled though."

"Who cares about the bike? We're just glad you're okay. We saw you racing out of the parking lot like a bat out of hell and someone screaming. We didn't see who, but we weren't gonna just stay behind and find out what's going on, so we followed you."

"I saw him put her in the car. I had to save her," he says.

"Who?" Rain asks again. Chase's eyes flick from Brody to Rain.

"I think I know who Lilly's mom is," Chase says.

"Lilly?" Rain asks, her brows furrowing before shooting up with worried surprise. "Is that the kid who was kidnapped?" Her eyes go wide.

"Yeah." I think Chase should also get checked out or something because he seems totally out of it right now. It could just be the shock of everything, or he could have hit his head in the crossfire.

"Well fuck, I'm glad you were there to see it and stop it. I would be devastated if she was taken."

"Do you know this kid or something?" Brody asks, looking between Rain and Chase.

"Lilly, like Lilly from the daycare when you guys volunteered?" I ask.

"Yeah." Rain nods.

"Damn," I sigh, rubbing the back of my head. "That girl really left an impression on you two."

"Hard not to, she's the best kid I've ever met," Rain says. "I can't believe this happened to her. Is she okay? You mentioned something about her mom, who's her mother?"

Chase turns his head in the direction of the ambulance. I follow his line of sight and my heart almost stops beating when I see a sobbing Ellie clutching a little blonde girl. "Ellie."

"What?!" Brody says, his voice laced with anger. What the hell is going on now?

"Shut up!" Rain shouts as the guys and I argue. We got back to our apartment a half hour ago. The car ride was pretty quiet as we all let the new information settle in, but as soon as we walked through the front door, Brody started going off.

We all shut up, turning to look at her with pissed off glares.

"Oh, don't look at me like that, you dummies. Sit the fuck down and let's talk about this like adults, because yelling at each other isn't going to solve anything."

"Fine," Chase mutters, flopping down on the couch next to her, kicking his feet up onto the coffee table and crossing his arms with a pout.

"Big baby," she laughs. He looks over at her and sticks his tongue out. She responds by flipping him off. He smiles at her and sits up straighter, grabbing a candy cane from his pocket.

"So..." I say, looking around at each of us. "Did that really just happen?"

"I'm gonna go with yes, seeing as how it was me who was chasing after the guy like a scene out of *The Fast and The Furious*."

"Yeah, that, but more specifically that you heard that little girl call Ellie 'Mama'. How the hell does Ellie have a child?" Brody asks. He's in a pissy mood now, not liking this new thing sprung on us. Me, I can't wrap my head around the fact that Ellie has a kid.

"You sure she's hers? Maybe Lilly is Theo's," I suggest. "If she's been seeing him for a while, it's not surprising that she would call her Mama. Girlfriends play a big role in step kids' lives sometimes."

"She's Ellie's kid, for sure. I can't believe I didn't see it before. She's a mini Ellie, she looks so much like her. There's no way that kid isn't one of ours," Chase says. Everyone goes silent at the thought.

It's the first time one of us has said it out loud. There's a strong possibility that we have a child we didn't know about.

"How old is she?" I ask.

Rain looks to Chase. "I think she said she was three, right?"

Chase nods. "Yeah, she's three, probably closer to four now."

"Okay, look, we don't know how old she is. She could have gotten pregnant after she left here. I think we need to talk to her before we jump to conclusions on whether she is ours or another man's," I reason. But the idea of that little girl being ours? It makes something inside me warm. We could have a little piece of us running around.

"I agree. We'll talk to her first. But I think we can all agree that the child is most likely Ellie's," Brody says.

"Rain, do you know what this means?" Chase asks her, a massive smile taking over his face. "Lilly could be ours! Our kid. I knew there was something special about her, but this? Wow."

Rain and Chase start talking excitedly, but then Brody has to go and ruin it.

"Or she could be Tim's," he says bluntly.

We all turn to look at him.

"What?" Rain asks with disbelief on her face.

"There's a chance Tim could be the father," he repeats.

"Don't fucking say that again," Chase growls, shooting to his feet. "Don't even think that!"

Brody stands too, taking a step closer to him. "I'm trying to be real about all of this."

"Shut up," Chase warns, his hands balling into fists. He's ready to snap.

"Well, what the hell do you want me to say? We just got two bombs dropped on us in the past seventy-two hours. What else is she keeping from us, huh? Maybe she's not the Ellie we used to know. Because *that* Ellie would never keep secrets," Brody snaps.

Brody doesn't see it coming. The crack echoes throughout the room as Chase punches him in the face, causing Brody's head to whip to the side.

"Fuck!" Chase hisses, shaking out his hand from the pain. It's the same hand that was busted up from before.

Brody stands there, a death glare in his eyes as he wipes the blood from his lip.

"You kind of deserved that," I say, standing up and stepping between him and Chase before they break out into a full on fist fight. They both now have busted up hands. They don't need any more injuries. "You need to stop seeing Ellie as the bad guy, right now or we're done. I can't do this anymore, Brody. Please."

"Fine." Brody grits his teeth. "That was wrong of me to say."

"Damn right, it was," Chase says, sitting back down next to Rain. She takes his hand to examine it.

"I'll wrap this again for you. It's bleeding," she sighs. I understand that there are all these different emotions going on right now. There's so much to process, but we can't turn on each other. We're family and we need to deal with this together.

We had thought we were just going to talk to Ellie about what really happened on graduation night, something I really don't want to think about right now. But instead, we find out she has a kid, a kid that could be one of ours.

"Lilly is mine," Chase says, looking over to us. "I don't care how she was conceived or by whom. She's mine. If she's Ellie's daughter, she's mine too," he says with all the confidence in the world.

"I'm with him," Rain adds.

"I have to agree with them." I look at Brody. "It doesn't matter to me who Lilly's biological father is, whether it be one of us or another man's. She's Ellie's, therefore, she's ours."

"Yours," Brody says dejectedly. "There is no 'me' involved in this. I'll be lucky enough if I even win her back as a friend. But there won't be anything more than that between us."

"Yeah, yeah, you don't deserve her. Blah, blah, blah. We heard you before," Rain says, rolling her eyes.

I try to hold back a smirk. He does say that a lot. But it's almost like he's trying to convince himself of that. Do I think she should forgive him easily? No, if anyone deserves to be forgiven soon, it's Chase, but I would hope that if she still loved Brody like she does Chase, then she would give him another chance some day. That she would give us all another chance. It may be selfish to ask, but I love her, and I would do anything to get another chance with her. If, in the end, she chooses not to, then as long as we can be friends, it will have to be enough. Even if it would kill me every day not to have her.

"It's not like I won't be involved in some way. I'd still like to be friends if she will have me, eventually. But I know I need to prove that I'm not the monster I've been the past few months. Maybe I can be the fun uncle or something." He shrugs.

Rain lets out this sound somewhere between a snort and her choking. "You, fun?" She doesn't bother holding back her amusement. "You're about as fun as a root canal."

"Oh, fuck you. I can be fun. Just ask Jax. He thinks I'm *really* fun." Brody gives me this heated look that has my cock stirring. I love it when he looks at me like he's ready to take a bite out of me. I miss him.

Since the party, we haven't really spent much time together. At night, I feel cold and alone, wishing I was in his arms. All I can hope for is that he takes the stick out of his ass and starts to change because I don't want to lose him. I love him so fucking much, it's soul consuming. But I felt the same way with Ellie, and I think I still do. At least, I know I want to get back to that point. But I can't do that being in Brody's shadow. If it means stepping back from him to earn Ellie back, I will. I just hope it doesn't come to that.

"Would you two get a room? Some of us aren't getting our dicks wet anymore," Chase mutters.

"And you're upset about that?" I ask, cocking a brow.

"Fuck no. I've had a taste of my girl again, and I'd wait for a million years to get another. This cock is claimed and all the other girls can weep in the sorrow that they missed out on the chance for the ride of their lives," Chase says, leaning back into the couch, looking like a cocky bastard.

"You're so fucking full of yourself," Rain laughs, shaking her head.

"I know someone who was full of me, and she came oh so perfectly on my cock." He gives her a shit eating grin.

"Chase," I warn. "Now is not the time. Don't talk about her

like that. I know we used to when we were all dating her, but I think, until that's the case again, just keep it to yourself and anyone else she's dating."

"You're right." He nods. "I'll be sure to mention it to Theo when the time is right." He grins.

"So here is what we're going to do. We give Ellie a few days, because I know this has shaken her up. Then we get a hold of her and get everything out on the table," I suggest.

"That sounds like a good idea and all, but Brody, you seem to be forgetting something. You say you want to keep in the background and all that, but what if Lilly's yours? What if she wants a DNA test and Lilly comes out as yours?" Chase asks.

"Then she's better off without me. She has you guys. I'm not meant to be a dad. I had a shitty example. Have you met my parents? You think I'll be any better? No." He shakes his head. "You guys would be what she needs, not me."

The reality of everything is hitting him hard, and he's trying not to show his emotions which he's way too good at doing. But I'm hoping once he starts spending time around Ellie without trying to tear her down, he will change his mind. He's not a bad guy. He's just done some really fucked up things. But I know the real Brody and I know Ellie did once, too. She just needs to see that part of him again. Brody may be a closed off, broody person, but with the people he's closest to, he loves hard.

But that will come in time. First step, talk to Ellie.

Chapter Eight

ELLIE

"YOU HAVE to go back to school, Ellie. And what about work? You missed last weekend, understandably, but are you going to call in sick again tonight?" Theo asks, pulling me into his arms as we stand in the kitchen. "I'm in no way telling you what to do, sweet girl, but I don't like seeing you like this. It's been a week and a half. I don't want you to lose everything you've worked so hard for."

"I know, but doing my classes online hasn't been so bad. And I can stay at home with Lilly all safe and sound," I say, looking up at him.

He smiles down at me, tucking some hair behind my ear. "But do you really get anything done with a little monkey running around all day demanding snacks?" He smirks, raising a brow.

"No," I grumble. "I just don't want her out of my sight, Theo. She was kidnapped; that fucked with me. It's not something I'm just going to get over."

"I know, my love, but you're not alone. You took Lilly out of daycare, and my mother has been calling me everyday asking if she can watch Lilly for you."

"I don't want to take advantage of her like that. She already does so much for us."

41

"But she wants to. She may not be old, but she's lonely. She loves my dad, but he has the restaurant. As much as my mom loves cooking, she loves hanging out with the kids more. She doesn't see it as a burden, or taking advantage. She loves it. And you still have Katie for when you're at work. But in order to pay Katie, you need to work."

He's right. I have some money saved up in case of an emergency, but replacing everything I broke when I had my meltdown cost a pretty penny. If I miss any more work, I won't be able to pay rent and bills next month. I know he would help me if I needed it, but I wouldn't ask him for money if I could be out there earning it myself.

"Fine. Are you sure she's okay with this?" I ask, double checking. He's right. As much as I love spending my days with Lilly, I don't get anything done until she's asleep. I've felt like a walking zombie.

"Yes, she is. And she said she will stay in the house with Lilly and keep her entertained all day."

"I know it sounds like I'm a crazy person, but I'm just not ready for her to leave the house yet and not without me with her, in my arms where she is safe."

"You're not crazy. You endured something no parent should ever have to. But she's safe. She's here with you. And from what the therapist says, the only thing she remembers is going for a ride with a scary man and getting saved by her best friend."

The day all of this happened, I went to pick up Lilly from daycare just like any other day. When I got there, one of the workers said they all went to the park across the street because they were getting some new equipment for the fenced off park they have. So, I went to go meet them, and when I got outside, I saw that they were coming back from the park. Only, by the time they got over to me, Lilly wasn't with them.

I lost my mind. Her teacher was saying that she had been at the end of the line. I yelled at her, and I yelled for Lilly. I felt like my soul was being sucked out of my body. Then I saw the car that the flyers warned us about.

It's why we've stopped going to the park by our house and have stayed after daycare for her to get some play time in before going home.

It wasn't enough. He ended up taking a kid, just like all of the local parents feared, and that kid was mine. All because one of the helpers turned their back for a moment. A moment that could have ruined our lives.

But then Chase came flying out of nowhere. God, I owe him my life for saving her. He chased the man down and got my baby girl back.

I know they did a lot to me in the past few months, but Chase was the only one trying after Brody put a stop to everything. He worked hard to get me to talk to him, finding me whenever he could. Let's be honest. He was pretty much stalking me, but it showed how much he regretted what they did, how much I truly meant to him.

And the night of the party with us? Fuck, it was a lot to unpack, but I don't regret it. It was amazing. It was like a piece of my soul clicked back into place.

I told myself to make him work a little harder, not to give in so easily, but after this? Call me crazy, but he's earned his spot back into my life. I want to go out on dates with him and get to know him again. I want to be with him. I've never stopped loving him, and I want him back. I'm always the logical one, trying to make sure everyone is happy. But it's time I make some decisions on things that *I* want. Life is short, and I don't want to live with a bunch of 'what ifs'.

As for the others, I still love them, even after everything they did. If they can show they want to change, that they really are sorry, then maybe I can get to where I'm at with Chase with them. But I'm not going to think about that yet. I still have to sit down and talk to them about everything.

But right now, I have so much going on, and I need to take one thing at a time.

The man who took Lilly was arrested. He was deemed mentally unstable. I guess his story is that he lost his little girl to cancer and his wife died in childbirth. He had no one.

I also found out that he wasn't scoping out the playgrounds for just any kid. He saw Lilly and me at the park one time, and got it in his head that Lilly was his daughter. It's sad to think about the amount of grief it takes to make you delusional enough to believe something like that, and a part of me sympathizes with him as a parent. I just hope he stays locked up, gets the help he needs, and stays the hell away from us.

But I have this little fear that he's going to get out and try this again some day.

Theo has been amazing, as always, keeping me as relaxed as he can and helping me with Lilly. We've been staying over at his place since that day, but Lilly was missing her toys, so we're back home for now. We've had a child therapist visit the house and talk to her, but honestly, I don't think she was as affected by it as much as I was. She hasn't had any nightmares and whenever she brings it up, it's about how cool Chase was and how he's her best friend. I guess being so young will help her forget things more easily.

"Knock knock!" someone calls from the other side of the door while knocking. I smile up at Theo before stepping back from his embrace to answer the door.

"Hey," I say when I see Val's bright and cheerful face.

"Hey, yourself. We've missed you but we knew with everything going on, you needed your space. But time's up, I just had to see your sexy ass. Oh, and that adorable kid of yours," she says pushing past me.

"Val!" Lilly shouts as she races over to Val's open arms.

"Hi, turkey butt. Auntie Val missed your squishy face."

"Hey, so did we," Cooper says as he, Lexie, and Tabitha come down the hall. "Hey, Ellie." He pulls me into a hug.

"Hey." I smile when he pulls back.

"Sorry about her. Sometimes I've thought of getting a leash for that girl," Lexie says, hugging me next.

"If you were a smoking hot m-a-n, I'd be totally willing to try that," Val calls from behind us.

I bite my lip, trying not to smile.

"What's this surprise visit for?" I laugh, going for Tabitha next.

"We needed to see our bestie. It's not the same without you at school, or life. We know you're not ready to be away from Lilly unless you have to, so we thought we would bring the party to you," Lexie says, walking into the house and plopping down on the couch.

"Soooo, *they* know? Everything?" Val just outright asks.

"Seriously, Val?" Lexie raises a brow. "Not in front of the kids," she whispers.

"Sorry," Val grimaces.

"Hey kids, why don't we go back over to my place, and we can make ice cream sundaes?" Theo asks them.

"YAY!" they both cheer as they drop their toys and run for the door, waiting by it with bouncing energy.

"Talk to them. They care about you and Lilly," Theo says, kissing the top of my head. "I'll watch these two little goobers."

"Good luck with that," I laugh. "They already look like they've had a bowl or two."

Theo chuckles. "Gonna have to put an interactive game on the TV to get them to burn it off."

I feel bad because normally, they would go to the park to do something like that.

"Hey," Theo says, cupping my face. "It's okay. You will be ready to let her go to the park again someday, but right now, it's too soon and that's just fine. No one can tell you how to deal with this, or how you choose to heal, or what to do with Lilly. You're her mother. You know best and we're here to help in any way we can."

45

Tears well in my eyes at his words, comforting my anxiety. "I love you."

"I love you more." He kisses my lips softly. "Now, go gossip like a bunch of old hens."

"Whatever you say, grandpa," Val calls over.

Theo smiles and rolls his eyes before taking the kids to his place.

"Okay, that's a total lie," Val says. "He does not look like a grandpa. He might be like what, eight years older than you, but he's fine as fuck. Just think when he is older though. I just know he's gonna be a silver fox. You're a lucky bitch," Val pouts.

"Thanks." I giggle, sitting on the couch next to my friends.

"Okay, now that the curious ears are no longer around, tell us everything."

And I do. Theo's given them the brief story about what happened, just enough to keep them from worrying.

I tell them all about the kidnapping and Chase racing after the man to get my baby girl back for me. And then about everything I've done while dealing with it up until now.

"Look, I know the others have been a bunch of turds, but Chase...damn girl, he's literally a knight in shining armor," Val swoons. "Get it? Because he's a Silver Knight and also rescued Lilly like a knight would?"

"We get it." Lexie rolls her eyes.

"God, you all need a sense of humor transplant," Val mutters.

"I owe him my life," I say, pulling my legs up onto the couch to my chest and wrapping my arms around them, then placing my chin on my knees. "He's been pretty persistent, but he's also made it known what he wants."

"And that's you," Cooper says.

"Yeah." I smile, thinking about the way he looks at me, and the things he said in the library that day when he told me he wanted me again.

"I agree with Val," Cooper starts.

"Wait, you do?" Val asks, looking shocked. "About what part?" She cocks her head to the side.

"About them being turds." Cooper grins.

"Ahh, and it's so true." Val nods.

"Anyways." Cooper shakes his head. "I really do think Chase has changed. I'd never tell you what to do, but you have mentioned working on forgiving them someday. I think he's a good place to start. And another thing Val was right about..."

"Look at me, I'm on a roll." She fist pumps the air, making us all laugh.

"He saved Lilly like your own personal knight, potentially risking his own safety. And, not to mention, there's a good chance she's his daughter. If not him, it's one of the other two."

"I think it's Chase," Val says. "He's got blond hair."

"So does Ellie, you nut," Lexie says, pointing at me.

"Oh. Well, still." Val shrugs.

"It doesn't matter who helped make her. I just hope they want her." I bite my lip, trying to hold back the tears. "The two things I've been trying to find a way to tell them about both came out, back to back, and in the worst possible ways. I just wanted to sit down and talk to them, but that choice was taken from me." Like a lot of things have been lately.

"At least they know now," Tabitha says, putting her hand on my shoulder.

"And it's driving me crazy wondering what they think. I know they waved a white flag and surrendered from their terror and want to make amends. But what if they don't want me now? What if I have too much baggage?" I wipe the tears away from my eyes.

"Then fuck them with a dragon dildo," Val growls. "You're the best thing that's ever happened to them, baby, and so will that little girl. If they can't see it, then let them be miserable assholes together."

"I feel like we're in the twilight zone, but even I have to agree with Val," Tabitha says.

"Hey, I speak wisdom and shit," Val defends.

"Sure you do, babe, sure you do." Lexie pats her on the back, making me giggle.

Val flips her off and sticks her tongue out at her.

"My plan is to go back to work, leave Lilly here with Theo's mom, and then start back with school on Monday. I'll talk to them, I will, I just don't know when."

"Can't hold off forever, babe. As much as they suck, they need answers," Lexie says with a sympathetic look.

"I know, and I will. There's no more avoiding it. I'll talk to them about what they found out at the party, and about Lilly, answer any questions they have, and then go from there," I agree.

"Sounds like a plan. Look at us. We're all adults and shit." Lexie grins.

Work is busy tonight. It's part blessing and part burden. I've been running around like crazy, trying to get everyone's orders in, while delivering food and drinks. But because my mind is concentrating on work, I haven't had much time to think about being away from Lilly.

"Ellie," Aria says as she steps up next to me while I grab a tray of drinks.

"What's up?" I smile. I've missed her. We still have yet to hang out outside of work but I'll have to fix that once everything settles down. If I'm lucky enough, that is.

"You've been working your sexy ass off all night. Go take your break."

"Are you sure?" I ask, realizing I haven't had anything to eat or drink since I started my shift.

"Yes, go." She laughs.

"Alright, thank you. You're the best. I'll drop this off in VIP first."

Grabbing the tray of drinks, I bring it to the customers. When I was told I was on VIP tonight, a part of me was afraid that Rain and the guys were going to be there. They weren't, just a group of college kids. Then I found myself disappointed that I didn't get to see them.

A month ago, I'd dreaded coming to work and risking seeing them, risking their harsh words and dirty looks. But now that all of that has ended, I find myself missing them. God, I'm so messed up.

"Rain, please." Laura's desperate voice has me pausing just as I enter the staff room. "Just give me another chance."

"Laura, how many times do I have to tell you? We were never together. There are no more chances to give because there were never any to begin with. We had fun, but it's over now," Rain answers back. What is she doing back here? And with Laura.

Before they can see me, I quietly slip over to my locker and out of sight. "It's because of her, isn't it? You were fine with things the way they were before *she* came back," Laura accuses, her voice growing angry. She must be talking about me. My stomach turns, waiting for Rain's reply.

"You wanna know the truth? Yes, part of it is because of Ellie. I love her, Laura. I've loved her since I was a kid, and I'm sorry if that hurts to hear. But I told you when we started our little arrangement that I wasn't looking for anything serious. You told me that was fine. We were friends. It was just sex, that's it. I'm sorry if it meant something more to you. That wasn't my intention."

She loves me? Still? Why does that have my heart pounding?

"But if you just give us a try, I know I can make you happy." Laura is borderline begging at this point, and it's kind of sad. A part of me feels a little sorry for her, just for a moment, then I remember how much of a cow she was to me.

"No, that's what you don't seem to be getting. You can't make me happy, because you're *not her*. I'm sorry." Hearing Rain say these words after thinking she hated me for so long has the fire in my soul slowly growing in size. Also, a part of me wants to get into Laura's face and say, 'suck it, bitch, she wants me, not you.' But you know, I'm too mature for that and all...right?

"You're gonna regret it. She's gonna hurt you, you know that? She's never going to forgive you after everything you did to her, and you'll be left heartbroken. But because I actually do care about you, I'll be here to pick up the pieces when she does."

Footsteps have me turning into my locker, trying to look like I didn't hear everything they were talking about. The staff door closes and I let out a sigh of relief which was short lived.

"Heard all that, huh?" Rain asks, moving to stand next to me and leaning against the locker.

"Maybe," I say, having no reason to deny it as I close the locker door and look over at her. Feeling like the air has been knocked out of my lungs, I fight to suck in a gasp. It's been a while since I've been this close to her. Her long, wild, red hair is hanging in messy curls that look so sexy and natural on her. Freckles cover her nose and under her eyes. Her eyes, damn it, they're like two emerald pools, hypnotizing me. They're filled with so many unsaid words as she watches me with an intensity that has me squirming. I clear my throat while tucking my hair behind my ears. "This is the staff room. What are you doing back here?"

"I came to see you," she says with caution.

"What about?" I ask, but I'm pretty sure I already know.

"Ellie." She smiles. "There were two pretty big bombs dropped in less than four days apart from each other. It's been a week, and we wanted you to take all the time you needed, but the guys..." She blows out a breath. "They are going mad, waiting to know answers to all their questions. We don't want to push you, but we would like to hear your side of things and talk about Lilly."

"You know, she's been talking about you and Chase a lot." I can't help but smile.

Rain's brows shoot up. "She has?"

"Yeah." I laugh softly. "At first, I thought she was talking about some friends at school when all she would talk about was Ace and Fire. But after...you know." I have to force my eyes from tearing up just at the mention of what happened with Lilly. "She kept bragging about how Ace saved her, and that Ace was her hero. Turns out, Chase was Ace, and I assume you were Fire. When I talked to Miss Macy about how Lilly knew who Chase was, she told me about you two volunteering at the daycare."

"She's an amazing little girl." Rain smiles. "She had our hearts from the moment we met."

Fuck. My eyes sting as I fight to keep the tears from falling. Knowing they already loved Lilly helps with the fear of them rejecting her. But would the other two feel the same?

"Tomorrow," I say, taking a deep breath to center myself.

"What?" Her brows furrow.

"Meet me at Bill's Diner tomorrow at noon. I have work at five and I need to be home to talk to the babysitter. With being away from school, I'll be too busy the next few days catching up to talk. So it's tomorrow or next weekend."

"Tomorrow then." She smiles. "Tell Lilly I said hi."

I don't say anything as she takes one last look before giving me a little wave. I give her one back before she turns and leaves. When the door closes behind her, I let out a breath, leaning back against the locker. Closing my eyes, I tip my head back.

"You got this, Ellie. It's time to get everything out in the open."

Chapter Nine

ELLIE

"WHY AM I SO NERVOUS?" I ask, fixing my hair in front of the mirror in the bathroom. "I feel like I'm going on a first date."

"Because," Theo says, kissing the top of my head then looking at me in the mirror. "These are people who meant a lot to you. People who have and probably always will own a part of your heart, whether you're together or not."

"Does it make me an awful person that the thought of seeing them gives me butterflies?" I ask, knowing that after everything they did, it shouldn't, but the whole situation was messed up and no one had all the facts.

"No. It just means you have a really big heart. You love hard, Ellie. It's one of the many things I love about you."

"I want to talk to you about Chase," I say, turning around in his arms to face him. I bite my lip, tasting the vanilla lip gloss on my tongue.

"Okay." He smiles knowingly.

"Are you really okay with this, if I'm with Chase and you at the same time? You don't think I'm selfish? Because Theo, I love you so fucking much, and you're enough for me." I feel like puking. Sweat is beading down my spine. I don't want to seem like a selfish person, but I'm also afraid he's going to change his mind.

"Yes, sweet girl. They owned your heart first, and it would be cruel of me to ask you to put that aside if it was something you wanted to have again. I just want to be one of the people you love and who can love and care for you back."

"You are, and you're never going anywhere. I'll track you down if you do." I smile up at him with watery eyes.

"Love, you're stuck with me. I'd haunt your sexy ass if I left this world before you."

"Shh," I say, slapping his arm playfully. "Don't talk like that."

"But really, love, what about Chase?" He pulls me closer into his arms, making me have to tilt my head back to look up at him.

"I think with what he did for Lilly and how sincere he's been the past few weeks, I'm ready to let him back in. Don't get me wrong, I'm scared shitless, but I don't want fear to hold me back if I don't have to."

"And I'll be here with you every step of the way. Just keep things open and honest and everything will be okay. I mean, no, you don't have to tell me what goes on between you two anymore." He grins and my cheeks flush. "But, if it's something that is a cause for change, like adding the others into your little harem, then I'd like to be made aware," he says, kissing my forehead.

"Always."

"Now, it's..." he checks his phone, "11:30, you told them noon, right?"

"Shit," I hiss, turning around to check myself over for the hundredth time.

"You look amazing, Ellie, stunning like always. Stop worrying."

Taking a deep breath, I nod. I'm in ripped skinny jeans that hug my body just right, a flowy pale pink top, and my hair is down in loose curls. I've added just a touch of makeup, not wanting to look like I'm trying too hard.

"Bug, come give Mama a hug," I tell Lilly who's coloring at the coffee table with Toby.

"Where you going, Mama?" she asks, playing with the hem of my shirt.

"Mama is gonna go see some friends, but then I'll be back to hang out for a bit before work, okay?"

"Okay! Have fun. Toby and I gonna watch a movie." She gives me a hug and a kiss. "Come on, Dada, let's watch Ariel," Lilly says, running over to Theo and grabbing his hand. She starts tugging him toward the couch. "'Mon, Dada, move," she grunts, tugging him harder, but we just stand there, shocked. Theo's eyes are wide with so many emotions at what she just called him. I'm so damn happy she feels so comfortable with him to call him her dad. I can tell by the look on his face right now, he's over the moon.

"Yeah, Dada, go watch Ariel," I grin, dabbing at the corner of my eyes.

"Umm. Yeah, yeah, let's totally watch some Ariel," Theo says, and I don't miss the emotion caught in his throat or the glimmer in his eye.

"YAY!" Lilly cheers. "Bye, Mama." And just like that, I'm forgotten. But I don't mind. This is a really big moment, and I hope Theo enjoys every second of it.

The whole drive, I resist the urge to pull over and puke due to all the anxiety I'm feeling right now. When I pull into the diner, I can see them all sitting at a table through the window.

"You got this, Ellie. You can do this," I tell myself. It's now or never. Turning the engine off, I grab my purse and keys.

I stop again when I grasp the door handle to the diner. With one last deep breath, I pull it open and step in.

The different aroma of foods fill the air, giving me a familiar feeling. This place is one of my favorite places to eat, and I have come to know the staff well, because it's mine and Theo's date night place. I'm just glad we don't have to go out of our way to hide our relationship anymore.

My eyes find them immediately. As if Chase can sense me, he looks up, his gaze locking onto mine. My belly flutters at the massive grin that takes over his face. I snort a laugh as he stands up in the booth, jumps over Rain and races over to me. He stops a foot away, bouncing on the balls of his feet with excited energy as he restrains himself from pulling me into his arms.

"Hey, Ellie Belly," he says.

And like a dork, I lose it. Throwing myself at him, he catches me, holding me tight.

"Thank you so much," I sob into his chest. "I don't know how to repay you for what you did."

"You never have to thank me, Ellie. I'll always be here." And I believe him when he says it.

Pulling back, I grip his face and pull him down to my lips, needing to taste him again and kiss him hard. He groans, his hands falling from my hips to my ass, pressing me tighter to him. Our lips move together with a desperate hunger. I love how he always tastes like a candy cane. I'm glad some things never change.

A throat clears from someone nearby, making my eyes snap open, realizing we are in the middle of a busy restaurant, making out like a couple of teenagers. I pull back with a blush creeping on my face. But Chase? He has a shit eating grin on his.

"Come on, babe. Let's get you something to eat." He wraps his arm around my shoulder and leads me over to the table. I'm not sure if I'll be able to eat. I'm so nervous right now.

Rain smiles when we get to the table, and I can't help but smile back shyly. She slides over in the booth, allowing Chase in the middle and me next to him.

"Hi," I say softly as I look over at Jax who has a small, nervous smile of his own, and Brody, who looks pissed. Or maybe it's just his face. I don't know, I haven't seen him smile since I got back here. I don't count the cruel grins he used to always cast at me.

"Hi," Jax says back.

"Hey," Brody grunts. Well, he's pleasant, isn't he? I knew he was always a broody man and I hope it's just the conversation we are about to have that is putting him off and not me.

"What do you want to eat?" Chase asks, sliding the menu over to me.

"Nothing, thanks." I smile up at him.

"So," Brody starts. "Thanks for coming to talk to us."

"Yeah." I let out a nervous laugh. "It's been a long time coming."

"First, I know this isn't the place to talk about him, but I am so sorry, for everything," Jax says, his eyes filled with so much remorse. "We didn't know."

"I know." I give him a sad smile. "I assumed that much from the start." I just wished they loved me enough to ask first.

"It was wrong of me, what I did. I saw what I wanted to see. Then I held onto that and made it my reality while also drilling it into the others. I regret it, every moment of it. If I could go back and change things, I would do everything different. I hope you know that." Brody's brooding look is gone, and I see it in his eyes that he really means it.

"Thanks. I know nothing can change the past. I just want to move forward and start over, in whatever way that means for all of you. If you wanna talk about it more later on, after we've spent more time together, I'd be open to it. Right now, I don't think I'm emotionally ready for that. What happened at the party the other weekend opened everything I've worked so hard at keeping locked up...but we are going to have to learn to get along."

"Babe, I think you and I are past that point." Chase grins down at me.

"Because of Lilly," Brody points out, ignoring Chase's comment.

"Yeah." The table is silent, and I really wish someone would say something to break the ice.

So, Brody decides to be the one to. "Is she Tim's?" Not the icebreaker I was looking for.

"What?" I ask, my eyes going wide. "No, of course not."

"Dude, really?" Chase growls at his friend.

"It was something we were all wondering." Brody glares at him.

"Yeah, but did you have to be so blunt? Damn, man, learn some people skills," Chase mutters.

"No. She's not his," I say, my stomach dropping at his name. "When I found out I was pregnant, the doctor told me I was sixteen weeks. Meaning, I was eight weeks along already on the night of graduation," I say, my voice going low into almost a whisper.

"Fuck," Chase curses. "It's taking everything in me, man. It's taking everything in me not to reach over the table and give you a set of matching black eyes." I can feel him vibrating right now. "She was pregnant with our kid, and we left her there." His voice cracks, and my heart breaks a little.

"Hey," I say, grabbing his hand under the table and lacing my fingers into his. "It's okay. You didn't know. I didn't know."

"It's not." His eyes are wide, and I just want to soothe him.

"Stop, please," I ask him. "No more blame. It was a messy moment in our past. The best we can do is try to move on. I want to work toward forgiving you all. Because I can't hate you, it hurts too much. It's toxic and I don't need that to taint my heart and my family." My eyes well with tears as I look at the others. "Let me tell you about your daughter, okay? She's pretty amazing." I smile.

"We know," Rain pipes up from her seat. "Well, Chase and I know." She smiles like she's remembering her time with Lilly.

"Deep down, I knew she was our kid," Chase says, his body starting to relax.

"You did not," Rain laughs.

"Yeah, because who else could help make such an epic kid?" Chase says. "She must be mine. I'm pretty damn epic."

I giggle and Jax's smile widens as he catches my eye.

"Oh, please," Rain says.

"I mean, maybe," I say, looking back at Chase. "You both do have pretty similar birthmarks."

Chase's grin grows. "You're right! I saw that and thought it was freaky. But in a good way."

"We don't know whose she is, but is that something you wanna find out?" Jax asks. "We talked about it, and if you don't want a DNA test, then we're fine with that. We don't care either way."

"You would be okay with not knowing which one of you is her actual father?" I ask, looking at the three of them.

"Yes, because she's a part of you, so therefore, she's ours, even if we weren't an option for being her father," Chase says, and Jax nods in agreement. My heart swells with so much happiness that they would be so accepting of her like this. I look at Brody, wondering if he feels the same way. He's let me know that he wants to have a ceasefire, but he's never told me if he wants to be friends eventually. Or more. I'm not ready for the 'more' with him, maybe I won't ever really be. But I would like to be friendly for Lilly's sake. And the others. They are family to each other, and I've never wanted to come between that.

"If you don't want a DNA test, then it doesn't matter to me," he says.

I relax a little. "Then I'd like to not find out unless we have to some day for health reasons."

"Agreed then. So, can you tell us about our daughter?" Jax asks, a hopeful look in his eyes.

We spend the next hour talking about Lilly, from the moment I found out about her, right up to the present. They laugh at funny stories and ask questions as I tell each story. And by the end of it, it feels like old times. And that scares me. I'm not going to open up so easily and let them back in. No, they need to work for it. So, I let them know.

"I hope this doesn't sound like a bitchy thing to say," I start, all the nerves are gone and the Ellie who stood up to all their bullshit the past few months is in place now. "But, just because we've agreed to get along for Lilly's sake doesn't mean I've forgotten about the past few months. What you did to me..." I look at Rain and Brody, "was really fucked up. Even if I did the things you accused me of, that never gave you the right to treat me that way. Hate me? Sure. Not wanting to be around me? I'd understand. But to act like I was nothing more than a piece of gum under your shoes..." I shake my head. "No, if you want to be in my life more than getting to know Lilly and eventually being a parent in her life, then you need to earn it."

"And he did?" Brody asks, nodding toward Chase, not sounding pissed, but generally asking.

"Yeah, he did. At least with me he has because he owned up to his mistakes pretty early on. He's been working on winning me back, and his role in all of this was different. He admitted he was a coward for not sticking up for me like he wanted to. And after what he did for Lilly, I have nothing to hold against him anymore."

"We're going to prove it to you," Jax says. "That we really are sorry, that we fucked up, and that we love you."

His words are something I both want to and don't want to hear. "Let's start with friends, okay?"

"Does that mean that maybe there's a chance for more?" Rain asks, and fuck, it's a punch to the gut at the vulnerable look in her eyes. Then I remember what she did, and how she's done nothing to show her remorse.

"Prove you're truly sorry, then we'll go from there," I answer her question and she nods. "I gotta go. I have work at five and I told Lilly I'd spend some time with her beforehand."

"When can we meet her?" Jax asks. "Well, I guess, when can Brody and I meet her seeing how they already met her?"

"I don't know. With work, school, and Lilly's birthday coming up, I have a lot going on right now." I don't mention the court case that I know I'll be having after I get in contact with a lawyer. I've decided to press charges against Tim, and work hard to get his rapist-ass behind bars where he belongs for good.

"Her birthday? When is that?" Chase asks.

"February fourth." I smile. "I was due at the end of January, but she was a stubborn little one and overstayed her welcome," I laugh.

"What are you doing for her birthday?" Rain asks.

"Umm. We were thinking of just a small party with Theo, his son, Toby, and my friends. Maybe rent out the bowling alley or something." I haven't talked to them about Theo and I or told them anything about him personally. They don't need to know right now. And it's not my place to talk about him.

"Can we come?" Chase asks hopefully.

"I don't know. I want to take this slow. Until I feel comfortable with it, Lilly will know you guys as my friends. It's gonna be a lot for her to get used to, and I don't want to confuse her." Also, seeing how she thinks of Theo as her dad now, adding three more and an extra mom she's never met is not something I'm going to do.

"We've missed so much of her life already. I don't want to miss anything else. We promise to just be there as friends." Chase gives me these big, puppy dog eyes. He's right, they missed out on all her important milestones as well as just being there as she's grown.

"Okay. Yeah. I can text you the details later. But remember, you're my friends, that's it."

"Got it!" Chase whoops, pulling me into a kiss. I melt into his touch, feeling lightheaded when he pulls away.

"I gotta get going," I tell them. "Thanks for meeting with me today. If there's anything else you feel like you need to know, please ask."

We all say goodbye but Chase insists on walking me to my car. I'm glad because I wanted a moment alone with him.

"So, me and you," I start.

"Yessss, what about me and you?" He grins down at me as he pulls me into his arms. I love being in his hold like this. It feels like home.

"I'd be okay with things being...more than friends, if it's something you still want?" I bite my lip, hoping it is.

"You mean, like dating?" His eyes light up. "Like you being my girlfriend again?"

"I mean, kinda? I think we need to spend some time together before we start putting labels on things, but yes."

"Fuck yeah, I do." Chase cheers, making me laugh. "I can't stop thinking about being buried deep inside you." His eyes grow hooded, and the mood shifts. Fuck. "I can't wait until I can take my time with you, and really show you how much I love you."

Now is not the time to be turned on, Ellie.

"Me too," I whisper.

"I love you, Ellie. I hope you know that," he says, brushing his lips against mine.

All I can do is sigh; I'm not ready to say it back, but I feel the same way. "I know. I know you do." He doesn't seem hurt that I haven't said it back to him.

"See you, baby girl." We kiss again, and fuck, it's everything I want and more. I don't think I can get enough of his candy cane kisses.

He leaves me panting, shooting his cocky smile, before saying goodbye, and joining the others inside.

The whole car ride home, all I can think about is how hot that kiss made me, and how I need to change my underwear before work.

Chapter Ten

THEO

"HEY, buddy, come sit next to me. I wanna talk to you about something," I tell Toby, patting the couch beside me.

Lilly fell asleep about a half hour ago, so while she's napping, Toby and I have played quietly with the toys.

He hops up on the couch next to me, looking at me with a tilted head. "What's up, Dad?"

"When Ellie left to go meet with her friends, Lilly called me something, and I wanted to see what you thought about it." When Lilly called me Dada, I just about passed out. I was so happy and excited, but terrified at the same time. But the look on Ellie's face eased my concerns a little. Seeing that she was okay with the new title sent a surge of pride through me. It means so much to me that that little girl feels like I am that role in her life now.

But it's not something I take lightly. I have a little guy of my own to think about. I want to be a dad to Lilly. She's an amazingly sweet little girl who I've grown to love as quickly as I did her mother, but I don't want Toby to think for a moment that he's being replaced, or that by Lilly calling me Dad, I'm no longer his.

"What did she call you?" he asks, his brows scrunching up.

"She called me Dada. Is that something you're okay with her calling me? If not, I can talk to Ellie."

"Yeah, Dad, it's fine." He rolls his eyes. I'm taken aback by his reaction.

"It is?"

"Duh, I told her she could."

"You did?" I ask, not expecting him to say that.

He shrugs. "She doesn't have a daddy. She told me she was sad about it, and I said we can share mine. She looked happy about that. You are the best dad, so she should have the best dad too. I can share. She's my best friend." Nope, not gonna cry right now. But I am so damn proud of my little man. Seeing his friend without and then willing to share something so important warms my heart.

"That was very nice of you. I'm sure it meant a lot to Lilly that you're willing to share me."

"Is it okay that you're her dad now?" he asks, sounding scared all of a sudden.

"I think if you are and Ellie is, then I am more than happy to be a dad to Lilly. She's a very sweet little girl, and I've grown to love her like my own."

"Are you and Ellie gonna get married?"

My eyes widen, not expecting the conversation to go in this direction.

"I don't know," I tell him honestly. And I don't. It's not that I wouldn't marry her in a heartbeat. I'd take that girl down to city hall right this second, but I'm not the only person in her life anymore, and there's likely going to be more joining in, eventually. I would never ask her to pick me for something so important over everyone else. It may be a good idea to talk about it at some point though, just to know where she stands.

"Will you still be together if you're not? I don't want Lilly to lose a dad like I lost my mommy."

My heart clenches at the mention of my late wife.

"Ellie and I are doing amazing, bud. We love each other very much, and we don't want to be without each other."

"Good." He nods. "I like Ellie. She makes you happy."

I give him a soft smile. "She does. Very much."

"I didn't like seeing you so sad after mommy passed. I think she would be happy you're happy." When did this little boy grow into such a wise little man? My eyes mist at his words.

"I think she would be too."

"Can we see Mommy sometime soon? I wanna talk to her about something."

"Of course, buddy, we can go whenever you want."

Toby has been going to Kristen's grave quite a bit. I've always made sure to keep her memory alive as much as I can. I tell stories, show photos, and we visit all the time to just sit and talk.

Toby goes back to playing, and I just sit and watch him for a while until Lilly wakes up from her nap. She stands in the doorway with a sleepy look in her eyes.

I'm about to say hi and ask her how her nap was, but she walks over to me, crawls into my lap and snuggles close before falling back to sleep.

Yup, this little girl owns my heart just as much as her mama. I'm done for, and I'm not even mad about it.

Ellie walks through the door with a shy smile on her face, looking like she is lost in her own little world.

"How was the talk?" I ask, her eyes snapping up to meet mine as my voice snaps her out of her thoughts.

"Oh, ah, it was... good." Her smile stays in place. "Some of them have more work to do than others, but they all want to get to know Lilly and be in her life. A part of me thought they wouldn't want to. There're still some things we need to talk about, but I didn't think telling them all the things they need to change in order for me to feel better about them being an active role in her life was a good ice breaker," she cringes.

"One thing at a time, my love. I think they will be okay with doing whatever it takes to be in her life. She's worth it."

"She is." Ellie smiles. "And I hope so, but we'll see. How was your day? Did they behave for you?"

"They did. We watched some movies and played some games. Lilly took a nap, and I had a little talk with Toby."

"Oh? About what?" she asks, hopping to sit on top of the counter.

"Lilly calling me Dada."

"Oh my God, I didn't even think of that. Shoot, is he okay? I don't want Lilly calling you that if it's going to make Toby upset."

"No, it's fine." I laugh. "Actually, he told me it was his idea."

"Really?" Her brows rise.

"Yeah. He said because Lilly didn't have a dad, he wants to share his with his best friend."

Her eyes go glassy. "You raised an amazing little boy, Theo. I'm so grateful he's willing to share you with my girl. He's a good kid, and he means a lot to me too, like Lilly does to you."

"I think it is one of the many reasons why our family works so well."

"Same," she says.

Ellie hangs out with Lilly for a little while before getting ready and heading to work. Toby and I go back to our apartment while Katie watches Lilly.

Ellie agreed to sleep at my place tonight, so after I get some papers graded and other work things done, Katie will bring Lilly over here.

I want them to move in with me, seeing how we spend more time at my place. It would save Ellie money on rent, bills, and food too. But, I know she's really into her own independence.

Now that she's slowly working on things with her exes, I don't know how she's going to feel about it. There's so much going on right now, so maybe I'll wait until life has settled again before bringing it up, until the time is right.

My eyes start to grow heavy. Looking over at the clock, I see that it's 11 pm. I put Toby and Lilly to bed around eight and got some extra work done. Looking down at my phone, I see that Ellie texted that she is on her way home.

Excited to see my girl, I put all my work things away and make her a late night snack, fried egg on a buttered bagel. It's one of her favorites and she's always hungry when she gets home because she's so busy, she forgets to eat. Even when she's staying at her own place, and me at mine, I'll still go by and make sure she has something to eat before going to bed. I don't like the idea of her going hungry.

"Yum," she moans as she walks through the door.

"Hi, my love." I smile at her as she closes and locks the door before coming over to the island where I set her food down for her.

"Hi, handsome. You spoil me, you know that?" she says, putting her bag down on the floor. She sits down on the stool and picks up the sandwich, taking a bite. "But I'm *so* not complaining." She groans as she chews. My cock twitches as she makes these sexy noises while she eats.

"Sweet girl," I say, my voice low and husky. I've been craving her for the few past weeks. We've both been so busy, and she's been so stressed out lately. I'd never pressure her for sex, and I've gone without it for a while before she came into my life, so it's not like I'd die if I didn't get some. But right now, the way her big doe eyes look up at me all innocent like... It has me wanting to see them water as she chokes on my cock.

"Oh," she says softly, her eyes going wide with understanding before flicking down to see my dick pressing painfully against my sweatpants. She bites her lower lip as her eyes grow hooded. "I was doing it again, wasn't I?" she asks, meeting my eyes.

"Don't be sorry. I find it sexy that you love the food that you eat."

"I can tell." She gives me a sassy grin filled with heat. "How about this, I'm gonna finish eating this and hop in the shower real quick, but when I get out, I want you waiting for me in bed."

"Oh, really?" I grin, loving when she feels confident like this.

"Yes, because you need help getting rid of that." She points to my erection. "And I would very much like to be the one who helps you out."

"You gonna suck me off, sweet girl?" I growl.

"Every last drop." Fuck my heart, and my dick, she's so damn perfect.

Laying in bed, I wait for Ellie while she showers. You would think because I've been waiting for ten minutes, my dick would have gone down some, but nope, it's still hard as a rock, because all I can think about is Ellie in the shower and her wet soapy hands all over her gorgeous naked body.

Yeah, there's no getting this to go away any time soon.

"Hey," she says, breaking the silence in my room. My eyes snap open to find my stunning woman standing in my doorway. She closes the door behind her, flicking the lock so no little ones walk in on something they shouldn't see.

"Hey," I say, moving up onto my elbows to get a better look. Her hair is still damp from the shower, hanging down over her shoulder. A towel hides her body, and I let out a groan as she drops it.

"I see you waited for me." She gives me a sexy grin as she looks down at my erect cock pushing against my boxers.

"Always. And I gave you easy access to all this too," I grin.

She bites her lip as she starts to crawl on the bed over to me, looking like a powerful goddess.

Her breasts sway with the movement, hypnotizing me. "Eyes up here, big boy." Her voice is seductive and full of need.

"You're so damn perfect, sweet girl." I groan as she covers my body with hers.

"So are you." She kisses me and I fall back onto the pillows, wrapping my arms around her and bringing her down with me. We mold together, arms and legs tangling as our tongues dance.

Her body moves against mine, grinding against my cock. It feels so fucking good, but I'd rather be inside her.

"Fuck, I need you, love," I growl against her lips, nipping her bottom one.

"Soon. But first, I want to taste you," she says in a breathy tone.

When we first got together, I was very careful with her. I didn't want to trigger her, or make her feel uncomfortable or scared. But as we started to become more intimate with each other, she became very encouraging of my sexual curiosity. When I was with Kristen, it was always good, but she wasn't into the kinds of things I wanted to try. Ellie seems to sense my desires to try more in the bedroom. She gave me her trust, and lets me take control in the bedroom. I was quick to learn that the way that I am in here versus the outside world are very different from each other.

As much as I love to have her a writhing mess under me, it's so fucking hot to see her take control like this, too. And I'm more than happy to have my woman please me as I do her.

"You can have whatever you want with me, my love," I say, my tone husky and full of need.

She shimmies her way back down my body until her face is hovering over my length. She looks up at me with hooded eyes before leaning over and biting my cock through my boxers.

I hiss, finding that it actually feels good. She gives me a

naughty grin that makes me want to slap her plump ass, but right now, my body is her's to do with as she pleases. I trust her, and the idea of her owning me like this has precum leaking out the tip.

"Now, now, are you gonna be a bad girl?" I ask as she pulls down my boxers, letting my cock spring free.

"Maybe." She shrugs, staring at my cock and licking her lips. "So fucking big," she says so quietly, I almost don't hear her. I bite the inside of my cheek, holding back my smug as fuck smirk that's threatening to take over at the hungry look in her eyes.

She looks up at me, making sure I'm watching her before sticking her tongue out and licking my cock from base to tip, then sucking the head into her mouth and taking me in on a bob.

"Sweet fuck, Ellie," I moan, bucking my hips a little at the sudden way she took me in one go.

Wasting no time, she starts to bob her head, sucking and licking. She feels amazing around my cock. Her lips and tongue are working me over, all while never looking away from me. She's enjoying this just as much as I am. My breathing is coming out choppy. Normally, I can last longer, but I've gotten so used to having a steady release that not having any for the past few weeks means it won't be long before I'm cumming down her throat.

Grabbing the base with her firm grip, she pumps me while sucking. And when she uses her free hand to roll my balls, I lose my fucking mind. Tossing my head back, my body tightens. Grasping the sheets, I try not to cum, not wanting this to be over before it starts, but damn it, it's really hard.

"Love, if you keep doing that, I'm gonna be cumming in seconds," I choke out.

She slows down a little, getting a nice and steady rhythm. My body relaxes slightly, but not completely because she's still rocking my world.

"Fuck, you take my cock so well, sweet girl. Look at you, taking me all the way," I groan as she deep throats me, holding herself there for a moment before pulling back.

She starts to hum, and that has the last of my restraint going out the window. I was already on the edge, but this is sending me flying over.

"Ellie. I'm gonna cum," I grit out, trying to give her a little warning in case she wanted to pull back and not swallow any, but she just goes faster, humming louder and I'm biting my arm, roaring her name as I cum down her throat. I can feel my cock jerk as she sucks down streams of my cum.

When I have nothing left to give her, she pulls back, her throat bobbing as she swallows the last of me, leaving a string of spit and cum as she does. *So damn sexy.*

"How was that?" she asks, her pupils dilated so wide, they're almost black. She wipes the bit of cum from the corner of her mouth with her thumb, then sucks it off. *This girl.*

"Amazing. Perfect. Mind fucking blowing," I huff out a laugh as she gives me a sexy grin.

"Good. I'm sad though." She pouts as she moves to hover over me, her tits so close to my face that I just want to bite them.

"Why?" I ask, rubbing her legs.

"Because, I'm dripping wet and you're too tired. Maybe I'll just take care of myself."

"Like hell you will," I growl. "Let me take away that ache between your legs, love."

"I mean...if you insist." She grins, rolling over next to me onto her back and letting her legs fall open.

I growl, moving so that my mouth lines up with her pussy. "Let's see how sassy you are when you're screaming my name, sweet girl," I growl again before diving in to have a late night snack of my own.

She cries out, her fingers tangling in my hair as I feast on her sweet pussy like a starving man. It doesn't take her long before she's cumming on my face. I make sure to lick every inch of her cunt, not letting her juices go to waste.

"I needed that," she sighs when I move to kiss her.

"Anytime you need some relief, I'm more than happy to lend a hand. Or a mouth." I grin.

"Theo, I need more," she whimpers, reaching down to grip my already hardened cock. "Don't hold back, fuck me, hard and fast. Please."

"Are you sure?" I ask, my eyes searching hers for any uncertainty. I want to, I crave it, but I need to be sure.

"Yes," she nods. "I trust you." I can see that she wants it and that she wants me to be a little rougher than normal. "I don't want you to hold yourself back with me anymore, Theo. I see the need for new and exciting things in your eyes. Do them with me. Let's explore together."

Our sex hasn't really been safe, I fucked her pretty roughly on my desk in my office that one time. But a part of me wondered if I took it too far. There's just something about her that brings out this primal side in me.

"I love you so damn much, Ellie," I say, capturing her lips with mine as I grab a hold of her hips with one arm and line my cock up at her soaked entrance.

She kisses me with a desperate need, making me growl into her mouth as I thrust forward. She cries out, her nails digging into my back. Pulling away from the kiss, I fuck her like she asked me to, the need to be deep inside her overwhelming. We watch each other, our eyes wild and crazed.

Our cries of pleasure mix with the sounds of our skin slapping together.

"Theo," she mewls, her eyes frantic.

"I know, baby. I know," I grit out. She's already close again, her pussy clenching around my cock. "I feel it too."

"Harder," she pleads.

Picking up the pace, I bite my lip as I fuck into her like a savage, but the glazed look in her eyes and the way she's babbling nonsense tells me this is just what she needed.

"Don't stop. God, please, Theo. Please, don't stop!" she begs, her eyes frantic.

"I won't, sweet girl. Fuck. I'll never stop," I growl, feeling my balls tighten and I thank the stars that she cums at the same time I do, making it so much more intense.

"Ellie!" I roar as she screams, "Theo!" Her pussy death grips my cock as she arches her back, her orgasm taking over her body, making her look like the fucking queen she is.

I still, my cock buried deep inside her, as I coat her inner walls with my cum, marking her as mine. The thought has my cock twitching harder.

Panting from the events of the night, we lie side by side, taking a moment to recover.

"I hope we didn't wake the kids up," she says, looking over at me with a sleepy smile.

"I put on some music near the door in hopes to drown us out." I laugh and her smile widens. "Come on, my love, let's get you cleaned up and into bed. You have school tomorrow."

"Right. School," she groans.

"It's gonna be fine. You have your friends and the others have put an end to their reign of terror."

"I know," she sighs.

Getting out of bed, I scoop her up into my arms and carry her to the shower. We shower and dress for bed, and as she brushes her teeth, I change the bed sheets.

"Theo," Ellie says, rolling over onto her side once we're back in bed ready for sleep.

"Yes, my love," I say, turning onto my side.

"I'm afraid."

"Of what?"

"A part of me wants to forget every bad thing they did and let them back in because they really didn't know what happened that night. I crave what we used to have. But then I remember that they should have loved and trusted me. That them treating me like a villain when I came back was immature and fucked up. Then I also think we were all young and dumb teenagers back then and people make mistakes. Ugh, I just don't know."

"I think you're off to a good start. Try taking it day by day.

Don't rush it, but also don't hold back if it feels right. Let everything happen naturally."

"Yeah, you're right," she says, snuggling into me. "They each need to prove that what they are saying is true. When did you become so wise?" she says with a laugh.

"Not sure, maybe it's because I'm so old," I joke, holding her closer to me.

"I love me a sexy silver fox," she says, kissing my chest.

"I'm all yours." I kiss the top of her head. "Sleep. I'll protect you while you do."

.

Chapter Eleven

RAIN

"WE SHOULD PROBABLY GO IN THERE, right?" I ask, my belly tight with nerves. We're just sitting in the parked car in the bowling alley parking lot. We got here about ten minutes ago, but none of us have made a move to go inside. Even Chase, who looks ready to explode with excitement to see both Lilly and Ellie, is displaying conflicting emotions on his face as he just stares at the door of the building.

After we got back to the guys' apartment, we all sat and talked about everything, replaying a lot of what Ellie told us about Lilly.

Brody tried to hide his excitement, but after a while, I saw a smile or two while Chase told him and Jax in detail about the week we spent with Lilly before we knew she was our daughter.

Our daughter? *Am I even allowed to call her that?* Ellie and I are nowhere near being at a good place in our relationship, not that we even have one at this point. Hell, me showing up at her work was probably the first time we've talked without me being a raging bitch.

I need to work on that. Maybe I'll start with talking to her alone again.

We've all been a mess this past week trying to come up with ideas for birthday gifts, stressing about how this day is going to go.

This is our first time seeing Lilly and spending time with her knowing who she really is.

Chase may be with Ellie now, and rightfully so—he's been working his stalker ass off to win her back for weeks now, and saving Lilly was probably the thing that solidified his place—but it's not even about all that. Yes, sitting back and doing nothing while we were scum of the earth was wrong of him, but I think Ellie knew that he was in a hard place, not that its any excuse for his choices. The fact is, he wasn't a monster to her. He always felt like there was something more with what happened on graduation night.

And he was right. *Boy, was he right.* Just thinking about what Tim did to her makes me want to scream, cry, and destroy him. But this isn't my pain. I have no right to demand anything. The best I can do is help her heal in any way she allows me to. We all vowed not to bring that night up again unless she does first. If she says she wants to move on, then bringing it up will only set her back.

Ellie truly is amazing because after everything that's happened, she's being so damn mature about the situation and allowing us to be a part of something important: a part of Lilly's life, especially after we missed out on so much, through no fault but our own. She's strong, beautiful, and so fucking amazing.

I hate myself for hating her for so long and without a reason. Years of thinking that she was the bad guy, when in reality, she was going through hell.

I regret every single moment of it. My gut turns when I think of all the bullshit I did. I sat back and watched while the other girls fucked with her and allowed it to happen.

My heart hurts knowing I did that to the girl that I'm so fucking madly in love with, just because I convinced myself to hate her; even though I've never stopped loving her.

And as much as I know that I don't deserve it, I want her back. I want a second chance to show her how sorry I *truly* am. I want my love, my best friend, and the only person who has ever really made me feel loved and wanted, back. I was so dumb back then, but I know better now, and I want to do better moving forward.

I'm going to do everything I can to show her, to prove to her, how I really feel, until she tells me to fuck off. Maybe I'll take a page out of Chase's book and stalk her sexy ass. I mean, as soon as I know she won't bite my head off for it.

"I don't like this feeling," Brody grumbles.

"What feeling?" Jax asks, looking over at him from his spot next to him in the front seat.

"Nervousness." Brody turns his head to Jax. Brody is all talk about how he has no right to Ellie and no right to Lilly, but I know he wants her, wants them both. He wants to be that little girl's dad. He wants to love Ellie, but he's so fucked up in the head, he doesn't think he has any worth, and it's affecting his and Jax's relationship.

I've seen them become a lot more distant since the night of the party. Jax is hurting, but there's also this other side of him that's changing, growing. I'm proud of him for using his head, having his own mind, and sticking up for what he wants. He's been more involved and excited when talking about our girls. He seems just as determined to prove to Ellie that he's as committed as Chase and I are.

Now we just need broody Brody to get the fuck over himself. To stop letting his shitty parents dictate his life choices, and move on from his past. And for him to use his brain for once.

"It's what we're all feeling." Jax gives him a reassuring smile. Reaching for Brody's hand, Jax laces their fingers together, brings them up to his lips, and kisses the back of Brody's hand. Brody looks shocked at first, telling me this is the first time they really had any contact with each other in a while. Both Brody's body and face relax at Jax's touch.

"Come on, let's get in there before we miss the whole thing and hate ourselves even more," Chase says, opening his door. "Leave the presents in here for now. We can get them whenever she's ready to open them." We all exit the car and stand together by the front door. I can hear the sounds of the bowling balls crashing against the pins and the cheers of people inside.

"I think we should just slip in, find them, and hang back a bit," Jax suggests.

"But, I wanna hang out with Lilly," Chase pouts.

"Wait until they come to us, okay? We kind of put her on the spot to come here," Jax argues.

"She's our kid. We should be able to come to her birthday," Brody mutters and Jax shoots him a look.

"Don't. We have no right to anything; we need to earn it. This is Ellie's child, who she has been raising for the past four years *by herself*. She's sacrificed so much to be a good mother to Lilly after everything we put her through. We will not undermine her parenting decisions, even if it's something we may not like or agree with, got it?" Jax says, giving Brody a stern look.

"Yeah," Brody grunts.

Chase opens the door and the sounds amplify as we step inside. The place is packed with kids running around laughing and screaming.

"Awesome, I can feel the headache coming now," Brody bitches.

"Seriously, man? This is for our daughter's birthday! Stop being a little bitch and man the fuck up," Chase growls.

A gasp comes from close by, and I look over to see a group of kids looking at us with shocked expressions.

"You can't say bad words here," a little girl sasses at Chase, putting her hands on her hips. I bite my lips, trying to hold back the grin that's threatening to take over my face at the look on Chase's face.

"Right," Jax says. "You're right, and he's sorry. Right, Chase?"

"Ahh, yeah. Sorry, kid," Chase says, clearing his throat. They all glare at him before turning around and running over to the little arcade area. "Well this is awesome," Chase grumbles. "We're going to have to watch how we talk from now on, aren't we?"

"Yup." I laugh. "At least when we are around Lilly, or other little kids. You did really well that one week. Now you just need to keep it up."

We make our way deeper into the place, eyes searching for Ellie and the others. We spot them at the very last lane. There's a table set up with some gifts and balloons, and a few streamers are hung on the wall above it with a sign that says 'Happy 4th Birthday, Lilly'.

"This is wrong," Brody says.

"What, why?" I ask, my brows furrowing.

"Lilly should have this day be about her, but she has to share her birthday party with all these other kids being around. They should have rented the place out or something."

I look back over and see Lilly step up to the lane, a little ball in her hands. She puts it on the dinosaur ramp and pushes it with all her might. It rolls down the ramp, then down the lane, hitting the middle pin that takes the rest of them down with it. Their whole group starts cheering, making Lilly squeal with excitement and that has my face slipping into a massive smile.

"Does it look like she cares?" I ask him, looking back at Brody who is also watching her. "Ellie works her ass off, goes to school, and is a single mother to that little girl. Do you think she has the money to be able to afford to rent this place out by herself?"

"Yeah, you have a point. But next year, we're going all out," he says.

Smiling, I shake my head. For someone who says he's probably only ever going to be an uncle-type figure to her, he sure is acting like an overbearing parent right now.

"Come on. There's an empty lane next to them. Go sit, and I'll get us some rental shoes," Jax says.

"Do we have to wear sweaty used shoes?" Brody's lip curls.

"Should have brought yours then," Chase laughs.

Yes, he does indeed have his own pair. We don't go bowling much these days, but we did a lot in high school. Brody bought his own shoes and ball, saying that places like these were a cesspool for bacteria. *Rich people.* I mean, Jax, Chase, and I were not bad off. Our parents had money, but nothing close to Brody's. But honestly, you could never tell he was a kid who came from wealth. Growing up, he never went out of his way to have all the new things, the *better* things. He was happy to just be out of his toxic house and be around us.

Brody goes with Jax, and Chase and I go sit and wait.

"Is it just me, or is this both really amazing and also super weird?" Chase asks, watching Lilly go again.

"It's not just you," I say. "I knew there was something special about that little girl."

"But I didn't think for a second that she was our kid," Chase says, looking at me with a big grin. "I never thought I'd be a dad, you know? I mean, I did at one point, and I imagined it would be with Ellie. Then everything happened and that dream died. So to find out that dream really did come true...it fills me with so much joy. But I'm also afraid. What if Lilly won't like the idea of us being her dad?"

"Dada!" Lilly calls out, making both of us look over to her as she runs over to Theo. "Your turn." She grabs his hand, pulling him toward the balls. Theo laughs, his face bright and happy as he follows her.

"Looks like she already has a dad," Chase growls.

"Down boy," I say, raising a brow at him. "From what Ellie said when she was telling us about Lilly, she didn't have a boyfriend until Theo. Meaning, Lilly never had a father figure before. Theo has been the only man in her life for the past five months. Ellie says Theo watches Lilly, and helps her care for her when she needs it. If anyone has the right to be called Dad right now, it's him."

"Fine," Chase grumbles, crossing his arms and slouching down into the chair. "But I will get that title someday."

"You will," I laugh. "But hey, at least you know she likes you already. That's a start."

"Yeah, true," he says, but he's glaring at Theo like he's trying to shoot lasers out of his eyes and into Theo's head.

The others come back, handing us our shoes, but we don't put them on. We spend the next half hour just observing. We watch Lilly play, looking so adorable in her little pink, puffy dress. Her hair is in pigtails and the ringlets bounce with her every step.

Ellie looks gorgeous. Her hair is in a sexy, messy bun, and she's in a pair of tight, light blue jeans that hug her ass so tightly, my hands itch to touch it. She's got on a shirt that says, 'Mother of the Birthday Girl'. A part of me feels happy for the guys that Theo doesn't have one that says father, not that I don't think he doesn't deserve it, it's just that I know it would make the guys feel even more out of place.

She just looks perfect, but she always looks perfect no matter what she wears.

I feel a pang of jealousy when I see how amazing she's doing without us, like maybe us coming back into her life will only mess it up. I mean, that's kind of what has happened the past few months. We have messed up her life.

What makes the feeling go away is knowing that she has had so many people on her side for every thing we did to her. She was never alone.

All her friends are here, Lexie, Cooper, Val, and Tabitha. There's a little boy here too. He must be Theo's son. But I'm most surprised to see that both of her parents are here too, knowing that they live so far away.

"So we're gonna just sit here and watch like a bunch of weirdos?" Brody asks.

"Yup, pretty much," Chase says. We don't actually want to bowl. We just want to watch Lilly be happy, smile, and enjoy her day.

Lilly is in Theo's arms when she looks over and spots us for the first time. Her bright, blue eyes light up, and my heart starts to pick up its pace. "Ace!" Lilly shouts as she wiggles in Theo's arms to get down. "Fire!" Hearing the name she gave me makes my eyes tear up. I've been worried because I honestly didn't know where I stood with her or what my place is supposed to be right now. I don't feel like I have the right to call myself her mother. I haven't earned that, and I'm not with Ellie at the moment. But the way she lights up when she sees me...it makes me so happy to know that I mean something to her, even if it's as just a really cool friend for right now.

They all look over at us as Theo puts Lilly down. They don't move as Lilly races over to us, launching herself into Chase's open arms.

"Hey, Lilly," Chase says, spinning her around. She giggles, making my heart swell.

"I missed you, Ace." She hugs his neck tightly before pulling back and kissing his cheek. The look on Chase's face is shock, but quickly melts into pure fucking joy.

"I missed you too, Lilly girl." His voice cracks with emotion. A tear slips from my eye as I smile, watching them together. My eyes flick over to Ellie who's watching them with a look similar to mine. She notices, giving me a small smile that's just for me and it has butterflies fluttering around in my belly. Fuck, she's so beautiful. Would it be weird if I went over and kissed her feet, begging for forgiveness? Yeah, probably not a good idea.

"Hey there, cutie pie," I say, tickling her side, making her giggle.

"Fire!" she squeals, jumping into my arms next. "I missed you too."

"And I missed you!"

She gives me a big squeeze then sits back on my lap, her little arms still around my neck. "Ace saved me from a bad, bad man!" she tells me, her eyes wide.

"I heard. That was so awesome of him."

She gives me one big nod. "Yup. He my hero."

I smile, looking over at Chase. I've never really seen him cry before, but he looks pretty damn close.

"Who's them?" Lilly asks, looking over at Jax and Brody who are sitting and watching with unsure expressions.

Ellie walks over to us and crouches down next to Lilly. "This is Jax," Ellie points at him. "And this is Brody. They are Fire and Ace's other friends. And they are Mama's friends too."

Lilly looks at her mother with a surprised look. "You friend with Ace and Fire too?"

"I am." She smiles. "Mama knew them since she was just a little older than you."

"Wow. Them too?" Lilly points to Jax and Brody.

"Yup." Ellie nods. Lilly wiggles out of my hold and goes over to the guys. They look down at her like deer caught in headlights. This is the first time they've met her, seen her up close.

"Hi." She waves.

"Hi," Jax says, giving her a soft smile.

"I'm Lilly." She grins up at him.

"I'm Jax."

Lilly looks at him for a moment like she's deep in thought. "No." She shakes her head at him, making his brow pinch in confusion. "You Axe," she says, then giggles.

"You know what? Axe does have a better ring to it." He chuckles.

She turns to Brody. "Hi."

"Uh, hi," he says, sounding unsure.

"I'm Lilly."

"Nice to meet you, Lilly. I'm Brody," he mumbles, looking so out of place. It's easy to tell he's never really been around kids.

Lilly squints at him like she's trying to decide something. "Nope, you not."

"I'm not?" he asks, raising a brow. "I think I know my own name."

"You're Broody. It sounds better." She nods.

Chase starts howling with laughter while Jax tries not to smile. I'm biting my lip, and Ellie snorts a laugh. Brody shoots her a look.

"What? She's got a point. Broody fits. You never smile, and you always look like something has pissed you off," Ellie says.

"Ohhh, shots fired," Chase says, raising his hand up to high five Ellie. She looks at it for a moment before a smile slips onto her lips and she high fives him back.

"How about some cake?" Theo asks as he comes over to us.

"Cake!" Lilly cheers, running back over to the other guests. The others watch us for a moment longer before bringing their focus back to Lilly.

"I'll get it set up and give you guys a moment," Theo says, giving Ellie a kiss on the top of her head. He looks at us. "You're getting a chance to make things right. Don't fuck it up. This is her life and her choice, but if you hurt her again, I'll make your life hell," he tells us, the look on his face saying he would do exactly that, before he heads over to the others.

"Well..." Ellie lets out a nervous laugh. "Thanks for coming. Lilly was so excited when I told her. She was sad because none of her daycare friends could come, but then I told her Fire and Ace would be here and that's all she could talk about." Ellie smiles.

"Thanks for letting us come. It means a lot," I tell her.

"I don't think she likes me," Brody mutters, watching Lilly stick her finger into the cake when no one is looking, scooping up a finger full of frosting, and shoving it into her mouth.

"She doesn't even know you," Chase says.

"She called me Broody," he huffs.

"And so? You are." Chase laughs.

"You're thinking too much into it. She gave us all a nickname that sounds like our names," Jax says.

"Well, not me," I point out.

"She should have called you Pain instead of Fire," Chase says, ruffling up my hair.

"Stop it, you asshole," I mutter.

"She likes your hair," Ellie says. Fixing my hair, I look up at her with a shy smile. "She says it's like a fire and she loves it. I think she picked a perfect name."

"Thanks," I say softly. My heart is doing weird things and my palms are sweaty. Her smile drops, like she just realized what she said.

"Anyways, you're welcome to come over with the rest of us and have some cake," she says.

"We don't want to impose," Jax says politely.

"Well, screw that. I want cake." Chase stands up and looks at us. "If you don't want to go over there, I'll grab you a slice." He turns around, but leaves a quick peck on Ellie's cheek before going over to Cooper and Ellie's other friends.

"Okay, well, if you want to join us at any time, feel free. We should be doing presents next," Ellie says, shifting from one foot to the other uncomfortably.

She turns to leave, but I get up and stop her. "Ellie, wait." Stopping, she turns to look at me. "Can I talk to you for a moment?" Probably not the best time to do this, but I need to say something before I lose my nerve and wait too long.

"Sure," she says. We walk away from everyone else, closer to the canteen.

"First off, I know no amount of times I say this will change anything, but I want you to know, I'm so fucking sorry for every-thing I did," I say, a ball of emotion. "I was wrong, *so fucking wrong,* and I regret how I acted. You didn't deserve any of it. And you were right at the diner; even if you did do what we accused you of, we had no right to be so cruel."

"Wanna know something?" she asks, her eyes growing glassy. "What Brody did, it hurt. It hurt really bad. It made me feel gross and dirty. But what you did? That was so much worse," she chokes back. Tears fall from my eyes, and I just want to reach out and hold her. "Because they may have been my boyfriends, and we were all close friends, sure, but Rain, you were more than that to me. You were my person, my best friend, my lover, the person I told everything to.

"You were the first person who I learned to love and trust with my heart out of all of you. It's no excuse for what he did, for anything he's done to me, but Brody's mind is a dark place. It always has been. His parents fucked him up good. But you, you knew me better than all of the guys. You, of all people, should have known I'd never in a million years do that to you. So, not only having you believe all that back then, but to go out of your way to be so cruel when I came back? That hurt my soul, Rain."

"I'm sorry," I cry. "I hate that I hurt you. It kills me knowing what I've done to you. I wish I could take it all back. Please, tell me what I can do to fix this." I've never felt despair like this. The fear of never having the one good thing in my life, the thing that meant the world to me, and still does.

She bites her lip, saying nothing, and I can't help but feel sick. I've lost her. I don't think I'll be anything more than what I am right now to her. And that idea crushes me.

Chapter Twelve

ELLIE

THIS IS NOT a conversation I was expecting to have today.

"Please, tell me there's something I can do to fix it. I miss you, Ellie, so fucking much, it hurts." Rain isn't one to cry. She's always so confident with everything she does. So seeing her like this, and remembering how she reacted the night of the party, I know she means it.

"How do I know you won't hurt me again?" I ask, my voice cracking.

"I promise, Ellie, I won't. I won't ever hurt you again. Just the idea makes me sick. Just let me show you. Let me prove it to you," she pleads.

"My life isn't going to be getting any easier. If anything, it's gonna get a hell of a lot worse before it gets better."

"What do you mean?" she sniffs, wiping at her eye.

"I'm going to use the video you guys took to press charges against Tim," I tell her, my belly flipping just thinking of that sick man and the idea of going up against him.

"You are? That's amazing, Ellie."

"So, you see, my life isn't like yours. I'm a mess." I huff out a laugh, a tear slipping free. "I'm a single mom who goes to school during the week and works on the weekend. I have PTSD. I go to counseling for my trauma and I have a therapist. I'm not the same girl you fell in love with, Rain. I'm not the same shy, easy going, quiet girl."

She takes a step toward me, getting so close, I can feel her breath against my face. My breathing picks up, my heart racing like the beat of a drum.

"No, you're not. You're so much more. You're strong with a big heart, and an amazing mom who did it on her own for so long. You're crazy smart, beautiful, and sexy. All the other stuff, that won't drive us away. Yes, we were partying all the time, getting drunk, and living life so carelessly, but do you wanna know why? We didn't care. We were without the person who made us whole. We weren't happy with that life. It's not what we want, it never was."

"And what *do* you guys want?" I ask, afraid of her answer.

"You," she whispers against my lips. She's taller than me so I have to tip my head back to see her eyes. They are still glassy, but they have a hint of lust and determination too. "I don't want to come off too strong, Ellie, especially after everything that's happened. But if you're willing to give me a chance to prove myself to you, I will spend the rest of my life showing you just how much I love you, because I do. Let me get to know the new parts of you, and fall in love with them too."

Fuck, my head is spinning, my body is humming. I want to tell her so many things, but my mind goes blank, so all I can get out is, "Okay." I breathe in, feeling light headed.

"Okay?" she asks, sounding uncertain.

"Prove it to me. Show me, love me."

"Always," she vows.

"I'm not going to make it easy," I whisper.

She grins and fuck if it doesn't make my heart flutter. "I would never ask you to."

Then she kisses me, and my world explodes. My eyes flutter closed as her lips meet mine, so warm and soft. It's sweet and slow, but burns like an inferno.

The kiss is over too quickly, and I find myself chasing her lips as she pulls away. "You're so perfect." Her thumb brushes against my lower lip. "I was blinded by my own toxic thoughts. Never again, Nori, never again." I just blink up at her, a dazed look in my eyes as she calls me her childhood nickname for me. It's been years since she's called me that, and only she has ever used it.

She gives me a sexy smile, reminding me of the Rain I fell in love with, and turns around, heading back over to Brody and Jax.

I stand there for a moment, trying to understand what the heck just happened. Then the sounds around me bring me back to reality. Shit, I'm in a bowling alley with kids everywhere. With my own kid. Shit. My eyes dart over to the lane we're using for Lilly's party. My friends are talking among themselves, my parents talking to Theo's, but someone did see. Two someones. Theo gives me a smile, letting me know he's okay with what he just saw. But then there's Chase, ugh. My cheeks heat at the shit-eating grin that he's shooting me right now, and my mind flashes back to high school for a moment. Rain and Chase used to love to tease me, get me all worked up, then take turns blowing my mind.

Rain is gay. She's not into men at all. But she's close with the guys, feeling like she's one of them, so she's never been shy about her body around them, and often took part in group activities. Of course the guys never touched her, never saw her in that way, but the smile Chase has...it's the same one he would give me when they left me lying there, spent and exhausted after making me cum until I couldn't move.

Shaking my head, I try to clear my head. I brush off my shirt and smooth my hair back into a bun then head back over to the party like nothing happened.

"Mama, can we have cake now?" Lilly asks, giving me her best puppy dog look.

"Yeah, Mama, can we have cake?" Chase says playfully.

Lilly looks up at him with a frown. "She not your mama. She mine."

Chase steps forward, leaning in close to whisper in my ear.

"You can be her mama, but you can also be my good girl," he says, his voice low and husky. My breath hitches, and damn him for turning me on right now! He nips at my ear lobe, making me shiver before stepping back with that cocky as fuck grin again.

"Cake!" Chase cheers, lifting Lilly and spinning her around which makes her giggle.

"I have a feeling that one is gonna keep you on your toes," Theo says, appearing at my side.

"Yeah," I breathe, watching Chase and Lilly together. "Some things never change."

We have cake and then bowl a little more. Brody and Jax stay where they've been all afternoon, but Rain comes over after a while. I can't look her in the eyes without blushing, and I think people are starting to notice.

"What are you doing, Ellie?" my mother asks as I watch Chase and Rain help Lilly bowl.

"What do you mean?" I ask her, giving her my full attention.

"With them," she says, looking at my exes. "After what they did."

"They know about everything now. We're trying to move forward for Lilly's sake." And partly mine.

"I just don't want to see you get hurt again, sweetie. It hurt your father and I to see you like that," she says with a sad smile. "But I know you're smart, and I know you will make the best choices for you and Lilly. I trust you. Just, be sure."

"I will." I hug her. "Thanks for coming, Mom. I missed you guys so much."

"Well, after missing Christmas, there was no way I was

missing my grandbaby's fourth birthday! I wanted to come sooner when we found out about the kidnapping."

"I know, but she's fine. We've made sure of it," I reassure her.

"I should thank that young man for what he did. He saved my baby girl."

"I owe him everything." I smile, looking over as Lilly knocks down some pins, causing her and Chase to do this little victory dance, and Rain laughing at their silly ways.

"I think you're even, wouldn't you say?" She smiles at me knowingly.

"Yeah, I think we are," I laugh. "The girl who got her heart broken wants me to believe that it's all just words and he's going to hurt me again. But I can see it in his eyes, hear it in his words. He loves me, and he's beyond sorry for everything that happened."

"So Theo is okay with it?" I know what she means. Me dating the others again.

"At first, I thought he only said he was okay with it because he was afraid to lose me if I thought he was going to make me choose. But now, I know he just wants me happy in whatever way that might be. He is supportive, and we keep a strong line of communication open."

"Would you leave him? If you got back with the others and dated like you did when you were teenagers?"

"What?" I ask, my eyes widening. "Never! As much as I love Rain and the guys, and I'll be the first one to admit that I never fell out of love with them in the first place, I love Theo just as much as them, maybe even more but in different ways. Theo loves me for me and has been supportive from the moment we met. He's never once seen me as a broken person because of my past, but as a warrior who's come out on top every time. No matter what happens with the others, Theo will always be with me as long as he chooses to be."

"Good." She nods. "I think he's a perfect addition to your harem." She smiles.

"Mom!" I blush.

"What? It's true. Chase, Jax, and Brody are still boys. They have a lot of growing up to do. But I think being around a man like Theo will help. Also, being in Lilly's life will show them what's important."

"Was I wrong to invite them? Was it too soon?" I ask, worrying my bottom lip as I glance over my shoulder. Jax and Brody are watching Lilly with Chase and Rain. A part of me feels bad that they are left out, but the look in their eyes tells me that they don't plan on having it be like this forever.

"I think you're in a unique situation," my mother tells me, drawing my attention back to her. "Do I think you should let them back into your heart so easily? No, make them work for it. Or at least make them show you that they mean what they say. But I do think you made the right choice in letting them come tonight. Lilly is already four and they lost a lot of time with her already."

"I didn't do it on purpose," I say, getting a little defensive.

"I know. It was one, big, jumbled mess. But now that you're able to move forward, this is the first step of many."

"Speaking of, I wanted to talk to you guys about something," I say, feeling my stomach drop.

"What's going on?" my dad asks, stepping into the conversation.

They know what happened to Lilly, and they know that Rain and the guys know the truth about what really happened on graduation night, but I didn't tell them *how* they found out.

"So, as you know, Rain, Chase, Jax, and Brody know what really happened that night."

My father's face turns into a mask of fury just thinking about it. "Yes."

"Well, they found out because they overheard Tim confessing everything a few weeks ago when he cornered me at a party."

"What?!" my father shouts.

"Shhh!" I say, looking around to see a few people glancing our way.

"Do not shh me, Eleanor. You're telling me that the man who assaulted you cornered you at a party?"

"Yes." My eyes water, but I take a deep breath, willing myself to be strong. I've always been open with my parents about most things in my life. "But, Brody got the confession on tape. Then, after Tim admitted what he did that night, he said he was going to do it again."

"What?" my mother gasps. "He didn't…"

"No, thankfully Brody got to him first. He ended up putting Tim in the hospital."

"Good," my dad growls. I agree.

"When everything happened five years ago, I didn't want to press charges. I wanted the pain to go away, and I wanted to pretend it didn't happen. I was convinced no one would believe me, because let's be honest, how many perverts like Tim get to walk free in the end? A lot. I was scared and alone with the loves of my life hating me. But now? Now, I have a whole army beside me. I'm stronger, I'm older, and I have something that could really help my case."

"So, what are you saying? Are you gonna press charges?" my dad asks.

"Yes, and I was hoping you could help me find a really good lawyer. I'll worry about the money later. Right now, I just want to put that fucker behind bars before he can hurt another person."

"Of course, honey. I think I know a few guys who would be a perfect fit for this case. Let me make some calls."

"Thank you, Dad," I say, giving him a hug. I've always been close with my parents, and they were amazing with helping me and Lilly from the start. I've missed them like crazy and wish we could be closer.

"I think it's time for presents, then to bring this party to an end," Mom says with a laugh. "Looks like someone is all partied out."

Looking behind me, I see Chase holding a sleeping Lilly, and my heart swells. I feared that they wouldn't want this big responsibility, but the look on Chase's face says that he's all in.

Theo and I clean up while my parents chat some more with his. Chase sits with Rain and the others, a sleeping Lilly still in his arms as they talk. My friends say goodbye, and I thank them for coming before packing up all the gifts into the car.

"She can open them at home tomorrow," I say to Theo, closing the trunk.

"No," Lilly whines, lifting her little head from Chase's shoulder. "I wanna open now."

"Yeah," Toby says, standing next to his dad. "Can't we open them now?"

"Toby, buddy, these are Lilly's gifts. She gets to open them," Theo says, ruffling up Toby's hair.

"No fair," Toby mutters under his breath with a grouchy face.

"We did bring some for her," Jax says. "Maybe she can open ours for now?"

"Pleaseeee," Lilly begs, giving me her big sleepy puppy dog eyes. How can I say no to that?

"Alright," I smile.

"Yay!" she cheers.

Jax grabs some boxes from the trunk, then the back seat.

"Wow!" both Lilly and Toby say in awe.

"This is from me," Jax says, putting a big box in front of her.

Taking out my phone, I video tape Lilly ripping off the wrapping paper, then opening the box. Her eyes light up. "Barbies!" she shouts. "So many!"

She starts to pull them out one by one. From the looks of it, he got her every Disney character that comes in Barbie form. Looking up at Jax, she says, "Thank you!" before running over and hugging his leg.

"You're very welcome."

"I like you. You're my new friend."

Jax looks up at me with a big smile, and I give him one back, trying to hold in my giggle at the excited look on his face. I love how much this means to him.

"Mine next, little lady," Rain says, handing her a box. Lilly opens it, revealing two remote control cars.

"Cool!" Toby says.

"I got you two in case you wanted to share with Toby."

"Thank you, Fire! You the best."

"Now, now, shortcake. You still gotta see mine!" Chase grins, running over to the trunk. He pulls out a pink and purple electric tricycle motorbike.

"Chase," I gasp, my eyes widening.

"What? I wanted her to have one like me," he beams. "Well, once I get mine back from the shop."

"Mama! Look," Lilly says, pulling me over to it. "Now I can save people just like Ace." She sits on it and admires it. I look up at Chase to see him staring at her with a big smile and glassy eyes.

"You're crazy, you know that?" I laugh.

"Yeah, but you knew that already." He grins, pulling me into his arms.

"Thank you." I smile at him.

"I loved that little girl before I knew she was mine," he whispers so the kids don't hear him.

"She loves you too. I can tell."

He kisses me quickly, not wanting to make a scene, but it still lingers on my lips when he pulls away.

"Go on a date with me," he asks, brushing some hair from my face.

"A date?" I do like the idea of that. "Okay, when?"

"Tomorrow morning, 6 am." He grins.

"What? No way," I laugh. "I love my sleep, and what the heck would we be doing at six in the morning for a date?"

"You know how you always wanted to learn now to surf back in high school?"

"Yeah..." I say skeptically.

"Did you ever learn?" I shake my head. "Good, then I'm gonna teach you."

Sleep. I really love my sleep. But the excitement in Chase's eyes is hard to say no to. Also, I think a little fun is in order.

"Okay," I say.

Chase whoops, and spins me around, making me laugh.

We hang around a little while longer while Lilly plays in the empty parking lot on her new bike before both of our parents leave, mine heading back to their hotel. They agreed to wake up early and watch Lilly for me. I'm excited about tomorrow, but I also have classes, so I'll have to come home and shower before then.

Everyone says goodbye to Lilly, then to me. Chase kisses me again, Jax gives me a smile, and Rain looks like she wants to do more than wave goodbye. As for Brody, he says nothing, but the way he looks at me, it's like he wants to say so much but won't.

"What did Brody get her?" Theo asks as we drive home.

"Nothing," I say, remembering him watching the others give their gifts to her with a pissed off look. He did have something in his hand, but he never gave it to her. "That's okay. I'm sure he just didn't know what to get a four-year-old little girl. Brody's never been around kids."

"Well, he's gonna have to get used to it," Theo says, taking my hand in his. "Because I don't think the other three are going anywhere from what I saw tonight."

"Yeah," I say, looking out the window. I'm not sure why I feel a little disappointed about how Brody acted today. I didn't expect him to be like the others, but he just looked like he felt so out of place, not even trying. But it's the first time, and this is Brody. Maybe after a little more time, he will come around.

I hope so.

Chapter Thirteen

CHASE

YESTERDAY WAS AMAZING. Spending time with my favorite little person, *my daughter*, was the best thing I've ever experienced. Watching her smile and laugh, it made me feel complete. The only person who has ever made me feel like that is her mother.

Who knew that I would go from someone who used sex as a way to numb the pain of my past to having the love of my life and a daughter in five short months?

I know life's about to change in some pretty big ways, but honestly, I'm happy.

Seeing my daughter smile, hearing her laugh, and having her call me her hero warms my heart. Every time she brings up me saving her, I feel a ghost of panic, but also a swell of pride knowing I did that. *I* saved her.

Partying, drinking, and sex, that's not a real life. It brings momentary endorphins, but the real high? It's having Ellie in my arms, on my lips, and my cock inside her.

So now I'm in the parking lot of Ellie's apartment with coffee in hand, and a candy cane hanging from my lips. I promised Ellie I would prove to her everyday how much I love her. And today, I'm taking her on a date. Her life has been shit lately, and with taking

Tim to court, she needs to have some fun; something to take her mind off the bad and replace it with something good.

We texted a little bit last night before bed when she sent me her address. She makes me feel like I'm on top of the world, like anything is possible. And horny, *so fucking horny.* I mean, just looking at her has my dick hard. And no, it's not because I'm a guy and all I think about is sex.

It's because of the bombshell of a woman, and sex with said woman.

What we did at the party, it plays on an endless loop in my mind. I want more, need more. Being inside her is where I belong. Well, at least where my dick belongs. It's hers now, only hers, to do with as she pleases.

Texting Ellie that I'm outside, I crank the music and start to belt out *Candy* by Doja Cat.

Five minutes later, I see her coming out of her building. As she gets closer, I grin as I take in the sight of her. Her hair is all cute and messy like she went to bed with it in a bun and didn't bother to fix it. She's in shorts, a baggy sweater, and flip flops.

The best thing about Silver Valley is that it's in South Carolina, so even in the winter we get warm weather. At least warm enough to go swimming and not freeze to death.

I snort at the look on Ellie's face. She looks pissed. It's the same face she always made when any of us would get her out of bed before ten am.

"Don't you look cute," I tease as she gets into the passenger's side.

"You suck," she grumbles, putting on her seat belt and crossing her arms with an adorable, grumpy face.

"Ahh, don't be like that. I got you coffee," I say, holding out the caramel latte I got her from Starbucks. Her eyes light up, and she snatches it out of my hand, immediately taking a sip. She groans, her eyes rolling into the back of her head, and I have to bite my lip from responding with one of my own at the sound. My dick happens to enjoy it just as much as I do.

"Baby girl, do you know how hard it is to surf with a stiffy?" I ask.

"What?" she asks, looking at me with her big, blue eyes. She looks down then back up at me with a blush.

"Sorry."

"I'm not." I grin, making her blush harder. "Ready to catch some waves?" I ask as I pull out of the parking lot and onto the main road.

"I was catching some zzz's, but I guess bobbing around in ice cold water for an hour or two is just as fun," she teases, flashing me a cheeky grin.

"I'll make it worth it, babe, trust me," I say, lacing my fingers with hers and giving them a squeeze. Touching her sends a rush of warmth through my body, and it settles over me like a comforting blanket.

"I'll take payment in coffee. And orgasms if they're on the menu," she jokes, then her eyes go adorably wide like she just realized what she said.

She bites her lip, her cheeks having a new rosy glow to them. I love how easily I affect her. She may have grown into this brilliant woman, but I still see that bit of the old Ellie, the best parts of her.

"I think that's something that can be arranged," I growl, bringing her hand up to my lips and leaving a lingering kiss that has her squirming in her seat.

The rest of the ride, we sing along to the radio. I keep glancing over at her, loving the way her face lights up when she smiles.

This, this right here. I'd do everything and anything to give her any ounce of happiness even if it's just for a small moment like this.

When we get to the beach, I'm happy to see the little parking lot empty. "Looks like we've got the beach to ourselves for now," I say, shutting off the engine.

"That's because people are smart and would rather be asleep in their nice warm beds than out here at six am, in a bikini about to die of hypothermia." Ellie cocks a brow with a little smirk.

"Don't be so dramatic. No one's gonna die. I'll protect you. I'm your Silver Knight after all, aren't I?" I grin over at her.

She rolls her eyes. "Yeah, yeah. Come on, oh great Knight Chase. Show me how to surf and let's hope I don't drown." She laughs, getting out of the car.

I unstrap the boards from the top of the car and take one of the surf boards down. "This one is for you," I tell her, handing her a blue beginners board.

"This looks new..." she says, taking it from me. "Did you just buy it?"

She's giving me a 'Don't lie to me' look. "No..." I say, and she tilts her head to the side, giving me some extra sass that just makes me wanna kiss her. "I got it a few weeks ago."

"Why? You already have one," she says, pointing to the one still on top of the car.

"Because, I maybe kinda have been waiting to ask you to come with me for awhile now, and I maybe kinda bought one because I didn't want to risk you getting hurt on mine." I grin sheepishly.

Her face softens. "Well, that was really sweet of you." She steps into me and leans up onto her tippy toes. She places a soft kiss on my lips, and it takes everything in me to not pull her into me to make it last longer. "But I don't want you spending your money on me."

"Baby girl, that's not fair. I wanna spoil you," I pout.

"You can," she laughs. "Just not with money. I don't need fancy things. Just being with you is enough."

"I mean, there was mention of orgasms. I feel like that's a great way to spoil you." I grin. She bites her lip, her pupils dilating.

"Let's surf," she says, blinking as if she's clearing her mind. "And maybe the cold water can get that to go down for while," she says, looking down at my boner that's tenting my swim trunks.

"Babe, when I'm around you, he never goes down. It's a curse and a blessing." I smirk.

She shakes her head and laughs. "You're such a hornball."

"But I'm *your* hornball," I tease.

"Yes, you are." She smiles softly.

I grab my board, and we head down to the beach. Finding a spot, Ellie puts her bag down on the sand, and I put my board down next to it.

"I forgot how beautiful the sunrise can be," she says, sitting down and hugging her knees as she watches the sun rising in the horizon.

"You look like you haven't seen it in years," I chuckle as I sit next to her and wrap my arm around her.

"I haven't. Not really. Sure, when Lilly was a baby, I'd be up before the sun with her, but I haven't really sat and watched it rise like this since...." She looks up at me. "Well, since before I moved away from Silver Valley."

"Really?"

She shrugs, looking back out at the water. "I've always been one who's enjoyed sleeping in, even back then. But you, the guys, and Rain would always get up in the mornings during football season for your morning runs, and I'd go with you. That's the last time I've really enjoyed one."

"If you hated getting up that early, why did you come with us?" I ask.

"Because I loved you all, and I hated that there weren't a lot of things we all enjoyed together. You all loved to work out, play, party, drink, stuff like that, and I was okay with just staying in and reading a book or watching TV. It's why I learned how to cheer so that I had something to do with Rain, but I chickened out of that. I was afraid that I would mess up and embarrass her or something."

"So you ran with us because it was something we liked?"

"And I just wanted to be with you guys. When you had ball, Rain had cheer, so I took any time I could get with you all that didn't involve the teams and parties."

I don't say anything, I just cuddle into her and enjoy the rest of the sunrise.

I hate that she thought she had to pretend to like things that we did to please us, to change who she was to feel better matched. I've never wanted her for more than who she was. I hadn't known she felt that way.

"Never change who you are to please us again, Ellie," I tell her, standing up and holding out my hand. "We don't have to like all of the same things. But, maybe try something first before writing it off? Like what we're going to do today."

She grabs my hand, allowing me to pull her up. "Things are different now. I'm older and I've come out of my shell a lot. There're things that may take a while to change, or may never change. I hate crowds, I hate being in close proximity to people with no exit, but it's something I've been working on. I've come a long way with work and the few parties I've been to since coming back. For the longest time, I didn't like being touched. The idea of someone putting their hands on me made me want to run and hide. Even with therapy, it wasn't until Theo came along that I was able to let someone hold me, kiss me, or touch me."

"I have a lot to thank him for. For being there for you when we weren't. For loving you when we couldn't. For seeing you for your true self, and accepting you completely. And for being the closest thing to a father our daughter has. But most of all, I want to thank him for sharing you with us. You two could go off, get married, and live happily ever after, you know."

"I love Theo. He's not going anywhere."

"I know." I pull her into my arms.

"But I love you too, Chase." Tears make her eyes sparkle in the sunlight. Hearing her say those words fills me with something so strong, I don't have a word for it.

"I love you, Ellie. I never stopped."

"Neither did I," she breathes.

Cupping her face, I kiss her hard. She moans into my mouth, gripping my shirt to steady herself. My tongue slips out, gliding along the seam of her lips, asking for entrance. She parts her lips for me, allowing my tongue to swipe over hers. We kiss until we're breathless and panting.

"So, ready to go surfing?" I ask, pulling back from the kiss.

"Surfing, right." She blinks up at me, her cheeks flushed and her blue eyes dazed. "Yeah."

Grabbing the hem of my shirt, I pull it off, revealing my naked chest. I smirk when I find her eyes roaming my body.

"See something you like?" I ask playfully.

Her eyes land on my dick. "Yeah, a whole lot of something," she mutters under breath before looking away to take off her own shirt.

I groan when I take in the sight of her body. She's in a black bikini that pushes her breasts up and barely covers her parts.

"See something *you* like?" she asks, biting her lip as she gives me a grin.

"We need to get out there right now before I fuck you on this beach," I growl, grabbing my board and jogging toward the water. I can hear her laughing behind me, and it's music to my soul.

"How does holding my boobs help keep me steady?" Ellie laughs as I hold on to her, helping her as she stands up with me.

"It's so you don't fall off, duh."

Just as I say those words a wave crashes into us, sending me and Ellie into the water. She comes up, laughing as she moves her hair from her face.

"I think that's enough surfing for now," Ellie says. "But I'd like to come back and try again. Maybe next time, I'll be able to stand for more than ten seconds," she laughs.

We've been out here for an hour, and the whole time was filled with lots of laughs and a lot of falling, but she never gave up. Every time she fell, she got right back up.

"But maybe we can go during the day. As much fun as this was, I'd much rather do it on a full night's rest and with the afternoon sun beaming down on me."

"I don't know. The cold seems to be working for you," I say, staring at her hard nipples against her swim top.

"Come on." She laughs and starts swimming toward shore.

When we get dried off, I notice that the beach has gotten busy.

"See, look at all of these people. They waited until at least eight am before coming to surf," Ellie says with a pout.

"Oh, it wasn't that bad." I laugh. "We got the water to ourselves, and we got to see a pretty sunrise out of it."

"Yeah, I guess you're right," she says. "Thank you, Chase."

"Anything for you, baby girl." I give her a quick peck on the cheek. "But there is one thing I wanna show you before we head back to shower and get ready for school."

"Okay, what?"

"Grab your bag and come with me."

We walk along the beach, the sounds of the waves crashing against the shore and the gulls' squawking fill the air.

"Chase, where are you taking me?" she asks, tripping over her feet in the sand as she tries to keep up.

"Almost there," I say, seeing the rocks ahead of us.

When we get closer, I hear her gasp.

"Is that..."

"Yup." I look over at her and grin. "Come on."

A big smile takes over her face and we both start racing toward the rocks.

"Leave the boards here," I tell her, leaning them behind one of the rocks. Grabbing her hand, I pull her into the little cave-like area the rocks have formed.

"I can't believe they're still here," she says, her voice soft as she runs her fingers over all of our names engraved on the rock wall.

"Remember when we used to come here, listen to music, drink, and spend hours just hanging out with each other?" I ask, coming up behind her and wrapping my arms around her.

"They were some of my favorite times. I loved it here, like our own personal hideaway from life."

"Remember that one time you, me, and Rain came here, just the three of us?" I ask, my voice filling with need just thinking about it as I kiss her neck.

She tilts her head to the side, giving me more access and letting out a little gasp. "Yeah."

"We drove you crazy. Made you scream our names over and over again."

"Until we got chased away by beach security." She laughs lightly, but her laugh turns into a moan as I suck her earlobe into my mouth, giving it a little nibble.

"I wanna hear it again," I taunt, my voice low and raspy.

"Hear what?" she whimpers.

"You scream my name so loud that it echoes off the cave walls." I kiss her neck, not wanting to push anything and make her feel uncomfortable. "Can I touch you Ellie?" I ask. She nods against my shoulder. "Words, babe."

"Yes." It comes out breathy, but I have no doubt that she wants this.

My hands slide up her shirt and under her swim top. I cup her breasts, rolling her peaked nipples with my fingers, making her breath hitch.

"Chase," she says, but more like a plea.

"I wanna touch you, Ellie." I move one of my hands down the front of her shorts. I slide my fingers through her slick folds, groaning at how wet she is. "Is this for me, pretty girl?" I ask, dipping my fingers into her pussy, loving the way she gasps.

"Yes," she says as her breathing starts to pick up.

She's so slick, so fucking wet. Grinding my cock into her ass, I start to fuck her with my fingers. "You're so fucking tight," I growl as I feel her tighten around my fingers, her body quivering in my hold. I pump my fingers faster, pulling back to play with her swollen clit before dipping back in while I pinch and pull at her nipple. Little cries leave her lips as I drive her crazy. But it's not enough, I want more. "That's it, love, fuck, you're dripping. Sing for me, pretty girl."

When I stroke her clit a few more times, she shatters in my arms, screaming my name like a prayer.

"You sound so pretty when you cum for me. Such a good girl." I pull my fingers from her shorts as she slumps against me, breathing heavily.

"Fuck," I moan as I suck her juices from my fingers, needing to taste her on my tongue.

She moves from my arms, turning around so that her back is against the rock. "Wanna taste, pretty girl?" I ask, rubbing the two fingers against her lips. She nods, surprising me as she opens her mouth. I slide them in and she closes, locking her lips around them and sucks them clean, her tongue getting every inch.

I groan, feeling my cock pulse. "Such a dirty girl. Fuck, Ellie, you make me fucking crazy, you know that? You drive me wild. Every time I see you, I don't just wanna fuck you. No, pretty girl, I wanna fucking consume you. You're my everything, and the need to touch you and feel our connection is out of this fucking world."

"Show me," she breathes, her eyes heavy lidded as she starts to unbutton her pants. "Show me how much you love me, Chase."

"Fuck," I hiss, watching her with a feral hunger as she drops her bottoms, leaving her bare pussy on display.

"The night of the party," she says, slipping her hand over her clit, giving it a few rubs and making her breath stutter. "It's like a part of me clicked into place when you were buried deep inside me. I wanna feel that again, Chase, please."

I watch her play with her freshly orgasmed pussy as I pull down my swim shorts. My cock springs free, slapping against my abs, hard and throbbing. Pre-cum seeps from the tip, desperate to be inside her. I take a step closer.

"Hold on, baby," I say with a growl as I grab her thighs and wrap them around my waist. Her arms come around my neck, her nails digging into my flesh as she clings to me. "How do you want it, Ellie?" I ask, my voice heavy with desire. Rocking my hips forward, I glide my cock against her pussy. "Hard and fast or deep and slow?"

She looks at me with wild pleading eyes. "Slow and deep."

I smash my lips into hers and pin her against the rock. Pulling my hips back, the tip of my cock finds her entrance and with one thrust, I push inside her completely. I swallow her cries before pulling out and thrusting back in. She's so tight, so wet...so fucking perfect. I meant it before when I said she was made for me. We fit together like we belong.

I do as she asks, fucking her slow and deep against the rock. "God, Ellie, you drive me wild," I say, gritting my teeth.

We stay like that for a while, both feeding off the other's pleasure as we titter on the edge of insanity.

"Chase," she moans against my lip. "God, I feel so full."

"Oh, I'll make you feel even fuller when I fill you with my cum," I growl, pounding into her a little harder, unable to resist as her pussy clenches my cock.

"I'm gonna cum," she whimpers, tucking her face into my neck. She clings to me, digging her nails into my shoulders.

"That's it, pretty girl, cum for me. Squeeze my cock with your sweet pussy," I encourage.

"Oh, yes, right there, Chase," she moans, her hips rocking into me, working with mine as she helps herself to the orgasm that's just out of reach. She continues to do that, each of us fucking the other as she uses me for friction against her clit. "Oh fuck, fuck, fuck, fuck. Chase!" she screams before biting my neck as she cums hard, her core gripping me so tight.

"Such a good girl," I pant out. "Sounds even better than I imagined." I can't hold back anymore. My balls tighten and with one last thrust, I push her ass into the rock, cumming hard with a loud groan as I fill her, sending jets of cum deep inside her core.

We stay wrapped in each other's arms, clinging together as we come down from our high, just enjoying being in each other's embrace. This is heaven to me. Being with her is like a sailor after being lost at sea. She's the light that guides me home, keeping me from rough waters and on safe grounds. She's my safe place, my heart, my home.

"Anyone in there?" a voice shouts from outside. We pull back, looking at each other with panicked eyes.

"Fuck," I say. I pull out of her, my cum gushing down her leg. But I don't have time to enjoy it. I grab her shorts and hand them to her. "Fuck, I totally forgot," I say as we rush to get dressed.

"Forgot what?" she whisper shouts.

"Security comes every morning to make sure there are no lingering homeless people. This spot is known to have people who hide."

"What!?" she shouts, eyes going wide.

"Come on," I say, grabbing her hand.

"Hello! I'm coming in," the man calls again.

I lead her out the opposite way we came in. The sun blinds us for a moment as our eyes adjust from the darkness of the cave.

"Chase, we're gonna get caught," Ellie says, her voice panicked.

"Not if I have anything to say about it," I say, dragging her around the rocks to where we left our boards. Just as we grab a hold of everything, he exits the cave the way we just did.

"Hey, you two!"

"Run!" I shout to Ellie, grabbing her free hand.

I laugh as we try to run in the sand toward the car. Thankfully, the guard doesn't seem to be in very good shape and is having some difficulty catching up.

Quickly, I put my board on top, then do Ellie's. "Get in the car," I tell her as I work fast to strap everything on.

She jumps in the front seat and a moment later, so do I. I start the car up and peel out of the parking lot and down the open road back toward Ellie's place.

"What was that?!" Ellie exclaims. I look over at her. We both just stare for a moment before bursting out laughing.

"I'd say it was a pretty perfect date, wouldn't you?" I grin.

"Yeah, I think so too," she says. The smile she gives me fills me with so much love, and I know at this very moment, I will never let this girl go again.

Chapter Fourteen

ELLIE

CHASE DROPS me off back at my place, giving me a heated, lingering kiss before I get out of the car.

"Thank you again for this morning," he says against my lips, my eyes still closed as I let out a content sigh.

"Thanks for taking me." I smile, blinking my eyes open. "I had a lot of fun," I blush. *Oh, boy, did I ever.* Back to back orgasms kind of fun. "Surfing, I had fun surfing," I add when he gives me a hungry look. "I can't wait until we can get out there again."

"Right, yeah, I totally had fun surfing too." He gives me a sexy, cocky grin and I'm reminded that I'm still currently sitting in his cum.

"I gotta go. See you soon," I say quickly, needing some air from this sinfully sexy, white haired, god of a man.

"I'll text you," he says as I get out of the car. "Don't feel like a stranger at school, you know."

"I won't," I say, not entirely sure if that's true.

Since Brody has made it known that I am off limits and the target on my back is now gone, almost everyone has left me alone. No one has tried to be my friend, but really, I didn't want them to. I have no idea who went along with Brody's bullshit and who stayed out of it.

However, there have been a few guys here and there who've asked me out for a good fuck, or catty girls calling me nasty names because they think I'm fucking all the Knights now. I just ignore them and walk on by. It's a lot easier to do now that it's not the whole school sniffing around like hounds ready to hunt their next meal.

"Ellie," he says just as I'm about to shut the car door.

"Yeah?" I ask, sticking my head into the car to look at him.

"I love you."

Biting my lip, I think for a moment. I know I said it back at the beach, and I *did* mean it because I've never stopped loving him...but is it too soon to say it? My heart says no. And with what happened to Lilly, I've learned to enjoy every moment in life because you never know how much time you're going to have with a person before you lose them, for whatever reason.

"I love you too," I say, almost a whisper, feeling like those were the right words to say. His face lights up like I just gave him the moon and I close the door, a smile of my own taking over my face.

I feel giddy the whole way to my apartment door. I can't believe that just happened; that Chase and I had sex in that cave. But God, it was amazing. The whole morning was. I don't think I've laughed that much in a long time. It was nice to just get away from reality for a few hours.

But I miss Lilly, and I have to go to school in an hour. I'm hoping she's up so that I can spend some time with her and my parents before I have to leave again.

Opening the door to my apartment, I snort a laugh as I remember the security guard chasing after us. We almost got caught, but the thrill of it all felt amazing.

"What's so funny?" my dad asks as I step into the apartment.

My eyes shoot up, finding my parents on the couch and Lilly

sitting on the floor watching some cartoons, totally engrossed in her show.

"Ah, nothing," I say. "Thanks for watching her. Just gonna shower and change for school, then I'll come hang out," I say, running to my room.

I grab a change of clothes and head to the bathroom to wash the saltwater from my hair.

As I clean the evidence of what Chase and I did from my thighs, I wonder if I should let Theo know that Chase and I slept together again.

He did say to only tell him what needs to be told. If Chase and I are together now...kinda...well sorta, I guess I don't have to. Right?

My core aches deliciously, and I find myself wanting more. Being with each of them always felt amazing in their own way, and I forgot how addicting Chase can be.

When he came inside me, I felt like he was marking me as his.

Then a thought occurs. He came inside me two times. I'm not worried about getting pregnant, I'm on birth control. But Chase has been known to be a bit of a man whore. *Fuck, how can I be so stupid?* I'm going to need to have a talk with him. God, that's going to be awkward, but I can't go around acting like nothing happened if there's something I need to be worried about. Something that he could have given me.

The thought makes me sick, just thinking of him with all of those women. But he's mine now and I'm enough for him, right?

Right?

The week goes by fast between school and home life with Lilly. After my parents left, we had a few more sleepovers with Theo.

I'm starting to wonder if maybe I should bring up moving in with him. *Is it too soon for that?* I'd help him with rent and bills, of course. And it's not just about saving money. It's because I love waking up with him in the morning and falling asleep with him at night.

But if I'm dating Chase now—and maybe, someday, the others again—then what does that mean if I'm living with Theo?

Ugh, I don't know. *Why does life have to be so complicated?*

Valentine's Day is next week, and all I can think about is, *what if they both ask me to be their Valentine's date?* Do I say yes to both, or turn them both down and spend the day alone when I have two men who love me? *Damn it!*

Standing in the hallway outside the food court, I hesitate to go in because I have no one to sit with today. Lexie and Val are working on an assignment that's due in their next class, Cooper had to leave early for his cousin's wedding this weekend, and Tabitha has an appointment right now.

I haven't been alone at school since I've made them as friends.

When I walk into the food court, I grab some fries with a side of gravy and a bottle of water before looking around for a place to sit. The table I normally sit at with my friends is empty, but I don't want to sit alone and possibly have all eyes on me.

Looking over at Rain and the guys, I see that the guys are chatting and laughing with some of their teammates while Rain talks to a girl next to her. Laura and Kayla aren't in their normal spots beside Rain, but are sitting at the end of the table instead. Chase mentioned that Rain's officially cut ties with them, knowing that they don't like me and because she doesn't want to be around people like that. A part of me loves that she's willing to stay away from people who are no good to me.

Just as I'm about to turn and leave to find a place to sit outside, Chase calls out my name.

"Ellie!"

I turn to look at him, only to find him waving like an excited golden retriever. The excitement on his face at seeing me has my nerves easing. But it doesn't last long before I feel all eyes on me and my nerves come crashing back into me.

"Come sit," he calls.

Well, it would be rude of me to turn him down. And I do have to start spending time with them if I wanted to get to know them. They each have asked me this week to sit with them, well, all of them except Brody, but I think it was more because he thought I'd say no. I've turned them down each time, not wanting my friends to feel like I was abandoning them. *But they're not here today, so what can it hurt?*

Trying to ignore the stares, I head over to their table.

"Hi."

"Come, sit with me today. Please?" Chase pleads, giving me puppy dog eyes and a pout much like Lilly does.

"How can I say no to that?" I laugh, then look to find no free seats. "Uhh, there're no chairs."

He takes my tray from me and places it on the table before taking my hand so that he can pull me down into his lap. I let out a little gasp of surprise as his arms wrap around me.

"I'll be your chair." He grins down at me.

Chewing on the inside of my cheek, I wonder if this is appropriate. But I'm with Chase now. If I want to sit like this with him, I have the right to.

We all make small talk, and after a few minutes, my body starts to relax.

"Eat," Chase tells me, dipping one of my fries into the gravy and holding it in front of my mouth. I smile and open my mouth for him. "Good girl," he says, kissing me on the forehead.

Wanna know something funny? If anyone else talked to me like that, I would have probably kneed them in the balls. But with Chase, and even Theo, I enjoy the praise. *Well, new kink unlocked.* You find something new about yourself everyday, I guess.

"You have a little something right here," Jax says pointing to the corner of my lip.

"Oh," I say, my face heating as I try to wipe it away. "Gone?"

"No," he smiles. "May I?" he asks. I look into his deep brown eyes and nod. Jax is so sexy. I can see his tattoos poking out of the top of his shirt, and from what I saw at the party, I know he's gotten a lot more ink since high school.

He takes his thumb, wiping at my lip slowly. My heart races and it takes everything in me not to squirm in Chase's lap and draw attention from the conversation he's having with another player across the table from us.

Jax, without breaking eye contact, sticks his thumb in his mouth and sucks it clean. *Fuck, why is that hot?* My face heats, but this time, it's not from embarrassment.

When he sits back, my eyes lock with Brody. He watched the whole thing. He doesn't look mad at the fact that his boyfriend was just touching me with a little-more-than friendly gesture.

He hasn't said anything more to me about him and Jax since the night I found them together. I just hope he knows I would never out them to anyone. It's their life and their choice with who they want to tell.

But how would that work? Jax has mentioned wanting to make everything up to me, to prove it to me, but does he want me like Chase and Rain do? The way he was just looking at me makes me think he does.

If he's with me, will he still be with Brody? I'd be okay with it because I just want everyone to be happy. I'd never ask one of them to leave the other because, how is it okay that I can date all of them, but they can't be with each other?

But if it was someone outside of the two of them, I don't think I could get on board.

"How's school been? Have people been leaving you alone since I called everything off?" Brody's gruff voice asks.

"Umm." I clear my throat, surprised he's actually talking

directly to me. "It's been good for the most part." I give him an awkward smile.

"For the most part?" he asks, frowning. "People have been giving you trouble still?"

"Well, I still get a few comments here and there, not very nice ones, but it's nothing I can't handle. It's not a big deal," I say, shrugging it off.

"It is a big deal," Brody growls, the sound sending a shiver through my body. "I gave an order that was intended for every single person at SVU to follow. If there are people that are going against my rules, then we have an issue."

"What's going on?" Chase asks.

"Is something wrong?" Rain adds, chiming in at the perfect moment. *It's like they choreographed it.*

"Looks like there're some people here that don't think the order to leave Ellie alone applies to them."

"What?" Chase growls. "Baby, who's been fucking with you?"

"It's really not that big of a deal," I say, not wanting to cause any issues.

"It is," Rain says, her face is a mask of fury. She stands up and my belly flips. "Everyone!" she shouts. "It's come to my attention that some of you are not abiding by our order when it comes to Eleanor Tatum."

Brody stands up too. "Ellie is off limits. She's not to be talked to or about in any rude or degrading way. You treat her with respect or just leave her the fuck alone."

"How can you go from ordering all of us to treat her like the trash she is to telling us to just pretend like nothing happened?" Laura argues, standing up from her spot at the table.

"Because," Brody snaps. "The reason we stupidly thought gave us the right to treat her badly was incorrect. Ellie is a good person, and she doesn't deserve what we did to her, what *any* of us did." He turns his attention to the room. "I am the captain of the football team. A lot of you look to me when it comes to how things are done around here. I steered you wrong. I asked you to do really fucking shitty things to someone who didn't deserve it. I was wrong, and I'm sorry that I asked you to do those things. But, I'm telling you here and now, so no one can mistake my words. Eleanor Tatum is off limits. If I find out you've been harassing her in any way, you'll deal with me. And trust me, you don't want that," he warns before sitting back down then Jax takes his place.

"One of the reasons you all look up to us, to Brody, isn't just because we're football gods but because Brody is a true leader. And true leaders are like role models and should do the right thing like admitting when they are wrong and make things right because that is what a good human being should do. And that's what we're doing now. It's a little late, but it needs to be said." Jax sits back down, shooting me a wink when he catches me watching him in surprise.

My heart feels like it's about to pound out of my chest, and my body has broken out into a nervous sweat. I hope Chase doesn't notice.

"Don't think it's just the guys we're worried about. I know some of you girls can be catty little bitches. I've seen it for myself," Rain says to the room, turning to Laura and then directs this last part to her. "Don't fuck with me. Don't fuck with my girl. Keep your mouth shut, and her name out of it. Got it? Good," she says, sitting back down looking like she's vibrating with anger. *Why does her calling me 'her girl' feel so good?*

"You okay?" I ask, my voice soft as the room breaks out into collective chatter.

"No," she huffs. "I'm pissed. We told them to fuck off, and they are still messing with you."

"It's okay," I tell her, placing my hand on her arm. She looks at it, then up at me. I can see her body relax under my touch and it sends a satisfied feeling through me.

Brody and Rain just told the whole school not to mess with me. There's no way people can do what they probably did before, delete the mass text Brody sent and ignore it.

Is this real? The people who had the whole student body after me for months just ordered them to leave me alone. It's not going to take away what's already happened, but I would like to think that I can now walk around without being worried that someone is gonna stop me and try something.

"They better leave you alone this time," she says.

"I think after that, they should." I give her a grin, and her pissed off look melts before I see a hint of a smile break through.

"No one messes with our girl," she says with a wink, and fucking butterflies erupt in my belly.

Yeah, no one but you, my inner thoughts think. Nope, not gonna go there. They are working toward making amends. I won't let toxic thoughts set me back. They're not just anyone. They are people who owned my heart from a very young age, and Lilly's parents. I need to do the right thing and be mature about this. And I hope they can too.

After lunch, I say goodbye to Rain, Jax, and Brody and promise to sit with them again next week.

"Can I talk to you alone for a moment?" I ask Chase.

"Sure," he says and follows me outside to the courtyard next to the food court.

"This is a little awkward to ask, but I need to," I say, hugging myself from the light breeze.

"Okay? What's wrong?"

"We've had sex twice now," I start

He grins. "I'm aware. I was there both times." He winks.

"Chase, this is serious." I cock a brow.

"Right, sorry, go on," he says giving me his full attention.

"We didn't use condoms. I'm not worried about pregnancy because I'm on birth control but...I know you had been with a lot of women before we had sex at the party. So I'm wondering if I have to worry?"

"About me being clean or other women?" he asks, brows pinching.

"Well...both, I guess," I say, feeling insecure all of a sudden.

"Ellie, all other women no longer exist to me. You are it, baby.

Only you, always you." He pulls me into his arms, and I melt into his hold, feeling a little better by his words. "As for the other thing, I'm clean. We have to get tested for the team regularly. But even if we didn't, I've always used condoms for everything I did. You're the only girl I've let touch me without one, even just your mouth. You're the only one I've wanted to be bare with. It's something I take seriously, and it's only ever been meant for you."

That means a lot to me, more than he will ever know. "Thank you for being honest," I tell him, leaning up on my tippy toes to give him a kiss.

"I'll always be open with you, Ellie; no more secrets."

"No more secrets," I agree.

As I'm heading to my afternoon class, I'm grabbed by the arm and pulled into a bathroom.

"What the hell!?" I shout when Laura pushes me up against the bathroom wall.

"Don't think that any of what they said applies to us," she sneers. "We know what you are, and that's a dirty, little whore. What, fucking a professor isn't enough? You gotta go for Rain and the Silver Knights too? What makes your pussy so special that you think you can have them all?"

She knows about me and Theo? What the hell?

"Fuck off, Laura," I growl, wrenching my arm out of her grasp. "You don't scare me. Call me whatever you want. It's just words, and at the end of the day, I know I'm better than you. And I don't mean it to sound full of myself. I say it because I am. I don't go around treating people like trash just for the fun of it."

"She's not gonna be happy with sharing you," Laura smirks.

"She loves the attention being on her and only her. And I've made sure she knows that I *only* want her. That she's enough for me, and I don't need the whole fucking football team in my bed to feel satisfied."

"You act like you know Rain so well, but did you forget the fact that I dated her first? That we were together for *years* while I was also in a loving, committed relationship with the guys? In all those years that we were together, she seemed pretty damn happy to share me with the others. Don't fool yourself into thinking you know anything about her. The Rain she's been with you is only a part of who she is. I know the real Rain," I say, stepping into her personal space.

"She's mine," Laura growls. "I almost had her until you came back. You ruin everything you touch!"

"Get over yourself; your crazy is showing." I smirk. "Now, if you don't mind, I'm gonna go to class and learn things instead of wasting my time threatening people."

I push past her and out the door, but before I can step through Kayla calls out, "Chase is mine! If you don't leave him alone, I'll find you."

God, these girls have a few screws loose. Something tells me this isn't the last time I'm going to have to deal with these two. They are obsessed with Rain and Chase, and they don't like the idea that I'm taking them away. *Not that they were theirs to begin with.*

But I'm not going to worry about it until I have to. I have bigger fish to fry, like getting my rapist behind bars.

ELLIE

Giggling and the sound of someone moving in the room wakes me from my sleep. Blinking my eyes open, I move to sit up in bed. My sleepy eyes take in the room before I let out a gasp of surprise.

"Happy Valentine's Day, sweetheart," Theo says, standing by

the door with Lilly standing next to him, a big smile on her face as she vibrates with excited energy.

"Theo," I whisper, emotion clogging my throat. My eyes water as I take in the room. There are tons of pink and red balloons lining the back wall, all different shapes and sizes. Rose petals are scattered on the bed and a few gift bags sit perched on the end of bed.

"Good morning, my love," Theo says, stepping into the room with a tray of food.

"I love you, you know that?" I say, wiping at my eyes. "You didn't have to do all this."

"Yes, I did," he smiles, placing the tray down on the bed. "Because this is our first Valentine's Day together, and what kind of a boyfriend would I be if I didn't go all out." He winks.

"You know I'm happy with just some sweet words and a kiss, right?" I tell him, but I do love what he's done for me.

"I know, and that's one of my favorite things out of many that I love about you. But I do want to spoil you every once in a while, is that okay?"

"I mean, I guess." I sigh dramatically, getting one of those husky laughs that makes my toes curl in response.

"First, I want to ask you an important question," he tells me.

"Okay..." If he asks me to marry him, I may freak out.

"Will you be my Valentine?" Oh thank god, not that I wouldn't love to marry him, but it's still too soon for that. I look at him and bite my lip. This is *exactly* what I was worried about. What about Chase?

"If I say yes, would you be offended if Chase asks me and I accept his offer too?" I ask, belly flipping with nerves. I know this is silly, but it's all so new. I've never dated more than one person who wasn't within my friend group. Theo isn't a part of that history, what we have is our own thing.

"Of course not," he smiles. "You can have as many Valentines as your heart desires."

"Then yes, I would love to be your Valentine." I smile up at him. He leans in and places a soft kiss on my lips.

"Ewww," Lilly says, climbing on the bed and snatching a piece of my bacon. I gape at her in mock outrage, but she just giggles as she eats my yummy bacon.

"Plus, you're not my only Valentine anyways," Theo says.

"I'm not?" I ask, cocking a brow.

"Nope. I asked little Miss Lilly and she graciously accepted." Theo grins over at her.

"Dada got me a bunny! And flowers! And chocolates!" she says excitedly, going for another piece of my bacon. *She's lucky she's cute.*

"I think she might have had a few when I wasn't looking." Theo laughs, adjusting his glasses. He's so damn sexy.

"I think so," I agree as Lilly grabs one more slice, shoving it in her mouth and taking off out of the room, laughing like a madman.

"I love that little girl," he says, shaking his head.

"I love that you do," I say, beckoning him with my finger to come closer. We kiss again, this time slow and soft. I savor the taste of him on my lips and tongue.

"Now, what did my handsome man get me?" I ask, pulling back.

He grins, grabbing the bags and putting them next to me. With giddy excitement, I open the first bag. "Theo..." My eyes widen at the beautiful heart pendant necklace.

"I noticed you don't wear one, so I thought I'd get you one. The stone also happens to be Lilly's birthstone," he says. There's a stunning purple amethyst that sits in the middle of the heart.

"Thank you," I tell him. "Help me put it on?"

He nods, taking the necklace out of the box. I gather my hair up and turn to the side for better access. Once he clips it, he places a kiss to the back of my neck.

"I love you, sweet girl."

"I love you too," I tell him, turning back around. "Okay, what's in this one?" I ask, pointing to the last bag.

"Open it," he laughs.

Reaching in, I pull out a rose-gold lingerie outfit.

Looking up at Theo, I can't help but grin at the pink tinge on his cheeks. "Umm," he clears his throat. "I remember you mentioning how you didn't have anything sexy to wear, but didn't want to waste money on something that would come off in a few minutes... I think if it's something you want, you should at least have one. So..."

"Thank you. I know I'm gonna feel sexy in it."

"You're sexy in anything you wear, Ellie. Could be a trash bag and you'd still be rocking it."

I burst out laughing. He really is amazing.

I finish my breakfast and get dressed for the day while Theo gets Toby ready for school.

As I'm putting my makeup on, there's a knock at the door.

"I'll get it," Theo calls out.

A moment later, Lilly yells out, "Ace!"

Chase is here? Butterflies erupt in my belly, and I quickly finish what I'm doing.

"Mama!" Lilly says when I get into the living room. "Look!" She's standing next to a giant pink teddy bear that's holding a heart that says 'I love you' on it. "Ace gave it to me."

"Wow, look at that! So cool and big," I say, smiling over to Chase who's looking at me like I'm the only person in the world.

"Only the best for my little buddy."

"Mama, I have two Valentines," Lilly says.

"You do?" I ask.

She nods. "Yup, Dada and Ace!"

"Oh, Ace asked you?" I say, looking back at Chase.

He just shrugs, giving me a smirk.

"I thought I could bring you to school today, is that okay?" he asks, looking at Theo then back to me.

"Ummm," I stammer, unsure what I should say.

"Go," Theo says, pulling me into his arms and kissing the top of my head. "My mom just called and she's on her way. I'll stay with Lilly until she gets here, then I'll drop Toby off before going to work."

"You're tall," Toby says to Chase. Chase looks down at Toby.

"And you're short," Chase grins.

Toby narrows his eyes at Chase then says. "You're not Lilly's best friend, I am!" Then he turns and runs down the hall.

"What was that about?" Chase asks, looking over at us.

"I think Toby is feeling a little jealous because you're all Lilly talks about," Theo explains. "It's okay though because he needs to learn that you're allowed to have more than one friend."

Chase nods then looks at me. "So, ride with me? Please?" he pouts. *Damn it, it's hard to say no to him when he does that.*

"Okay," I laugh, "just let me grab my bag."

I grab my things and say goodbye to Theo and the kids before following Chase down to his car.

"That was really sweet of you to ask Lilly and bring her a gift," I say as we drive to school. Waiting to see if he'll ask me is killing me. Maybe he won't, I mean, he doesn't have to. Maybe he thought Theo already did and he can't ask too. Or maybe I'm just overthinking everything and making a big deal out of nothing.

"She's my little lady, I had to spoil her," he says, looking over at me with that sexy smile I love so much.

"I think you've definitely managed that with her birthday gift," I say with amusement. "She's always asking to go down to the paved area in the back of the building to drive it. I think some of the other kids in the apartment are getting jealous."

"Only the best for my girl."

His girl. Seeing Chase love Lilly as much as he does already makes me so happy. I feel bad that he and the others missed out on so much of her life.

When we get to school, Chase walks me to my first class. "I'll see you at lunch okay? Sit with us today, please?"

"Okay."

He gives me a kiss that has me weak in the knees and a little bit dazed before taking off down the hall. This is going to be a long morning.

"Theo did good," Val says as she admires my necklace while we wait for Chase and the others to get to the food court. Class ended a little early so we decided to get here before the rush of people.

"It's so pretty," Lexie agrees. "And the way he woke you up, ugh, swoon! I feel bad for any man who tries to date me because if they're not Theo-level, I don't want them."

"Oh, stop." I laugh. "Not everyone is the same. I'm sure you can find a good guy out there who will treat you right."

"Think there are any female versions of Theo?" Tabitha asks. "I need me one of those."

"Speaking of women, how are things going with the Queen Bitch?" Val questions.

"Val," Lexie hisses. "We talked about this."

"Look, I know we did, but just because she's trying to work things out with them for Lilly's sake doesn't mean Rain didn't still do what she did. She's a bitch. And she fucked with our best friend. I'm not nice like Ellie. I still want to cut a chunk of her hair off and throw it in her face."

I love my friends, and I love how fiercely they love and protect me. If it wasn't for them, I don't think I would have been able to be at this school without going mad the past few months.

"Rain is changing," I inform them. "I haven't forgiven her just yet, she has a lot of work to do, but she's made it known what she wants along with what she's going to do to get it."

"What does that mean?" Lexie cocks a brow. "What did she say?"

I bite my lip, thinking back to the other week when she kissed me. *It was a really damn good kiss.*

"She's blushing!" Val gasp. "What happened? Spill!"

"She told me how sorry she was, then told me she was gonna win me back," I shrug.

"And...?" Val says, waving her hand at me to continue.

"Then she kissed me." My cheeks get pinker. I feel like a love sick fool again. I don't want to get excited at the idea of being with Rain again, but the way she treated me, I knew that wasn't the real her. I don't want to make excuses for her, even though the way she acted was that of someone who had their heart broken for all the wrong reasons.

"I still vote we go paintballing again so I can take a few more tit shots," Val says casually, making me snort a laugh.

"I'd like to see Brody dance like a little monkey again," Tabitha adds.

We all burst out laughing and chat for a little while longer before Rain walks over to the table with Jax.

"Hey," she says, making us all look up at her.

"Hi." I give her a small smile.

"So, Chase is gonna be a little late, but he asked if I could get you over to our table to wait for him. Is that okay?"

I look at my friends and they nod. "Yeah, sure," I say, grabbing my bags. "See you girls later," I tell them, then follow Jax and Rain toward their table.

"I'm watching you, she-witch!" Val calls from behind.

My eyes widen and Jax snorts out a laugh while Rain lets out a grumbling huff.

"Sorry about her," I say, scratching the back of my head as we sit down.

"Don't be. She's just being a good friend. I love that you have people who care about you like that. And I deserve it."

I look over at the table we just left to find Val glaring at Rain. She does the 'I'm watching you' thing with her fingers before turning away to talk to the girls.

"They're all pretty amazing. I don't know what I'd do without them."

"Looks like you're not the only one we have to win over," Jax grins.

"Yeah, I think it would be for the best," I laugh. "Val isn't someone you want on your bad side. She's got a way with words and they are not always pleasant."

"Noted," Jax chuckles.

"So, where's Chase?" I ask. The food court is full now, and I look to see if he's arrived yet.

"He should be here any second," she says, looking at the food court door. A moment later, Chase walks in and he's holding something... *Is that a boombox?*

My eyes narrow on the object as I see him put it down on one of the tables, not caring about the people sitting at said table. And he's a Silver Knight, so they don't ask questions.

"What's he doing?" I ask, looking to Jax then to Rain. They both have matching grins, but won't look at me.

Chase presses a button on the stereo and a song starts to play. It takes me a moment before I recognize what song is playing, *Can't Take My Eyes Off Of You* by Frankie Valli.

Chase turns to me with a mic in his hand and starts to sing. A thrill runs through my body as he starts walking toward me. When we were younger, I had an obsession with the movie, *Ten Things I Hate About You*. And the scene when Patrick sings this song to Kat was my favorite. I thought it was adorable and funny while the guys would always tease me about it.

So seeing Chase do this right now, it means everything.

I watch with a grin so wide, my cheeks hurt. Just like at the pool party, this song's lyrics are how he feels; I can see the truth shining in his eyes.

Then the song picks up a little and he starts to dance around. He jumps up onto one of the tables and loudly sings, "I love you, baby, and if it's quite alright, I need you baby..." It's not the best singing, but I love it.

He keeps going and dancing around the table. Then he starts to jump from one table to the other. When it slows down again, he starts to make his way over to our table. Once he gets to us, the song picks up again. He looks right in my eyes and belts out the rest.

When the song is over, the room bursts out into cheers and cat calls.

"So, Miss Tatum, will you do me the greatest honor and be my Valentine?" he asks. "Because I love you and I need you baby." He winks.

I burst into a happy laugh, nodding my head. "I would love to."

"Fuck yeah!" Chase whoops and leans down to give me a soul consuming kiss right in front of everyone.

If anyone had any questions on what Chase is to me, all of them have now been pretty much answered.

"This is bullshit!" Kayla cries, and storms out of the room, but no one pays her much attention.

This means more to me than he will ever know, and I love him so much more for it.

Chapter Fifteen

BRODY

TODAY IS VALENTINE'S DAY, and I'm freaking the fuck out. I've thought a lot about what I'm about to do, and even though I'm going to man the fuck up and do it, I'm still nervous as hell.

I'm not the sweet romantic type, and I don't do the lovey dovey bullshit. It's not me. Loving someone is hard enough for me to do. I didn't have a good example of a loving relationship growing up, and I've fucked up a lot over the years. The only two people I've ever loved are currently not very happy with me.

Things with Jax and I haven't been the same since Ellie came back, and I know it's my fault. But since the party and everything came out, we've been extremely distant. So much so that I'm starting to worry I'll end up losing him too.

I can't lose him. I love Jax more than words can say, and if I lost him, then what else do I have? Ellie is better off without me, and Lilly has three other dads. She doesn't need me. But Jax, even though he's also probably better off leaving me to be with Ellie, I won't let him go. There's only so much I'm willing to give up.

I've stopped drinking since the night I got that damn tattoo. I was pissed off at first. *I mean, who tattoos a drunk person?* Don't they know drunk people make stupid decisions, like I did? But after a while, I've grown to like the tattoo. It's a really epic piece, so the artist might be shady to take the money, but he's damn good at his job.

Jax was right about my drinking, but I'm too stubborn to tell him that. I was drinking too much, and it wasn't helping my problems; it only made them worse. I refuse to believe that I'm an alcoholic like my dad, though. Plus, there is the fact that I wanted to stop, and I did, just like that. *So that's proof enough, right?*

Do I often want a drink? Sure.

But have I actually consumed that drink? No.

Now I'm in my car with Jax's gift in hand, about to walk into the food court at school and ask him to be my valentine...in front of *everyone*. It's so fucking corny, but I know it will mean a lot to Jax. *I hope.*

As I said before, I've been thinking about this a lot, and Jax deserves better. We've been keeping things with us to ourselves because I care too much about what people think about me; about us. Me, the football captain and the quarterback with one of my teammates.

On the other hand, I don't want him to think that he's my dirty little secret. I've been a dick, and I've hurt him, but not anymore. I'm lucky enough to have an amazing man like him who loves and cares for me, sticking by my side through everything, when he doesn't have to.

I mean, he fucking cleaned up my drunk ass and put me to bed. The man's a damn saint.

And I don't blame him for taking a step back from us while working on getting Ellie back. I've made it hard for him to do both, but I've put my issues with Ellie to rest. There are no issues anymore.

He wants her. He loves her. I'm gonna help him get her back, but I love him and want him too. I don't think she would be the type of person who would try and come between us, although that's something we're going to have to talk to her about because I will fight for him.

I want to fight for her too, but I can only be so selfish. She has amazing people who love her. She doesn't need me.

It's like the moment I had nothing to hate her for, the hate I'd been harboring turned into an obsession and it's getting harder and harder to keep myself from throwing my hat into the ring.

But I've done fucked up, horrible, and unforgivable things.

I think about her all the time. Her smile, her voice, her laugh. The way she looked when I used to fuck her, the pure bliss that would twinkle in her eyes.

A part of me wishes Jax and I were together when we were all dating. I would have loved to fuck his tight ass while he fucked her pussy, watching them both break beneath me.

Awesome, now I have a fucking boner.

Letting out a harsh sigh, I get out of the car and slam the door behind me.

"It's now or never. He better know how much I love his sexy ass after this," I grumble to myself as I head into the school.

When I reach the food court, I get to watch the tail end of whatever the fuck Chase planned to do to ask Ellie to be his Valentine. I overheard him and Rain talking about it, but the little shit was tight-lipped when it came to me. Whatever it was, she looks so damn happy that I almost trip over my feet when I see her beaming smile.

Fuck, being around her is gonna be harder than I thought.

Taking a deep breath, I head right for our table.

"Hey, there you are. I was wondering where you disappeared to," Jax says looking up at me.

He looks delectable today in a black t-shirt that hugs his muscles, and puts his arm tattoos on full display. I just want to trace every inch of them with my tongue. His brown eyes stare up at me, waiting for me to answer.

Before I know what I'm doing, I'm leaning over the table to grab the back of his head, fisting a handful of hair and crushing my lips to his.

He moans softly like he just can't help it as I slip my tongue into his mouth and over his. It's a short kiss, but it had an effect.

Whispers break out around the room, but I ignore them as I pull back to look into Jax's shocked eyes. "Mine," I growl, then bite his lower lip before standing back up.

I can see Chase's massive grin out of the corner of my eye. Ellie is sitting on his lap, a cute smile on her face like she approves of what I just did. "About damn time," Chase chuckles.

"Fuck," I sigh. "That's not how I planned to do this," I mutter.

"Do what?" he asks, his voice in awe as he blinks up at me. "Do you even know what you just did?"

"Yeah, I just showed the whole school whose man you are. You're mine, Jax Hunter, and it's about time I stop hiding that fact. You're not my dirty little secret, and I'm proud to call you my boyfriend. And if anyone has an issue with it, then I'll smash their stupid faces in," I growl before pulling up a chair to the table to sit across from him.

The look on his face makes the awkward feeling that is rising within me right now worth it.

"I love you," he tells me. The look in his eyes tells me what I just did means more to him than I'll ever understand.

Say it, man, just fucking say it. Looking dead in his eyes, I tell him something he's been craving for me to say. "I love you too, Jax. So fucking much."

His eyes water, but he blinks it away.

"So, umm...you want to be my valentine or whatever?" I ask, scratching the back of my head, feeling really out of my element right now.

"Awww, who knew Brody was a softie," Chase teases.

"Fuck off." I flip him off, making him laugh.

"I'd love that," Jax says, grabbing my hand under the table and lacing his fingers through mine.

"Here," I say, handing him an envelope. I have something else for him, but I want to give that to him in private.

"What's this?" he asks, opening it. He takes the paper out and reads it over, his eyes going wide. "Brody, are you serious?"

I shrug. "I know you wanted to get some ink from him someday, and he was running a special, offering up a gift certificate to a selected few. I got one for you."

"But this is Alex Russle. He's one of the best tattoo artists, like, ever."

"I know." I grin.

"He costs a fortune! Brody, this is too much."

"You're worth every penny and more. Now, be a good boy and accept my gift," I grin.

"You're fucking amazing! You know that, right?" he says. "It's taking everything in me not to kiss you again."

"Later." I shoot him a hungry look.

Because I don't think I'll be able to keep my hands to myself anymore. It's been too long since I've felt his mouth on my skin, since I've tasted him. I'm dying to feel his tight ass grip my cock so tightly that I pass the fuck out. To hear his moans, his screams of ecstasy, as he falls off the edge with my name on his lips.

It's gonna be hard, fast, and oh-so-fucking perfect.

Why does the drive home feel like it's taking forever? "Move!" I shout at the cars in front of me, laying on the horn.

"It's a red light." Jax laughs next to me. "What's the rush?"

The rush is that I need my cock inside you like yesterday, that's the fucking rush.

"I just want to get home." I sigh harshly as I honk the horn.

"Babe," Jax says, his hand finding my thigh. "Relax, this isn't gonna get us home any faster. It's just stressing you out." He rubs his hand up and down my leg, getting awfully close to my growing cock.

"Watch what you're doing, Jax. You go any higher then you're gonna have to finish what you start," I growl, giving him a warning look that's filled with more heat than anything else.

He gives me a bratty smirk and moves his hand further up, slowly.

"Jax," I say sternly, but he just bites his lip. He looks so fucking sexy as he cups my cock, giving it a squeeze.

"Fucking brat," I hiss, pressing down on the gas pedal the moment the light turns green. I let out a deep groan as he slowly starts to pump me through my pants. "You're gonna pay for this. I hope you fucking know that."

"I'm so scared," he taunts, being a smart ass, and getting another growl from deep within my chest.

We get to our apartment in record time. I park the car and hastily open my door, slamming it shut before storming around the car to Jax's side. Flinging it open, I glare down at his amused but excited smirk.

"See this?" I tell him, pointing to my dick. "You fucking did this. Now you're gonna get your ass up stairs. Right. Now," I demand.

"Yes, Sir," he sasses back before getting out of the car. We head inside the apartment building and into the elevator. He stands there, smirking at me the whole fucking time. I just want to bend him over my knee and smack his ass until it turns a pretty shade of red.

Finally, we get to our floor and Jax struts out in front of me, walking toward our place like he's not about to get punished for teasing the hell out of me.

Once we get to our door, he goes to put his key into the lock, but I grab him by the shoulder and spin him around, pushing him up against the door. My hand closes around his neck, and I squeeze lightly.

"You think it's funny to tease me like that?" I growl.

His eyes grow hooded, and his breathing starts to pick up.

"I asked you a question."

"No," he rasps.

"Then why did you do it? Do you want me to punish you?" I ask, my face less than an inch from his. I press my body against his, feeling his hard cock against mine.

"Yes," he breathes.

"Well, if that's what you want, then get your fucking ass in that apartment. Now," I growl.

I add a little more pressure to my hold, getting a whimper from him that has my cock pulsing.

Letting go, he rushes to do what he's told. Once the door is open, I grab him by the arm, hauling him inside and locking the door behind us before shoving him up against the door again.

"Teasing is all fun and games until you're the one on the receiving end," I tell him, running my hands down his chest. I grip his shirt with both my hands, getting a good grasp before ripping down the middle to reveal his tattooed chest. He lets out a gasp, his eyes widening. "It's been too long, Jax. It's been far too fucking long since I've tasted you." I lean in and suck on his nipple, swirling my tongue around it and flicking the tip back and forth.

"Brody," he groans.

I bite down, getting a hiss in response. "Did I say you could talk?" I challenge.

He shakes his head frantically.

"Then be quiet, or you get no release." I would never be so cruel to leave him wanting and unsatisfied, but he doesn't need to know that. Moving my mouth back to his fine body, I kiss my way down his chest. "Before I'm done with you, I'm gonna have memorized every inch of your tattoos by touch alone."

By the time I get on my knees before him, my face level with his cock, he's panting like a bitch in heat and I fucking love it.

"You wanna tease me?" I ask him, unbuckling his pants,

137

making sure to brush my hand against his erection as much as I can while doing so.

Once they're undone, I slowly pull them down along with his boxers. His cock springs free, heavy, thick, and leaking with pre-cum. *So fucking tempting.*

"Then I'm gonna tease you." I wrap my fist around his cock, giving it one firm stroke and his knees almost buckle. His velvety, warm skin feels soft against my rough hand.

"Look at you, dripping for me." I look up at him, and god, it's taking everything in me to take this slow instead of bending him over and fucking him. His eyes are frantic, and his pupils are blown wide. "I need a taste." My tongue darts out, licking the pearl at the end of his shaft. "So fucking good," I groan. "I think I'll have some more."

Wrapping my lips around the head of his cock, I give it a little suck before taking him all the way in. The sound he makes have my own cock weeping. But I'm saving that for his tight little hole.

I bob my head, sucking and licking to drive him wild.

"You like this?" I ask, pulling back with a pop. He nods, but that's not what I want. "Answer me when I ask you a question."

"Yes," he croaks. "So fucking much."

"Good." I give him a smile before taking him again. His eyes are squeezed shut, nails digging into the door behind him. I continue to tease him until I feel his cock start to twitch. He's going to cum any second, and that's when I pull back.

"Brody," he cries.

"Now, now, little pup, I'll give you what you need when I think you've earned it," I tell him, getting to my feet. When he opens his mouth to protest, I cut him off. "Shhh." I cup his face, stroking his cheek with my thumb. He looks pissed, but I know he fucking loves this back and forth. We don't play games like this a lot because we both love to give the other what we want, but I know the release will be so much fucking sweeter since it's been a while. "I love you so fucking much, do you know that?" I ask him, brushing my lips across his. It's like now that I've said those three little words, I can't stop. And he deserves to hear them all the time. "You're so fucking amazing, so needy, so desperate for my cock. Such a good boy."

I suck his bottom lip into my mouth and give it a bite.

"Now, we're gonna go into your room. You're gonna lay down on your back and open your legs nice and wide for me. I'm gonna fuck your tight ass, watch the torture on your face as I bring you to the brink of ecstasy, then you can have your release," I inform him, my voice pure sex.

"Yes, Sir," he whimpers.

"Run along, pup," I tell him. He takes his pants off the rest of the way and runs to his room. I let out a deep chuckle, loving how fucking eager he is. I undress as I follow him, naked by the time I reach his room.

He did what I asked him, laying in the middle of the bed, his cock so painfully hard and waiting against his stomach.

"You even have a bottle of lube waiting for me." I grin, kneeling on the bed. "Good boy. Now, get me nice and wet for you. I wanna slide right into that tight ass of yours."

He moves to sit up, grabbing the bottle of lube and putting a heavy amount on his hand. I move between his legs so that my cock is level with his face. He stares at it, a hungry look in his eye like he would like nothing more than to have a lick. "Not today," I tell him, and he gives me a pout. I cock a brow and nod down toward it. He licks his lips, then starts to coat my cock in the lube. "Fuck," I hiss at his touch. "Lay back now," I tell him once I'm nice and ready. "This is gonna be hard and fast, are you ready?" I ask.

"Always," he breathes. I know he loves it any way I give it to him, but I can't do slow and sweet very often. It's not how things are between us, but I do enjoy it from time to time. Only, right now is *not* that time.

He lays back, and I move myself in position. Grabbing the pillows behind him, I place it under his ass so that it's higher up and at the perfect level. Then I take his legs and put them over my shoulder.

"Ready?" I ask again.

"Yes," he rasps.

Lining my cock up with his hole, I slowly start to push in. We both let out this loud, pained moan as I inch into him.

"Damn it!" I growl. "You're gripping my cock so fucking good."

"Brody," he pleads.

"I know, baby, I know." I rub his legs to soothe him, giving him a moment to adjust. "I'm gonna fuck you now. I'm gonna fuck you raw until you're limp and exhausted under me."

"Please," he begs.

Gripping his legs, I pull back and thrust back in. His eyes roll into the back of his head. *God, he feels so fucking good, so fucking perfect.*

Something takes over me, a pure primal side as I start to pound into him. I need this; so does he.

"Never again," I grunt, my hips slapping against his ass. "Never again will we go this long without each other, do you understand?"

"Never," he moans.

"Touch yourself," I demand. "Stroke your thick cock as I fuck you, but don't cum until I do."

He grabs ahold of his length, grasping it tightly, and starts to jerk himself off in a frenzy.

"That's it baby, choke on that dick," I growl. I start to rut into him, my fingers digging into his thighs.

We fuck like this for a few minutes, the room filling with our sounds of pleasure. But I know he can't hold back anymore, and neither can I.

"Cum for me, Jax," I demand, slapping his ass hard. "Coat yourself in your seed as I fill your ass with mine."

I'm almost there, so fucking close.

"Brody!" he moans loudly. His back arches and his eyes roll back as he cums hard, sending jets of cum onto his abs.

"Good boy," I praise, thrusting one last time before I still, roaring out my release as my cock twitches in his ass, filling him with my release.

"Fuck's sake, Brody," he breathes, his chest heaving. I put my forehead against his leg, giving it a kiss before letting them drop. "I was so close to losing my shit. There's a reason why we don't edge," he chuckles, his eyes still closed.

"Well, next time, don't be a fucking brat."

"Yeah, fat chance of that." He gives me a sleepy grin.

"Look at all this," I tsk, looking at the cum on his chest. "So messy."

His eyes open and he looks at me. "That's a week of no release."

"You didn't touch yourself?" I ask.

"No." He shakes his head. "I tried, but it wasn't you, so I didn't want to."

Fuck, I love the sound of that.

"Well, let's not let this go to waste shall we?" I growl, then lean over him to lick a line of cum off his abs. "Delicious," I say, licking my lips before cleaning him completely.

"Damn it, Brody, you have me hard again," he groans.

"Well, we can't have that." I give him a wicked grin before taking his cock into my mouth.

We fuck a few more times. After a while, it ends up being more like making love. As I fuck him soft and slow for the last time of the night, finally giving him a break, we find a happiness in each other that was temporarily lost. Afterwards, we clean each other up, then the bed.

As we lay in bed, I realize I almost forgot his other gift.

"Where are you going?" he asks as I get out of the bed.

"Just a sec," I tell him, going out to the living room to grab my pants.

Chase it sitting on the couch with headphones on. When he

sees me, he gives me a shit eating grin. I flip him off, grab what I need, and head back to the room.

"Give me your finger," I tell him, opening the box that I had in my pants.

"Okay?" he says, and holds out his hand. I slip a shiny, metal band on his ring finger, and he stares at it like it's an alien about to eat him alive.

"Brody, what's this?" he asks, looking back at me.

"It's me promising to always love you. To become a better man for you and the others. To never give up on us, and always fight for what's right."

"Brody," he says, his voice filling with emotion.

I put my forehead to his. "I love you, Jax, and I'm sorry if I ever made you feel like I didn't care or that you didn't mean the world to me. I've never been ashamed of you, or what we have, and I know that I should stop letting my head fuck over my heart. You're mine, and now, the world knows it. I will never hide you from the world, instead I'll have you at my side."

I pull him into my arms and we kiss. It's lazy and soft, but filled with every good feeling in the world. We fall asleep in each other's embrace.

And I dream all night of *her* between us, filling that missing piece of my heart.

Chapter Sixteen

ELLIE

LIFE HAS TAKEN a 180° turn since I moved back here five months ago, and not in a bad way. I know I have a lot coming up, and my fight isn't over, but for the first time in a while, I feel like I can finally breathe.

My dad found me a really good lawyer, and during our conversation over the phone where I sent him the evidence, he told me that he thinks we have a really good case.

We've went ahead and taken the next step. Now, I'm just waiting to hear back from my lawyer.

Valentine's Day was amazing. Chase and I hung out after school for a few hours, then I went out for supper with Theo. It was honestly perfect.

Since then, I've been splitting my lunch time between my friends and the others. I refuse to be the kind of girl who chooses her boyfriends over her friends, because these girls and Cooper are the real deal, and I wouldn't give them up for anything.

I've found this perfect balance, juggling my time between school, Lilly, Theo, my friends, work, and Chase. I've surprised myself with how well this is working.

At school, I see Chase and the others as well as my friends, then at night, I'm with Lilly for a few hours and when she's in bed, I'm with Theo. On days I work, sometimes my friends come in to see me. I have yet to see Rain and the guys there. Maybe it's for the best. I'd probably get too distracted.

Work is work. I've been making it my mission to keep away from Laura and Kayla. I told Aria about what's going on, and she's been helping by assigning them jobs that keep us away from each other.

Today, I'm scheduled to eat with Chase and the others. They haven't seen Lilly again, but I'm kind of glad I get to spend this time with them before they start coming around her. I want to know I can get along with them before they become a big part of her life. It would be horrible if we couldn't at least get along as friends.

The more time I spend with them though, the more I wonder how they even got to the point of being so cruel to me, because the people I've been around lately have been anything but cruel. They have really been showing me that they can change, and a part of my heart loves the little glimpses of what they were like back when we were together.

Sometimes I catch myself watching Rain interact with other people, not seeing a cold hearted bitch but the fun, vibrant, confident person she really is.

Jax has been talking to me a lot more. Even going as far as finding things to have conversations about, not liking when things get too quiet between us. And I find him easy to talk to. We can talk about anything, and it never gets boring.

Chase...is Chase. Funny, silly, and very affectionate. But I crave it. I can't seem to get enough.

As for Brody, right now, he's just there. He doesn't talk to me much, but he doesn't make me feel like I'm not wanted either.

It's a weird feeling to be around him and not worry about what horrible thing he's going to say or do next.

It's taken a lot of strength from within myself to give them this chance, and taking things slow has been really working well.

Am I ready to forgive Rain and Brody? No. The only things

Brody has really done to show he's changed is call the school off and continue to be civil with me. It's not even close to earning my forgiveness.

As for Rain, she's done a little bit more. She's working on getting to know me better, asking questions and engaging in conversations. She's made it known to the school where she stands. She does have the love of my daughter, and I'd say Lilly is a pretty good judge of character. Trust me, toddlers are brutally honest little things. They will tell you straight up if you're a shitty person.

Today, for lunch, the others wanted to sit outside in the court-yard, so we got our lunch and are now sitting at a picnic table.

"So, I've got some exciting news," Jax says, looking at all of us with a big smile as he grabs Brody's hand, lacing his fingers through Brody's.

Since Brody made it public knowledge that he and Jax are together, I've seen Jax come out of his shell a little more, and I've seen a softer side in Brody that he didn't really have even when we were together. A part of me feels robbed of that, but I'm also proud that he's growing and capable of being an affectionate lover.

"What, you're gonna be a grandma?" Chase asks, stealing one of my grapes. He gives me a wink as I stick out my tongue at him.

"What? No, what the fuck does that even mean?" Jax asks, his brows furrowing in confusion. Chase just grins, giving him a shrug. I giggle knowing Chase is just fucking with him. "I got a call from one of the scouts that was at the last game of the season. He was with the Black Ravens. They are a minor league football team, and they're offering me a spot on their team."

"What!? That's amazing!" Rain says.

"Yes! That's what I'm talking about!" Chase high fives him.

"I'm so proud of you," Brody says, gripping the back of Jax's head and pulling him in for a hard kiss.

I can't help but watch. Just like when I caught them at the party, it still turns me on. I shift in my seat and look away, catching Chase's eye. He gives me a look that's a cross between a shit-eating grin and a knowing one that makes me blush.

"I'm so happy for you," I tell Jax, giving him a beaming smile when he and Brody break apart.

"It's not the NFL, but it's a stepping stone," Jax says.

"You're gonna get there, baby. I know it. They would be fucking stupid not to have you on one of their teams. You're amazing," Brody tells him.

"So, Ellie, are you trying out for the Storm River Cheer Team this spring?" Rain asks, taking a bite of her fry.

"Actually, yeah. I think it would be a lot of fun. I know it's going to be a lot of work to cheer for them if I make their team *and* the school team, but life is short and I love to cheer. Plus, Theo's offered to watch Lilly during the summer camp." I shrug.

"You know, we can watch Lilly too," Chase mumbles, taking a bite of his pizza.

"I know." I give him a smile. "But this is still new, and you guys need to spend some more time around her. Right now, you're strangers, and that needs to change before you take her by yourself. It's not that I think you wouldn't be able to do a good job, just that I'd rather Lilly feel comfortable with whoever is watching her."

"That girl you have watching her while you work is a stranger," Brody says.

"At first, yes," I say. "But I had Katie come over a few times to spend time with Lilly, with me there, before I had her start working. I needed to know that my daughter felt safe when I left her alone with Katie. That goes for everyone else too."

"Alright, I see your point." Brody nods.

"Well, I think she's pretty good with me and Chase." Rain grins.

"Stop rubbing it in, fire crotch. We get it. You two have an advantage." Brody tosses a fry at her.

"Fuck you," Rain says with a laugh.

"Nah, I'd much rather fuck him," Brody says, looking over at Jax whose cheeks have pinkened a little.

This is weird, but a good weird. It feels so much like old times.

"I'd like to say something regarding the two of you," I say, looking from Brody, whose smile drops, to Jax who now looks panicked.

"And what would that be?" Brody asks with warning.

"Well first, I'd like to say, I think what you two have is amazing, and I'm proud of you both for not hiding it and embracing it. As someone who was out in the open with Rain, I know sometimes it might not be easy."

"Oh." Brody's defensiveness deflates. "Thanks."

"And second." I look at Jax. "This might be a little too early to be asking this, but it's something that's been on my mind. What do you want in regard to you and me?"

"Umm." His eyes widen, and I feel bad for putting him on the spot. "Well, I, uhh." He scratches the back of his head, and I feel my gut sink. Maybe I thought too much into what he said back at Bill's diner when he said they wanted to prove that they are sorry and that they love me. Not the sorry part, but the love.

"You know, never mind," I tell him, feeling like an idiot. "Forget I said anything." I let out an embarrassed laugh.

"Wait. Ellie," Jax says, and I look back up at him. "You want to know what I want from you? What I want in the end?"

I don't say anything, just nod while biting the inside of my cheek.

"I want you. I want to be with you. I want to take you on a date, get to know this new amazingly strong, talented, smart girl who grew into a stunning woman. I want to love you everyday for the rest of our lives. I know it might come off a bit strong, but that's how I feel. I love you, Ellie. I've never stopped." I can see how sincere he is by the look in his eyes.

My eyes water. "Really?" I ask, voice cracking.

"Yes." He smiles.

"So you want me, and you want him? Kind of like how I'm with Theo and Chase?"

"If that's something you're okay with. I'd never want to choose, Ellie. It would hurt too much," he says, looking from Brody to me.

"I'd never ask you to choose, Jax," I tell him, and I can see some tension leave Brody's body. "You never made me pick back then, and I refuse to pick now, so I'd never ask you to do it."

"Thank you," Jax says.

"I won't come between you two either. I want Jax to be happy. If he wants you, then I'm supportive of that," Brody says. "But do you...do you want me like the others?"

I shrug, not committing one way or the other.

Doesn't matter, Ellie. You love him, sure, but after everything he's done, he needs to work for it. So far, he's showed nothing but just wanting to be friends. You are not going to be chasing after him. You're better than that. You're worth more than that.

"Okay, well, now that that is out of the way, I have to ask you something," Rain says, gaining my attention.

"Okay?" I ask.

"Would you be alright if I was on the Storm Rivers team with you? Because, I kind of already am." She gives me a half smile.

"I know." I smile back. "And it's okay. This was your team first. Are *you* okay if I'm a part of it?"

"Yes!" she says quickly. "You're like fucking amazing. And I'm 100 percent jelly of it. But, like damn, you kicked ass this year."

I smile, finding myself really liking her approval in this aspect. "Thanks. It was a lot of work, but totally worth it."

"Did you mean what you said? When you confronted me when you tried out?" Rain asks. The look in her eyes tells me the answer to this means something to her.

"That I originally learned to cheer so that I could join the high school team with you?" I ask and she nods, biting her lip. "Yeah. I wanted to do something with you. The guys had football and you had cheer. All I had was school and reading. Sometimes,

I'd get it in my head that you guys would realize that I'm too different and want someone who liked more of the same things you did. So I spent the whole summer learning all the basics. Turns out, I actually loved it. Too bad I was too chicken shit to actually try out." I laugh.

"It never mattered to us that you weren't into the same things we were," Brody says, and I turn to look at him. "We didn't love you because you liked cheer, or ball, or partying. We loved you because you saw the real us, and still loved us back."

Well, fuck, this is the most real I've seen Brody. I look to Jax, "You're good for him," I say. Jax grins, and Brody frowns.

My phone rings, and I grab it off the table. "Oh, I better get this," I say, seeing that it's Jeff McWilson, my lawyer. "Jeff, hey, what's up?"

"*Hey, Ellie, I'm calling with some good news. We have a court date set.*" My stomach drops, and my body starts to tremble.

"Really?" I ask, my voice barely a whisper.

"*Yes. April 15th.*"

That seems so close yet so far away. I don't know how I'm going to be able to sit and wait over a month.

"Oh, wow. Okay, well, what do we do next?" I ask, looking around the table to see everyone watching me with worried expressions.

"*Right now, nothing in regard to your case, but I did get a call from Brody Creed's lawyer. He wants to know if you're willing to testify at Brody's hearing. But there's something you should know. Because Brody's charges are connected to your charges against Tim, they might postpone deciding his sentence until after your hearing. However, I do think it would be a good idea to be there and be a character witness. What both of you say at this hearing could be beneficial.*"

"Okay, yeah, I can do that. When is it?" I ask, my body breaking out in a nervous sweat. I feel a panic attack coming on just thinking about confronting this officially.

"*March 5th.*"

"What?" I squeak, my eyes widen. That's really soon, like in a week.

"Is that going to be a problem? I can be there to help if you like."

"No, no problem. I can be there, and yes, that would be wonderful, thank you."

"Sounds good. I'll contact you closer to the date."

I hang up the phone, and place it on the table. Closing my eyes, I take some deep breaths to calm my nerves. This is becoming all too real.

"Ellie, baby, are you okay? What's wrong?" Chase asks. His hand meets my arm and he gives it a soothing rub.

"I'm okay." I give him a reassuring smile, but I'm not sure he believes it. "That was my lawyer. They have a date set."

"That's good, right?" Rain asks.

"Yes, but I'm also terrified," I admit.

"We're going to be there, you know, right by your side through it all," Brody says. I'm surprised it's him who vows that.

"My lawyer also said your lawyer asked for me to be at your hearing on your behalf."

"Fuck's sake," Brody hisses. "I told him not to," he growls.

"Why?" I ask, head tilting. "If I can help, I'd like to."

"Because, Tim is going to be there. I don't want you to have to be around that pervert any more than you already have to with your own case happening."

That's the main reason why I'm trying not to lose my shit right now.

"At best, I'll tell my events of the night and that's it. I won't have to look at him or talk to him."

"Unless his lawyer tries to start shit." Brody looks pissed. Not at me but over all of this.

"My lawyer said he will be there to make sure it doesn't become about me," I tell him. "I'm just not sure how I'm going to pay for the extra hours." I sigh, not even wanting to think how many zeros are going to be on that bill.

"Don't worry about it," Brody tells me. "I'm paying for it."

"What?" I ask, my brows furrowing in confusion. "What do you mean?"

"I mean, I'm paying for it. For the whole bill. Don't even argue about it, you won't win. I know you're proud, and that's one of the things I admire about you. I know you can handle your own, but this is on me. You wouldn't even have to be pressing charges if I was a better person back then. This is on me," he repeats.

I want to tell him no, that I can do it myself, but really, I can't. I was going to have to dip into savings and possibly get another job just to pay Jeff's bill off and that could still take years. So, I'm going to push aside my pride and take his offer.

"Okay. Only because if I don't take this offer, I'd have to use the money I've been saving for Lilly and other things. I don't want to make my life more complicated than it already is," I tell him. "But, thank you." My eyes tear up. "This is really going to help me. I didn't know how I was going to pay for the whole thing."

"If you need money, for anything, not even just for Lilly, come to me. I may not flaunt it around, but I have money, more than I know what to do with. I want to help," he tells me and his offer is making it really hard to remember the shit he's done to me. Because this isn't that cruel Brody. Hell, this isn't even the one I remember dating.

"Thank you." I give him a watery smile.

I can breathe a little easier. Only now, I'm going to have to face my attacker sooner than I was expecting. But one thing is for sure. I'm so damn lucky for all the support I have at my side.

JAX

"I think I'm going to ask Ellie out on a date for tomorrow," I tell Brody as we get out of the car and head toward the lecture hall. We have our first class of the day with Theo, or do we call him Mr. Munro?

We don't really know him outside of school except through Ellie, and even then, we haven't spent time with him other than at Lilly's party.

I guess if he's going to be a big part of both of their lives, we're going to have to get used to being around him too.

Not that I think he's a bad guy or anything. Actually, it's the opposite. He loves Ellie and Lilly and has done so much for them. He was there for her when we were the worst to her. I have a lot of respect for the man.

It's just going to take a while to get used to the fact that we have to share her with someone outside of our group. I've never had an issue sharing because it's what's worked best for our group, but it's always *only* been with my best friends. Sharing Ellie was easy because she was one of us and we always hung out with each other.

Now, we'll have to split time with Theo unless we get to a point where we include him in our little group. We'll have to make the effort to get to know him first.

"And do what?" Brody's question brings me back to the conversation at hand and I look over to see him giving me a side eye. "Take her to a movie?" he snorts.

"No, but what would be wrong with that? We're pretty much treating this relationship as if we are strangers getting to know each other while going on dates and stuff like that. Dinner and a movie is something lots of people do."

"True." He shrugs. "I guess I wouldn't really know. We've never been on a date, now that I think of it."

I take a moment to think. He's right, we haven't. We kind of just found our way into something more than friends during a really hard time in our lives, and it kind of just evolved from there.

"We should change that," Brody says. "Dinner, movie, then I'll take you home and make you scream my name. Sounds like a perfect date to me." He gives me this sexy, devilish grin that's pure sex, and I'm trying really hard to will my cock to stay down because sitting in class with a stiffie for the next hour isn't my idea of fun.

We stop outside of the lecture hall when Brody pulls me to the side. He slides his fingers into my hair and grips a handful, making me stifle a moan at the light sting. "How does that sound? I'll wine and dine you, then fuck you until you see stars." His voice is seductive and it does nothing to stop my growing issue down below, only adding fuel to the fire. And now, I'm completely hard.

"Yes," I breathe as his lips brush against mine before pressing them together in a heated kiss.

"Gay," someone coughs as they move past us to head into the same class we were going to.

Brody breaks apart from me and has the guy pressed against the wall in a flash. His arm is pushing into the guy's throat as he pins him to the wall.

"Brody, let him go. He's not worth it," I try to reason with him.

"No, I think our friend here wanted to tell us something," Brody says, looking at me with rage in his eyes before turning back to the guy he's pinned. The guy looks pissed, but I can see some worry. "So...sorry about that, I was a little distracted. What did you say?" Brody asks the guy and when he doesn't respond, Brody pulls him back from the wall just to slam him back against it again.

"Gay," the guy finally says. "I called you gay."

"That's what I thought," Brody growls. "But here's the thing, we're not gay. We're bi. There's a difference, but even if we were gay, there's nothing wrong with that. So, I don't appreciate you using the word in a derogatory way."

"Is there an issue?" Mr. Munro asks as he steps outside of his classroom, taking the situation in.

"No issue, sir," Brody says, letting go of the guy who starts to cough, patting him on the shoulder. "Just educating this fine, young gentleman that it's not okay to make people feel bad about being gay."

Theo looks to the guy. "What's your name?"

"Bentley," the guy says, rubbing his neck.

"Well, Bentley, I think it's a good idea to listen to Brody here. I don't stand for homophobic behavior in my class," Mr. Munro says.

"Yeah. I'll do that," Bentley says, side eyeing Brody.

"All of you, get in here. My class is about to begin," Mr. Munro says before standing back to let us pass.

Bentley heads inside, but Brody gets stopped. "Be careful how you react, especially when there are witnesses. Ellie is taking a big step out of her comfort zone to be there for you this weekend. Don't fuck this up by adding more to your name."

"I won't," Brody says.

"Thanks, Mr. Munro," I tell him.

"Theo," he says. "Seeing as how you're going to be dating my girlfriend, I think we're past the formalities." He grins.

"You have a point." I smirk back.

We all head inside, and Brody and I take our seats. Theo is a good teacher. I enjoy his classes, but maybe that's because he's a good guy too. I think we could actually be friends. At least for Ellie's sake.

"Are you busy tomorrow?" I ask Ellie as I sit down next to her. She's eating with her friends today, but I didn't want to just call or text her to ask.

"Well, hello to you too." She laughs, looking at me with a beautiful smile and shining blue eyes.

"Sorry." I smile back. "Didn't mean to intrude on your time with your friends."

They're all glaring at me, giving me a feeling I'm not really welcome. They've started letting Chase around, but I think I still have some more work to do.

"That's okay," Ellie says. "As for plans, umm, well, I don't have work until Thursday, so I was just going to hang out with Lilly. Theo will be home, but he's grading papers all night. Why, what's up?"

"I was wondering if you wanted to go out with me?" I ask, scratching the back of my head, feeling awkward as her friends continue to stare at me.

"Like on a date?" Val asks, cocking a brow.

"What else would he want?" Lexie asks her friend.

"I don't know. Maybe he wants to drive her out into the middle of the woods and kill her," Val replies, then turns to me. "Do you? Do you plan on taking my girl and chopping her up into tiny pieces then leaving her to the animals?"

"Val, seriously, have you lost it?" Cooper asks. "Because this is *too* much, even for you."

"I maaaaaay have had a weed cookie," Val says. "Or two."

"That will do it," Tabitha says.

"Guys, relax. Jax is not the enemy here," Ellie giggles.

"Maybe not yours," Val mutters.

These girls are some oddballs, that's for sure.

"No, I'm not going to hurt Ellie. I never want to do that again," I reassure them then look to Ellie. "I wanted to take you out paintballing. You seemed to have a lot of fun last time."

"Yeah, because we got to shoot Rain in the tits," Val cackles.

"And don't forget taking out Brody's man jewels," Lexie laughs.

"Oh. Well, I don't really have anyone to watch Lilly. I don't want to ask Theo's mom because she's already going to be spending the day with her," Ellie says. Chase told me about Ellie not having Lilly in daycare anymore. I can understand her worry. I also think they should have kept a better eye on her.

"Rain and I would be more than happy to watch her. I know you're not ready to leave us alone with her yet, but if Theo is down the hall, we can call him if we need anything," Chase says as he takes a seat across from us next to Val. "Come on, babe. My boy here is dying to get some time with you. You should see him around the apartment, pouting like a sad puppy. 'Oh, I love Ellie. I miss her. I just want to schmooze her and show her how amazing she is,'" Chase mocks, making Ellie giggle and me glare at him.

"I'm gonna kill you," I growl at him.

"Nah, because then Ellie would be sad." He grins, and I flip him off. "Fries, yum," Chase says, taking one of Val's fries and opening his mouth to inhale it.

"Mine!" Val says, snatching back her food. He just shrugs.

"I guess," Ellie says slowly. "I'll have to talk to Theo first and see if he's okay with it. How about I text you tonight with my answer?"

My face splits into a massive grin. "Sounds good," I tell her. "I'll let you enjoy the rest of your lunch with your friends." I get up and go over to Chase who looks like he's about to get his hand bitten off as he reaches for Val's food again.

"Come on, man, let them be," I tell Chase.

"Fine," he pouts and leans over the table to pull Ellie into a kiss. "Catch you later, Ellie Belly."

"Bye." She blushes.

"Later, firecracker," I tell her, my old nickname for her slipping out. Her eyes widen slightly, but she gives me a smile nonetheless.

"Later."

"Things are looking good, man," Chase says, tossing his arm over my shoulder. "I'm proud of you guys. Who knew you all had it in you to not be raging assholes?"

"Oh, fuck you," I laugh. He knows our behavior toward Ellie wasn't who we are. It was disgusting behavior we never plan to repeat again. But he is right. Things are starting to look good with everything. Having her around has been exactly what I've been missing.

I just hope she can go out with me tomorrow. I want to spend time with her, but I also want to give her a little fun before Monday. I know it's going to be hard on her, and if I can distract her for a few hours, then I want to be able to do that for her.

"I'm nervous. Is it weird that I'm nervous?" Chase asks as he looks at Ellie's apartment building out of the front windshield.

"No, because I am too," Rain says. "It's different hanging out with Lilly knowing she's your guys' daughter."

"She's yours too, you know," Chase says, looking at her over his shoulder.

"I don't think I've earned the right to consider her that," Rain sighs.

"Soon," I tell her, meeting her eyes in the rearview mirror. "It may take you a little bit longer than us because, let's be honest, you have more to make up for."

"I know," Rain mutters. "Trust me, I know."

"Come on, there's a little monkey up there that I need to see!" Chase says with a sudden burst of excitement, making me laugh.

We all get out of the car and head up to Ellie's apartment. I knock on the door and smile when I hear Lilly scream, "I get it!" and Ellie reply, "Oh, no, you won't."

The door opens, and I chuckle when I see a giggling, wiggling Lilly under Ellie's arm. "Hi," Ellie says, sounding out of breath.

"Hi." Her hair is a little messy, her shirt seems to have what looks like frosting on it, and she looks a little tired. And, I don't think I've ever wanted her more than I do right now. She's grown up so much since she's been gone. She's a mom now and it looks amazing on her.

"Sorry. I'm not really ready," she says, holding the door open so we can come in. "We were making cookies, and well, Lilly got into them before I had a chance to put them away." She looks to Chase and Rain. "She might be a little hyper." Ellie puts Lilly down, and she launches herself into Chase's arms.

"Ace!" she cheers. "Mama said we having a playdate."

"That's right, little lady. You ready for some fun?" Chase confirms, adding more excitement to Lilly's cheer.

"Yay!" Lilly cheers and looks to Rain. "Can we play makeup?"

"Ahhh..." Rain says, looking at Ellie.

"It's okay," Ellie laughs. "It's kid's makeup."

Lilly wiggles down from Chase's hold and takes off into another room.

"Warning though, I don't think she even tries to do anything but make you look like a clown," Ellie says with amusement. "And be prepared to have her laughing at you for a good five minutes because she thinks it's the funniest thing ever when she thinks she's pranked you."

"Pfft," Chase says. "I'd rock that look, and we all know it."

"What look?" Rain asks. "Isn't being a clown your everyday look?"

"I don't know, I think that's more you. With the red hair and all," Chase volleys back with a cocky grin.

Rain gapes at him.

"Chase!" Ellie slaps his arm. "Be nice. Plus, Rain's hair makes her look like anything but a clown. It's sexy and I like it."

"You do?" Rain asks, a smile threatening to take over her lips.

Ellie blushes a little, and it's pretty adorable. "Well, yeah. I mean, I've always loved it." Ellie shrugs. "And so does Lilly."

"See?" Rain sticks her tongue out at Chase. "Ellie loves it, so kiss my ass."

"Ass!" Lilly cheers. "Ass, ass, ass."

"Oh my god," Rain gasps, her eyes going wide. "I am so sorry."

"It's okay, we just gotta be careful what we say because Lilly has become a little parrot lately. Theo said the word, p-e-n-i-s, to Toby and of course, it's not a bad word. But coming from a four year old little girl who starts to run around screaming it, yeah, that makes for some interesting looks when we're out in public."

Chase bursts out laughing. "I wish I could have been there for that."

Ellie smiles and shakes her head before crouching down to Lilly's level. "Lillypad, what did mama say about naughty words?"

Lilly is vibrating with energy right now. "Not to say them."

"Right. And that word is a naughty word. Let's say bum instead, okay?"

"Bum, bum, bum," Lilly starts to sing and dance around the room.

Ellie stands back up and sighs. "If she's gonna be too much for you, I'm okay with not going."

A pang of disappointment takes over, and I glare at the back of Rain and Chase's heads, willing them to take one for the team. I mean, it's not like they're not going to have to deal with this anyways at some point, with us all being her parents.

"No, we'll be fine. Go, have fun. Jax has been dying for his chance to start making things up to you," Chase says, pulling Ellie in for a kiss.

I really want to slap him every time he puts me on blast like that. But also, a part of me thanks him for bringing it up, even if it makes me look a little desperate, because at least she knows how I feel, even if I'm too chicken shit to say it myself.

Ellie tells the other two things to do and not to do, showing them which apartment is Theo's, and anything else they might need to know before running back into her room to get changed.

"Ready to go?" she asks, a big bright smile taking over her face.

"Sure am. Where's your gear?" I ask, seeing that she only has her purse. I knew the marker was hers because the facility doesn't rent out that good of a brand name.

Her smile drops a little before she hides it. "Oh, I don't have any."

"I was sure that you did last time. Maybe I saw wrong?" I tell her, trying to back track this conversation.

"Ah, yeah." She shifts uncomfortably and looks over at Rain, who's listening in, before looking back to me. "I sold it. I used our savings to get my hair fixed, and well, I started to panic that we wouldn't have enough money for rent if something happened and I was unable to work, so I sold what I had left of my gear to replace it." She shrugs. "But I can rent some, it's no big deal." She forces an excited smile, and now I feel pissed off toward Rain.

I shoot her a glare when Ellie heads toward the door. Right now, Rain looks like she's feeling miserable about what she did. Good. What she did was fucked up.

I hate what she did to Ellie. And knowing now that she was a single mom struggling to pay bills makes me even more angry.

The car ride is a little awkward. This is the first time I've been alone, hanging out with her in years. She looks out the window, singing along to the music under her breath, and I smile as she starts to get a little louder as the song goes on, really getting into it.

Glancing over at her, she turns her head at the same time. I meet her eyes, and she stops singing.

"Don't stop on my account," I laugh lightly.

"I can't help it. I love Avril Lavigne." She laughs.

"I know." I cast her a smile. "That one time when we all slept over at Brody's place when his dad was gone on a business trip, you woke up before all of us to make us breakfast. You were blasting the song, *Smile* by her. You looked adorable and sexy dancing around the kitchen with a spatula in your hand like a mic. I stood in the doorway watching from the cracked door. You looked so free, so happy that I didn't want to ruin it."

"Oh." Her voice goes soft.

"How come you never did that around us?" I ask as we pull into the parking lot of the paintball arena.

"I guess I didn't have a lot of confidence back then," she says looking out the window. "I didn't wanna look stupid around you guys. You were all so perfect at everything you did." She looks back at me. "I guess I didn't want to stick out."

My heart hurts at that. "Ellie, we only ever want you to be yourself. We love you, no matter how silly or carefree and confident you wanna be. I know it would have been the same back then."

"Well, you don't have to worry about that now because I love myself, and I don't care what anyone thinks." She grins. "I spent way too long locking myself in a box, thinking no one would like my true self."

"Then I'm very excited to get to know this side of you, Miss Tatum. Care to show me?"

"Why not?" She winks.

Something tells me this is going to be one of the best dates I'll ever have.

Chapter Seventeen

ELLIE

WE GET out of the car, and I see that the place is packed. "Normally, I'd say the less people the better on a date, but we will be on the same team and the more people that have to get out, the longer the game can last," Jax says as he opens the trunk and grabs his gear.

"No, I'm excited." I grin, feeling the adrenaline starting to pump in my veins. There's just something about paintball that brings out my wild, competitive side. "Too bad we're on the same team though," I say, looking back over at him with a grin. "I would have loved to whoop your ass again."

"Next time, firecracker," Jax says, stepping closer to me. He tucks a piece of hair behind my ear, his finger lingering on the shell of it. "I know how much you love to play. I'll make sure we come here more often, bring the others too. Maybe this time we can have a less violent game." He grins.

I bite my lower lip, and his eyes follow the movement. "Sure thing, Jax. We'll make sure to go easy on you next time." I giggle, and step past him toward the rental booth.

"I'll need one of everything please," I tell the man behind the counter, getting my card out and trying not to think about how much of my tips this is going to cost me.

"Put it away," Jax tells me, grabbing my card from the counter and handing it back.

"What, why?" I ask.

"Because, I'm paying. This is a date, Ellie. Normally, the person who asks the other person pays." Jax gives me a playful smile. "Also, we have a lot of spoiling and making up to do, so get used to it."

I've always been determined to do as much as I can for me and Lilly without taking any handouts from anyone else. I'm not used to so many people being so insistent on wanting to help or doing things for me.

But it's kind of nice. I've never realized just how much I've taken on until recently. Going to school, working, and taking care of Lilly is a lot of work. I often find myself exhausted by the end of the day.

Also, it's not like I'm asking, they're offering. Might be rude to turn them down and possibly offend them.

"Fine. But I'm paying for dinner." I narrow my eyes at him playfully, and he gives me a sexy smile in return.

"You're a stubborn one, but I like it. Fine, you get dinner," he chuckles.

Jax rents my gear and pays for us to play. We head into the waiting area and put everything on before joining the group of people waiting.

"Alright, split up into two groups of ten. You've got one hour. Be safe, be fair, and have fun," a worker says.

"Come on," Jax says, grabbing my hand and guiding me over to a group of people.

"Jax!" a guy I've never seen before shouts. "What are you doing here, man?" They do one of those guy hugs before stepping back.

"Taking my girl out on a date," Jax says, then smiles down at me.

The guy gives Jax a confused look. "I thought you were with Brody?"

"I am." Jax's smile slips, his face becoming more defensive. "But I'm also seeing Ellie."

The guy looks to me, then back to Jax, realization taking over his face. "Like how you all used to date in high school?"

"How do you know about that?" I ask.

"Umm," he says, looking a little sheepish. "I was on the football team with the guys in high school. The whole school kind of knew."

"Oh. Sorry. I didn't really know a lot of people in high school." I give him a small smile.

"We sure did know about you. You're all the guys talked about. It got annoying sometimes," the guy laughs.

"Shut up, Mark," Jax laughs, then looks down at me. "It is true though. Even Brody would talk about how sexy you were, when he had a few beers. How smart and sweet you were, and how much he loved you."

My cheeks burn with everyone staring at me right now, but knowing that Brody used to talk about me like that to other people makes me feel warm inside.

"He doesn't do that anymore," I mutter, looking away. Jax gently grips my chin and turns my head so that I'm looking at him.

"He's sorry for everything bad he's done. I hope you know that. I'm not gonna defend him, but I know that despite his stubborn ass denying it, he loves you like the rest of us do. None of us ever stopped. He will come around. You're hard to resist." He leans over and brushes a kiss across my lips. Just when I think he's going to press further, the whistle blows and our group starts running into the arena.

Jax grabs my hand, and we start running with everyone else.

"We gotta hide," Jax shouts and brings me behind a fort-like set up.

We stay there for a bit, letting everyone else find their spot, then we start the game.

Over the next hour, I have the time of my life. We work

together as a team, hunting people down and taking them out. We should be trying to get the other team's flag, but at this point, we're just trying to see how many people we can get out. At one point, we got so into it, we almost got one of our own team members out.

We're running, trying to find cover when paintballs come flying our way, hitting the trees in front of us. "Duck!" Jax shouts, and I drop into the little trench. We grab our markers, searching for whoever is taking fire. I find someone hiding behind a tree through the scope on my gun.

"There," I say, pointing in the person's direction. Another person steps up next to them and I grin. "You take the one on the left, I'll take the right."

We wait, only the sound of our breathing and other people in the distance as we concentrate on our targets. When they move just enough to get a good hit, we let loose.

"Damn it!" one of them roars.

"Fuck!" shouts the other.

"We gotta find a new place," Jax says, and I follow after him. We both laugh as we run. Jax leads us to the broken down bus on the far side of the area.

"We should be good in here to catch our breath for a moment. I think we almost got everyone," Jax says as we climb the steps. We move to the back of the bus where that part is hidden more into the wooded area of the arena. Jax slides into the seat and pats the spot next to him.

"This was exactly what I needed," I admit. I've been so stressed with everything going on in my life that I just needed a day of fun. An hour to get out of my head and do something I love.

Theo has been amazing with helping me de-stress. He's so loving and attentive. I seriously don't know what I'd do without him. Chase has been trying to distract me in very Chase-like ways like sending me funny videos or memes. There's been a few times he's pulled me into the co-ed bathroom and helped me de-stress in more rewarding ways in the form of orgasms. He's really good at that, and does not seem to mind that I'm the only one receiving any relief. I've offered because the idea of taking him into my mouth and bringing him pleasure is just as much of a turn on for me as it is for him, but he's refused to let me get down on my knees on the bathroom floor.

I'm going to have to start seeing them outside of school. Spring break is the first week of April, so I'll have some time off. I'm going to have to make sure I spend some time with the others.

My parents plan on coming down for that time, so I'm sure they would be more than happy to watch Lilly. They've even said so in the past. They really are amazing, and I'm so blessed to have two amazing, supportive, and loving parents. I don't know how I would've been able to do the whole single mom thing without them.

"I'm glad you're having fun," Jax says, taking off his face guard and I do the same.

"Thanks for bringing me. I've always loved coming here with you and the others, but there's just..." I pause looking up into his brown eyes. He's so sexy. His hair is a little sweaty, making his curls flatten a little and giving him that wet look that makes girls drool. "I always enjoyed playing with you more. You have a love for the game that matches mine, and it just makes it more enjoyable."

He smiles at me, a sweet one that makes my belly flutter. "I've always felt the same way. I saw it as our thing, you know? The others enjoyed playing, but with you, it was more. The joy on your face, the way you come out of your shell and really let loose, leaving reality at the door."

We stare at each other for a beat, neither of us saying a word, but I can feel the tension growing by the second. Jax wasn't innocent in what was done to me, but he wasn't as bad as Rain and Brody. I'm not ready to jump into a relationship with him, but he's shown that he's sorry, that he cares for me. And right now, all I can think about is straddling his lap and taking his lips.

So I do. Without thinking too much about it, I move until I'm sitting on top of him. His hands find my thighs, and he grips them with a little pressure. My eyes bore into his, full of so much fucking emotion I may burst. I want him. I love him; I've never stopped. Spending this time around them all has been heaven and hell.

"Ellie," he rasps, his hands moving to rub up and down my thighs. "I don't want you doing anything you're going to regret. I love you, baby girl, but I don't want you to think I won't wait for you."

"I know you will." At least I tell myself that. "But I want this. Kiss me, Jax, please," I breathe, my heart pounding painfully against my chest. He lets out this growl, low in his chest, that has my clit throbbing before his hand slides into my hair. He grips it lightly and brings my face down to his.

His lips are soft and warm, tasting like a thousand promises. We move together, slowly at first. It's like coming home after years of being away and feeling like no time has passed.

My hands find his shirt and I grip it with both hands, holding myself to him. I whimper into his mouth as his tongue prods at my lips to open for him. And I do, our tongues dancing together.

This feels right, perfect, and I want more. I feel like a hunger has woken inside of me. I've had a taste of the past that I desperately want back.

Rocking my hips, I can feel his cock hard as a rock under my core. He groans, his hands finding my hips, and he grips them as he helps me move against him. Running my fingers into his hair, I grip him back while our kiss becomes more intense.

We moan together, chasing that feeling I know we both want. That need to consume the other. To mold together and become one.

My pussy is soaked, and my clit is throbbing to be touched by his big, inked fingers. I use his cock for friction, bringing us both to the edge of pleasure.

If we keep doing this, I know I'm going to cum; maybe he will too. Our breathing becomes erratic, our cries of desire grow louder.

"Jax," I breathe, feeling my orgasm just out of reach.

"Fuck, Ellie," he moans. "God, you're so fucking perfect, so beautiful. Cum for me, baby girl, give it all to me." He rocks me harder, my thrusts becoming faster and faster.

My eyes go wide, wild, and frantic as I'm tossed off the cliff, free falling into ecstasy. My mouth parts to let out a cry, but Jax pulls me down to silence me with his mouth. I whimper out my release, my body jerking as I cum, hard. He holds me through it, still rocking me gently with one hand. A moment later, he presses me down hard, letting out a long groan as he cums too. I can feel his cock jerk under me even through the clothes.

We break the kiss, chests heaving as we try to catch our breaths and just stare, lost in each other.

I don't even hear the sounds of the others around us until someone bursts into the bus, shooting me in the shoulder and Jax in the back, snapping us out of the trance.

"Ouch," I hiss, rubbing my shoulder. "I'm not used to getting hit," I pout. Jax lets out a husky chuckle as I look at the red paint on my shoulder.

"Same," he says, looking down at his own red splatter. "That's gonna bruise." He looks back up at me. "But it was totally worth losing, at least this time."

"Yeah. I agree. Just this one time." I grin.

We accept our defeat and head out of the arena, opting out of another round.

"So, I know we said we would go get dinner and stuff, but ummm..." he says, looking down at his crotch as we drive back to Silver Valley.

Right. I just dry humped my ex and got myself off, as well as making him cum in his pants.

"Hey," Jax laughs softly when my cheeks go pink. "I don't regret it. That was one of the hottest things I've ever done. And Ellie, baby, you look so gorgeous when you cum."

He's not helping with the pink cheeks which are now red.

"You can just drop me off at home. We don't have to do dinner," I tell him, knowing it must be uncomfortable sitting in his release.

"Would it be too much to ask for you to come over to our place? We can rent a movie and order in. I'm sure Brody won't mind keeping you company while I shower and change."

"Yeah." I give him a smile. "I'd like that."

Well, not really the time alone with Brody, that's going to be weird, but I don't want this date to end.

I call up Chase and he tells me that everything is going fine and that Lilly is being good. I tell him I'm going over to their place for a bit and he tells me to have fun.

When we get there, Brody is surprised to see me.

"Date over so soon?" Brody asks, pausing whatever he's watching on TV.

"Ah, yeah," Jax says. "Change of plans. Ellie is gonna hang out here and watch a movie while we order in," he says as he starts to take off his clothes.

I quickly avert my eyes, meeting Brody's. He looks at Jax then back at me with a knowing smirk. When Jax disappears into the bathroom, Brody asks, "Why so shy all of a sudden? You made my man cream his pants. Don't act like you're some Virgin Mary."

I glare at him, taking the spot next to him.

"What we do is none of your business," I mutter, bringing my knees up to my chest and hugging them as I avoid Brody's stare.

"I suppose it's not," Brody agrees. "But if you're ever curious about what we get up to together when we're alone, I'd be more than happy to fill you in," he says, letting out a husky laugh before getting up and heading in the direction Jax went to shower.

"THAT MOVIE WAS SO STUPID," Brody mutters after we get done watching some cheesy horror movie.

"It was," I agree with him. "But it was so bad, it was funny."

"What was funny was you screaming at the TV for her to turn around and run." Brody's eyes shine with mirth.

"Well, who the hell goes toward the creepy sound in their house? If I was her, I would have ran away like my ass was on fire, getting the hell out of the house full of demons. Problem solved."

"One, she couldn't hear you no matter how many times you told her to run, and two, if she just left, there wouldn't have been a movie," Brody points out.

"Maybe that would have been better. It was almost like she wanted to get possessed and slowly eat herself alive." I shake my head. *It really was a bad movie.*

"We better get you home," Jax says, laughing at me and Brody as he turns off the TV.

"Shit," I say, grabbing my phone off the coffee table. There are no missed calls thankfully, but there is a picture that Chase texted with him, Rain, and Lilly. Both of their faces are covered in makeup, looking like some of the ugliest clowns I've ever seen. But my face slips into a grin so wide, it hurts at the pure joy on

Lilly's face. I choke back a ball of emotion because this is something I've gotten to experience with her, but it's different getting to see their own firsts of all the things they do with her.

"Everything okay?" Jax asks.

"Yeah," I laugh, showing him the photo. He grins and chuckles.

"You need to send me that. That's a keeper."

"Let me see," Brody asks, and I show him. "Cute," is all he says, but I can see the hint of an amused smile.

Looking at the next text, I see it's from Rain. This time, it's a photo of them all with no makeup. Lilly is holding up a paper that says 'I love mama.'

"Ready?" Jax asks, grabbing his wallet and keys off the counter.

"Yeah. I need some sleep. I have an early start at school, then work. I'm picking up an extra shift during the day at the restaurant."

Brody says, "Thank you again, for doing this for me. I'm not even sure if they will end up calling on you, but my lawyer said it's a good idea to have you there, just in case they need to ask you anything."

"It's really not a big deal. If I can help you get the charges dropped, then I want to help."

"It *really* is a big deal. You're already going to have to deal with him because of your own case, but being there on Monday means you may have to see him a month earlier. So thank you, and I wish it didn't have to be this way. You can still back out, you know. I'd understand. You don't owe me anything," Brody insists.

"I'm going to be there," I tell him. "And I never did thank you."

"Thank me?" Brody's eyes furrow in confusion. "Thank me for what?"

"For stopping him." My eyes water. "He said some..." I take a deep breath. "Some pretty fucked up things, and I'm not sure how much my fighting him off would have helped. So...thank you."

After Lilly was born, I took some free self-defense classes at the rec hall by where we lived. I learned some basics, but I'm not sure how good it's going to do me if I freeze up in panic or shock.

I get up and grab my purse, about to follow Jax to the door, when Brody stops me.

"I'm sorry," he says. "For not stopping him on graduation night." His eyes are filled with regret that has my pulse fluttering.

"But you were there this time." I give him a small smile. "It counts for something."

We don't say anything more, just look at each other for a moment before I turn to leave. The drive home is too quick, and once we get home, I find myself wishing the night didn't have to end.

"Can we do this again soon?" Jax asks. "Not just paintball, although I would love to play again soon, but you, hanging out at our place. It was nice. I missed this."

"I missed this too." We stop outside my front door. "I want to come over more, and maybe you guys can come by and spend some more time with Lilly? I think after tonight, it's about time you came around more."

"We would love that," Jax grins.

"Spring break is coming up in a few weeks. We should hang out or go do something. I haven't been out in a while." I did start to enjoy going to parties. It was nice to just let go of stress and hang out with my friends, but then the last one went to shit. I'm not going to let him ruin that for me.

"Sounds like a plan. Thanks for saying yes to paintball," Jax says.

"And thanks for coming with me," I say. His eyes widen, and my cheeks heat as I realize just how that sounds. "I mean, thanks for taking me with you," I rush out.

"I'd come with you anywhere, Ellie, always." He grins, stepping closer. "Can I kiss you goodnight?"

He's taller than me, so I have to look up at him with how close he is to me. Jax looks at me like I'm the only girl in the world, and the idea of that excites me.

"Yes," I whisper.

He cups my face and leans in, kissing me with one of the most tender kisses I've ever experienced. "I love you, Ellie. And I'm never going to stop fighting for you. I made that mistake in the past, but never again," he says when he pulls back from the kiss. He brushes his nose against mine, leaving me light headed and dazed.

When we get inside, the TV is playing, but everything else is quiet.

"Look," Jax whispers, nodding his head toward the couch.

"Oh my god," I breathe, my heart feeling full as I take in the scene. Chase is laying on the couch with Lilly on top of him, cuddling into his chest. Both are sound asleep. "I need a photo of this," I whisper, taking my phone out and freezing this moment in time. I know Chase would love this, so I quickly send it to his phone.

The bathroom door opens, and Rain walks out.

"You're back," she says, giving me a soft smile. It widens when she looks at the two on the couch. "Aren't they just the cutest?"

"They really are." I turn back to watch them. I crouch down next to Chase and brush the hair on his forehead out of the way before leaning in to kiss it. "Chase, love, wake up."

His eyes blink open. "Am I dead? I didn't know angels were this sexy," he says, his voice cracking with sleep.

"Nope, not dead. But thank you. You're pretty sexy yourself," I grin. Standing back up, I carefully pick Lilly up off of Chase's chest and carry her to our room. After tucking her into bed, I head back out to say goodbye.

"Thanks for watching her tonight. How was she?" I ask.

"She was hyper for a little while, but we got her all played out. We remembered some of her favorite things to do, and we had a lot of fun. If you ever need us to watch her again, we would be more than happy to," Rain says.

"Hell yeah, I love that little goober," Chase says, pulling me into his arms. "So babe, how was your date?" he asks, wiggling his eyebrows. I blush and bite my lip. He watches me and his eyes light up. "Oh, what did you two get up to? Did you kiss?" he asks, looking from Jax to me, making my face heat even up more. His eyes widen. "Did you guys fuck?!" he asks, a shocked laugh.

"No, we didn't fuck!" I gasp, slapping Chase in the chest.

"You sure?" Chase grins. "Your face is telling me more than just a kiss happened."

"Leave her alone, Chase," Jax warns. "If she doesn't want to talk about it, drop it."

"So there *is* something to talk about," Chase says a little to excitedly. "Fuck yeah."

"Why is this making you happy?" I ask, finding myself laughing at his reaction.

"Because, baby, that's two down, two to go." He wiggles his eyebrows. "Then everything will be right in the world."

Somehow, I don't think it's going to be that easy.

"Sweetheart, you look great. You don't need to change again," Theo says as I rush around the apartment like a mad woman. The hearing is in an hour, and we are leaving soon.

"This is court, Theo. I can't look too casual or no one will take me seriously. And I can't look over-dressed or I'll look like I'm trying too hard."

"Baby, you have on a nice dress. It's perfect for something like this," he tells me, putting his hands on my shoulders to keep me still.

"Are you sure?" I ask, my belly in knots. I feel like I'm sweating buckets. Theo tried to get me to eat something, but the idea alone had me wanting to puke.

"Ellie, baby, look at me," he says to me in a calm voice. "Breathe." And I do, taking a few deep breaths. "You've got this. We're here with you. Everything is going to be okay."

I nod, taking another deep breath. "You're right. I'm getting so worked up over nothing. This isn't even my hearing."

"Come on, let's get going before you trash your closet again," he says.

The whole car ride there, I'm on pins and needles. And when we get out of the car in front of the court house, I find Rain standing there, dressed in a pencil skirt and blouse, her long red hair up in a professional looking bun. *Why now, of all times, am I having naughty secretary fantasies?*

I guess when your mind is running a mile a minute, nothing makes sense.

The guys look handsome in dress clothes. The last time I saw them looking like this was when they dressed up for graduation.

"Ready?" Theo asks, moving to stand next to me.

"With you there with me, always." I give him a shaky smile as I slip my fingers into his, and we head over to the others.

"Hey, babe," Chase says, pulling me into his arms and kissing the top of my head when we reach them. "How are you feeling?"

"I'll be honest, I'm a bit of a mess." I let out a nervous chuckle. "But I've got all of you here with me. I think I'll be fine."

"You don't have to do this, Ellie," Brody says, stepping forward. His normally messy brown hair is tamed, and the dress shirt he's wearing hugs his muscles tight. *Why does he have to look so good, and be a raging dick?*

"I said I'm doing this," I tell him. "So suck it up because I'm not going anywhere." I raise a brow and lift my chin, daring him to argue with me.

"Eleanor Tatum?" someone asks from behind me. Turning around, I see a well-dressed man who looks to be in his forties walking toward us with a briefcase.

"Yes, that's me," I tell him as he stops before me.

"Hi, I'm Jeff McWilson."

"Oh, hi, it's nice to meet you in person. Thank you so much for coming," I greet him, taking his hand to shake it.

"Of course. Seeing how Mr. Creed's case and yours play a big part with each other, I thought it would be best. Can we talk for a moment?"

"Sure." I turn to the others. "I'll meet you inside." Then I look at Brody. "You should probably go meet with your lawyer as well."

"Yeah." Brody nods, but hesitates to leave. "If at any point you don't feel comfortable, it's okay to leave. Don't force yourself to be in there if it's going to hurt you. I don't want you getting hurt any more, especially if it has to do with me."

"I will, I promise." I give him a reassuring smile. He nods, then turns and takes off inside the building. The others follow, leaving me and Jeff to talk.

"Now, all we want out of this is for you to explain what Tim said to you that night. I don't want you to bring up what happened five years ago. That's for your case. Only say what was said that night to validate Mr. Creed's story. If Tim's lawyer tries to dig deeper and starts interrogating you, I'll shut it down fast."

"Okay." I let out a shaky breath.

"Ready?" he asks.

"Not really." I force a laugh. "But I have to be."

Chapter Nineteen

ELLIE

WAITING for everything to start is making my nerves go crazy and causing my stomach to turn inside out. I feel like I'm about to have a panic attack.

Theo's hand meets my thigh, giving me a comforting touch and a soothing rub, reminding me that I'm not alone in this.

I love this man so much, and his love and support for me takes so many of my worries away, bringing me some much needed peace. I can breathe a little better knowing he's here next to me. Chase is on my other side, and he takes my hand in his, bringing it up to his lips to place a kiss. "Love you," he mouths.

I smile at him, feeling my heart flutter as I mouth it back.

"All rise for the honorable Judge Mathews," the bailiff says, breaking the almost deafening silence that had filled the room.

We all stand until he takes his seat.

"You may sit," the judge says. Just as we take a seat, the door opens again. My heart stops, and for a moment, I wonder if I'm going to be able to get it to start again.

In walks Tim. He's not chained up like a prisoner should be. He's dressed in a sickeningly fancy suit as he strolls in here like he doesn't have a care in the world.

He doesn't notice me right away as he heads toward his side of the room. But just as he passes us, his eyes scan Brody, shooting him a hint of a smile before carrying on back to the audience where I'm sitting and locking eyes with me.

It takes everything in me not to puke as he looks me over and licks his lips. I'm shaking, my hands are clammy, and I don't think I'm breathing.

"Sweet girl," Theo whispers in my ear, so low that only I can hear. "Close your eyes and listen to my voice." I do as he says. "Take a deep breath." I do. "And I want you to remember this. You are strong. You are a fighter. No one can tear you down unless you let them. You are beautiful, caring, loving, and brave. You are Eleanor Tatum, and don't let anyone take your crown."

My eyes sting with tears. His words mean so damn much, it hurts but in a good way. I don't know where this man came from, but I thank the gods everyday that he was brought to me.

The hearing starts, but I zone out, focusing on my breathing and trying to get the ringing out of my ears. I'm playing with my fingers, trying not to look up while also trying to avoid seeing *him* as much as I'm able to.

I'm not sure how much time passes when Theo gets my attention. "I'm sorry, what?" I ask, looking up to see all eyes on me.

"I asked you if you would be willing to come up here and tell us what you remember from the night of the incident," the judge repeats.

"Oh, yes. Sorry, your honor," I say, my voice giving away my nerves. Theo takes my hand and gives it an encouraging squeeze.

"Look at who's talking to you, or us, don't pay him any attention, okay?" Theo reminds me. I nod and stand on shaky legs. I make my way over to the stand and get sworn in.

"Eleanor, may I call you that?" Brody's lawyer asks me as he walks a little closer to me.

"Ellie, I prefer to be called Ellie," I answer.

"Ellie." He smiles. "On the night of January 7th, did you happen to see Brody attack Tim?"

I look at Brody, his eyes hard as he stares not at me but at his lawyer. Turning my attention back to the man asking questions, I answer, "Everything happened kind of fast."

"Can you replay the moments leading up to the event? Only what's relevant to this incident."

"Umm, well." I take a deep breath. "I was dancing. Someone I didn't want to be around started bothering me." I will myself not to look Tim's way or get into any further details. I don't want to have to re-tell this again at my own hearing.

"And who was that person?"

"Tim," I say. "Tim Hightower."

"Is he here in the room right now?"

"Yes. He's sitting right there," I tell him, pointing to Tim.

He nods, then continues. "And what happened next?"

"Tim followed me outside when I left to get away from him. When I was out there, Tim cornered me and said some things that made me feel like my safety was in trouble. Then Tim put his hands on me, and a moment later, he was gone. That's when I looked over to see Brody on top of Tim."

"Thank you, Ellie," his lawyer tells me. "Just one more question, is that alright?"

"Yes." I nod, gripping my hands together to keep them from shaking. My whole body feels alive and not in a good way. I want to leave. I want to get far away from the monster who's only a few feet away from me. I want to hold my daughter, cuddle up to her in bed, and forget about all the bad things in my life.

But I can't. Brody doesn't deserve my help, but the fact is, he did save me. I might not owe him anything, but I'm not the kind of person who would let him suffer for doing the right thing.

"Do you feel that if Brody didn't remove Tim from the situation the way he did that your safety would have been in jeopardy? Do you believe Mr. Hightower would have harmed you if no one had intervened?"

As if I have no control over my own body, my eyes slide to Tim as I answer, "Yes. I believe that if no one was there, he would have followed through with every horrible thing he said he would do to me," I say with far too much confidence, it makes me sick.

Tim sneers at me. The look in his eyes is woven with regret that he didn't get to do what he wanted to do to me. I can't look any longer, a wave of nausea taking over.

"Thank you, Ellie, that is all."

The judge asks Tim's lawyer if he has any questions for me but he declines for now.

I'm dismissed from the stand, but instead of going to sit back down, I run from the room, my hand over my mouth as I burst into the hallway. I find the nearest trash can and throw up.

"Ellie," Theo's voice comes from behind me. "Love, are you okay?"

"I'm fine," I groan, feeling anything but.

"Sweetheart, you're shaking."

"I just need to sit down," I tell him, letting him help me to the bench nearby. "I'm sorry."

"Sorry about what?" Theo pulls me into his lap, his arms coming around me in a warm comforting embrace, protecting me from the rest of the world. "You did amazing, Ellie. Just like I knew you would."

"Really?" I let out a humorless laugh. "Then how come I'm out here, puking like a drama queen?"

"Enough," he says softly, kissing the top of my head. "You were in a room with your attacker. Anyone would have reacted the same, or worse. You were brave and strong."

"What about the hearing? Did I ruin it?"

"No, love, I'm sure if they need you again, they will find you, but everything else is on them."

"I think I'm ready to go to one of those meetings I was talking about," I tell Theo after a few moments of silence. "I know they are going to ask me exactly what happened the night of graduation, and I've told my therapist everything, but I don't know, maybe talking to other survivors will help me when it comes to my hearing."

"Only *you* know what's best for you. But I think it's a wonderful idea. We'll find out when the next meeting is, and I'll make sure someone can watch Lilly."

"You don't have to, Theo, I can," I tell him, moving so that I can look into his eyes.

"Ellie, Lilly is just as much mine as Toby is. I want to help her in any way a father does, if you'll let me. We're in this together, sweet girl. You're not alone."

My heart, my heart is so damn full, everything that just happened is completely forgotten in this moment. "I love you so much, Theo," I tell him as I hold back tears. "Thank you for being so amazing to me and Lilly."

"Always, my love, you never have to thank me."

We sit and talk for about half an hour before the courtroom doors open and everyone starts to come out.

Theo helps me stand as we wait for everyone to make their way to us. "How did it go?"

"It got postponed until after your hearing," Brody says. Just what we thought. "I can't go anywhere past Spring Meadows. If it was just me Tim had to worry about, he would be free to walk around, but the judge doesn't seem to like rapists. So he's ordered Tim to stay in his parent's custody. He has to take a leave of absence from school. Meaning, he's pretty much on house arrest until after the hearing." *Good.* I'm glad he's not going to be out wandering the streets and lurking in the shadows. But I still won't feel safe until he's behind bars.

"Did you see his face?" Chase asks with a laugh. "Might have been a few months ago, but his nose is still totally bent as fuck."

"Good." Brody grins.

"Ellie," Jeff calls out, getting my attention. He says goodbye to whoever he's talking to before heading over here. "You did great. And I'm sure they told you that Brody's hearing is postponed until after your hearing. But I've just gotten some other news. It turns out that the news of the charges you have against Tim have gotten around. Ellie, there've been five other women who have come forward to press charges. This helps our case *big* time. Not that I didn't think we couldn't have won without it."

Five other girls. My eyes burn and a sob breaks free.

"Ellie?" Chase asks, catching me before my knees give out.

"Five," I croak, looking up at him with blurry eyes. "*Five* other women. Who knows how many more. I said nothing and he hurt more people."

"No." Brody's strong tone has my eyes snapping to his. "Don't you dare take the blame for any of this. You are not responsible. You don't know when these women were assaulted. And even if it was after you, that's on him. You did nothing wrong. Do you understand me?"

I want to agree, but I feel the weight of the world on my shoulders, like I'm to blame for those women getting assaulted. If I had just said something, maybe it could have been avoided.

I'm unable to keep the tears in anymore, the emotions of the day taking over. Chase gathers me into his arms as I start to cry into his chest. He rubs my back, whispering sweet and loving words in my ear, kissing my head in between.

More hands find my back and shoulders as Theo, Rain, and Jax join in.

This is why I felt like I could finally come forward. Knowing I have so many people who will stand with me by my side through it all, no matter the outcome, gives me strength.

"Ready to go?" Theo asks me after I calm down.

I nod as I move my face from Chase's chest. "Sorry." I wipe my eyes. "I ruined your shirt." I cringe.

"Don't worry about it. I have another one." Chase winks at me.

I smile, and he leans down to place a kiss on my lips.

We leave the courthouse, and as soon as we get outside, a lady in a way too tight black dress steps in front of us.

"What the fuck are you doing here?" Brody growls.

"Is that any way to talk to your mother?" she gasps. *His mother?* It's been a while since I've seen her. She looks like a

184

woman who can't accept the fact that she's aging and is trying to look twenty years younger than she is.

"How many times do we have to go over this? You might have given birth to me, but you're no mother of mine," he sneers.

"You're so ungrateful. And after I bailed your useless ass out of jail," she scoffs.

"I don't think that getting on your knees and sucking the police commissioner's cock counts as bailing me out," Brody says. "And *I* paid the actual bail money."

"Why did you waste that much money? You were free. You could have used it for other things."

"Like what?" he asks. "I have everything I need."

"You could have given it to me. I gave birth to you, after all. I think I'm owed for having you ruin my body!"

Brody snorts a laugh. "I think all the cock and random dick you take is the cause of that."

She glares at him, her lip pulling back. "You stupid little—" She raises her hand to slap Brody, and I let out a little gasp.

"Don't fucking touch me," Brody says, grabbing her hand before she can make contact.

"I should have let you rot in that cell. I hope they charge you and you get sent to prison. No one would care if you're gone. Do the world a favor and leave."

My blood starts to boil, and I really want to say something to her. Brody's jaw ticks as he breathes heavily through his nose.

"I don't care what you think. If anyone needs to fuck off for good, it's you. When will you get it through your vapid head that no one wants you around? You use Dad like an ATM and fuck anything that looks your way. You offer nothing to this world but STDs. Get the fuck out of my face."

"I should have aborted you," she shouts, snatching her hand back.

"Yeah, yeah, I've heard it before. Now, get lost."

"Maggie?" someone asks.

Brody's mom looks up, and her face turns into a fake smile.

"Oh, Bob, honey," she coos, running over to him.

Brody starts to laugh. "And she's fucking Tim's lawyer now. This is just fucking perfect."

I feel bad for Brody right now. I've known his mom has always been an issue for him, but in all the years I knew him, I only saw her a handful of times. He never liked to talk about her, and when I did see her, it was in passing. Brody always made sure we left when she was around.

They come back over to us, her arm wrapped around Bob's waist. "Ellie, honey, I didn't even see you over there. Look at you. You've grown into such a beautiful young woman."

I don't say anything, my own jaw is clenched tight.

"I'm so glad you dumped my son. He was never good enough for you. That boy has some anger issues, and I don't think he treated you like you deserved. Then to get angry when you found someone better. I was sad to hear you didn't give poor Tim a chance. He's a nice young man from a good family. He would have given you more than Brody ever could. I still can't believe Brody attacked him like that! I hope the judge does the right thing and gives Tim the justice he deserves."

"You're kidding me, right?" I gape at her. *Is this woman for real?* "You do know Tim raped me, right? That's what all of this is about." I'm shocked, damn near stunned right now.

"Oh, hun, you really shouldn't use that word so carelessly. It could cause real damage to a young man's reputation. I think you might have had a little too much to drink that night, and misread what was going on."

The others start going off on her, making her jump back in shock like she's confused as to why they are acting like that.

I stand there, numb, wondering if she really just said all that.

"Get the fuck away from her!" Brody shouts. "You crazy cunt."

"Brody," Jax says, stepping in front of him. "Let's go. She's clearly off her rocker. It's all bullshit to get a reaction out of you. You know that."

Brody looks like a raging bull right now, and for the first time, I understand why Brody is the way he is. Having to endure that fucked up verbal abuse all the time from someone who should love and care for you...with them reminding you every chance they get that they regret having you, that has to leave deep and mangled wounds. My heart hurts for him. *God, this woman is a real piece of work.*

"Brody," I say as I reach out and touch his arm. "Don't let her get to you. Remember where you are. You don't want to do something you're going to regret. Let's go, I'm hungry. How about we all go out to eat?"

He's not pissed, he's enraged. But the longer we look at each other with both mine and Jax's hands on his shoulders to stabilize him, I can see him start to simmer down.

He looks at his mom and Bob. "Hope you know you're fucking a married woman. And that married woman is not only fucking you, but half the town, if not all. Enjoy your used cunt." Brody takes off toward his car as Bob guides Brody's mom away from us as she screams nonsense. Jax looks at him, then back to me, and I can see he's conflicted on what to do.

"Go, it's okay. Meet us at Bill's Diner if he's up for it?" I give him a smile.

Jax steps forward and places a kiss on my forehead. "I love you," he says before taking off after Brody.

"Are you okay?" Chase and Theo ask at the same time, then look at each other with a frown. But it makes me laugh, which is something I needed at this moment.

"Yes. But god, is that woman always that awful?" I ask, watching Bob shove her into the car as she fights him.

"That's not even the half of it," Rain sighs, watching too.

"Has she always been like this?" I ask. Chase and Rain look at each other as if they're wondering what they can tell me.

"I'd never agree with what Brody did to you. But the reason why I didn't kick him out of my life is because I know that's not the real him. Years of that woman in his ear telling him he's better off dead and no one will miss him, it did things to his head," Chase says.

The idea of Brody having to deal with that, the hurt he must feel, my heart breaks. No one deserves that.

"I never knew it was that bad," I tell him, watching Brody's car take off out of the parking lot.

"He didn't want you to know. We've seen it since we were little kids. He didn't want you to see him differently," Rain says.

"But he's trying," Chase says. "He hasn't drank since the night after he was released from jail."

"Really?" I ask, sounding surprised. Brody always had a drinking problem; it's one of the only things we used to argue about. It was an added issue with what happened on graduation night that had me parting ways from my guys and Rain.

"I'm not asking you to forgive him, because he has a lot to make up for, but maybe now you can see why he can be the way he is sometimes?" Chase asks.

"Yeah." I nod. "I don't think I have it in me to forgive him yet, because what he did, it was soul crushing. But I will be more open to seeing him try."

"You're amazing, babe, you know that?" Chase says, pulling me in for a kiss.

"Eww." I laugh. "I just puked, you know."

He just shrugs. "Sorry, I just love you so much. It's been like what, an hour since I've had my lips on you? I was pretty much dying. But don't worry, that just brought me half way back to life."

"Oh, really?" I laugh, loving how he can make my crappy mood vanish. "And what would I need to do to make you fully alive?"

"Well, I mean if you really want to know..." He gives me a mischievous grin as he wiggles his eyebrows.

"How about you try not to ravish my girlfriend in a court-house parking lot?" Theo asks, and I look back at him, giggling as he cocks a brow at Chase. He doesn't look pissed, just amused.

"I'm pretty sure you mean our girlfriend," Chase responds.

"Are you two using titles now?" Theo asks with a grin.

Chase's brows furrow. "Are we?" he asks me. "Are you my girlfriend?"

Before, I wasn't ready for it to be so official, but now?

"Yes. I think it's about time you called me your girlfriend," I grin. His face lights up like I've just handed him the moon.

"Fuck yeah!" he whoops, then turns to a group of people walking by. "You hear that? My girlfriend is Eleanor Tatum. Be jelly."

"Chase!" I laugh at his antics as he scoops me up into his arms and spins me around.

"No kissing!" Theo says before Chase's lips crash into mine. "If you start, I know it's gonna be a bitch to get out of here."

"Fine," Chase pouts.

"Later," I tell him, biting my lip at the idea of being with him again.

He gives me a heated look before Rain grabs him by the arm. "Come on, hornball. Let's get going. You're gonna see her in a few minutes."

"Bye, girlfriend!" Chase shouts across the parking lot. "I love you!"

I wave bye, the smile on my face so big it hurts.

"You know, seeing him like that, it reminds me why I'm okay with you being with the others," Theo says. "He might be a goofball, and has some growing up to do, but I think he's good for you."

"He is," I tell him, giving him a kiss on the cheek. "Just like you are."

"I know we both have something in common," he tells me, brushing my hair off my face.

"What's that?"

"We both love you with everything we have. And we would burn the world down just to see you smile."

And just like that, I fall in love all over again.

Chapter Twenty

ELLIE

"YOU GOT THIS, Ellie. Everyone in that room is going through the same thing you are, but in their own way," I tell myself, taking a deep breath as I stand outside the building that is holding the meeting I'm attending.

I was happy to hear that they had something like this in Spring Meadows. But this building has different offices for different meetings like alcohol, drug, and sex addictions, and so much more. It makes me hopeful that if there's a place for people who need help or more support, then they can get it.

Gathering all my courage, I grab the handle to the front door and pull it open. Looking down at my phone, I remember to get the room number right before heading down the hall.

One of the things I really liked about this set up is that you keep what's going on behind the door private. So, if you come in here asking what goes on behind door 33, they won't answer. Only the people who sign up know what it's for. I can see how it could help people feel more comfortable about going without having to worry about someone seeing you walk out of the room and know you're a sexual assault survivor. It's no one's business but your own and who you choose to share it with.

When I get to the room, I walk in and I'm greeted by a lady with a nice smile.

"Hello," she says.

"Hi." I give her a smile of my own.

"Welcome, and I hope you find comfort in attending today. We ask you to please leave any recording devices here in this basket," she says, pointing to the one on the table next to her. "We will keep them safe until after the meeting. It's to make sure all of our members attending feel safe to talk freely."

"Of course," I tell her, getting my phone out of my purse and placing it in the basket.

"Thank you. There's coffee and donuts on the table over there if you would like any. The meeting is about to begin."

I thank her and head into the room. I'm shocked to see how many people are here. There has to be a good thirty people, maybe more.

My heart clenches as I think about all of them being here for the same reason as me. Knowing that so many people have been taken advantage of, and this isn't even a number on the scale of how many people have had this happen to them, is sobering.

A man gets up in front of the room to start the meeting, introducing himself as Marty, so I slip into the empty chair in the back so as not to disturb him.

Over the next half hour, I listen to stories from different people. I cry for each of them. None of them happened the same way, but all ended with the same results. They are so brave to get up there and tell their story. That won't be me today, but I'm hoping if I keep coming here for the next few weeks, I'll be ready to tell mine. It will never be easy to relay what happened that night to anyone; it's bad enough to live with the memories, but to say them out loud in front of people I don't know well, as opposed to the people who mean the most to me in this world... it's terrifying. But I'm hoping to maybe heal a small part of my heart by coming here.

I'm not looking forward to having the ones I love know the details, though. My lawyer warned me there's a high chance I'm going to have to reveal everything during my hearing.

"I wanna thank everyone who came today. It's okay if you're not ready to tell your story yet. Keep coming here. We want to see your beautiful faces, and maybe someday, you will be ready to share. And if you don't think that will ever be the case, that's okay too. There is no requirement to talk. If sitting here and listening helps, then we are happy to help with that too. There're some refreshments left on the table, and we hope to see you again next week. Feel free to mingle with each other for a little while, there's no rush to leave," Marty finishes up.

Everyone stands up. Some leave, some find other people to talk to. I get up and grab myself a coffee. When I'm ready to leave, I get in line to get my phone when someone says my name.

"Ellie?" a shocked voice asks.

I spin around to find Aria standing there, her eyes widened in shock.

"Aria," I breathe, my eyes stinging with the knowledge of why she's here.

"Well, this is...an interesting place to meet outside of work," she says with a nervous laugh as she wrings her hands together.

"A little," I smile. "But I'm happy to see you either way."

"Same." She smiles back. "So, looks like we have something in common." Then she cringes. "Sorry, that's a horrible thing to say."

"It's fine," I laugh. "Wanna sit?" I ask her, pointing to a few empty chairs.

"Yeah," she says, and we sit. "First time here, I'm guessing?"

"Yeah. I thought it was about time to see if maybe coming here could help."

"I've been coming here for a few months now, but I still have yet to speak. I want to. I've wanted to talk to someone who knows the pain I'm feeling, you know?" She shifts in her chair. "My

193

parents know, and they are supportive and everything, but they don't understand."

"Trust me, I know that feeling. My parents are amazing, and they've been there for me for years through it all, but it's not the same."

"Every time I think I'm ready, I freeze up when Marty asks if anyone wants to share."

"Well, I don't know if you will feel comfortable telling me, but I'm always happy to listen. Maybe talking to one person versus a room full of people might help."

"Really?" she asks, her eyes glossing over. "You would be okay with that?"

"Of course." I smile at her. "And if it will help you feel better about telling your story, I can tell you mine?"

"You don't have to. Don't feel pressured. I know I'm ready to talk about it, it's just finding the guts to do it."

"Aria, what happened to us is horrible, no matter the story. It's okay to *not* be okay with sharing."

"I know."

"But, if you're ready, I'm more than happy to be your conversation starter." I grin and she laughs.

"I don't know. Sometimes, I feel like my story isn't as big of a deal as most."

"Don't say that. Your story matters too. Wanna tell me?"

She lets out a heavy sigh before nodding. "It happened about eight years ago. I was in a relationship with someone. At that point, it was about four years in. Things weren't the best. We kind of were only together because we share a kid. After years of feeling unloved and unwanted, I went back to my hometown for a wedding. I realized how unhappy I was, and broke up with my boyfriend.

"Well, while I was there, my first boyfriend from high school wanted to see me. He was the love of my life at some point, my first everything. We ended like any other high school relationship, but at the time, it felt like the end of the world," she laughs. "I never fell out of love with him, or so I thought at the time. He asked me to come hang out with him. So I did, because I missed him.

"He told me everything I had ever wanted to hear. He told me he loved me, wanted to get married and have kids with me. He didn't care that I already had a three-year-old son. He wanted us both. I had years of feeling like I wasn't loved or wanted, so a part of me jumped at the chance.

"We'd hung out a few times the week before it happened. It felt like old times and, after having sex with him again, I wanted to see him more. He invited me to his brother's birthday party, and of course I went. I always loved his mom. She was so nice to me when we were dating, and she was happy to see me.

"I brought my son with me because I was there on vacation and didn't have anyone else to watch him. I was sick with a cold, and later on, I took some cold medicine because I felt like crap, but didn't want to miss out on the party because he seemed so excited to have me there.

"For the most part, the night was fun. My son played with the toys he had there for his own son. And when it got late, I put him to bed in my ex's son's bed. I didn't have a way back to where I was staying because everyone was already drunk and the buses weren't running. I could have called a cab, but I was on a tight budget and the cab would have cost too much.

"So, I said I'd stay the night on the couch. He still lived with his mom, so her and her boyfriend left the party early to go to bed upstairs, already drunk themselves. The party ended and everyone else left. My ex was drunk too, so I helped him up to his room."

Aria pauses, looking down at her fingers, and I know this is where things are going to take a darker turn. I hold out my hand, offering her support, my heart hurting to see her in pain. She takes it, giving it a squeeze like I'm her anchor during this conversation. "As I went to leave, he grabbed my arm and pulled me down on top of him. He started telling me how sexy I was, how much he loved me and wanted me. I told him I didn't feel like it tonight, that I didn't feel well and just wanted to go to sleep.

"He ignored me, kept trying to get me to sleep with him. He was a big guy, and his grip on my arm was strong. I tried to pull away, tried to tell him no, but it was like he didn't hear me or was too drunk to care.

"The thing is, my son was sleeping right next to us. I was afraid that if I was too loud or put up a fight, he would wake up and I wouldn't have been able to help. I couldn't risk him getting hurt. Everyone else in the house was passed out drunk.

"I felt like there was nothing else I could do. My head was fuzzy from the meds I took on top of already feeling out of it from the cold itself."

Tears are streaming down her cheeks now. I bite the inside of my cheek to ground myself, telling myself to stay strong for her.

"I can't remember how it got to this point, but I ended on top of him. He kept grabbing me, holding me to him. He moved my clothes out of the way and forced his way in. I cried, I kept saying no, I kept trying to get out of his grip. But the fear of my son waking up and seeing this kept me from trying harder. I didn't know what he might do to my son with him being so drunk.

"He ended up passing out after a while. And when his grip loosened, I got off him and went down to the couch. I cried myself to sleep. But what I should have done was grab my son and leave. I felt like the worst parent because I didn't. When I woke up, I grabbed my son so we could go back to my friend's house where we were staying.

"My ex asked me where I was going, and I told him I was leaving. He asked me why, so I asked him if he was joking. Reminded him what happened that night, and he played it off like he had no idea what I was talking about. That he was drunk, and didn't remember.

"I told him he raped me, and because he didn't remember the

night, he denied it. And I kept pressing that he did, but he made me feel stupid, like I was a liar."

"You're not," I tell her, my voice strong with emotion, and I give her hand a squeeze. "You're not a liar. I believe you."

"Thank you." She gives me a watery smile. "As I was leaving, he asked me not to call the cops. He said that my lies would just end up hurting him. He would lose his job, and his son. In the end, he guilted me out of calling. How fucked up is that? I get raped and he makes me feel guilty about getting justice." She laughs, wiping her eyes.

"What a fucking monster," I seethe. A part of me wants to find this guy and kick his ass.

"Yeah, tell me about it," she says. "So I left, never seeing him again. I told some friends what happened. A few of them felt bad for me, but said it wasn't rape."

"What!?" I ask her, my eyes going wide with disbelief. "How the hell wasn't that rape!"

"They said because I had sex with him the day before and was so willing to do it, and the fact that I didn't fight hard enough to get him to leave me alone, that it wasn't rape. That I had the chance to scream for help, to fight more but didn't."

"That doesn't matter! You said no. He kept going. You had your son next to you!" I say, my anger growing for her. "Fuck what they think. You were assaulted, and they can go suck a dick," I growl.

She laughs at my last comment. "Thanks for believing me. It took me a long time to see it for what it is. I ended up thinking that it wasn't assault, so I gave up talking about it. But then I started doing research and read a lot of other people's stories. I realized it was rape. I had said no. I was afraid for my child, and manipulated into not saying a word after."

"Good. I'm glad you saw it for what it was. Don't let anyone make you feel like just because it wasn't as graphic or violent as some other's that it isn't what it is," I tell her.

"The thing that pissed me off the most is a few years later, I ended up talking to his ex, the mother of his son. Turns out, he did something similar to her when they were dating. My ex used to bitch about her to me, saying she was so mean for keeping their son from him at first. Now I know why. I feel bad for ever agreeing with him on that."

"I know how you feel about finding out he did it to someone else. I just found out that my abuser attacked at least five other people. I can't help but feel like if I had just said something, then they would have been safe," I tell her, my own tears are falling now.

"Hey, don't think like that."

"It's hard not to, you know? But I plan on fighting hard to get him behind bars. I'm going to win this case, I just know it." At least I hope so. *I really fucking hope so.* "Thank you so much for trusting me with your story. I guess it's only fair if I tell you mine."

And I do, trying not to go into too much detail. By the end of it, she's just as mad for me as I am for her.

"So you get assaulted and they say you're cheating," she scoffs, her face filled with fury.

"To be fair, they didn't know that part. It's a really messy situation, but we're starting to move past it now that they know."

"Brody is a dick, make him pay. And don't go easy on Rain. Make that girl work for it."

"Don't worry, I will," I laugh.

"What about the other two? What's going on there?"

"Ah, Chase and I are together, and Jax and I are dating," I say, waiting for her judgement...but it doesn't come.

"On top of that fine ass teacher of yours? Damn, girl, I wanna be you," she says.

"I'm pretty lucky." I smile. "They are amazing. It's nice to feel some peace after all these years, you know?"

"Yeah." She smiles. "My son's father and I ended up getting back together when I got back from my trip. It took some time, but we ended up falling in love. Now, we are married and have a daughter together too. Life's pretty good for the most part."

"That's so exciting! I'm so glad things have worked out for you," I tell her.

"We should get together and have a playdate. My youngest is seven, but she just loves little kids," Aria tells me as we leave the room and head toward the exit of the building.

"Theo's son is six, and just loves Lilly. I think they will get along. I'll set something up for sure! But, maybe after the trial?"

"Sounds good. See you at work. And remember, you've got this."

We grab our phones then hug goodbye, and she leaves before me. I text Theo, telling him I'm going to pick up some food on my way home before leaving the building.

"Oh, sorry," I say as I step out, walking straight into someone.

"Watch where you're going," someone shouts. "Ellie?"

I look up to see Laura and Kayla with a few other girls. *Just fucking awesome.*

"What are you doing here?" she laughs. "You do know this building is like a breeding ground for addicts."

"Oh my god. Are you a druggie?" Kayla gasps. "Wow, how trashy."

"I don't do drugs," I snap. "And you don't know what people are going through, so you have no right to judge."

"Sure." Laura laughs. "Must be an alcoholic then."

"Or maybe she's here because she's a raging slut and needs help for her sex addiction," Kayla says.

"You know what, I don't have time for this," I tell her, moving to step past.

"Hope Chase knows he's dating a whore. Don't worry, he will realize soon enough that he deserves someone who wants him and *only* him," Kayla says.

"And that's who, you?" I laugh.

"Chase will be mine. He just needs to get you out of his system," she sneers.

"Keep telling yourself that, lady." I roll my eyes. "Now, if you will excuse me, I've hit my quota of bitch for the week."

They can say what they want, but I know it's all bullshit and lies. I just feel bad for Chase and Rain for getting stuck with these two crazy chicks. *Good thing they have me.* If I ever get like that, I hope someone puts me down.

Chapter Twenty-One

ELLIE

MARCH IS FLYING BY FAST. We're already halfway through the month, but I feel like it was just yesterday that Brody had his hearing.

A lot has happened, and I've been kept busy for sure. With work, school, Lilly, friends, two amazing boyfriends, and Jax who's working his way back into my heart, I don't think I've had a moment to myself.

A part of me is glad because when I'm alone, my mind wanders and I think of all things that get my heart racing and not in a good way.

This Saturday is St. Patrick's Day, and I'm kind of bummed that I'm working because Rain, the guys, and all my friends are going to be at the club to celebrate. I might not be able to hang out with them, but at least I'll be in the same place as them.

I could have booked the time off, but it's a holiday, and one that usually involves a lot of drinking so that means it'll be a packed house. And a packed house means crazy tips which I just couldn't turn down.

"Ellie!" Jax shouts from behind me as I head to my next class.

"Hi." I turn around to smile at him. His black curls bounce as he jogs the last few steps toward me.

"I wanted to catch you before your next class," he says, his breath a little uneven, but as a football player, it would take a lot more than that to tire him out.

"Well, you're in luck." I laugh lightly. "I'm just about to head to it. What's up?"

"Umm." He suddenly looks nervous as he rubs the back of his head. "What are you doing tonight?"

I grin. "Gonna ask me on another date?"

He gives me a small smile. "Kinda?"

"I was just gonna do some homework and hang out with Lilly for the night, maybe have Theo stop by."

"So, my dad's birthday is today. He's having a barbecue at his place with his girlfriend and her family. He asked me to go, and I was wondering if you and Lilly would like to come? I've told him about Lilly, and he would love to meet his granddaughter. But don't worry, I've told him Lilly doesn't know about any of this yet so he won't say or do anything to mess with that."

"Oh," I say. I've always liked his dad. Jax's parents were amazing when it came to our unique relationship back in high school. Chase and Rain's were also the same, as well as mine. The only ones who didn't have an opinion were Brody's parents, but we never saw them really. And if we did, they were never together.

"I know it might be a lot to ask, but I'd love for you to come. I'm still not used to being around my dad's girlfriend's family and having you and Brody there would make it easier."

"Brody is going to be there?" I ask.

"Is that going to be a problem?" he asks, then lets out a sigh. "Fuck, of course it is. I'm sorry, I didn't even think. I just wanted the three people who mean the world to me to be there."

"No, no, it's fine. I gotta get along with him anyways, so why not try this in a setting that's outside of school," I say, giving him a reassuring smile. "You know what? I think some hot dogs and hamburgers sound better than the mac and cheese I was going to have tonight." I laugh. "Lilly would argue otherwise, but she will eat just about anything."

"Really?" His whole face lights up, and the little bit of unease that I was feeling ebbs away. "My aunt is going to be there with her little ones, so Lilly should have a few kids around her age to play with."

"Now I'm sold." I laugh. "Lilly has been going stir crazy with just being around us. She has Toby too, but I know she's been dying to get out and run around." Guilt sinks deep into my gut. "I've been pretty selfish with keeping her from daycare and the park. It's just, anytime I think about letting her run around, my mind starts to think 'what if someone is sitting and waiting for me to turn my back for a second?' Because, Jax, it only took a second. A single second for someone to take my baby girl." Tears fill my eyes, and I start to feel an anxiety attack coming on.

"Shh," he says, pulling me into his strong tattooed arms. Wrapping my arms around his waist, I hold myself tight to his chest. "Breathe, Ellie." His large hands rub up and down my back to soothe me. "You're not selfish. What happened with Lilly was a horrifying event for you both. It's more than normal to react this way afterwards. As Lilly's parent, you've been doing what you feel is right to help her keep safe. Don't be so hard on yourself. You're an amazing mom, Ellie."

"But I can't keep her locked up in a little bubble forever," I murmur into his chest. "She's going to be starting school next year, and I know she misses hanging out with other kids her age. She loves Toby, and Chase and Rain have been a big help, but she's been asking about Miss Macy a lot. She's an amazing teacher, and she wasn't the one in charge of the kids at the time, so it wasn't her fault."

"Do you think you will be ready to put Lilly back into daycare any time soon?" he asks as I move back to look into his chocolate, brown eyes.

"Maybe? I think I need to warm up to leaving her somewhere."

"How about next week we take her to the park?" he asks, then quickly adds on to what he was saying when he sees the slight panic in my eyes. "We all take her. Rain, the guys, Theo, you, your friends, and me. We will have a whole team looking out for her," he explains, grinning down at me and my heart fills with what he's offering. I know my friends will be more than happy to do this. They love hanging out with Lilly.

"Really?" I ask, my voice conveying all the emotions he's bringing out of me.

"If it helps you feel better about bringing her to the park, of course. I want to spend more time with her anyways, we all do. I think this would be a perfect time to do that."

"Okay." I nod. "I'll talk to Cooper and the girls and see what they think."

"So, about tonight?" he asks, his eyes filled with a hopeful look that I don't think I'd have the heart to turn down.

"Count us in." I smile up at him.

"Thank you." His grin is so wide, it's adorable. "Brody has a meeting with his lawyer after class, but I will come pick you and Lilly up around four. Is that okay?"

"Sounds perfect."

"Ellie?" he asks, his eyes searching mine.

"Yes?" The way he's looking at me feels light and airy.

"Can I kiss you?" he asks, his voice low. "It's all I've been thinking about since our date."

"Yes," I breathe, my heartbeat picking up in pace.

His eyes drop to my lips as my tongue pokes out to wet them out of nervous habit. His pupils dilate with need. *Why am I so nervous?* I dry humped this man just a few weeks ago. Now is not the time to be acting like a blushing virgin. But fuck, the longer he takes to kiss me, the more my heart starts to pound. My palms get sweaty and my belly does somersaults.

Finally, *finally,* he lowers his lips to mine. I close my eyes the moment he makes contact and sigh as he pulls me flush against his body, his other hand moving to the back of my head to hold me in place. Our lips move together, exploring each other. He tastes like watermelon gum, the sweet flavor made more intense when his tongue slides between my lips to caress my tongue with his.

I whimper into his mouth as I grip his shirt, needing to steady myself. I keep forgetting how this man always consumes my mind and body every time he touches me.

Our kiss grows heated, and I can feel his erection against my belly. I want him; *man do I want him.*

A throat clears behind us, breaking the spell we are under. We pull back and stare at each other, both panting from the heated kiss. His eyes are hungry, and he looks pissed that we were interrupted.

"Sorry to ruin the moment. But you're standing in the middle of the hall and now you have an audience," Theo says, his voice makes my eyes widen. I bite my lip, my face heating up pretty damn close to how hot that kiss was.

"Hi," I squeak, looking over Jax's shoulder to my boyfriend.

"Hi, sweet girl." He grins.

The people around us move on now that the show is over, and Theo steps closer.

"Now, if you're done getting my girlfriend all worked up, I think that maybe you two should be getting to class," he urges Jax, cocking a brow, and I don't think my face could be any more red than it is right now.

"Right," Jax says, clearing his throat as he tries to subtly adjust his hard on. "I'll see you tonight," he says, giving me a quick peck on the cheek before leaving.

"Bye," I call after him then turn to Theo who's looking at me with a playful grin.

"I see you two are making progress."

"We are," I tell him. "After our date, we've gotten closer."

"I'm glad. So what was he talking about seeing you tonight for?"

"Oh, he invited me to a barbecue for his dad's birthday. His dad wants to meet Lilly."

Theo's face lights up. "That's awesome. I'm glad they want to get to know her. It's always nice to have family on your side."

"It is." I smile. "Jax's parents are amazing." My smile falls. "I guess it's just his dad now. His mother passed away a few years ago."

Theo looks in the direction Jax took off in. "Poor guy." He looks back at me. "Has he told you about it?"

I shake my head. "No, but I would like to know about what happened whenever he's ready to tell me himself."

"I'm sure he will." Theo leans over and kisses my forehead. "Now, don't you have a class to get to?" he asks, pushing his glasses up his nose with his pointer finger, and looking adorable while doing it.

"Right," I laugh. "Got a little side tracked. Won't happen again, Sir." I bite my lip, giving him a playful grin.

He lets out a low growl in his chest that excites me. "You're a naughty girl, aren't you?"

"I don't know, why don't we test that theory out tonight?" I giggle, leaning up on my tiptoes to kiss him quickly on the lips then dancing away from him before he can grab me. "See you later, Mr. Munro," I say in a seductive tone before taking off down the hall, giggling harder as he lets out a "Fuck," of sexual frustration. I'd love to help him with his little...I mean *big* issue, but we have to keep our relationship friendly while at school, and what I want to do to him is anything but.

The rest of the day, I have trouble trying to keep my mind on my school work. It often drifts to that kiss with Jax and the idea of taking care of Theo.

Sex wasn't something I really thought about or wanted in a very long time, not until I found people I felt comfortable to share myself with again.

It's like, now that I've taken that part of my life back, I can't help but embrace it and enjoy myself while doing so. There's nothing wrong with being sexually curious or free. It's not like I'm having sex all day, every day—not that there's anything wrong with that either. But I am finding myself craving their touch more often, even if it's just little brushes of arms and hands.

What happened to me controlled so much of my life, and not by choice, so if I'm able to find ways to heal that includes being intimate with the people I love, is that wrong? I don't think it should be. I don't see it that way.

When class is done, I gather my things into my bag and head out to my car to find Chase waiting for me.

"Hey there, pretty mama." He gives me a panty-melting grin that has my belly fluttering.

"That's a new one." I laugh as I open the back seat to my car to throw my backpack in.

"What are you up to?"

"Just got done with class, now I'm heading home to get ready for tonight," I tell him, stepping up to him and allowing him to pull me into his arms.

"Oh? And what are you doing tonight?" he asks as he brushes my hair back from my forehead and places a kiss there that has my eyes fluttering shut and me sighing in contentment.

"Jax asked me to go with him and Brody to his dad's birthday party," I tell him and he cocks a brow. "His dad wants to meet Lilly. And I like the idea of Lilly getting to know more family, even if she doesn't know they're family just yet."

"I think that will be good. I know Jax will appreciate it. He loves you, you know. Both you and Brody mean the world to him. I haven't seen him this happy in a very long time. Hell, probably not since before you left. After his mom passed, he was in a bad place; so bad that I don't know if he would have made it through it without Brody."

My heart hurts at the idea of him losing his mom and feeling so alone; with the pain of me being gone and then someone who meant the world to him, also passing away... "I wish I could have been there for him and it hurts knowing I couldn't."

"You're here now, and that means something to him."

"I'm nervous about going tonight," I tell him truthfully. "His dad must know enough about what happened for him to know about Lilly, and Jax and I being in each other's lives again."

"None of our parents think differently about you. They understand now, and Rain and my parents have been hounding us to see you too. They always loved you and were crushed when you left. They haven't stopped talking about having a granddaughter that they are dying to spoil." Chase grins.

"We should all get together soon, maybe have one big party or something?" I ask.

"How about we invite everyone over to celebrate locking that fucker up behind bars?"

"I think I like that idea," I say, plucking the candy cane from his mouth and sticking it in mine. I suck on it, making an overly dramatic show, trying to be funny, but his eyes only fill with heat.

"Fuck me, baby girl, don't start something you're not prepared to finish," he groans.

Heat swirls inside my belly, and as much as I'd love to drag him into the car and suck on *his* candy cane, I need to get home and get ready.

"Sorry about that." I grin, taking one last suck of the candy cane before putting it back into his mouth. "I gotta get going, but I'll see you soon." I lean up on my tippy toes and place a heated kiss on his lips, but pull back before he can grab me, holding me to him. "I love you," I call out to him as I get into the driver's seat.

"I love you too," he calls back, a sexy grin on his lips and a tent in his pants that he proudly shows off.

Shutting the car door, I giggle as I start the engine and head home.

When I get here, Lilly is watching TV while Theo's mom cleans the kitchen.

"Hello, hun. How was your day?" She smiles over at me as she wipes down the counter.

"It was a good day." I smile back, placing my backpack on the floor by the door. "You don't have to do that," I tell her, feeling bad that she's cleaning on top of watching Lilly all day.

"Nonsense." She waves her hand. "I made the mess, I'll clean it."

"Mama!" Lilly calls out as she gets up off the couch and runs over to me. I crouch down and hold out my open arms. She collides with me, giggling her little head off as I scoop her up and spin her around.

"I missed you, my little Lillypad," I tell her, peppering kisses all over her face and making her giggle harder.

"Missed you."

I place her down on her feet and lower myself so I'm level with her. "Remember mama's friends, Jax and Brody?" I ask her.

She tilts her head to the side in question. I laugh to myself, forgetting her names for them. "Axe and Broody," I correct.

"Oh, yes!" She smiles wide.

"How would you like to go to a party with them? There will be some kids there for you to play with too."

"Yay! We go now?" she asks, her body starting to vibrate with an excited energy. My gut springs with guilt that I've been depriving her of socialization with other children by keeping her so limited on where we go.

"Not right now, bug," I laugh. "Soon though. Wanna come with me to pick out something to wear?"

"Yes!" she cheers, then takes off into the bedroom.

"A party you say?" Theo's mom asks with a soft smile on her lips.

"Umm, yeah," I tell her. "Jax's father is having a birthday party, and they want to meet Lilly."

"That sounds nice." She smiles.

"It does?" I ask, a wave of nerves coating my body. "You're okay with all of this? With me being in a relationship with others as well as your son?"

"This is Theo's life, not mine. He makes his own choices. Do I think this is an ideal situation? No. This is different, and something I'm not quite accustomed to. But he's happy, and honey, he'd been hurting for so long until you came into his life. If he's okay with this, then so am I. I just wanna see my boy happy. And you make him happy."

"I love him, you know? What I have with anyone else doesn't take away from that. He owns a big part of my heart and soul; it's his, forever. I will love him, care for him, and always remind him of the amazing man he is. And I'll always show him how much I appreciate everything he does for Lilly and me."

"I know you will, dear. I've never doubted that."

"And about watching Lilly, I wanna thank you again for everything you've done for us." She's an amazing woman, and I'm so glad Theo has her as his mother.

"I love that little girl. In my eyes, she's my grandbaby." She steps toward me and takes my hands into hers. "You're family now, both of you. And I will always do everything for my family." She gives my hands a squeeze.

"Thank you." My eyes water with how grateful I am for this woman. "I'm slowly working to bring Lilly back out into the world. It's hard, but I know keeping her locked up all the time isn't healthy for her. I can't let fear control our lives. I'm hoping by the time the hearing is over, I'll feel better about her going back to daycare."

"Whenever you're ready."

We say goodbye and I head into the bedroom to get ready. I put Lilly in a pair of leggings and a pink and purple flower sundress, pairing it with a jean jacket. After putting her hair into pigtails, I get myself dressed. Picking out a pair of light, white washed, ripped jeans and a maroon form fitting shirt, I grab my own jean jacket to finish the look.

"Look, Mama! We match," Lilly says.

"We do." I smile. "And we look pretty good, don't we?"

Lilly nods, and the buzzer to the apartment goes off. "Looks like Axe is here."

"Yay!" Lilly shouts and takes off into the living room to get her shoes. I buzz Jax in, and gather my phone and purse as I try to get the nervous flutter in my belly to settle. I've been around Jax's dad and even his aunt before, but it's been a very long time.

There's a knock at the door and Lilly takes off toward it, snapping me out of my own thoughts. She flicks the lock and throws the door open.

"I really need childproof locks," I mutter, rushing over to join her.

"Well, hello there, little lady." Jax grins down at her. My eyes roam his body and I bite my lip as I take in what he's wearing. He has on black jeans that fit him just right and a white short sleeve dress shirt that shows off all his arm tattoos along with a few poking out through his shirt from the first few buttons undone. This man is a tattooed god, and he wants me.

"I'm gonna lick each of those tattoos someday."

"Really now?" Jax asks, amusement thick in his voice. My eyes snap up to his, filled with horror.

"Did I say that out loud?" I ask, dying of embarrassment.

"Mama, that's gross." Lilly looks up at me with her nose scrunched up. "You said no licking things that's not food," she adds.

Jax snorts a laugh, and I shoot him a glare.

"You're right, Lillypad. Tongue to yourself," I tell her as I grab her backpack and usher everyone out the door.

As I lock the door behind me, Jax leans in. His hot breath against the side of my neck sends a shiver down my spine before he whispers, "Don't feel like you need to apply that rule to yourself, firecracker. You can use that tongue on me anytime, anywhere."

Closing my eyes, the heat in my belly grows with need. These men are gonna be a handful, that's for sure.

"I'll keep that in mind," I say, my voice sounding a little more breathy than I was intending.

We head down to the parking lot and toward my car. "I have to grab her car seat first."

"Come on, Lilly, let's wait for Mom at my car," Jax tells her, taking Lilly's hand. Looking back over my shoulder, a wave of emotion fills me with warmth at the look of pure love he has for our daughter while he talks to her.

I'm glad that they smartened up with everything because it would have hurt to keep Lilly away from them. But I needed to make sure they were mature enough to be in her life. I'm starting to see that waiting was a good idea because when I first came back here, they was anything but.

After getting the car seat set up, we take off to pick Brody up at their apartment. He's standing by the front door, and when he sees us, he moves away, heading right toward us.

"Why is he always wearing long sleeves? Doesn't he ever get hot?" I ask. It may be March, but our cold months are over with. Heck, even in this jean jacket, I'm starting to sweat. But I've noticed since the pool party, he's been wearing a lot of warm looking clothes.

Jax chuckles under his breath, his face slipping into a grin as he watches his boyfriend head toward the car.

"Must be cold or something," Jax says, his eyes finally looking at me. There's more going on, and I have no idea what it is.

"Hey," Brody says, getting into the back seat of the car next to Lilly.

"Hi!" Lilly says, and I look into the rearview mirror at the both of them. Brody looks at Lilly and just stares at her for a moment.

"Umm. Hi," he says back.

"You said that," she points out, and I bite my lips to hold back my smile.

"Yeah, well, I wasn't talking to you," Brody says, putting on his seat belt.

"Then who?" she asks, her little brows furrowing.

"Ah, to Jax," he says, looking back at her.

"Why not me and Mama?" she asks, her cute little face growing angry.

"I said hi," he grumbles back.

But Lilly looks away, crossing her arms and looking out the window.

"Well aren't you a little ball of sass," Brody mutters.

Lilly looks at me. "Mama, Broody being mean!"

"I am not!" Brody says, a shocked look on his face.

"Uh huh!" she volleys back.

I can't help the giggle that slips from me. "Now, now, you two. Don't make us turn this car around."

"We didn't even leave the parking lot yet," Brody grumbles, turning to look out the window, his attention away from Lilly. She glares at him, sticking her tongue out before looking out her own window.

I look at Jax, and we share a look of understanding. Those two are going to take some time. Brody isn't used to kids, and Lilly isn't used to people whose energy doesn't match her own.

But I'm hoping with more time around him, Lilly will be able to bring the grumpy bear around.

JAX

The party is loud with kids running around and screaming. There are a lot more people here than I thought there would be. But they're mostly Wendy's, my dad's girlfriend's, family—apart from my aunt and some of my dad's co-workers.

When they got here, Lilly gravitated toward the other kids and has been busy playing with them since.

I went around saying my hellos, but Brody and Ellie stayed back. I could tell they both needed time to get used to being here before meeting a bunch of people who are strangers to me, as well as to them.

"How are you doing?" my dad asks after I get done greeting my uncle and am about to head back over to my lovers.

"Hey, Dad. Happy birthday." I give him a hug. "I'm doing good."

He looks over at Lilly who's playing. "She's a cute one. Looks just like her mother," he says, looking over at Ellie who is talking to Brody. And by the not so brooding look on his face, and the small smile on hers, I think they are actually getting along.

"She's an amazing kid," I tell him.

"Shame you didn't get to help raise her," he tells me, looking back at me. I narrow my eyes, getting irritated with him already.

"You know what happened, Dad. That's in the past now. We're working on things, and we're in Lilly's life now."

He nods. "I know. I don't mean to sound judgmental or anything. But you can't be upset with me for being shocked. You told me you're a dad. That you all are."

"No, I know. It came as a shock to us too, but it's also the best thing that's ever happened to us. They both are."

"So...you're all with her again?" he asks, taking a sip of his beer, but he doesn't seem put off by that.

"We're all showing her that she means the world to us. That we love her, and we're sorry for not trusting what we had in the past. Everything is in her hands."

"So you're not dating her?" He grins.

"Well, yes. I mean, no." I sigh, taking a sip of my own beer. "I don't know what we are really. We went on a date, and she agreed to come here. I know we're friends at least. We've gotten really close over the past few weeks. I know I love her, and I want to be with her. And I think she wants the same. Chase has worked his way back into her heart, so I have hope I can prove myself too."

"And what about Brody?" he asks.

My face heats. "What about him?"

He chuckles, shaking his head. "You're my son, I'm not blind. I see the way you two look at each other, and it's not how someone looks at their best friend."

I have nothing to hide; I'm not ashamed. So I take a deep breath and tell him, "Brody is my boyfriend. We've been a thing for a few years now."

"Since your mother died," he corrects, and something inside me breaks all over again.

"Yeah," I tell him, looking over at the only thing that kept me from crumbling in on myself after my mom died.

"He helped you through a lot. He was there for you when I wasn't able to be," he says, and I turn back to see his eyes shine with regret.

"Don't be so hard on yourself. You were dealing with the death of your wife. I know if Brody or Ellie passed, I would be nothing; just a shell of my old self."

"I know, and it was hard. The worst pain I've ever felt, but you are still my son. I should have been there for you. I'm so sorry." He pulls me into a hug, holding me tight.

I can't be mad at him for finding love after my mom's passing. He deserves love, deserves to find someone to help put him back together again. And he did pick a good woman. I think Mom would've approved.

"I forgive you. And as hard as that time was, something amazing came out of it. I love him, Dad. I love them both."

"Well, I'm happy for you. Whatever you all had back then worked for you. And I have no doubt that if you really want it to, it will again."

"Thanks, Dad," I tell him.

"Now, go see your lovers. They look like they would rather be anywhere but here," he chuckles.

I say goodbye and head over to the two of them. "How are you two holding up?"

"We're okay." Ellie smiles.

"It's weird," Brody says, looking out at the backyard of people. "I don't know anyone."

Ellie looks at him and cocks a brow. "You think I do?" She laughs.

"If it makes you feel any better, I don't really know any of these people either," I say.

"Well, I can tell by the look on your dad's face, it meant a lot for you to come. So that's what matters," Ellie says.

"Yeah. I miss him, you know?" We take a seat on the chairs

nearby and watch the kids play. "We were always pretty close, but it was my mom who I saw as more of a best friend," I say, her smiling face flashing across my mind, and I'm hit with a wave of heartache.

"I always loved her," Ellie says, grabbing my hand and giving it a squeeze.

"She was the best." I smile. "I miss our Sunday suppers. I miss going to the farmers market every weekend with her. Now I can't step foot near the place."

"How come? Too many sad memories?" Ellie asks.

I turn from watching Lilly playing with my cousins and meet Ellie's eyes. "That and it's where she died." My voice cracks with emotion, and I feel like a ball is clogging my throat. My eyes burn, but I don't look away. "We were out getting supplies for supper like we did every weekend. She was so excited about this one because she made some new friends at church, and she invited them over." I laugh as I remember her non stop chatter as she told me all about them. "We were heading back to the car that was parked across the street and she forgot something. I don't even remember what it was, but I offered to run back and get it. After I was done paying, I turned around just as she was crossing." I can't help the tears that well in my eyes. Ellie has tears of her own falling down her cheeks and she climbs into my lap, holding me tight.

I wrap my arms around her, closing my eyes tightly. My eyes open again when I feel Brody's hand on my thigh, giving me a comforting touch and I continue.

"Someone ran a red light. She didn't have time to move, to react." I'm crying now. Ellie puts her face in my neck, giving me soft kisses as she runs her hand up and down my back. "I saw it all; it was like it was playing out in slow motion. Even if I started to run, there was no way I would have been able to get to her in time. She was too far away. I should have walked her to the car first or had her go back and get what was missing. I should have been the one crossing the street, not her."

"Don't say that," Ellie says, her voice stronger. She moves so that she can hold my face in her hands. "There was nothing anyone could have done. And I know for a fact that your mother would have been destroyed if it was you. As a mom, I would always give my life up for Lilly, and she would have done the same thing for you."

"I know." I nod. "It's just hard not to feel like that sometimes."

"I'm so sorry you had to see that, and to feel everything you went through. I wish I could have been there for you." She learns forward and kisses the tears away from under my eyes before placing a soft kiss on my lips. Her touch settles something deep within me that has always felt out of control.

"There were so many times I wished that also. But I wasn't alone." I give her a watery smile before looking at Brody. I take his hand in mine. "I had the others, and it helped, but this guy right here, he saved me. I don't know if I would have made it through that part of my life without him."

Brody is not an open person, and he doesn't talk about his feelings often, but by the look in his eyes right now, I know it means a lot to him that he helped me through that time of my life.

"You helped me too," Brody says, leaning over to grip the back of my neck. "You've saved me time and time again. I love you." My heart thuds against my rib cage at his words. I'll never get tired of hearing him say them. He kisses me, and even though it's hard and fast, I can feel the love and passion in it.

"I'm glad," Ellie says, looking at Brody as we break apart. "Are you okay with not being the only one who's there for him?" she asks.

"Yeah, I am. Because he deserves the world and an army of people by his side. And so do you."

They stare at each other, and I have to bite the inside of my cheek to hold back the smile that's threatening to break through. They want each other, but Brody is being a stubborn ass. He's working hard to win her over, but not in the way he wants her. He keeps playing the friend card, but there's too much history and feelings for there to only ever be a friendship between them.

As for Ellie, I know she loves him. I can see it in her eyes; the way she looks at him when she thinks no one is watching. Brody does the same thing. I don't know what she wants from Brody in the end, but I'm glad that they've come this far. I want them to find their way back to each other. I want us all to be together. But in order for that to happen, Brody needs to get his head out of his ass and fight for her the way he needs to.

I don't think Ellie is ready for that right now though, so he has a little time. But he better realize it soon, before it's too late. I'm not going to give up hope.

Chapter Twenty-Two

ELLIE

THE PARTY IS NICE. We eat, talk, and watch the kids play. But I mostly agreed to come to be here for Jax.

His story about his mom broke me, but I tried my hardest to keep it together for him. I love that he felt comfortable enough to tell me. And the love and support between him and Brody is amazing to see.

Brody and I have a long way to go, but the more time I spend with him, the more I see the man I fell in love with years ago. I'm starting to see more of why Brody can be the way he is sometimes and it sheds a light on things that are helping me to understand him better. I didn't know the others tried so hard to hide what Brody's parents are really like. I wish they didn't; maybe I would have understood more before now.

I can tell he's remorseful with how he treated me, and I can see the changes in him. But it's not like with the others. The others are working toward winning my heart back, but he's just trying to be a friend. And I appreciate that. It's helpful with being around everyone as a group and when it comes to being parents for Lilly, but a part of me is hurt that he doesn't want me like the others do. Call me selfish, but a big part of me wants that part of my past back. Even thought he hurt me.

I guess that's not completely true. I can tell he wants more, but he's holding himself back. *Why, I'm not sure.*

Brody gets up to walk over to the cooler to grab another beer when the kids come running past him. One of them bumps into him and his ice cream cone goes flying, hitting Brody right in the middle of his shirt.

"Damn it," Brody hisses, his arms raised as he looks at the dripping mess on him.

"Sorry," the little boy says.

"My shirt is ruined," he growls, looking at his shirt. The little kid is already crying as he runs away. I don't think he meant to direct it toward the kid, but Lilly walks up to him and crosses her arms, tilting her head up, and gives him a mean mug stare.

"You made him cry!" Lilly states strongly.

Brody looks down at the little ball of sass. I feel bad for him at the moment, but Lilly is like her mama and doesn't put up with mean or rude people.

"I didn't mean to," he says, and I know he means it.

"You say sorry!"

Brody looks back at the kid crying by his mother and then to Lilly. "Fine." He lets out a frustrated sigh and takes off toward the boy. Lilly watches him, a smug as fuck grin on her face, proud of herself for making the broody man do something nice.

I smile, also proud but of my girl for sticking up for others.

Brody crouches down and the little boy peeks his head out from his mother's chest, his face red from tears. I can't hear what they are saying, but by the time Brody stands back up, the little boy has a smile on his face and runs back to the other kids. Lilly grabs the boy's hand and takes off to play again.

"I think you have a little something on your shirt," I tease Brody, giving him a grin.

"Ha ha," he mocks, but I see a smile of his own creeping onto his lips. "I can't stay in this," he grumbles, flicking some of the ice cream off. "Jax still has some of his things here in his room. I'm going to go get changed."

Brody takes off into the house while I check my phone, answering a few texts and then I check on the kids. Jax is over with his dad and a group of guys talking about football and the position he was offered on the Black Ravens. He looks happy, a big smile taking over his face as he talks about something he's so passionate about.

When we've hung out and ate lunch at school, I've heard the others talk about what they want to do after school. Chase is going to work with his dad at his dealership. His family owns Rivers' Auto, a line of dealerships and auto shops. Chase wants to run the one in Spring Meadows, but he seems more excited to work on the cars themselves than actually running the business. I know he would make a good salesman. He just has a way with words...and people.

Brody has been offered a coaching job at the university next fall. He said he didn't really have anything planned for his future and took the job because it was more than he was expecting to find. I hate that he doesn't see much within himself. He's a smart man, and I know if he put his mind to something, he could do it. But at least football is something he loves. I just wish he didn't sell himself so short. Chase has also agreed to be an assistant coach.

Rain is in school to become a children's therapist, but she also wants to go back to school next year to become a pediatric nurse. I love that she loves kids and loves working with them. She's really amazing with Lilly.

She has been trying to hold off on pressuring me, giving me the space I need, but I can tell she wants to move on from where we are in our relationship.

She's made it clear what she wants from me in the end, and I want that too. The kiss is consistently on repeat in my mind, and I find myself craving more. But I'm not going to give in until I feel like she's proven herself.

I should give her more of a chance to do that. I've been waiting for her to ask me to hang out, just the two of us, but she hasn't.

We talk a lot when we all hang out, and when we laugh together, I'm filled with a happiness I've missed so much.

We've also caught each other looking at the other a few times, always filled with longing or heat.

She's gone out with her friends a few times, gotten drunk and left a few voice mails that had me in tears, but not necessarily in a bad way. She would go on about how she hates herself for what she's done, that she loves me so much and plans on doing everything she can to get me back.

I hate what happened, and I hate how it tore us apart. Now only *I* have the power to bring us back together. But before that can fully happen, I need to know that we can't be broken so easily next time.

"Hey, you guys ready to go?" Jax asks as he comes over to me a few minutes later. "Where's Brody?" he asks, looking around.

"One of your cousins spilled ice cream on his shirt. He went inside to find a clean one of yours."

"Oh." Jax makes an amused grimace. "I'm guessing he didn't take that too well."

"Don't worry, Lilly chewed Brody out until he apologized to the kid," I laugh.

"Way to go Lilly," he chuckles.

Lilly comes running over, but skips past me and goes right to Jax. "Axe," she says as Jax lifts her up into his arms. "I sleepy." She cuddles into him, and the look on his face melts my heart.

"I'll go find Brody, and then we can take Sleeping Beauty home," I tell him, wanting to give him this moment with his daughter. He gives me a look like he appreciates it before I turn and head inside.

I make my way to Jax's room, remembering exactly where it is. We spent a lot of time here when we were kids, so much so that it became like a second home at one point.

When I get there, I see the door cracked open, and the sounds of drawers opening and closing drift through the crack. "He's got to have something," Brody mutters.

Looking in, I find a shirtless Brody crouching down in front of the closet, searching through a box. I notice something on his arm. It looks like a tattoo and it's big. My feet have a mind of their own, and I find myself walking over to him, drawn to see it up close for myself. "This will have to do," he sighs. As he stands up, I get a side view of his arm, and my eyes go wide when I see what the design is. It's a night sky with a galaxy feel to it. But what has my heart racing like a drum is the name spelt out in stars within the night sky.

"Holy shit," he says, jumping back when he notices me. "Don't sneak up on people like that."

"What is this?" I ask, ignoring his comment and pointing to the tattoo. His eyes widen slightly and he looks to his arm.

"Nothing," he grumbles, trying to turn away and cover it with the shirt.

"It's not *nothing*, Brody," I tell him, grabbing his arm to keep him from turning away from me.

He doesn't fight me as my fingers brush along the stunning artwork. "When did you get this done?" I saw him at the pool party without a shirt on, and a piece this big is not easily missed; I would have seen it.

"After I got out of lock up," he tells me. My eyes flick up to his, and my heart races a little faster seeing the intense emotion in his eyes.

"Why?" I ask, my voice barely above a whisper. He has my name on him. *My name*. And this tattoo looks like it cost a pretty penny.

"I was pissed, drunk, and had the money," he says, putting his shirt on as I let my hand drop to my side.

"But why my name? Why this design?" I press. This isn't something I'm going to just let go. This is a big deal.

He lets out a harsh sigh, his eyes blazing. "Why? Because I love you, Ellie. I've never stopped, and I hated myself for that for so long because at the time, I thought you did something that ruined us, *all* of us. But I still found myself thinking of you. All the fucking time. Every night, your face was haunting my dreams, reminding me of the person who owned my fucking heart.

"When I found out what really happened, I went on a bender to try to forget about everything, to clear my mind, but it didn't work. Drunk Brody went on and on about you, remembering how much I love you. So, I came up with a brilliant idea to get a tattoo. At the time, my mind thought *'Hey, what better way to prove to the girl you love, who you spent months making her life a living hell, than to get a tattoo of her name.'*" He huffs out a humorless laugh, taking a seat on the bed.

My mind is buzzing. I want to be mad, to tell him how dare he do something like this after the way he treated me. But as I look at him, sitting on this bed with a look of hopeless defeat, I don't find myself angry or upset. I mean enough to him to do this to his body. Drunk or not, it's still a big fucking deal.

"Why this design?" I ask again.

He looks up at me like the weight of the world is on his shoulders. "Because you're my star, my whole world. You shine the brightest, like a galaxy." He stands up, stepping into my personal space. "I've been trying my hardest to deny how I feel about you, but it's so fucking hard. I love you, Ellie, so fucking much, it hurts because I know I can't have you. The others...they deserve another chance to be with you, but me? I don't. I was a monster, and you don't treat the person you love the way I did with you. I don't even deserve to be able to call myself your friend, but I want to try because of Lilly. I might not get to have you as my lover again, but I know I *need* you in my life."

My eyes are blurry with tears. So many things are running through my mind. We're so close, and I want to reach out and grab him, pull him down to me, and kiss him.

As if he can see that for himself, he takes a step back, and it hurts me more than I thought it would.

"Friends?" he asks, taking a seat on the bed again. "If you'll have me as that?"

His mother has gotten it into his head from such a young age that he's worth nothing in this world. My heart breaks for him because despite what he did to me, I know that's not who he really is. He made bad choices, but he's not a bad person.

He's worth so much, and a life without him in it would make not only Jax and his friends crushed, but me as well. I've missed him more than words can explain. Having him back in my life, on good terms, started to settle something deep inside me that was caused from being away from them.

"That's all you want from me? Is to just be friends?" I ask, stepping up into his space until I'm standing between his parted legs. He looks up at me, his nostrils flaring like he's holding himself back from touching me. I lean forward so that my mouth is by his ear. "Because we both know that's bullshit, Brody. You want me, I know you do, you said as much yourself. You can keep telling yourself that you're not worthy of me, never have been, never will be, but you've already shown that it isn't true. You're not as bad as you make yourself out to be. Don't let monsters whisper nasty things into your ears and keep you from the people you love. It will only hurt the ones around you." I turn my head to the side slightly, just enough to leave a feather light kiss on his cheek. "You have more people on your side than you let yourself believe. Remember, Brody, you're not the only one in this equation. I have feelings too."

I stand up straight and take a step back. He looks up at me with stormy eyes, his breathing heavy, and his fists clenching. "We gotta get going. Jax is ready to go and Lilly is down for the count," I tell him before turning around and heading toward the bedroom door. "Oh, and Brody?" I ask, turning back around to look at him.

"Yeah?" he grunts.

"I haven't given up on you, so please don't give up on yourself."

At the end of the day, five people each hold a piece of my heart. Without all of them, I don't think I'll ever be whole. I don't plan on holding what happened against Brody forever, I never did. It's not who I am. Life is short, and if a person is remorseful and works to redeem themself, then I believe in second chances. Now, is Brody going to fight for his? Or will I always be missing that one part of my heart, never feeling whole again?

ELLIE

"VIP three wants another round of their last order!" Aria shouts to me over the buzz of the club.

It's St. Patrick's Day, and this place is packed to the point that we had to start turning people away. Not only is the club full, but the restaurant is as well.

I feel as if I'm running around like a chicken with its head cut off, but the crazy amount of tips I'm getting makes up for it.

"Got it," I shout back as I place the empty tray of glasses on the counter and replace it with a full tray.

I'm surprised that I'm not covered in alcohol by now with how little room I have to move.

As I start to move through the crowd, my friends pop up out of nowhere again, and start forming a circle around me. "Move it!" Val shouts. "Liquid gold coming through, handled by a sexy bitch!"

I snort a laugh, smiling so wide my face hurts. I really thought this night would suck but my friends are amazing and have been doing this all night. So, not only have I gotten my job done without the hassle of trying to weave my way through a crowd, but I get to be around my friends too. They take their dance breaks, but always seem to find me when I have big orders.

"That's right, move it, coming through!" Lexie shouts.

"You guys are crazy," I laugh when we get to VIP three.

"But you love us." Tabitha grins.

"That I do." I smile at my bestie.

"Oh, look! It's that crazy hot tattooed guy I made out with in the library the other day." Val grins. "Hey, you! Get away from him," she shouts and takes off toward the guy who's started dancing with a blonde girl.

My eyes widen and I laugh. *That's totally Val though.*

"Does she mean he's like crazy hot, or he's a hot guy who's also crazy?" Cooper asks as he watches our friend hip check the blonde girl and wrap her arms around the man. He grins down at her before diving in for a kiss.

"I'm leaning toward the second one. Cooper, come dance with me so we can keep an eye on her. She's not quite drunk, but she's getting there," Lexie says, grabbing Cooper's hand and pulling him onto the dance floor.

Shaking my head with a grin, I give the customers their drinks before finding Tabitha waiting for me where I left her. She's looking at something with heat in her eyes. I follow her line of sight and grin when I see a really hot chick eye-fucking my bestie.

"Go dance with her," I tell Tabitha.

"What?" she asks, blinking over at me. "Me?"

"Yes, you," I laugh. "Girl, she wants you."

"No, she doesn't," she laughs nervously before flicking her eyes back over to the girl who's still watching her.

"Yeah, she does. Go," I encourage her.

"She is really pretty," Tabitha comments. "Should I?"

"Yes!" I giggle.

"Alright, here goes nothing," she says before taking off.

Letting my friends do their thing, I head back over to the bar to see where else I'm needed. "VIP one has requested you." Aria smiles, giving me a knowing look. "There's a blond football player who's very insistent that it be you who serves them."

"Gotcha," I laugh and take off toward VIP one. When I get there, I stand back and watch for a moment, no one noticing my presence just yet. Jax and Brody are talking, their faces close to each other. A smile takes over Jax's face as Brody runs his hand up and down Jax's thigh before pulling Jax's legs over his lap. Rain tosses her head back while letting out a musical laugh, her red hair wild just like her. Chase is pouting, glaring at her like he's the butt of her laughter.

"Hello," I greet them in a friendly and playful tone. "What can I get for you all tonight?"

They all turn to me, their faces all lighting up in different ways that has my pulse racing, but I keep my smile in place.

"There she is," Chase says, getting up from his seat. "My girl." He pulls me into his arms and kisses me. My head spins, my knees are weak, and there's a fire in my lower belly whenever one of them touches me.

"Chase," I breathe, pulling back from the kiss. "Later," I tell him, knowing that once we start, it's hard to stop.

He pouts, but lets me go. "Fine."

Jax gets up and comes over. "Hey, pretty girl," Jax greets, giving me a kiss on the cheek, but the look in his eye tells me he wants to do so much more.

"Hi." I smile, then look at the others. "What can I start you off with?"

"I'll have a beer, my fine lady," Chase says, giving me a wink. I grin, shaking my head.

"I'll have a vodka and Sprite," Jax says, sitting back down next to Brody.

"And you?" I ask, locking eyes with Rain. She bites her lip, her eyes trailing down my body. I'm in the themed work uniform they made us all wear. It's a green, strapless tube top with gold, glittery, booty shorts. On the top it says *'Kiss me, I'm Irish.'*

"I'll have you...if you're on the menu," she says, her voice filled with hunger. My cheeks burn, and I have to resist the urge to squirm under her greedy eyes.

"Don't mind her. She had a few drinks before we came here. She was a little nervous to be back here after everything. Don't worry, I'll make sure to keep the horny bitches' paws off her on the dance floor," Chase says, giving me a smug smile. A feeling of possessiveness flares inside me at the idea of another girl touching Rain.

"Chase," Rain growls, glaring at her bestie.

"What? It's true," Chase defends himself.

"She doesn't have to worry about that anyways because the only person I wanna dance with is the sexy as fuck goddess standing before us," she tells Chase before looking back at me with lust filled eyes. "But since you're not an option at the moment, I'll take a rum and Coke, please."

She leans back, her gold dress rising as she crosses her legs. My eyes follow the movement, taking in her long legs. I've always loved them, especially how soft and smooth they were when my face was between them.

"Nori," Rain says, her voice thick with want.

My eyes snap up to hers, and I feel the blush all over my body. Knowing I can't recover from that, because the look on her face tells me she knows exactly what I was thinking, I turn to Brody. "And what can I get you?"

"Just a soda, please," he says. "No alcohol."

Not drinking? That's the first that I've not seen it in a while.

"B-man, here, has decided to get clean," Chase says.

"Just because I don't feel like drinking anymore doesn't mean shit. I'm not addicted, you asshole," he snaps at Chase.

"Sure, keep telling yourself that, dude. But remember, the first step is admitting you have a problem."

"Chase," Jax warns, anger filling his eyes in defense of his boyfriend.

"No problem," I tell Brody with a smile, trying to play off the moment. "Anything to eat?" I ask, then turn to Rain. "I think you should eat something if you're going to keep drinking."

"Aw, worried about me?" Rain purrs, and my eyes widen at how that sounded.

"Sorry, I didn't mean to tell you what to do. I just don't want you to get sick or anything."

"No, it's okay," she replies, moving to lean forward and resting her forearms on her thighs, making her breasts push forward. "I like that you care. I'll take an order of fries"

My eyes linger too long, making Chase chuckle. "Right. An order of thighs." I shake my head, horrified by my flustered mind. "I mean fries. I'll go get your drinks," I say, groaning as I rush out of there like a bat out of hell, hearing Chase cackling behind me. *Fucking asshole.*

But damn, they all look so good tonight. Since we all found ourselves in a good spot, I can't help but allow myself to open up my mind to other thoughts about them.

Thankfully, because their order isn't big, I don't have to worry about spilling a large tray. When everything is ready, I bring it back to their section only to find it two people short.

"Rain loved the song that was playing so she dragged Chase out onto the dance floor," Jax says, breaking apart from his heated make out session with Brody. My eyes can't help but find the two very large erections they are sporting. Biting my lip, I look back up. Both of them have heated looks in their eyes. I'm not sure if it's from what they were just doing, or the fact that I'm enjoying what I'm seeing. Maybe both?

Turning to look out into the crowd, I find my friends. Tabitha is still dancing with the girl from earlier, but it looks more like sex on the dance floor. Good for her. I'm glad she's enjoying herself.

Lexie isn't dancing with Cooper anymore since they both found dance partners of their own. Val is still with the tattooed guy, but another guy who could pass as his twin has her sandwiched between them, and she looks like she's in heaven.

A flash of platinum white hair catches my attention. Chase stands out in the crowd making it easy to find him dancing with Rain who has her eyes closed, swaying to the music without a care in the world and a smile on her face. That's when I see stupid Laura heading toward her and my blood starts to boil. My eyes widen, and I choke on a laugh as I watch Chase booty bump her out of the way, sending her flying on her ass as he plays it off like he was just dancing. Hard to do when afterwards, he yells down at her, "Not today, Satan!"

Laura gets off the ground and starts yelling at Chase. He ignores her, pulling Rain into his arms and starts to grind on her. Laura lets out an angry shriek, stomps her foot, and takes off into the crowd.

"You know, he doesn't have to be out there watching her. Drunk or not, she wouldn't dance with anyone that wasn't her friend. She really does love you. We all do," Jax says, turning his gaze to Brody with the last part.

He just glares at him before looking out to the crowd.

"I'm starting to see that," I say, smiling when I lock eyes on Chase and Rain. Rain is laughing with her eyes closed and head tossed back as Chase twerks. I love seeing them so carefree with each other.

"I should get back to work," I tell them, getting closer and leaning down to kiss Jax. I kiss him slowly, loving the feeling of his warm lips against mine. A low growl leaves Brody's chest, and I break the kiss, raising a brow at him. "Jealous?" I ask with amusement.

"Oh, he is, baby girl. But not of you kissing me, more like the other way around." Jax's chuckle is low and husky. I need to get out of here.

With one last lingering look at Brody, I say goodbye before heading back to the bar.

For the next hour, I take orders to tables, mostly the VIP sections. Rain and the guys have stayed in their spot for the most part, and I feel a bit of relief when I see Chase making sure Rain is eating and drinking water.

"Hey," Aria says as I put in an order for a table. "Why don't you give me that, and take the rest of the night off?"

"Really?" I ask, looking over to see my friends are still here at their own table, then over in the direction of the VIP section.

"Yes, you only have what, half an hour left? Go, have fun with your friends and those lovers of yours," she says, giving me a wink. "God knows you deserve to let loose and have some fun with everything that's been going on in your life."

She does have a point. I start to get excited about the idea of being able to just dance and hang out with them.

"You're amazing, you know that? I totally owe you!" I holler, blowing her a kiss before taking off through the crowd, heading for the staff room.

"Hey," someone says, stepping in front of me just as I break free of the crowd and pass the bathrooms on this side of the club.

"Oh, hi?" I say, looking up at a tall man with black hair. His eyes are bloodshot and red. I'm not sure if it's because he's drunk or something else.

"I've been watching you tonight, running around here all sexy and flustered," he says, taking a step toward me, and I step back. *What a creep.*

"Look, I gotta get past you. I'm still on the clock," I tell him, giving him a forced smile. "My co-worker is waiting for me to help her with some tables," I lie. I don't want to be here right now, talking to him. My heart starts to race faster the longer he doesn't move out of the way.

"Come dance with me." He reaches out to touch me, but I move my hand out of the way. "Just one dance. You can't prance around here looking like that and leave a man like me hanging."

"I'm sorry, but I'm working. I can't." *Please leave me alone. God, just make him take a hint.* I haven't been triggered in a while, but being this close to a man who doesn't seem to know how to take no for an answer is making me start to panic.

"Don't be a tease." He grabs my arm, pulling me toward him. My fight or flight instinct kicks in. And just as I'm about to start swinging and scream for help, someone grabs his wrist.

"Don't fucking touch her!" Brody roars, making the man let go of me. Brody bends his arm back at an awkward angle, making the creep scream out in pain as Brody brings his other hand up, and punches him in the nose. I hear a crunch and blood starts gushing down his face. Brody then grabs him by the throat and throws him against the wall, holding the guy in place by his throat.

I watch, eyes wide with shock and my heart pounding in my chest.

"How fucking dare you put your fucking hands on my girl," he snarls, getting into the man's face. He's breathing like a mad man, his eyes wild with fury. "I should fucking kill you." Brody's grip is so tight around the man's throat that he's starting to turn blue.

"Brody!" I shout, snapping out of my frozen state. I grab a hold of his arm, trying to pull him off the guy, but it's no use. Brody is a football player and is as solid as a rock.

"No," he growls. "He touched you. You said no, and he fucking touched you."

"I know," I agree in a tone as calm as I can muster. "But look, I'm fine," I urge him. His eyes flick over to mine, and I have to suppress a gasp as I lock eyes with a black void. The whites of his eyes are practically gone. He looks at me for a beat before looking down at my arm where the guy grabbed it.

A feral growl rumbles deep in his chest, making me look at my arm. "Fuck," I breathe, seeing the red hand print.

Brody lets out a roar before bringing his hand back and punching the creep in the jaw.

"Brody!" I shout.

He's about to take another shot at him when Jax comes out of nowhere and grabs a hold of his arm mid air.

"Enough!" Jax booms, momentarily stunning Brody long enough for Jax to be able to pull him away from the man. The creep drops to his knees into a coughing fit. He doesn't get away though because Chase shows up, grabbing the guy by the arm.

"He fucking put his hands on her!" Brody shouts at Jax.

"What?" Chase growls, looking at the man in his arms, to me, then my arm, and then back to the guy.

"She said no. And he didn't take that as an answer," Brody says.

"Are you okay?" Chase asks.

"Yes, I'm fine." *Thanks to Brody.*

"I'm gonna take this fucker to security. I'll be back." Chase grabs the guy, twisting his arm behind his back and starts to push him into the crowd.

I turn back, my body shaking with adrenaline. I'm proud of myself that I didn't fully freak out and break down.

Jax is wrestling with Brody, trying to hold him back from going after them. "Brody, you need to calm down. You're gonna get yourself arrested again."

"I don't fucking care," he spits. "I wanna kill him for putting his hands on her."

"Enough," Jax barks.

"Brody." His eyes snap over to mine. He looks like a beast trying to get loose. "I'm fine. I'm okay. You saved me...again." I take a few steps closer, moving slowly like I'm approaching a wild animal because that's what he seems like at this moment.

I reach up, gliding my fingers through his brown locks. "I'm fine," I say in a calming tone. He's breathing heavily, but he stops fighting Jax. "I'm okay." Jax moves to the side, giving me more access to Brody, but not much in case Brody tries to take off.

His eyes start to return to their normal golden brown. My hands slide up to cup his cheek. "Thank you," I tell him, "for being my dark knight." I don't hesitate as I lean up and place my lips on his.

I'm not sure what comes over me. Maybe it's the intensity of the moment or the fact that once again, this man has saved me from being attacked by a man who tried to take what's not his. Whatever the reason, I have a need to show my appreciation for what he has done for me.

He releases a pained moan before his hand finds the back of my head. He tangles his fingers into my hair, kissing me with everything he has. But he doesn't hold me to him, his touch is more gentle than I would have thought after what just happened.

Pressing my body against his, I wrap my arms around his neck, my tongue running along the seam of his lips, looking for more.

He opens and our tongues clash together. We both moan, but his hold on me stays gentle as if he wants me to know I can get away whenever I want.

We kiss like no one is around until his body is no longer shaking with anger.

When I feel like he won't go taking off to finish the creep off, I break the kiss. We're both breathing hard, our breaths coming out in heavy pants.

"You good?" Jax asks, a grin taking over his lips.

"Yeah," Brody grunts, his eyes never moving from me.

"I don't want you getting arrested, okay? Promise me you won't do something that takes you away from us," I say.

He doesn't say anything for a moment before answering. "Fine," is all he huffs out.

I turn to Jax, giving him a look that tells him to keep an eye on Brody. "Go find Rain. Dance a little," Jax says. "Aria told us you were getting off work to hang out with us. Don't let a bastard like him ruin your night. We'll find you soon; just give me some time with him."

"Yeah." I nod, letting out a breath. That kiss did far more good for my state of mind in this moment than I want to admit. Not only did Brody keep someone from possibly assaulting me, but he was also able to bring me back from a triggering moment. I look back at Brody, the taste of him lingering on my tongue and my lips tingling from our kiss. I have no idea what this means, but I can't think about that right now. I just know I enjoyed it a lot. "Thank you," I tell him again before turning around and heading over to find Rain.

My brain is still trying to wrap around what just happened.

"Ellie!" Lexie shouts, and I look over to find her and Cooper on the dance floor.

"Hey!" I shout back over the music. "Where are the others?"

"Rain said Val went to rest in their VIP spot, and Tabby went with her. I'm glad because I don't want to play babysitter again tonight."

"And you shouldn't have to. You're just a really good friend, babe."

"So are you!" She smiles. "Dance with us?"

I laugh, and Lexie and I sandwich Cooper between us. We probably look silly, but who cares? We dance for a few songs before someone taps me on the shoulder. Turning around, I find Rain. She has a glow to her, probably from all the dancing, but she looks so good.

"Wanna dance?" she asks with hopeful eyes. I smile and nod, letting her take my hand and pull me toward her. She spins me around, pulling my back against her. She puts her hands on my hips, and we start to dance to *Don't Stop The Music* by Rihanna.

She moves my hips, grinding me into her. A flush takes over my body while heat grows in my lower belly. Her hands are all over me, and I don't mind at all. I love her touch, crave it, and when her lips meet the back of my neck, I can't help the breathy moan that slips past my lips.

"I love you," she murmurs into my neck. "It's been complete and utter torture seeing you everyday, being inches away from you, and never being able to touch you." She leaves an open-mouthed kiss on my neck, and I tilt my head to the side, giving her better access as I close my eyes. "But I deserve it," she tells me. "I deserve all the torture in the world for what I did to you."

I move, turning around so that we are facing each other. Wrapping my arms around her neck, I put my mouth to her ear. "I forgive you," I tell her, and I know deep in my heart, I do. It hurts more not having her in my life than it does keeping her at arm's length. She's stuck up for me on more than one occasion, spent the past few months getting to know me again, and I've loved seeing the real Rain shine bright. I know she's sorry. I know she hates herself, and I don't want her to hurt anymore.

Her arms tighten around me, and I feel her body jerk with sobs. My eyes tear up as we hold each other, no longer dancing. She cries, telling me how much she loves me, how sorry she is and that she promises never to fail me again. My heart does funny things as we move from one step to the next in our path toward the end goal of getting back together.

When she calms down, I move back to look into her eyes, finding them tear stained.

I reach up and brush a stray tear from her cheek before grabbing her hand and leading her to the VIP area so that we don't have to shout over the music for this next part. We don't go in but stand just outside so that my friends don't hear.

"Can we start over? Start anew? I wanna go on dates, hang out, just the two of us. I don't need to fall in love with you again, Rain. Because I never stopped, but I want to get to know each other again. You and me."

"Yes," she says, smiling so wide my heart does a flip. "I'd love that."

"Rain," I tell her, leaning up so that I can brush my lips against hers. "I'm sorry your heart hurt for so long, but I hope we can heal it together." I kiss her, and my body ignites like fireworks exploding in the sky. She kisses me back with just as much passion, our mouths in a battle as we try to chase all the moments we missed with this one kiss.

I don't know what's going to happen tomorrow, or the next day, but what I do know is that I want to take on every new adventure with the people who own my heart at my side.

Chapter Twenty-Three

THEO

"SWEET GIRL, YOU NEED TO BREATHE," I tell Ellie as I rub my hands up and down her arms. She nods, taking a few deep breaths, but I know she's feeling anxious about being here. Her eyes aren't even on me; they're looking over my shoulder, scanning the area like a hawk.

Lilly is in the car with Toby, both of them starting to go stir crazy while everyone is checking out the area to make sure nothing is odd or suspicious.

"Can't we just ask everyone to leave?" she asks, looking at the kids playing on the playground.

I chuckle. "No, love, we can't. It's a public place. But everything is going to be fine. Your friends, Rain, and the guys are all out there making sure everything is good."

As soon as those words leave my lips, Cooper pulls up with the girls in the car and Brody pulls up with Rain, Chase, and Jax.

"Everything is good to go," Chase says as he gets out of the car, closing the door behind him and making his way over here.

"But what if someone was waiting until you left, and now they're there?" Ellie asks, biting the side of her thumb. I take her hand and pull it away from her mouth, then bring it up to mine to place a kiss on the back.

239

"Ellie, someone will always have an eye on Lilly, and be right behind her while others watch the whole park. Everything is going to be fine."

"Okay," she breathes. "Let's do this before I go crazy about it."

"Wait, this isn't you crazy?" Rain asks, giving her a playful grin. Ellie smiles, her shoulders relaxing. Rain steps up to her and cups her face, brushing her nose against Ellie's. "We won't let anything happen to her, Nori. Promise." She kisses Ellie, making Ellie melt into her touch.

It should bother me, seeing my girlfriend with other people like this, but it doesn't because with each person she adds, it's like a part of her heart is being put back together. How can I be mad when she's so happy and keeps getting happier by the day? Also, all of us together have been doing a good job at keeping her distracted from thinking about Tim and the trial coming up. Spring break starts Friday, and she will have a full week off from school.

She's going to be going out this weekend with Rain, the guys, and her friends. I suggested she needed some time to let loose.

When she told me about what happened at work the other week, I was fuming, but then she told me what Brody did, and it made me hate the guy a little less.

She also told me that her and Rain are going to be officially trying to work on their romantic relationship as well.

I'm not sure what it's going to be like later on, but right now, I'm the one who spends the most time with her. I know it's not going to stay like that, but I think it's been a big help with adjusting to each new change. One thing I know for sure is that her love for me hasn't changed any by giving her heart to more people; if anything, it's expanded.

"Are you ready to go?" Jax asks Ellie when she breaks apart from Rain.

"Yeah." She nods, but I can tell she's still unsure.

"Alright, little monkey, you ready to play?" Rain asks, opening the car door.

"Yes!" Lilly screams from the top of her lungs before launching herself out of the car and into Rain's arms. Rain laughs, spinning her around before getting her situated on her hip. Toby climbs out after her and looks at Chase. "You're still tall," he says before taking off toward the playground.

"Yeah, well, you're slow!" Chase shouts back, running after him then passing him.

"Hey!" Toby shouts and starts to run faster.

"You know, they might pick on one another, but I think they like each other." Ellie laughs as she watches them reach the playground. Chase runs up on the equipment, and the two of them start racing down the slide.

"He's like a giant child," Brody says, shaking his head with a hint of a smile.

"But it's one of the things I love about him." Ellie smiles over at him. They look at each other, a moment passing between them. I'm not sure what's going on with those two, but I already feel the shift in their relationship and I have a feeling it's headed in a good direction.

She hasn't mentioned anything about Brody becoming a part of the equation yet, so I don't think they've made it as far as the others.

"Ellie!" Val shouts from across the playground, waving her arms. "All clear over here. No creepy men looking to kidnap any kids!"

"Oh my god," Ellie groans. "Come on, we better get over there before someone calls the cops." Rain giggles, taking Ellie's hand. Ellie looks over at me. "You coming?"

"Yeah, I wanna talk to Brody for a moment, I'll be right there," I tell her, placing a kiss on the top of her head. She looks from me to Brody before nodding and taking off with Rain and Lilly.

"I'll go make sure Chase gives the poor kid a chance," Jax says, kissing Brody on the lips before running in the direction of the playground. He stops long enough to kiss Ellie real quick, then continues over to Chase and Toby.

"They're gonna have to talk with Lilly soon," Brody says, watching his boyfriend leave. "They're spending more time with Ellie as her boyfriends. It's gonna get confusing."

"I think Lilly will surprise you with how she feels about all of these new people in her life. I've seen her observing sometimes, but she hasn't said anything. I think she just likes seeing her mother happy," I tell him.

He nods. "So, what did you want to talk to me about?" he grumbles.

"I want to thank you. Ellie told me what you did for her the night of St. Patrick's Day."

"He touched her, and he would have died for it if Jax didn't pull me off of him," he growls.

"Thank you for caring enough about her to protect her."

He steps closer to me. "Of course I would. You think I'd just let her be assaulted? I would never stand by and let that happen to anyone, but with her? It's not even a question," he seethes. I can see it in his eyes that he wanted to add 'not like before' but he stopped himself.

"I didn't say you would," I tell him, cocking a brow. *Am I trying to get him worked up?* Maybe just a little. He's being stupid, for what ever reason. And he may be thinking that by keeping himself from Ellie in a romantic way, he is helping because he's not good enough, but it's only hurting her.

"I know you don't like me. That you think I'm some piece of shit. But Ellie is with my best friends. They are the parents of her child. I'm not going anywhere," he says, crossing his arms and jutting his chin out.

Now I'm getting annoyed. "Don't put words into my mouth. I've never said I hated you. Are you my favorite person? Fuck no." I scoff a laugh. "You hurt my girl, pretty fucking bad. I'll admit, at the time, I wanted to smash your pretty boy face in. But things are different now. It's not me you have to impress; it's not me you have to prove yourself to. If Ellie is okay with you, then so am I."

"I don't get it," he says, narrowing his eyes. "How are you okay with all of this? Your girlfriend is in love and dating multiple people."

"How were you okay with it?" I ask.

"She's Ellie," he shrugs. "She loved my friends, but she loved me just the same. I couldn't imagine my life without her. So I would rather share her with the people I love than not have her at all. She makes everything better."

"And there you have it." I grin. "I'd rather have her in my life than not. Meaning, I'll do whatever I can to make this unique dynamic work. Some may think I'm crazy to go along with all this with a girl I just met seven months ago, but I see a strong, amazing woman with so much love in her heart. Why keep her to myself when she can do so much good with the others who she loves? If anything, it would hurt more to see her unhappy by keeping her from them, or making her choose. So I chose, and I *chose* her. I choose to love her, be there for her, and take care of her the best I can because she does the same for me. Loving you guys hasn't made her love me any less."

"You're a weird man, you know that?" Brody says. "But I'm glad she has you. You're good for her."

"If I'm weird for being okay with all this, then so are you," I chuckle.

"Well, I'm not part of that," he says. "She has all of you. She will be fine without me."

"Look, man, life's short. You made some mistakes, but you've been doing the right thing by making up for them. No one is perfect. But you need to stop punishing yourself because you're only going to end up hurting yourself and the ones around you. You love her. I'm not stupid, none of them are. We all see it. Now, you just need to get over whatever is keeping you from her, because she loves you too." I don't know if I just over stepped by telling him that, but it's not hard for anyone to see it by the way they look at each other.

He doesn't say anything, just stares at me like he wants to tell me off or punch me. *Speaking of punching...*

"Also, this is the second time you've gotten yourself into some sort of fight, as far as I know. You need to be careful or you're going to end up in a heap more trouble than you already are. They can spin what you did to Tim as a form of defense, but if you keep throwing hands, you're not going to be credible in the court's eyes."

"You just want me to sit by while people make homophobic jokes or assault Ellie?" Brody says through gritted teeth.

"No, just be smarter with how you handle it. Also, make sure there are no witnesses." I smirk before turning around and heading toward the park to catch up with the others.

ELLIE

"Lilly, baby, don't go over there!" I shout, starting to panic as I watch Lilly head to the outside of the sand box next to the open field.

"Relax, Nori," Rain says, wrapping her arms around me from behind. She kisses my neck, and I melt into her touch. "Look." A second later, Jax and Chase are both standing next to Lilly. They sit down on the edge and start to play with the sand toys we brought. "We've got this. We're all working as a team okay?"

After about ten minutes of me following Lilly around everywhere, she stopped, turned around, looked up at me, and with all the sass she could muster, she said, "Mama, chill!" Then turned and ran after Toby and Chase.

It was then I realized I was hovering so much that I was keeping her from having fun. So I've been watching while she has the time of her life with everyone, and I don't mind. Watching her like this has helped ease my worries a little.

"Also, there's like no one else here but us now," Rain says. "Val has pretty much scared everyone away." She chuckles.

Looking over my shoulder, I see Val sitting at a bench talking to a woman who has a small toddler with her in a stroller. I can't hear what she's saying, but I can see her lips moving a mile a minute. The woman looks extremely uncomfortable, and I don't know if I should feel sorry or laugh. A few moments later, the woman gets up and takes off with her child. Val watches them leave before getting up and heading over here with the biggest smile on her face.

"Alright, that was the last one," Val says, looking proud of herself.

"Did you really go up to every stranger here with their kids and talk their ear off until they left?" Rain asks, cocking a brow.

"Yeah, I did," Val says, lifting her chin. "Ellie said she would feel better if it was just us here, so I made it happen."

"Val, babe, I was kidding." *Well, not really.* "But I love you so damn much for doing that." I really do have the best friends a girl could ever ask for.

"Anything for you, boo," she says, blowing me a kiss. "I mean, my mother always said I have the gift of gab; I thought I'd put it to good use."

"Thank you," I laugh.

"Alright, off to get some play time with the little lady. Those boys have been playing with her long enough. Auntie Val needs some loving." She takes off over to the guys who are making a sandcastle with Lilly. But instead of making them leave, she sits and plays with them too.

Looking around, I see that Theo, Brody, and Cooper are the only ones keeping an eye out at the moment, but they have pretty much the whole place under watch.

I leave Lexie and Tabitha on the swings with Toby as they have a contest to see who can go the highest.

Lilly giggles then cheers, and I look over to see her wrap her arms around Jax's neck, hugging him, then doing the same to

Chase. "Look, Axe, look, Ace. It's so big!" she says, looking proud of the sandcastle.

"I shouldn't have waited so long to bring her back to the park," I tell Rain, turning to look at her. "She loves the park, and look at her, she's never been so happy." My eyes start to water and a tear slips free.

"Hey," she tells me, cupping my face. "You are an amazing mom. Something horrible happened, and you reacted out of love for your child. No one expected you to just go on like nothing happened. But look at you now." She smiles, wiping the tears away with her thumb. "You're trying. You realized it was time to try to get Lilly's life back to normal, and that's what matters. I'm so proud of you, baby." I love this woman so damn much. The weight that's been lifted off my shoulders now that we're in a good place feels amazing.

"I love you," I tell her, giving her a watery smile.

Her own eyes flash with emotion, and she bites her bottom lip before answering me, "I love you too, Nori. So fucking much." She tries to apologize again for how she treated me; she does it every moment she gets. I could tell her she doesn't need to tell me so much, but she needs to say it as much as I need to hear it, at least for now.

She leans in, kissing my tears before kissing me, but it's short lived.

"Fire!" Lilly shouts.

We break apart, and turn to see Lilly standing there with a confused look on her face. "You kissed Mama!"

"Oh boy," Rain says, looking at me with panicked eyes.

We've never talked about what we would tell Lilly and have been keeping the PDA to when she's not looking.

"Well, who's ready to have this talk with Lilly?" I laugh nervously as the others all start to head over, hearing Lilly's outburst. "Bug, can we go sit down on the bench and talk?" I ask, holding my hand out to her.

"So, you know how Theo is Mama's boyfriend, right?" I ask

her, her bright blue eyes wide with wonder. She nods. "Well, so are Chase and Jax."

"They are?" she asks, her eyes getting even wider as she looks at the two. "You love my mama?"

"Very much," Jax tells her, crouching down next to her.

"More than she will ever know," Chase tells her, picking her up and placing her on his lap.

"And Fire? Fire your boyfriend too?" she asks, looking back at me. We all laugh.

"No love, she's..." I look up at Rain. We're not officially a thing at the moment, but wanting to get to know each other a little better before we start to label anything. "She loves Mama like the others."

"Is Broody too?" she asks, looking at Brody.

My heart hurts to say these next words, but I won't lie to her. "No, baby, he's one of my best friends."

She glares at Brody before wiggling down from Chase's lap to stalk over to him. Crossing her arms she says, "Be mama boyfriend too!" Chase snorts a laugh.

Brody looks at her in shock. "Ahh." He looks over at us.

"Now!" she demands.

"Alright there, little sassy one, let's go play some more before we have to leave," Jax says, scooping her up and racing off into the playground.

"Alright. I think she took that wonderfully," Val says from her spot close by. "But hey, meathead, the little monkey has a point," Val says, cocking a brow at him as she gives him a once over.

Brody says nothing, his jaw ticking before looking at me. Why does he work so hard to deny things? I can see it in his eyes at this very moment. He loves me. Why can't he just let himself be *with* me?

Chapter Twenty-Four

ELLIE

SPRING BREAK IS HERE, and I don't think I've been more relieved for some time off of school. It's going to be a busy week, but I'm so excited.

"So, what do you wanna do for the first day of break?" Theo asks, wrapping his arms around me from behind.

"What about moving in with you?" I laugh. "I feel like I spend more time here than at my own apartment."

His body tenses, his lips hovering over my neck, and his warm breath makes my skin pebble. "Really?" he asks.

Biting the inside of my cheek, I wonder if I should try to play this off as a joke, but I'd be lying if I said I haven't thought about asking him if we could move in together. I just never wanted to impose on him; he already does so much.

Turning in his arms, I tilt my head up to look at him. "Do you want me to?" I ask, my belly doing a little flip, hoping he doesn't reject the idea.

A grin slips across his handsome face. "You wanna know if I'm okay with having the love of my life living with me? Knowing that every night, you'll fall asleep next to me and that I'll wake up with you still there? Ellie, I've been wanting to have you move in for a while now, but because of how life has been with all the new changes, I didn't want to add more."

"So, we're doing this?" I smile, an excited feeling washing over me. "Lilly and I are moving in?"

"I think it would be an excellent idea. Why pay rent and bills there when you're always over here anyways?"

"You do know I'll be paying half of everything here, right?" I ask, cocking a brow. If he thinks that we're going to move in here and not help at all, he's got another thing coming.

He lets out a playful dramatic sigh. "I know." He rolls his eyes before smirking. "Even though I'm more than fine with paying everything myself like nothing has changed, I know you're not. But it does make me feel better that you are saving half. That way, if you need time off for anything, you don't have to worry as much about missing work."

He does have a point. I may only be working four days a week, but with school and Lilly on top of everything else, it's a lot.

"But what about Chase and the others?" he asks.

"Well, it's not like they come over here much anyways. When we meet up with Lilly, it's normally outside somewhere. Plus, we can always go over there to visit."

"They are welcome here too, you know. They aren't as bad as they used to be, I'm starting to see their appeal."

"They have changed a lot. I'm glad. It wasn't just what they did to me that hurt, it was seeing the people who I loved so much being capable of being so cruel to someone they claimed to love at one point."

"Hey," he says, cupping my cheek. "They're not that way anymore now, are they? Haven't they shown you that they regret it, that they were wrong?"

"Yeah." I can't help but smile. "They have. Even Brody. Although he's not after the same things the others are," I tell him. I feel hurt, but I know Brody has so much baggage in his mind because of his mother. But it's not going to be something he deals with on his own anymore. He's so damn stubborn.

There's no hiding that tattoo, either. *I still can't believe he got that done.*

"Do you love him?" Theo asks me.

I take a moment, already knowing the answer, but it sounds odd saying it out loud to Theo. "I do."

"And do you want him like you do the others?"

My heart starts to race faster. "I do," I say, my voice breaking a little.

"You, in no way, should feel like you have to do any of the work to get him back. He should be on his knees begging you for a second chance, but I don't think he will because in his eyes, he will never be good enough for you. So, I guess the question is, do you wanna try to make the effort to get him out of his head and show him what he could have, or do you sit around, hoping that he comes around?"

Fuck. So much to think about.

"I don't know," I breathe. "But, that's for another time. How about we take the kids to Chuck-E-Cheese to celebrate the move and maybe run off some of that energy before bed. I'd hate to leave you alone with these hyped up terrors." I giggle, watching Lilly chase after Toby like she's a monster.

"Hey, kids!" Theo calls out. They both stop and look over at us. "Wanna go to Chuck-E-Cheese?"

"Yay!" they instantly cheer and jump around.

Theo looks at me with a grin. "I think that's a yes."

We had some pizza, but the kids didn't stay still for long. After buying a bunch of tokens and giving them each their own, we set them free, but not before making them promise to stick together.

Not that I'm worried because no one is here at the moment, and we plan to leave before the dinner rush starts trickling in. Also, it helps that we can see everything from our booth. A part of me wanted to follow them because the first thing that came to mind was that someone would kidnap them, but Theo asked the girl working to let us know if anyone else came into the building. I love that he's doing all these silly, little things just to put my crazy, overactive mind at peace.

"You gotta flick your wrist," he says, stepping behind me and helping me position the basketball at the game we were playing. He does the motion and the ball sails through the air. It misses the hoop, bounces off the backboard, and goes flying onto the ground, making me jump back with a laugh.

"You sure?" I smile, raising a brow. "Didn't seem to work."

He grins, giving me a shrug. "Who knows, I heard someone say it on TV. I don't play basketball."

I shake my head and laugh some more, grabbing the ball.

We play more games, getting very competitive with each other. By the time we are ready to leave, we are both laughing so hard, my face hurts from smiling.

"I love seeing you smile," he tells me, kissing my forehead then my lips. Theo starts the car then looks back to me.

"It's easy to smile around you, Theo. With you, everything is right," I tell him as I buckle my seat belt.

We stare into each other's eyes, a million unsaid words passing between us that we've used many times before.

"You know, one of these days, you're going to have to come out with us," I tell him as we take off from the parking lot.

"Umm, love, no one wants to party with me. I'm a teacher," he says, looking over at me like I'm crazy.

"A *sexy* teacher," I say, giving him, what I hope, is a sexy smile. Lowering my voice, I say, "Don't you want to get all hot and sweaty with me, Sir? You can hold me from behind while we dance."

His eyes flash with hunger before looking back to the road. A little growl slips from deep within his chest, and my lower belly heats with want. It's been a few days since we've had a moment alone, and I can't wait until we can celebrate just the two of us.

"You have no idea what you do to me," he says, his knuckles turning white as he grips the steering wheel.

My eyes trail down his body, stopping at his lap where he tries to hide his erection. "I think I have a good idea," I say, trying not to giggle.

"You're gonna get that sexy ass of yours slapped soon if you keep that up," he warns, and my body tingles with excitement. A part of me wishes we could go put the kids to bed so I can take him up on his offer, but I'm going out with Rain and the guys.

They said normally they take a trip to somewhere tropical, but because that's not an option for me, at least not this year, they want to stay close and use this time to hang out with Lilly and me. At least where we live it isn't cold, and we can still go to the beach. Tonight, we're kicking off Spring break by going to a party. I'm a little nervous because the last one didn't go so well, but this time I have everyone around me. Plus, I'll feel better knowing Tim isn't allowed out of his house. That is a *huge* plus.

"Mama, you bad?" Lilly asks. "You get bum taps?"

My eyes go wide, and I choke on a shocked laugh. Theo turns to me with a look much like mine.

"Daddy, what did Ellie do? I thought we don't do spankings. It's mean. You might make her cry," Toby rambles.

"No make mama cry!" Lilly shouts.

"Kids, it's fine. No one is gonna get a spanking. Mama is sorry, right, Ellie?" Theo looks at me, grinning like he loves this.

"Right. I'm so sorry. Please, don't spank me." I bite my lip, giving him a bratty smile.

We get back home and I get out, making my way around to Lilly's side to get her when Theo gets out as well. As I'm about to open the door, his hand cracks across my ass.

I gasp, turning to him with a shocked expression, but he's

already going to Toby's side with a pleased and smug as fuck smirk.

"Oh, you're gonna be the one paying for that later," I warn him.

"Bring it on, baby." He winks. Fuck, this man makes my panties melt right off.

"Hey, baby," Chase says as he opens the door to the guys' apartment. He closes the door behind me before lifting me up by my thighs, making me wrap my arms around his neck as he picks me up. I lock my legs around his waist and smile, raising a brow at his hardening cock against my core.

"What can I say, one look at you and I'm fucking hard as stone, baby girl," he says, his voice husky while his peppermint scent envelopes me with each of his words. He invades my space and growls as he pushes me back against the door, rolling his hips into me. A little moan slips past my lips, making his chest rumble with a groan as his lips meet mine. He kisses me like a starved man until my lips are sore, my panties are wet, and I'm very tempted to tell him that we should move this into his room.

"Alright, hornball, let the girl breathe," Rain says as she walks into the room.

Chase lets my feet drop, and he pries his lips away from mine leaving us both panting.

"Cock blocker," Chase mutters over to his best friend.

Rain just grins as she pushes him out of the way before pulling me into her arms. Her hands find my ass as her lips meet mine, and I'm sent back into a dizzying state that gives my whole body a delicious hum to sing to.

"What the fuck, Rain? So much for me being the hornball. Maybe you should let the girl breathe and stop trying to suck out her soul," Chase protests while unwrapping and shoving a new candy cane into his mouth.

Rain breaks the kiss, and I feel like I'm high. "Oh, I'd love to suck something into my mouth, but it isn't her soul. Although, by the time I'm done with her, she will feel like it left her body." Rain gives me one of the filthiest smiles, and I swear I just came.

I keep forgetting what they are like. Some things never change, and one of those things is Rain's dirty talk. I love how confident she is, and she never fails to speak her mind when it comes to how she feels about me; whether it be sweet and loving, or hot and dirty.

"You guys ready to go?" Jax asks as he leaves Brody's room, stopping in the middle of the living room. "What is going on?" he asks, looking between all of us.

"Nothing. Just turning Ellie's panties into Niagara Falls, aren't we, Ellie Belly?" He chuckles, and I blush.

"Leave her alone," Brody says as he follows after Jax. They don't look like they were getting up to anything *fun* in there, but both of them have wet hair, telling me they showered together.

"Look at her!" Chase says. "She's lighting up like a Christmas tree." He turns to me with an evil grin. "Were you wondering if they were doing dirty, *dirty* things to each other, babe? Because I can almost guarantee they were," he chuckles.

"Fuck off," Brody flips him off before coming over to me. "How are you feeling?" he asks, his voice growing softer. My heart flutters at the genuine concern on his face.

"I'll be okay." I give him a small smile. "I'll have you guys and my friends will be there too."

"We won't let anything happen to you. Only a stupid person would fuck with you now," Brody growls.

I haven't told them how Laura and Kayla haven't been listening to the order they put on the school. But they're just catty girls, and it's nothing I can't handle. I don't want to make a bigger deal out of it if I don't have to.

"I know you won't. But I don't want to think about anything bad happening. We are gonna go out and have fun. And this time, I'm *actually* gonna be hanging out, drinking, and dancing with you guys instead of finding a quiet place to read." I look at each of them, and I can see it in their eyes as they think about our past.

"It's like old times, only better," Chase says.

"I missed out on a lot of things back then, but at the time, that's what I liked and how I wanted it. Now, things are different. I enjoy going out and getting some adult time every now and then. As much as I love playing dress up and being Lilly's snack bitch, I enjoy these moments too," I laugh.

"Hey, this week, we get to be her snack bitches," Chase grins.

"But you know we're gonna love every moment of it," Rain laughs. "We can't get enough of her."

"Well, now that she knows that we're dating you, it feels like it's one step closer to her knowing who we really are to her," Chase says.

They all look at me like they are waiting for me to tell them when that will be. "I don't know if Lilly will understand. She knows that it takes a mama and a dada to make a baby. I don't know if telling her she has three more dads and another mom will confuse her or not."

Rain's face lights up when I include her as one of Lilly's mothers, and my heart hurts a little because of how she must have felt during this whole thing and where her place was.

"But, I think if we sit down and talk, see where the conversation leads, we could possibly tell her soon."

"I'm gonna be real for a moment. Theo is an amazing man, and he deserves the title Lilly has given him. It doesn't bug me that she calls him Dad, but I want that title too, you know? As much as I love being Ace, being Dada would make my world." His normally joking persona is gone, and I can see the real vulnerability in his blue eyes.

"I know how much you love her." I wrap my arms around his waist. "And she loves you too, Chase, so much. I know she will be proud to have you as her dad." I turn to the others. "She adores all of you. It's not that she won't like that you're her parents that I'm worried about, it's her being confused by it all. But we will try to explain it the best way we can. And if she doesn't understand, because even though she is a very smart little girl, she is still only four, she will still know she has all these amazing people who love her."

"Well, she loves all of us, except Brody," Chase points out. I swing my attention back to him, glaring at him for his hurtful words. I'm about to say something in defense for Brody when Rain does it for me.

"What the fuck is your problem?" Rain hisses, hitting Chase upside the head. "Brody and Lilly are doing a hell of a lot better than before. God, not everyone is a giant child like you. Some people take longer to get used to being around kids."

"Ouch," Chase groans, rubbing the back of his head. "That hurt."

"You deserved it," I tell him, pulling away from his hold. He looks at me like a hurt puppy, but he can't say things like that. It's one thing to be joking around, but not like this.

"I'll meet you in the car," Brody mutters, opening the front door and slamming it behind him.

"Way to go, Chase," Jax growls, ready to go after him.

"I'll go," I tell him, grabbing a hold of his arm lightly to stop him. Jax looks down at me, a war waging on his face, but he nods and lets me go.

Chase starts cursing behind me, saying he's sorry, but I ignore him and head after Brody.

I find him waiting in the car, sitting in the back, looking out the window with his signature broody face. Only this time, it's different.

"Hey," I say, sliding into the back seat next to him.

"Hi," he grunts, not moving to look at me.

"What Chase said...he was wrong," I state with confidence, hoping he hears me.

He turns this time. "No, he's not. I know at first I just wanted to sit back and let the others take on that role, but the more time I spend with her, seeing her fall in love with them, the more it hurts. Because as much as I know I'm not a good fit to be a father, that she would be better off without me, the fact is, I am her father. And I don't want to be like my parents. I don't want my kid to hate me."

"She doesn't hate you, Brody," I tell him, scooting closer. "She can tell you're unsure about this whole situation. She doesn't know what's really going on behind the scenes. She doesn't know that this is all new to you, being around kids, and the fact that she's the kid you didn't know about."

"You see how she is with me. She doesn't like me," he insists. I hate seeing the hurt on his face, but I know Lilly doesn't mean to make him feel like that.

"Lilly has only ever been around me and my parents. We're very upbeat and positive people. Lilly is an energetic, loves life, sees the best in everyone kind of little girl. You don't have that vibe." He gives me a dirty look that just makes me laugh. "It's true, and you know it. I mean, dude, she calls you Broody, and she's not the only one I've heard say that."

"I'm not a sweet, easily approachable person like Jax or a hyper ball of sunshine like Chase. This is who I am."

"I know it is. But I've also seen a side of you that you have yet to show her. I know you can be loving, caring, and although it's been a while, I know that face is capable of a smile."

He just glares at me harder.

"Oh, come on, Mr. Grumpy Gus, give me a smile. I know you can do it."

"No," he grumbles.

I move so that my thigh is touching his and angle my body so that it's facing him. I start to tickle him. "Come on, give me a smile. I know you can do it."

"Ellie..." he warns, but I can hear it in his voice that he's trying not to laugh.

"Oh, are you ticklish?" I grin, going for his side.

"Ellie!" He starts to laugh as he grabs me and pulls me into his lap. We both go still as I feel his very hard cock under my ass.

"I knew you could smile," I tell him, my voice low. "Try it more often. It makes me happy when you're happy."

Jax hops into the front seat and turns to look back at us. He grins, turning back around before starting up the car.

Clearing my throat, I move back to the middle seat as Chase gets into the front passenger's side and Rain gets in next to me.

We start up the music and take off for the party. My body hums with excitement and a little bit of nerves. But I know one thing is for sure. I won't let what that monster did to me ruin all the fun things life has to offer. This is my life; I have control of it, and I won't let him take another thing from me.

Chapter Twenty-Five

ELLIE

THE NIGHT HAS BEEN AMAZING SO FAR. When we got here, I found my friends right away, and they've been hanging out with us. For the most part, they all seem to be getting along. Brody, however, has made multiple comments that all boil down to 'why would a gay man be so touchy feely with me and the others?' Each time, I rolled my eyes and laughed because that's just how we are. Cooper is like one of the girls at this point.

I'm two coolers in, feeling relaxed and enjoying myself. I'm not drunk, not even tipsy, but it has helped take the edge off.

Everyone has been so sweet with wanting to make sure I feel safe and that I have a good time. Brody has been insistent on getting my drinks himself and verifying that they were unopened. But then he also stood there and made me drink the *whole* thing in front of him. He said it was so that there was no chance someone could slip anything into it. As if they would with everyone watching me like a hawk.

After the first hour, my friends broke off to find people of their own to have a little fun with, leaving me here with Rain and my guys. Now, I'm sitting on the couch between Jax and Brody while Rain dances with Cooper. I'm happy to see that my friends are starting to come around to everyone.

"Come dance with me, my sexy queen," Chase says from the dance floor, holding his hand out as *Champagne and Sunshine* by PLVTINUM and Tarro starts playing through the speakers.

His smile is all sex and dirty fun. Giving him a playful smile back, I get up and go to him, taking his hand in mine. He pulls me to him so that my back is to his front and wraps his arms around me, holding me close like he's trying to mold his body to mine.

Like he did the night of the pool party, he starts to sing against my neck. The vibrations of his words make me shiver, and goosebumps break out all over my body. I love the effect he has on me.

Closing my eyes, I put my head on his shoulder, tilting it to the side so he has better access, and I let him move us how he wants. I can feel his hardened length against my ass, and when the song says '*Rough sex on the bedroom floor,*' I roll my hips, moving my ass against his cock. He growls out the next line, and my core lights on fire. He's getting me all worked up, and he's loving it.

We dance, he sings, and it's perfect. As if I can feel eyes watching me, mine flutter open, locking with two hungry stares. Brody and Jax are watching me like I'm a little rabbit and they're the hungry wolves looking for a meal. *And that meal is me.*

My belly heats more, and with how Chase and I are moving, I'm finding it very hard to *not* rub myself against him, looking for the friction I desperately need right now.

The way they're looking at me makes me feel powerful, desired, and sexy. Brody can act like he doesn't want me all he wants, but the look on his face says otherwise.

So when *Dip It Low* by Christina Milian starts playing next, I decide to have a little fun. Moving away from Chase's hold, he stands there and watches me. I start to sing the song, looking at Jax while I do, slowly walking to him in time with the beat. When I reach him, the song says '*dip it low*' and I turn, dipping down with my ass right in front of him. I'm so glad I decided to wear shorts because the groan from the two men sends a thrill through me and makes me want to keep going.

I follow the lyrics as if they are instructions, making sure to roll my hips like fucking Shakira. When the main chorus of the song plays, I turn back to face them, continuing to sing while moving my body with the beat.

Their eyes follow my every movement as I run my hands over my body. I lean forward, and when the song says '*take him by the hair*,' I grab a fist full of Jax's hair, forcing his head closer to me and level with my tits. His eyes are wide as saucers. I sing a few more words before licking up his neck, stopping at his ear. Taking his ear lobe into my mouth, I suck on it before biting down, getting a growl from Brody and a moan from Jax. Looking over at Brody, I take Jax's lips and kiss him with everything I have.

When it's time for the chorus again, I break the kiss, and this time, I straddle Jax's lap backwards so that my back is to his chest. My ass meets his hard cock. I do what I did before with my hips, but now my ass is grinding all over Jax's thick length.

Leaning back against Jax, I grab another handful of his hair as I wrap my arm around his neck, and I continue to dance like this, my body grinding against him until the song is over.

When it is, I get up and stand before them. My body is on fire, my panties are drenched, and my nipples are so hard they could cut glass. But the only thing I want to do right now is take my man into one of those empty rooms and fuck him.

I hold my hand out to Jax and he takes it without question, getting up and standing beside me.

"Where are you going?" Brody asks, his voice husky and thick with lust.

Looking over my shoulder, I give him a sassy smirk. "You don't think I'd just leave our guy wanting, would I? What kind of girlfriend would I be?" My smirk turns evil, and Brody growls.

"You think I'd be missing that?" he says before prowling after us.

BRODY

Like fuck she was gonna take my boyfriend into a back room, get down on her knees, and suck his cock. At least, not without me there, she isn't.

Watching her dance like that, so sexy and free...fuck, my dick has never been so damn hard. The way she moved against our boyfriend, teasing him so perfectly, I've never seen anything so erotic.

Until now.

Ellie leads Jax through the house and down the hall. The rooms are normally off limits, but the party is being held by someone on the football team, so the normal rules don't apply to us.

She enters the first room that has an unlocked door, opening it and slipping inside. I follow after. My mind brings me back to a few months ago when she watched me do something very similar to what's about to happen. Only this time, *I'm* the one who gets to watch.

"Did you like the dance?" Ellie asks, brushing her hand across Jax's face, then trailing her finger down his chest. He nods, his chest heaving. He looks so sexy, all flustered and turned on. I can see his cock straining against his dark jeans, and it's taking everything in me not to rip off his black shirt and pants, bend him over on this bed, and fuck his tight ass until we're both cumming.

But I want to see her take care of him so much more. The idea of sharing Jax pleases me more than I care to admit. It's hard to keep denying shit to myself when it's blatantly obvious that I'm, at the very least, attracted to her. She's a fucking goddess, how could I not? But seeing her and Jax together like this...is mind fucking blowing and they haven't even started yet.

I step closer to him as Ellie lowers to her knees, a starved look in her eyes as she looks up at him, then straight ahead where she is eye level with his crotch. "This looks so uncomfortable," she says, looking up at him with her blue eyes. It's dark in here, but the moonlight streams through the open window, casting a light over the two of them. It's not enough, so I flick on the lamp on top of the dresser behind me.

"How about I take care of that? Would you like that?" she asks. Jax is a sub, rarely does he have a dominant bone in his gorgeous body. So her talking to him like this, he's fucking living for it.

"Yes," he croaks out then swallows thickly, his throat bobbing as he looks down at her with desperate need.

She undoes the button on his jeans, slowly pulling the zipper down. Grabbing the waist of his pants, she pulls both them and his boxers down. His cock springs free, hard and already leaking pre-cum. Her eyes stare at it like she's being offered her favorite lollipop. She wraps her small hand around his shaft, her fingers not quite touching, and gives him a few pumps. Jax groans, his eyes closing and head falling back.

My hand has a mind of his own, and I reach for his cock, needing to touch him too, but Ellie slaps my hand away, giving me a glare. *Brat.* Without looking away from me, she takes him inch by inch into her mouth. A growl slips free from my chest as I watch him disappear down her throat. She doesn't take him all in though, because he's fucking big. Not as big as me, but still big.

She lets out a little gag before pulling back, saliva dripping down her chin before taking him in again, making him curse. My cock twitches at the eagerness to take our man, to please him.

"How does she feel?" I ask Jax, my voice husky as I step up behind him and look down at her over his shoulder.

"So fucking good," he chokes out as she starts to bob her head, her pupils taking over her eyes, the bright blue almost gone.

"Is she wet?" I breathe against his neck. "Is her mouth all wet and warm? Does her tongue glide perfectly against the bottom of your cock?"

"Yes," he moans. "So fucking perfect, so wet and warm."

His breaths are coming out short and choppy as Ellie works

him over, her moans making pre-cum leak from the tip of my cock.

"Grab a handful of her hair, Jax. Get a good grip on her," I tell him. He looks down at her, and she nods her permission. With a shaky hand, he threads his fingers through her hair and grasps a good chunk of it around his fist.

"Now, fuck her mouth, Jax. Make her gag for your cock. I bet she's wet for you, fucking soaked. If you were to stick your fingers into her pretty little pussy, I bet they would be coated. Am I right, Star?" I ask her.

She moans, nodding her head as she shifts her thighs together. God, I am so turned on right now. So much so that I would not be surprised if I cum in my pants like a virgin boy.

She lets go of his cock, and I see her jaw slacken in preparation for Jax to do as I command him to do. *So damn hot.*

He pulls his hips back, letting out a shuddering moan as he thrusts into her mouth at the same time that I start to suck on his neck.

"That's it, baby, fuck your girl's mouth. Look at her choking on that thick cock," I purr in his ear, biting his lobe.

"Fuck's sake, Brody," he breathes. "With her being so fucking perfect, and your dirty talk, I don't think I'm gonna last long."

"Don't cum just yet," I tell him, my hand sliding down and over his ass. I grab a handful of his cheek, giving it a rough squeeze before a hard slap.

"God," he moans. His attention is on the girl whose pretty pink lips are wrapped around his cock. I can't help wishing it's my cock that's disappearing down her throat.

"Fuck, fuck, fuck," he chants. He's close, and how can he not be? She's looking at him with so much want, lust, and love in her eyes that it does fucked up shit to my cold heart.

"Are you close, baby?" I ask him, sticking my fingers into my mouth, getting them nice and wet.

"Yes, yes! Ellie, fuck, I'm gonna cum soon. If you don't want it, I need to pull it out," he pants. But she just grips his thighs and bobs her head, encouraging him to keep going. He moans, his hips moving faster, and he sucks in a sharp breath as I slip my finger between his cheeks, brushing the tip against his tight hole.

And just when I feel his legs shaking, his body trembling, I thrust my finger into his ass at the same time, I growl, "Cum."

And he does. He roars out with a tight grip on her hair as he shoots his load down her throat. She locks eyes with me while tears run down her face and spit drips down her chin. She does her best to swallow everything he gives her until he stills his hips, his cock still deep in Ellie's throat.

When he's done, I remove my hand, and he pulls back from her mouth. She sucks in a breath, her mascara smeared, her hair a mess, and some of Jax's cum in the corner of her lips. I've never seen anything so heavenly.

"You were such a good boy," I tell Jax, gripping the back of his head and pulling him in for a scorching kiss, tongue and all.

Then I look down at Ellie. Leaning over, I use the hand that wasn't in Jax's ass to wipe the cum from the corner of her lips before sucking it clean from my fingers, savoring the flavor of my man on my tongue. Meaning every word, I look deep into her eyes and tell her, "I've never seen a more beautiful sight."

Chapter Twenty-Six

ELLIE

THIS WAS NOT how I thought this night would go. My body is on fire. I'm so turned on that I'm ready to beg one of them to get me off, but we've been gone from the party for a while now, and someone is going to come looking for us soon if we don't get back out there.

Just as the thought pops into my head, the door opens.

"Oh, there you guys are..." I turn my head around to see Rain standing there, her green eyes blinking in surprise. She looks to the guys then down to me. A slow smile takes over her lips. "What's going on in here?"

"Ummm..." I struggle to think of something, anything, as I get up off my knees. "Nothing?" I say, not sounding convincing at all.

She laughs. "Babe, your hair is a mess, there's makeup running down your face, and your lips are swollen. Not to mention, you were just on your knees."

My hands fly to my hair. I try to fix it, running my fingers through my hair. God, I must look like a mess right now.

"Hey," Jax says, cupping my face. "You look gorgeous." Jax gives me a sweet, lingering kiss, making my heart race for a completely different reason. I can't believe I just sucked him off,

269

let him fuck my face while Brody took control, and spoke of dirty things that has my pussy weeping.

This is something I would never have done before, but since they've come back into my life, I've found myself doing a lot of things that are out of the ordinary for me. I've loved coming out of my shell and exploring.

Giving up control, especially with sex, is a big deal, so I surprised myself by agreeing when Brody told Jax to take control of my hair, my mouth, me. Something inside me knew that I was safe, that they would never force me to do something I wasn't comfortable with. And I loved every moment of it. Except for the fact that they left me wet and wanting.

"I'll meet you outside," Brody tells Jax, giving him a kiss on the lips before locking eyes with me. He doesn't say anything, but the way he's looking at me, like it's taking everything in him not to fuck me against the wall right now, makes a whimper threaten to escape my throat. He breaks eye contact and leaves the room.

"We should get out there. I'm sure Chase and the others are looking for us," I tell Jax, wiping under my eyes and inwardly groaning when I see the black makeup that came off. *I really need to find that bathroom and clean up.*

"Are you okay?" he asks, giving me a look of concern, like maybe I'm regretting what we just did.

"I'm fine," I promise him. "I just need to go to the bathroom to clean up."

"I love you," he tells me, pulling me in for a kiss.

"I love you too," I tell him. He gives me a beaming smile before turning and leaving me with Rain.

"So, have fun?" She gives me a knowing look, wiggling her eyebrows. I can see why Chase and her are the closest of the four.

"Yes." I smile. "Only now, I'm horny and have to go out there with wet panties," I mutter under my breath, walking out of the room. Rain follows me down the hall and waits outside the bathroom while I go inside.

I get to the mirror and groan at the sight of myself. I really do look like a mess. Grabbing some tissues from the box on the counter, I wet them and try to get as much of the smudged makeup off as I can. When I look less *hot mess* and more *party girl*, I get to work on my hair.

The bathroom door opens, and my eyes shoot to whoever just walked in. It's Rain, and her playful smile is gone, replaced with one that resembles Brody's before he left.

I watch her in the mirror as she locks the door, my heart kick starting. Her eyes meet mine, and she walks over to me until she's standing right behind me.

"Hi," I breathe, my voice shaky as I wait to see what she's going to do.

"Did those mean, mean boys leave you wet and wanting?" she asks me, her voice husky. She ignites the fire in my belly that had turned into a low simmer. "I would never do that," she promises. My breathing picks up, and I suck in a breath as her hands slide down my sides and over my belly. She's taller than me, not by much, but enough that I have a perfect view of her face in the mirror.

"I can't just leave you like this. It's cruel." One of her hands slips lower as the other one spreads against my belly, holding me in place. "Can I do that? Can I take the ache between your legs away?" she asks, kissing the side of my neck.

"Please," I whimper. Fuck, I need her. I need her badly. The idea of her getting me off because the guys have me all worked up makes this more erotic to me, turning me on even more.

My eyes flutter shut as she uses her fingers to undo the button on my shorts. Once she has the zipper down, she slips her hand inside, past my panties and over my pussy. I moan as her fingers play with my folds. "God, baby girl, you really are fucking drenched," she growls. She dips two fingers inside me, making my knees buckle as I suck in a gasp. But she catches me, holding me up with her arm around my waist. "Shhh. I've got you." She kisses a spot on my neck before her tongue licks and she begins sucking at the sensitive skin.

She starts to fuck me with her fingers, and it feels so, so good. When she pulls out to rub my clit, I cry out her name. "Rain," I pant.

"That's it, baby, such a good girl," she whispers against my neck. Alternating between my clit and thrusting inside me, she works me over good. I feel my orgasm building fast. It won't take me long to cum. I'm already so worked up. I'm in heaven, pure bliss.

I feel it, just out of reach. My pussy flutters around her fingers, and she instructs me, "Open your eyes, Nori. I wanna see the look in your baby blues as you cum around my fingers."

My eyes snap open, my chest heaves, and my body goes haywire. Her eyes lock with mine in the mirror, hungry and lust filled. "Rain," I moan as she uses the heel of her hand to grind my swollen bud, her fingers still moving inside me.

"That's right, say my name. Better yet, scream it," she commands and I shatter. My orgasm rips through me like a title wave.

"Rain!" I moan so loud, I wouldn't be surprised if the whole party heard me as I clench around her fingers.

"So fucking beautiful when you cum," she says as I sag back against her, my eyes still locked with hers through the mirror.

I'm breathing in short breaths, my body feeling like I ran a marathon. But she's not done with me, not yet.

Pulling her fingers from my shorts, she brings them to her mouth and sucks me clean off. *God, it's so fucking hot.*

"You taste like heaven," she moans, her eyes rolling back, and the fire in my belly is back again, ready for more. "I need to taste you," she tells me, spinning me around. "Can I?"

Is she asking what I think she's asking? I have no idea, but I'd let her do anything to me at this point, I just want her. I nod and rasp out, "Yes."

She gives me a smile that's pure sex before ripping down my shorts. I let out a shocked gasp as she picks me up and sets me on the marble counter of the sink.

"Hold on, baby, this is gonna be messy, but I'm starving, and you're the only thing that will satisfy my hunger," she growls before dropping to her knees so that her face is level with my core. She opens my thighs wider, and I shake off my flip flops, putting my feet on her shoulders.

She doesn't seem to care about them being close to her face because her mouth is on me in seconds.

"Rain," I cry out, falling back onto my forearms as she laps at my pussy, licking every inch before thrusting her tongue inside.

The sounds that leave me sound foreign to my ears as she eats me out.

I can feel my second orgasm approaching already, and then she takes my clit into her mouth as I lock my legs around her head.

But she just keeps going, fucking and licking; flicking her tongue back and forth until I'm crying out again, cumming all over her face. I'm positive I squirt, but that only has her letting out a lusty moan.

"Fuck," I groan as I lean back against the mirror. My body is covered in sweat, and I don't think I can move.

Rain gets up off the floor, her face covered in my release. She looks so fucking sexy. Her eyes are still blazed, her nipples hard against her crop top. If I had the strength, I'd pull her over to me, lift up her top and suck one into my mouth. Damn it, I really want to touch her too.

She must see the want on my face because she winks saying, "Next time. This was all about you." I shake my head back and forth before she stops my protests.

"Like I said, Nori, this was about you," Rain says firmly, grinning like she knows what I'm thinking.

"But I wanna touch you," I pout.

There's a bang on the door that makes me jump. "Open up!" someone screams frantically. That gets my body in motion. I hop off the sink, grabbing my shorts from the floor and quickly put them on while Rain moves to open the door. Just as I button them up, the door swings open wide.

A girl comes racing into the room and over to the toilet, barely making it in time before she starts heaving.

"Yeah, I think it's time to go," I tell Rain, grabbing her hand and pulling her out of the bathroom. *Moment totally ruined.*

Rain laughs behind me, and I can't help but smile too. We race through the house, back toward the living room and I bump into Chase. "There you are," he says, grabbing a hold of my shoulders to steady me. "I was looking for you. Ready to go?" he asks, then stops to take a closer look. He scans me over slowly, then looks at Rain who's grinning like the cat who got the cream. And I guess in her case, she did. That thought makes my cheeks turn bright red knowing my release is still on her face.

"You found them," Brody says, and I turn around to find him and Jax behind me.

"What did you all do?" Chase huffs. "And how come I didn't get to play?" he grumbles.

"You always get to play," Jax says. "It was our turn." Jax grins at Chase, making Chase narrow his eyes.

"And it smells like someone else got to also," Brody says, looking at Rain with a raised brow.

Smells. He can smell me on her? *For fuck's sake!*

"Yup, time to leave," I say, needing to get some fresh air and away from this awkward situation. My body is still high off everything that's happened tonight, and I feel like I could sleep a full day away.

When we get out to the car, Chase hands me my phone when we get buckled in. I check my text messages. There's some photos of Lilly and Toby playing, an adorable selfie of him and Lilly, and one of her sleeping snuggled up to the stuffed dog she loves so much.

"Let me see?" Chase asks, leaning in and looking over at the phone. "Wait a minute. That dog looks familiar."

I laugh softly, exiting out of the text message, then go to my photo album and click on the one I made with all Lilly's photos. "That's because it is." I show him the first photo I have of her pulling it out of the box, then all the other ones. With each photo she looks older and older, but she always has a big smile on her face as she holds her best friend. "It's her favorite. Just like it was mine when you gave it to me."

He looks at me with shocked eyes. "You kept it?"

I give him a small smile and nod. "Never had the heart to throw it away."

"You know, I really wanna kiss you right now, but I'd rather not know what Jax's cum tastes like," he growls in frustration.

My eyes widen, and I choke on a laugh.

"I'd rather that too," Brody says as he looks at us in the rearview mirror. "That's for Ellie and me only." He gives me a dirty smirk before looking back at the road. Jax lets out a husky chuckle and damn it, now I want them again.

"You all suck. I'm the only one who was left out," Chase sulks.

I roll my eyes, but with a smile on all our faces, Chase, Rain, and I look through baby photos of Lilly all the way home.

They drop Rain off at her dorm. She gives me a kiss goodbye and a promise to see me tomorrow.

When we get to their apartment, Chase and Jax get out. "Want me to bring you home?" Brody asks.

I stare at him for a moment and shake my head no. We already planned for me to stay the night on the couch. The couch was my idea, much to Chase's displeasure.

After we get into the apartment, I say goodnight to the guys and watch them go into their rooms. I lay there just looking at the roof for a while when a door opens. Looking over, I see Brody leaving his room and heading into Jax's.

Watching the door, I feel the urge to go in there. After everything we did tonight, I feel like something shifted in our relationship.

Debating with myself, I finally give in. I get up and quietly walk over to Jax's door. When I open it, I find Jax on his back, his chest rising and falling as he sleeps. Brody is on his back, but his head is facing Jax's. His arm is under his pillow, his hand poking out, his fingers threaded through Jax's hair.

Chewing on my bottom lip, I just stand there and watch them. They look so peaceful.

Swallowing my nerves, I move over to the bed and crawl between them. They don't move, and I remember how deep of sleepers they are. That's kind of concerning. Someone could break in and kill them in their sleep.

Wow, Ellie, that took a dark turn.

I've always been in the middle, always able to sleep through thunderstorms and car alarms. But since I had Lilly, I wake up to the smallest noise. My mom said she was the same way, that most moms are.

I wiggle down under the blanket and put my head on Jax's chest. Then I take a deep breath and relax. He smells like fresh soap with a hint of aftershave.

I'm almost asleep when I feel Brody move. He molds his body to mine, and I know he's asleep because he wouldn't do this otherwise. His mouth is close to the back of my neck, his warm breath tickling me.

"Ellie," he mumbles in his sleep, snuggling closer to me. "I love you."

My eyes fill with tears at his words, my heart both filling with joy and breaking apart at the same time. *Why can't he just admit that out loud? Then, maybe everything would be different.*

Chapter Twenty-Seven

ELLIE

MY BODY FEELS LIKE A FURNACE. Well, like I've been sleeping next to two all night. The sounds of light snores slowly wake me from my slumber. Blinking my eyes open, I'm met with two brown eyes staring at me like he's been watching me for a while now.

"Good morning," I whisper, trying not to wake up Jax, but also not wanting my morning breath to make its way over to Brody.

"Morning," he says a little louder. His voice still thick with sleep.

"Ah, I hope you don't mind that I snuck in here last night?" I ask him, searching his eyes.

"It's fine." He looks over at Jax as Jax's arm tightens around my waist, pulling my ass back against his hard cock.

Jax lets out a sigh as he grinds himself into me. I'm partly turned on by the feel of him, but I'm also biting my lips and trying to hold back my giggle. Brody cracks a smile as Jax nuzzles his face into my hair.

"He hasn't slept this well in years," Brody tells me, his eyes meeting mine again. "I think having me in here with him helps

277

with the nightmares, but I don't think he's slept all night without waking up at least once...until now."

My heart hurts for Jax. Having to see something so horrifying, then having it on repeat, haunting you while you sleep every night, having to relive it and know you can't change the outcome. It's got to be pure hell. I hate that he has to deal with that.

"You had a sleepover and I wasn't invited!" Chase's voice has me and Brody sitting up. "Next time, I wanna join," he demands, a big grin taking over his face as he dives onto the bed. I squeal, which turns into a giggle, while moving my arms up to block my face as he lands between Brody and me.

"Get the fuck off of me," Brody grumbles, pushing at Chase. Jax mutters next to us and sits up.

"Oh, Brody, is that for me?" Chase gasps, looking down at Brody's morning wood. Now that the blanket is moved out of the way, we can all clearly see it tenting his boxers. "I'm sorry, man. I'm flattered, but I don't swing that way," Chase says, staring at Brody's cock before turning to Jax. "Dude, that thing is huge. How the fuck does it fit in your ass?"

"That's it. Get the fuck out of here," Brody says, grabbing Chase and tossing him on the floor, then he grabs the blanket to cover himself up.

"Ouch!" Chase mutters, getting up off the ground.

"Is there a reason you're in here?" Brody growls at Chase. I look at Jax who's watching me with a big smile like he's over the moon to find me here. I grin back then peck a kiss on his cheek before snuggling into his side, needing his warmth. He wraps his arm around me, holding me closer to him.

"Actually, yes. My mom called and invited us over for supper tonight...*all* of us. Rain's parents are gonna be there too," Chase informs us, crawling back into the bed and cuddling up next to me so that I'm now sandwiched between Chase and Jax again.

"Whatever," Brody grumbles and gets out of the bed. He's shirtless, his cock still jutting out against his boxers. I can't help but stare as he stretches his arms over his head, his tattoo of my name on full display. "I'm going for a shower. But I'm good with what everyone else decides," he says before disappearing into Jax's bathroom.

"How about it, Ellie Belly?" Chase asks. I look away from the closed bathroom door down to Chase's bright, blue, puppy dog eyes. "You down for supper with the fam-jam? My parents really wanna meet Lilly, and they are excited to see you and meet Theo."

"Theo?" I ask. "You want him there too?"

"Well, yeah. If you're dating him, he's a part of the pack too; he's family. So is that little ball of energy of his. I like that kid. He reminds me of me at that age."

I can't help the smile that takes over my face at the fact that he called Theo and his son family. It gives me hope that this will all work out in the end. Now, I just gotta tell them I'm moving in with Theo. I mean, some day I'm sure we will all get a place together, probably after we graduate, but for now, this is for the best.

"I can ask him," I tell Chase.

"Awesome! Supper with all your boyfriends and girlfriend," Chase says, then his brows scrunch together in thought. "Jax is your boyfriend now, right? I mean, you sucked his dick."

My eyes widen. *How does he know exactly what we did?* You know what, I don't wanna know. I look over at Jax who's watching me with a nervous but hopeful look. I smile at him. "How about it? Wanna be my boyyyyyfriend?" I ask playfully.

"More than anything in this fucking world." He laughs, then dives in for a kiss. I forget all about morning breath and moan into his mouth at his touch.

"Me next," Chase says, gripping my chin and bringing my face to his. He kisses me slowly, and if I was able to get a boner, I'd have one right now.

"Is anyone home!" Rain's voice shouts from somewhere in the apartment.

Chase breaks the kiss and curses. "Why did we give her a key again?"

I giggle, and Jax chuckles as Rain makes her way into the room. "There you are. Why is everyone in here?"

"I was just inviting them to dinner tonight at my parents' place. My mom invited yours too."

Rain's eyes light up. "Really? My mom is dying to meet Lilly. I thought I was bad with the non-stop talking about her, but every time I show her photos, she never shuts up with how cute she is," Rain laughs.

"So, now that Jax is your boyfriend again too, where does that leave Rain?" Chase asks, sitting up.

"For fuck's sake, Chase, way to put someone on the spot," Jax mutters.

I look at Rain who's face slips into a panicked look like she thinks I might reject her.

"I mean, I wouldn't just do what we did in that bathroom with anyone. That's more girlfriend material," I tell Rain, giving her a grin.

"Really?" Her face lights up. She jumps onto the bed and scrambles over until she's on top of me. She starts to pepper my face in kisses. "I promise to be the best girlfriend ever. I love you." She kisses me some more, then moves back to look me in the eyes. "And I can promise more of what we did last night whenever you want it."

My body flushes, my face burns more with lust than embarrassment. I really did forget how they were when it came to us as a whole. But I love it.

I was able to keep up with four loves before, what's one more?

CHASE

I'm excited to be bringing Ellie and Lilly home to meet my parents. They've been asking me about her, and the best I've been able to do was show them videos and photos. I didn't want to pressure Ellie into bringing her by. But now that Lilly at least knows we're dating her mom, it's not too weird to start doing group things.

So, with her agreeing to come, I was over the moon. Theo also agreed, and now, I'm at my parents place waiting for them to arrive.

Jax's dad is working, so he wasn't able to make it, leaving just mine and Rain's parents here. Brody banned us from ever inviting his parents to anything, *ever*, so it's not even a thought to try and include them.

Not like our parents want to be around them anyways. They used to be friendly with Brody's dad, but as time went on, his dad's drinking became worse, as did his mother's bad behavior.

Our parents still love Brody like he's one of their own. And even though he always turns us down when we invite him home for holidays, we still do it anyway, wanting him to know he will always be a part of the family.

"Chase, honey, relax," my mom says as she sets the table.

"I can't," I tell her, not looking away from the window as I stand here, watching and waiting for Theo's or Ellie's car to pull up.

"They said they are coming, just give the poor girl time to get ready. And getting a toddler ready too is not an easy feat. It's not like she can just grab her purse and keys and race out the door," my mom says, then walks over to me and takes the candy cane I just popped into my mouth. "You're gonna spoil your dinner."

I frown then let out a sigh. "I know. I just miss them, that's all."

Rain's mom laughs as she walks in with Rain. "You just saw the girl a few hours ago."

"True, but it's been a few days since seeing Lilly. We miss our daughter," Rain says, coming over to stand next to me. We both watch like creepy stalkers. She's been on cloud nine ever since last night, but when Ellie made things official with her this morning, she won't shut up about it.

I'm not bothered by it, because I was the same way. Rain is my best friend, they all are, but Rain and I are the closest. I hated seeing her so unhappy for years. Just these few months since Rain's been back in Ellie's good graces have been the happiest she's been in years. I'm glad that when she smiles and laughs, it's not forced or faked anymore.

Also, now I have someone to obsess over Ellie with.

"You guys are going to have the neighbors worried," Jax says, walking into the dining room.

"They know we're weird. It's nothing new," I respond.

"That's sad, you know that right?" Brody comments.

I just shrug. A moment later a car pulls into the driveway. "They're here!" I say, my face splitting into a grin.

Racing to the front door, I fling it open, and run down the steps all the way over to the car. It's barely parked for a second before I'm opening the back seat. "Hi, little lady." I smile at Lilly.

"Ace!" She giggles. I unbuckle her and get her out of the car before going to the other side to unbuckle Toby. "Hey, little dude."

"Hi, Ace!" he says, and they both start giggling like crazy as I tuck them both under my arm and carry them into the house.

"The prince and princess have arrived," I announce while setting them back on their feet.

The moms stay back so they don't scare Lilly by over-whelming her, but I can see the tears in their eyes as they look down at her, smiles taking over their faces.

"This little lady is Lilly, and her best friend, Toby," I intro-duce them to our moms.

Toby says "Hi," and moves over to his dad's side who has just entered the house.

They all greet Ellie and Theo, making my heart feel full as I see our mothers fussing over Ellie like they used to. They always loved Ellie, and as much as they hated to see us hurt, I think they always knew there was something off about the whole 'graduation night' fiasco. They are still really good friends with Ellie's parents, so maybe they said something, but didn't mention anything to us. Doesn't matter now, that's in the past.

"You Ace mama?" Lilly asks, tugging on my mom's hand. She smiles down at Lilly before picking her up.

"I am."

"He saved me!" Lilly tells her. My mom knows the whole story, and she was so upset over it. But she was so proud of me for saving Lilly. I would have done it for anyone.

My mom fakes her surprise, playing into Lilly's story. "He did? That's so cool."

Lilly nods and goes into detail about everything, her little mouth going a mile a minute. I'm not sure if my mother understands half of what she's saying, but she's loving every moment of it.

"She really doesn't seem to be affected by the fact that she was taken. She only ever points out that you saved her," Ellie says, coming up next to me. I wrap my arm around her, pulling her to my side. I kiss the top of her head, then look down at her.

"I'm glad that she's fixated on something positive about the situation. She doesn't have any nightmares, does she?"

"Nope. Other than her stories like this one, it's like it never happened. The therapist said she could be suppressing what happened, but she thinks that because she was so young, it won't have any lasting effects."

"Mama," Lilly calls out, now in Rain's mother's arms. She really is a people person. "Ace mama said we having gettie!"

"Yum! I can't wait," Ellie laughs as they take the little one into the dinner room. She looks up at me. "Did you tell them one of Lilly's favorite foods is spaghetti?" Ellie laughs.

"Yeah. I wanted to make sure there was something we could all eat. It was that or dino nuggies." I chuckle as we follow everyone, and we all take a seat at the table.

"Hey, I love those things." She grins, taking a seat between me and Rain.

Supper turns out to be a lot of fun. Brody and Jax mostly talk to themselves about football. Rain, Ellie, and I talk about a little bit of everything. But the oddest of all is how Theo gets along with our dads. Theo kind of falls into the middle of everyone's age group, so I can see how it's easy for him to get along with everyone.

"I'm gonna go to the bathroom," Ellie says, getting up from her spot.

"You remember where it is?" I ask.

"Down the hall, fifth door on the right?"

I nod, and she kisses the top of my head before taking off.

Rain watches her leave, a dopey, love struck look on her face.

"I still don't think it's fair that you got to be with Ellie last night, that all of you did but me," I mutter to Rain. Her eyes meet mine, and she fucking smirks at me.

"You're such a big baby. You act like you're not inside her any chance you get."

"True." I grin. We've had sex a few more times since the beach, every time just as amazing as the time before. "And I think I'm gonna go see if she needs any help."

"Peeing?" Rain laughs, looking at me like I'm nuts.

I just grin and excuse myself from the table. My cock has been hard this whole supper. Ellie wore a sexy, yet classy, white dress with black and pink flowers on it. It covers her breasts, but while sitting next to her, I was able to look down the bodice. And what can I say, she has nice boobs. Boobs I love to shove my face in and suck on. Fuck, my cock twitches in my pants.

Am I really about to find my girlfriend, bring her into my childhood bedroom, and make love to her like we used to? Fuck yes, if she's down for that.

When I get to the bathroom, Ellie is just getting out. She looks at me with a curious look. Giving her a mischievous grin, I bend and throw her over my shoulder.

"Chase!" She laughs as I slap her ass, racing toward my room. After crossing the threshold, I close and lock the door behind me before tossing her on my bed. She squeals as she bounces, her blonde hair a mess covering her face. She brushes it back so that she can see, revealing her eyes that are lit up with joy.

"What are we doing?" she asks, looking around the room. Everything is the same as I left it when I moved into the guys' and my apartment. Band posters line the walls, football trophies displayed on my desk.

"Well, I know what I want to be doing, and that would be you, pretty girl." I grin, my knees hitting the bed as I start to crawl toward her. "What do you say? Wanna be naughty teens again?"

Her pupils dilate, and I know she's considering the idea. "But everyone is down the hall," she breathes. "What if someone hears us?"

"Then we're just gonna have to be quiet," I counter, my body hovering over hers. She looks up at me with lidded eyes, her tits threatening to spill out of her dress. I groan, lowering my face to the soft skin of her breasts. I kiss each one before nuzzling my face between them. She sucks in a gasp, writhing between me as her thighs open, allowing my hard cock to nudge against her panty covered core.

"Chase," she moans, her fingers threading through my hair.

"That's not very quiet, babe," I murmur into her tits, then look up. "Also, you didn't answer my question. Can I take you? Make you cum? Own your sweet body?"

"Yes," she breathes. "I'm yours, take me. God, Chase, please?" She whimpers as I start to grind against her.

"I wanna taste you first," I tell her, capturing her lips with mine before I shimmy down the bed until my face is in view of her soaked panties. "All I've been thinking about tonight is getting between these creamy thighs. This dress has been tempting me all night, baby girl."

"That's why I wore it," she pants as I kiss down her thigh.

I grin against her leg. "You naughty little minx. Did you hope one of us would ravish you tonight?"

"Yes," she moans as I brush my nose against her swollen clit. "You."

A growl leaves my chest; she wanted *me*. She was hoping for me tonight. Something primal in me preens at that. The need to taste her, fuck her, and own her takes over me. I don't have the patience to take off the scrap of fabric keeping me from what's mine, so I move to my knees, grasp it in both hands, and pull, snapping the strap of the thong.

She gasps in shock, but it turns into a moan as my lips and tongue meet her sweet pussy.

After lapping up any juices she's already spilled, I remind her of our game. "Remember to keep quiet, baby girl." She grabs the pillow next to her, holding it close just in case. "Can you be a good girl for me?" She nods, her eyes wild with lust. "If you listen and follow the rules, I promise your reward will be worth it."

Her hand grips my hair as I start to eat her out like a starved man. She's writhing under me, her legs shaking, and it doesn't even take her a full minute before she's slapping a hand over her mouth to cover her cries.

My mind has one mode right now, and that's making her cum on my face. I lick and suck her pussy, plunging my tongue in and out of her before sucking and nibbling on her clit as I fuck her with two fingers.

I know she's close when I feel her start to clamp around my fingers. My eyes flick up, finding her back arched and she grabs the pillow to hold it over her face as she lets out a sexy scream mixed with my name before her body locks up and she cums. Her hand grip my hair tightly as her core pulses around my fingers. Her release coats my face, and I do my best to get every last drop.

My cock is hard as fucking stone, and all I want to do is slide it into her pussy.

"So fucking perfect," I tell her, moving so that I'm covering her body. I remove the pillow from her face. She looks up at me, her chest heaving, eyes black, and her face flushed.

"Did I do good?" she asks, her voice laced with the need for approval, and my cock fucking twitches.

"So good, baby; you were such a good girl," I growl, kissing her hard. She moans as she tastes herself, our tongues dancing together.

"Chase," she whimpers. "I need you, please."

"Shhhh," I soothe her, kissing her once more before adjusting my body so that I can pull back the top of her dress. Her breasts spill out, and I groan. "No bra?"

"Don't need one with this dress."

Her nipples are hard as diamonds, just begging to be sucked. So I do. Leaning over, I take one into my mouth, sucking hard. She gasps loudly, and my eyes shoot to hers. She slaps a hand over her mouth, and I grin at her eagerness to keep playing this game.

I play with her perfect tits, sucking one nipple while plucking and pulling at the other. I'm driving her mad but I want her dripping before I take her perfect body.

When she's whimpering and pleading for more, I move back on my knees. She lets out a whimper. "On your hands and knees, baby girl. I wanna see that sexy ass jiggle as I pound into you." My voice is thick with need. Her eyes flash with excitement as she scrambles to get into position.

I bite my fist, letting out a pained groan as I get a full view of her ass. Her pussy showing, dripping with need, and my god, it's the most amazing sight.

Leaning over, I bite her ass cheek and get a breathy moan in return.

"Do you want it slow and sweet or hard and fast, baby girl?" I ask her, moving so that I'm right behind her. I undo my pants and take my throbbing cock out, wrapping my hand around it. I give it a few strokes, hissing as the heat of her pussy meets the tip of my cock while I glide it up and down her folds.

"Hard," she moans. "I wanna feel you deep inside me. I want to feel you days from now. Fuck me like you own me, Chase. I'm yours."

A rumble erupts in my chest as I grab her hip with one hand and position my cock with her entrance with the other. In one hard thrust, I enter her completely. We both moan as her pussy takes me all the way in. She grabs the pillow, trying to cover her sounds, but I grab a handful of her hair. "Not so fast now, baby girl. I want to see you work for it."

There's a mirror above the headboard of my bed, and I had never understood why it was put there. However, in this moment, I've never been so thankful for it because this view is making it really hard for me not to cum in an instant.

She is fucking gorgeous. Her tits sway as I start to pound into her. My hand is holding her head back so that she can see us too. We watch each other in the mirror, and the look of pure bliss on her face eggs me on.

My hips pound against her ass, making her cheeks jiggle with each thrust. "Fuck," I hiss, my mind on overdrive. *So good, so fucking good.* I slap her ass, making her bite her lip harder.

"Not so easy, is it?" I ask her, gritting my teeth as she suffocates my cock. She frantically shakes her head. "Do you need to scream, to cry out?"

She nods yes. I shove her face into the pillow, and the moment I do, she screams out my name, moaning, whimpering, begging me to go harder, faster. I rut into her, grunting like a wild fucking animal. I let go of her hair and grip her hips.

A tingle takes over my body, and I can feel my balls draw up. A few more thrusts, I enter into her one last time before moving my head to bite my arm so hard I taste blood on my tongue. I smother my roar as I fill her with jets of my cum, coating her insides, and marking Ellie as my girl. *Mine.* All fucking mine. It doesn't matter to me that she's theirs too, because she's still mine.

She follows after me, screaming into the pillow as her pussy locks around my cock, trying to milk me for every last dtop.

"Look at you," I tell her, kissing down her spine as she sags into the bed. "You listen so well. I'm so proud of you."

"Do you think they heard?" she asks, moving her face to the side to look at me.

"No, baby girl, you played my game just right." It's not a total lie, I don't think they would have heard her scream, but the sounds of flesh slapping together wasn't exactly quiet.

I pull out of her, watching my cum drip from her pussy. My cock twitches at the sight. I take my two fingers, swiping it up, and push it back into her, not wanting it to leave her so soon. She whimpers, and I remove my fingers, holding them out to her. She gets up and takes them into her mouth, licking them clean.

"My dirty, perfect girl," I growl, then slap her ass hard enough that I hope I left my hand print before soothing the sting. She moans, *fucking moans* at that. There's so much more I want to do with my girl.

But a knock on the door reminds me where we are, and why we are here.

"I know you two are fucking in here, but if you don't get out here soon, the parents are gonna start asking questions," Rain's voice sounds from the other side of the door.

That gets Ellie going. She jumps up, fixes the top of her dress, and I pout as she puts the girls away.

She laughs. "Chase! You destroyed my panties," she says, holding up the scrap of soaked fabric.

"That's not the only thing I destroyed." I grin.

"Chase," she growls, sending a shiver down my spine. "I have your cum dripping down my leg. I can't go out there like this."

"Fine." I laugh, loving the annoyed glare she gives me. "If you must clean yourself of me, I'll take you to the bathroom."

I open the door, giving Rain a shit eating grin as Ellie darts from behind me and rushes over to the bathroom. Just as she goes to open the door, Theo walks out.

Ellie looks up at him with a mortified, stunned look, and my spine goes ram-rod straight.

He looks her over as Rain and I stand there waiting for him to react. Will he be pissed?

His face morphs into a smirk. "Did he make you cum, sweet girl?" he asks, surprising the fuck out of me. My eyes widen in shock.

She stammers, not sure what to say, but finally answers, "Yes, two times."

"Good," he nods. "Only the best for our girl," he says, kissing her lips. The lips coated in her release that was transferred there from my lips. Like he knows the taste of her, he licks his lips, savoring the taste. "Go clean up, love. I'll keep the others talking."

She nods, and he lets her into the bathroom, closing the door behind him.

He looks at me, gives me an approving nod before taking off down the hall.

"Did that just happen?" Rain asks, watching him leave.

"Yeah, it did." I'm starting to like this man. He has my seal of approval.

Chapter Twenty-Eight

JAX

"THANK you so much for doing this," Ellie says, grabbing her purse and keys.

"Babe, we told you this before. We want to hang out with her, to spend time with her. We're not babysitting, we're doing our job as her parents," I tell her, cupping her face and placing a soft kiss on her lips.

She nods. "I know. I'm sorry. With the hearing being only a week away, I've been a little on edge."

I pull her into my arms, holding her close to my body. "Everything is going to be okay. I know this will be hard, and I hate what you're gonna have to say and do, but in the end, he will get what's coming to him. I know," I say hoping to reassure her.

"I hope so."

"Now go, have fun with your man while your other lovers have fun with the princess," I say.

She steps back from my embrace and laughs. "You know, that should sound weird, but it doesn't."

"Nope, because it works for us, and that's what matters." I smile

"I know you haven't been here before, but feel free to snoop if you can't find what you're looking for." Theo grins as he steps into the kitchen from the hallway. "We stocked the place with food, so feel free to help yourselves."

Ellie moved in with Theo a few days ago. She told us during supper at Chase's parents' house. She looked worried like we would be upset, but none of us were. It makes sense. She'll save money, and when we're all out of school, or when we've been together a little longer, we will see about where to go from there. For now, living here is the best thing for her. Also, they said we are welcome here anytime, and we told them they are welcome at our place too.

We already changed things around a little bit back at our apartment. Brody moved into my room, and we renovated his into a room for Lilly. We want her to feel like no matter where she is, she's always welcome and at home.

As for Ellie, she's free to sleep with one of us, or share with Lilly. We wanted her to have her own space, but it's not really the right time for us to be moving into another rental. But we did get a bunch of things for her. We cleared a spot in the bathroom for her stuff, and stocked the place with girly products like tampons, pads, and other things she might need.

"Come on, Axe!" Lilly says from the living room where she already has Rain and Chase decked out in dress up clothes. "I found a crown for you!" she says proudly, holding up one that looks like Elsa's crown.

"We made sure to get some extra dress up things for you guys." Ellie giggles as Chase adjusts his crown.

Ellie says bye to everyone and takes off with Theo, leaving us alone with Lilly. Last time it was Rain and Chase watching her. Brody and I haven't done this yet.

"So, what do we do?" he asks, leaning against the counter in the kitchen as he watches Lilly play with the others.

"Well, it can't be that hard, can it?" I grin. "Keep her alive, feed her, water her...easy peasy."

He cocks a brow, a smile hitching at the corner of his lip. "She's not a dog or a plant."

"Nope, just a very smart, energetic little spitfire like her mama." I look over at Lilly, my heart filling with love as she giggles while Chase tickles her. It's the sweetest sound I've ever heard.

"Come on, guys, it's tea time," Rain says, holding up a toy teacup.

I chuckle and go over to them, sitting on the couch. "Hi, princess Axe. I princess Lilly."

"Hello, princess Lilly. I would love to look as beautiful as you. Can you help me?" I ask, playing into her game.

"Oh yes! I have perfect thing," she says, running over to her toy box. She pulls out a white feathered boa, fairy wings, and a silver plastic crown with different color gems before she runs back over to me. "You be the very special fairy princess."

My smile is so wide that my face hurts, but I don't care one bit. Lilly wraps the boa around my neck, almost choking me and making me cough out a laugh. I lower my head so she can place the crown on my head, then she stands back and looks at me. "I don't think this gonna fit," she says, holding up the wings. "You're big."

Chase snorts out a laugh. "Yeah, little monkey, his big gorilla arms might rip the straps."

She studies me then the wings before taking off over to her little beauty table then back over. She climbs on the couch behind me and grabs my shirt. "There," she says with excitement.

"How did you get it to stay?" I ask her.

"Mama's hair clip. It looks like a spider, but she says it's not." Lilly shrugs. We all laugh and she giggles. This little girl has the power to make me go out in public like this, and I wouldn't fight her on it if I got to see that smile. Anything she asks, I would agree to in a heartbeat. Every time.

Brody hangs back, watching us play. I hate that he feels like the odd one out, but I think he just needs to keep trying and take things slow.

We play for a little while before Lilly says that she's hungry.

Brody makes everyone mac and cheese for supper, and when we're done, we all sit down to color.

"Axe," Lilly says my name, getting my attention. I look up from the page of a kitty and puppy that I'm coloring to meet her big, blue eyes.

"Yes?"

"Why don't Broody like me?" she asks, her eyes growing sad, and my heart sinks.

"What makes you think he doesn't?" I ask.

"He always so mad. He never talk to me, or play like you, Ace, and Fire do. I do something wrong?" She's almost in tears now, and my heart breaks. I look up at Brody and his face is crushed. He looks at me with pleading eyes, asking me what he should do.

"Brody is always like that. It has nothing to do with you, sweetie. You and Toby are the first kids he's been around."

"Oh. Okay," she says, her voice so sad as she goes back to coloring. The mood shifts as the others look at me with matching glum moods.

Brody gets up and grabs something from the fridge then closes the door but doesn't turn around. I follow him into the kitchen, and when he feels me behind him, he speaks, just barely loud enough for me to hear.

"I thought she didn't like me. But to hear that she thinks I hate her," he says, his voice broken. He turns his brown eyes on me, and this time, my heart clenches with how much pain he's showing. "I don't want her to think I hate her. I love that little girl so fucking much, it scares the shit out of me, Jax. I'm afraid that I'm gonna let her down, that I'm gonna fail her, and she'll end up hating me like I do my parents."

"Brody, she doesn't hate you. You need to spend time with her, try to get to know her. Show her what kind of dad you can be."

"But how?" he asks, sounding defeated.

"Just sit down and play. You might feel like it's stupid or silly, but Brody, she's four. These are the kind of things kids do," I tell him, grabbing his hand and lacing my fingers through his. Bringing his hand up to my lips, I place a kiss on the back of his hand. "Go over there and ask her if you can color."

"What if she says no?" he asks, his eyes flicking over to Lilly.

"Won't know if you don't try," I encourage him. "Come on." Tugging his hand, I drag him over to the living room.

I let go and sit on the couch. When he just stands there, I jerk my head toward her, motioning him to ask.

He clears his throat. "Ah, Lilly?" he asks, sounding unsure. Her little head looks up at him, and she waits for him to continue. "Can I...Can I color too?"

She looks down at the table where the others are coloring, who are acting like they are minding their own business but we all know they are not, then back up to Brody.

"No more coloring books," she tells him, and Brody's shoulders slump. "But you color on mine?" she asks, pointing to the other page in her book that has a pineapple with sunglasses.

He smiles, a real smile and fuck, my heart explodes. The back of my eyes burn as I try to hold back the wave of emotion while watching my man and our daughter bond.

Brody sits down next to her, and she stands up. "You don't fit in," she says, putting her finger on her chin as she looks over the big, muscled, football player of a man before going back over to the box of stuff. She comes back with a rainbow boa and a pink fuzzy tiara. "Look, Ace! Broody has crown like you!" she exclaims to Chase who has a fuzzy blue crown atop his head.

"It's what the cool kids are wearing," Chase grins.

Lilly rolls her eyes. "I cool too, dahhhh."

"Yes. Yes, you are. The coolest," Brody says, and she looks at him with a beaming smile that makes Brody's whole face light up.

She sits down next to him and starts to explain all the reasons why the house she's coloring needs to look like a house made out of candy. Brody nods along and asks questions. That's when I know everything will be okay. No matter what happens, we have each other, and Lilly has all of us. We won't let anyone down again.

ELLIE

"I still think that was Elvis Presley," Theo says as we head back to the car. We went to an early movie, then got a bite to eat at one of the nicer restaurants in Spring Meadows.

"Babe, if Elvis was still alive, he'd be in his eighties. That man has gotta be no more than forty," I laugh.

"It could be him. Elvis has money, his family has money. Technology is crazy these days, babe. He could have been put into some kind of freezing machine that preserved his body until he was ready to be out in the real world again." Theo grins as we get into the car. I buckle my seat belt and turn to him.

"Yeah, and he chose to live out his life as a restaurant owner in Spring Meadows?" I ask, raising a brow in amusement.

"Anything is possible," he chuckles.

We drive to the pier and walk along the beach holding hands, enjoying each other's company and forgetting all about the fact that I've got to back to school tomorrow or that the hearing is next Monday. One last night of fun before life becomes a shit show again.

"Wanna get some ice cream before we head back home?" Theo asks, pulling me into his arms. I wrap mine around his waist and look up at him with a smile.

"Sounds yummy," I tell him, my hair and dress blowing in the wind. It's a warm breeze, a perfect night, I wish it didn't have to end.

"I love you, Ellie," he tells me, capturing his lips with mine. I let out a soft moan before he pulls back.

"I love you too," I say breathily.

"Everything is going to be okay, you know that, right? No matter the outcome, you have us by your side, all of us. I'll be honest, I had my doubts about the others after everything they've done to you. But I see how truly sorry they are, and how much they regret everything they did. I'm glad that they make you happy. That's all that matters to me."

"I know I tell you this, like a lot, but you truly are amazing. I'm so damn lucky to have you."

"It's me who's the lucky one." He smiles.

We walk hand in hand to the little ice cream shop on the pier. "What kind do you want?" he asks me. "Cotton candy or strawberry?"

"Umm, I think I'm in a cotton candy kind of mood," I laugh.

"Two scoops coming right up." He kisses me on the cheek and takes off inside while I wait out on the wooden deck.

Moving to stand by the railing of the deck, I watch the sun start to set. The waves crash on the beach, and it's beautiful. Getting my phone out to take a photo, the photo booth photos we got from the movies slip out, blowing across the deck.

"Fuck," I hiss as I start to run after them. I run down the side stairs and manage to grab them by the side of the shop. "Thank god," I breathe, tucking them back into my purse.

"Well, well, well, look who we have here," a slimy voice makes my body go rigid. It's been months since the last time I saw this sick fuck, but I'd know his voice anywhere. It haunts my dreams.

Ricky.

I turn around to face him, and I'm not at all surprised to see his pervy friends, Vin and Luke, standing next to him, all with matching leering looks.

"What do you want?" I say, giving them a look of disgust.

"Justice for our friend." Vin says, taking a step forward. "He's locked up at his parents' place, can't do shit."

"Oh, boohoo. The big, bad rapist can't come out and play," I pout. "Excuse me while I try to find some fucks to give."

"Listen here, you little bitch," Luke says. "You think you're gonna win? Nah, Tim's family is loaded. He's gonna get out of this, and you're gonna be made to look like a fool."

I should feel scared. I should feel the panic in me, but I don't.

I feel anger, fucking rage that these micro-dick fuckers get to walk free.

"Boys, I think we should teach this whore a lesson," Ricky taunts. Just as he's about to step toward me, Theo comes around the corner. Theo grabs the back of Ricky's head and smashes his face into the side of the building. He drops to the ground with a girly screech. Then Theo whips around and uppercuts Vin before bringing his knee up, hitting him hard in the crotch. Vin groans and also drops to the ground.

"Look, man, we were just messing around," Luke says, trying to defend himself. His eyes widen with fear as Theo starts to stalk toward him, his chest heaving like an angry bull.

"You fucked with the wrong woman," he growls. "I know who you are, and you're lucky I don't put a fucking bullet between your eyes. All three of you."

Luke backs up a few steps before turning, trying to make an escape. But he doesn't get far because Theo tackles him, knocking him to the ground.

"You're gonna stay away from Ellie, do you understand me?" Theo roars, shoving Luke's face into the sand. I'm in shock. The only thing I can do is watch with some sick fascination while my boyfriend steps up to defend me. "If I find out you so as much looked at her, I will break into your house and gut you in your fucking sleep," Theo says, putting his face close to Luke's ear.

"Yes," Luke sobs like a baby. "We won't go near her again."

Theo stands up with a frustrated huff, giving Luke a kick to the gut before turning around to face me.

Worse time ever to be turned on, but my god, that was one of the hottest things I've ever seen.

Theo fixes his glasses then runs a hand through his rumpled hair, his dress shirt untucked from his jeans. He looks so damn sexy.

"You okay?" he asks, his eyes worried as he searches me over.

"Yeah, better than okay." I take a breath, blinking the shock away. Theo looks down at the other two moaning on the ground. He spits on Vin, then kicks sand in Ricky's face.

"Come on," I tell Theo, grabbing his hand.

"Where are we going? What about the ice cream?" Theo asks as he follows me.

"Fuck the ice cream," I say. When we get to the car, I push him up against it, thankful that the parking lot is empty, and our car is far away from any others. "Do you understand how fucking hot that was?" I ask him, my eyes blazing with lust. I don't feel like myself right now, I feel high off the adrenaline, and all I want to do is ride my man, my king.

"What? Really?" he asks, looking adorably confused.

"So fucking hot. I'm unbelievably wet for you right now," I breathe, running my hands down his chest.

The confused look on his face fades, replaced with one of hunger.

"Wanna show me how wet?" he growls.

"Yes." I open the back seat of the car and look back at him. "Get in."

He gives me a dirty look before ducking in. I look around, my body humming with everything that just happened. I need this. I need to feel him. I need him to calm my soul, my mind, my body. I don't care how coping this way may look, it's better than having a panic attack and feeling like I can't breathe. He's one of my anchors, one of the few who can ground me.

The sun has set, leaving us alone under the cover of darkness. The sounds of people laughing and singing songs around a fire are distant; they're most likely whoever these remaining cars belong to.

When I feel like we're safe enough, I get in the back seat with Theo, closing the door behind me.

Straddling his lap, I immediately feel his hard cock against my already soaked core. We look at each other, eyes blazing, hearts beating out of control.

"Thank you," I tell him, breaking the silence as I take his

glasses off and put them on the center console so they don't get broken.

"For what?" he asks, his voice husky, sending a shiver of need through my body.

"For saving me back there. For beating the shit out of them. I've never been so turned on by a fist fight before," I explain, running both hands through his hair. He groans, his eyes closing as my fingers graze his scalp. I give his hair a light tug, making him grunt.

"You never have to thank me for defending you, sweet girl. I will always be ready to slay any demon that might come your way," he growls, his hands gripping my hips. "You're so fucking strong and brave, but love, don't think I would just stand by and allow someone to diminish your worth."

Fuck, this man. I smash my lips to his in a desperate need. His hand grips the back of my head, holding me there as I slip my tongue into this mouth. He groans, swirling his tongue around mine before sucking on it, making me whimper as I grind against his cock. I need him, I need him inside me.

My hands frantically work at opening his jeans as he kisses me with an animalistic need. Teeth clashing, tongues battling, all so fucking dirty.

When I get his zipper down, I lift my hips so I can pull him out. Wrapping my hand around his hot, velvety shaft, I give him a few pumps, making him growl against my lips. "Fuck."

"That's what I was aiming for," I tease, my words coming out in a shaky, breathy way.

"Smart ass, huh?" He gives me a grin that tells me I just lost any control over this and I whimper, my thighs growing slicker by the moment. "You want me to fuck you, sweet girl? You wanna ride my cock in the back seat of this car?" he asks, his words thick with desire. One of his hands slips under me and pulls my panties to the side. The other goes under my ass cheek, lifting me up until I'm hovering over the tip of his cock. I can feel his pre-cum against my entrance, and I nod. A moan slips free as I bite my lip.

"Then ride me, love. Ride me until the windows are fogged up and dripping, just like your tight pussy." With those words, he shoves me down on his cock. We both cry out in pleasure, and my eyes roll into the back of my head. He's so fucking big, and I feel so damn full. I love the burn, the line of pleasure and pain we tip-toe over.

"So fucking perfect," he growls as I sit there, adjusting to his size. He pulls down the top of my dress, sucking my nipple into his mouth, giving it a bite and making me suck in a sharp breath before doing the same thing to the other one. "Hands behind your back, love."

I do as he says, and one of his hands grabs both of my wrists from behind.

"Now, let's see how hard we can rock this car. Bounce those perky tits for me, Ellie. Hypnotize me," he purrs.

Well, fuck me; his dirty mouth makes me gush as my pussy grips him. My hips start to roll, and I moan as his cock hits me in that perfect place. He continues to praise me as I pick up the pace.

I'm riding him with urgent need, my clit grinding against his lower belly. I'm lost in a haze of lust and pleasure that I never want to leave.

His eyes lock with mine as I fuck him hard, fast, and my breasts do exactly what he wanted, shifting with every roll of my hips. Before long, I'm bouncing on his cock, my arms still behind me and even though it may look like he's in control, I'm the one with all the power.

I feel like a damn queen with how he's looking at me. It's like I'm the most precious thing in the world, a rare find that needs to be protected at all cost.

"That's it, sweetheart," Theo groans. "You ride my cock so fucking well. You own this cock. It's all fucking yours."

His words settle inside of me, setting off this need to please him, the praise turning me on. He moves his free hand down to play with my clit, and the sensation has me falling forward. He lets go of my arms, allowing me to lay against his chest as he continues to massage my sensitive bud. Wrapping his arm around me to hold me to him, he starts to thrust up into me.

I'm a sobbing mess. My body is on fire with everything this man is doing to me. *Pure fucking ecstasy.*

"Theo," I cry. "I'm gonna cum."

"I know, love. Let it out, cum for me. You can do it, sweet girl," he grunts as his thrusts get deeper, harder, faster.

It's all too much. Between his cock, his hand, and his dirty words, I'm a fucking goner.

I scream his name into his neck before biting down hard and sobbing out my release. My body starts to twitch and writhe on top of him as I have one of the best orgasms I've ever had in my life.

He keeps fucking me, chanting my name. "Good girl, Ellie," he pants. "Just like that, love. Fuck, choke my fucking cock. Argh," he roars with one last thrust. Theo holds me tightly to him as he stills, his cock pulsing out his release, coating me with jets of hot cum.

We stay like that, wrapped in each other's embrace with only the sounds of our heavy breathing filling the silence in the car.

"Well, look at that," Theo lets out a husky chuckle. I open my eyes to see one of his hand prints on a steamed up window, the condensation dripping down the window. "I thought that only happened in the movies."

I move back, his cock still inside me as I put my breasts back in my dress. Looking down at a very sexy, messy haired Theo, I raise a brow.

"Have you never had sex in a car or something?" I ask with a joking laugh.

His face turns sheepish, moving me with him as he sits up straight. "Ah, actually, no."

"Really?" I ask, my brows shooting up in surprise.

"As you know, Kristen and I didn't have a very adventurous sex life. She always wanted to play it safe. So no, I've never done this before."

"You know, I love that I get to be your first with so many things. I love that I get to help you find out what you like and experience new things you wanna try. Anything you wanna do, you know I'm always willing to try for you. Who knows, maybe I'll find something new I like too."

"I love you so fucking much, Ellie," he says, his hands rubbing up and down my thighs. "Thank you for being so amazing."

Just as I'm about to lean over and kiss him, there's a bang on the window.

"Security!" a male's voice comes from the other side. Our eyes go wide and dread fills my gut. "Don't think I don't know what is going on in here. I'm gonna need you all to please leave before I have to call the cops."

Theo's face turns beat red, and I try to hold in my giggle. He clears his throat and says, "Sorry about that, sir, we will leave right now."

"See to it," he says, and I clear off the window to make sure he's gone.

"That's also a first," Theo chuckles. "I've never been *caught* before."

"Come on, bad boy, let's get home and see how much damage Lilly did to Rain and the guys."

The car ride home is relaxing. My mind and body is clear, not letting what happened earlier have any control over my life. I might not be able to do anything about those other three douche bags without proof of their involvement, but I have every intention to bring down the leader of their pack.

When we get home, I was completely expecting Lilly to be passed out. I didn't tell them they had to put her to bed before we got home, just in case Lilly needed me there for bedtime, but sometimes she tires herself out.

But when we walk through the front door, I'm brought to tears, happy tears.

Brody has Lilly in his arms, both of them dressed up in princess clothes as they dance and sing to *Frozen 2*.

My hand covers my mouth as a big smile takes over my face, and Theo's arm pulls me to his side.

Brody spins Lilly around, a look of pure happiness on his face as he locks eyes with me. His smile doesn't fade as we have this moment of understanding between the two of us.

Things are changing, changing for the better, and I'm excited to see where this new adventure takes us.

Now, to just get over the nightmare of facing my enemy in a courtroom first.

Chapter Twenty-Nine

THEO

"BREATHE, SWEET GIRL," I tell Ellie as we wait outside the courtroom for the hearing to begin. She was doing so well this morning right up until this moment. The moment her lawyer told her they were about to begin. I can tell she is about to have a panic attack.

The others are already inside waiting, but I'm staying out here with Ellie until she absolutely has to go inside.

"Breathe? You want me to breathe? I'm about to walk in there and tell a room full of strangers, as well as my lovers, what really happened to me that night. Theo, I can't breathe," she says, her eyes tearing up.

"Look at me when you tell your story, not anyone else, just me. You've got this, Ellie. You're so brave and strong. After this is over, you don't have to talk about this with anyone else, ever again, if you don't want to. And as hard as this is going to be for you, if it gets him behind bars, isn't it worth talking about it?"

She closes her eyes and nods as she takes a deep breath. My heart and soul hurts for my girl. I wish I could just make all of this go away and get the ending we want without her having to go through all of this. I feel so helpless, but I know I'm not. I'll always be here for her, with whatever she needs. I'm not going *anywhere*. There's nothing she can say in that room that would make any of us see her differently.

This past week, Ellie has been using school and work to keep her mind off of today, but the week went by in the blink of an eye. I was up half the night with her in my arms, unable to sleep, as I thought about everything that scum bag's lawyer is going to say. He's going to find any way to make it seem like Ellie is lying, or mistaken about what happened and I'm going to have to bite my tongue to keep from telling him to go to hell.

The thing that pisses me off the most is that Tim's little lackeys aren't up there with him. I asked Ellie if she wanted to press changes on them too, and I think she wanted to say yes, but she didn't. She said there wasn't any evidence other than the one time they mentioned it at the football game where Jax scared them off. She said that Tim was the big fish she wanted to fry, and that he was the main focus.

I told the guys what happened at the pier, and they were not pleased at all. Jax had to hold Brody back from going out and finding them.

Brody holds a lot of power and not just in his school. He sent a blast out all over the internet, calling them out for what they are without broadcasting what they did to Ellie.

We're hoping it helps bring forward anyone else who might have been a victim of theirs. I grew a whole lot of respect when Brody said if anyone comes forward and wanted to press charges, he would help pay to get the survivor the right representation if they needed it.

"Ellie," Jeff says, stepping outside the courtroom. We both look over at him, and he waves us over. "We're ready for you now. The hearing is about to begin."

"Okay," she says, letting out a breath and looks up at me. "Ready?"

"Only if you are," I tell her, lacing my fingers through her hand and kissing the back of it.

We walk over to the door and with one last deep breath, we walk in. There's a low hum of chatter but luckily this is a closed hearing, meaning only people from each side were allowed to have people here. Ellie's side has Rain, the guys, her parents, and her friends. My mom and dad are at home with the kids.

Tim's side is empty in comparison with only his parents sitting there to support him. It just shows what people really think about him.

He's already sitting with his lawyer, huddled together and talking. When Tim notices us enter the room, he stops and looks over.

"Eyes straight ahead, sweet girl," I tell her, moving to her side so that the creep can't see her.

She nods, and we continue to walk until we get to the front row. Ellie slides inside next to her dad and sits. I sit down next to her, leaning over to give her a kiss on the side of her head and a squeeze of encouragement to her shoulder.

"You've got this," I whisper in her ear. She nods and turns around to see the others in the row behind her. They all look nervous. Everyone but Brody, who is glaring over at Tim like he wants to murder him.

"Brody," I whisper. His head snaps over to me, and I shake my head. He gives me a glare before his face softens, eyes landing on Ellie.

As much as hearing all of this is going to break my heart, I'm not her parents, or a lover who had mistaken the situation and left her there with Tim. I can be the strong one, holding back my emotions for the right time and place. *Is it going to be easy?* Not a fucking chance. But if that's what she needs, I'll be that safe place for her.

"All rise for the honorable Judge Mathews," the bailiff says. We all stand and in walks the same judge who is proceeding over Brody's case.

Everyone sits, and the judge rattles off a case number, the legal terms for both sides, and what Tim is being charged with before giving Ellie's lawyer the floor. There is no jury, just the judge, so everything will be directed toward him.

"Thank you, your honor," Jeff says. "We are here today to get Miss Tatum the justice she deserves. Ellie, would you please take the stand?" Jeff smiles over at her.

Looking over at Ellie, I give her a look of encouragement before she takes a deep breath and stands. She walks over to the stand, her head held high, and I'm so proud. She gets sworn in, and when she takes a seat, she looks solely at Jeff, ignoring everyone else in the room.

"How are you doing today, Ellie?" Jeff asks.

"I'm good," she says softly.

"I know being here today must be very stressful. I'm so sorry you have to deal with this, but let's work together and get your story told, how does that sound?" Jeff asks.

"Good." Ellie smiles.

"Now, Ellie, can you tell me everything that happened on June 18th, 2018? I'm going to need you to tell me in as much detail as possible, please," Jeff instructs her. She nods, looking down at her hands before moving her gaze over to me.

That's my girl. I give her a loving smile and nod my head. "It was the night of my graduation. Some friends and I went to a party. It was at Robby Nolan's house. I'm not really one to party, but my friends wanted to go. It was our last high school party, and I knew how much it meant to them, so I went. When we got there, we all split up."

"And why is that?"

"Like I said before, I'm not one to party. I wanted them to enjoy themselves, so they found their team members and hung out with them while I stood in the background, watching," Ellie says.

"And at this party, did you have any alcohol to drink?"

"I did. I had two coolers. I'm not much of a drinker, and because it was a special occasion, I kept it to two coolers."

"And were those drinks consumed in a time that was close together or far apart?" Jeff asks. I know it may look like he's grilling her, but I think with him asking her as much as he can, it leaves less for Tim's lawyer to harass her with.

"They were spread out over the span of a few hours."

Jeff nods. "At what point in the night did you see Mr. Hightower for the first time?"

"Not too long after we got there. I saw Tim and some friends show up. After that, I spent the night trying to avoid him."

"And why is that?" Jeff asks, titling his head to the side.

"For a while before this night, Tim was pretty friendly with me, always trying to talk to me, to get to know me and be my friend."

"And you didn't want to be Mr. Hightower's friend?"

"At the time, I thought he was a nice enough guy, but I had a close group of friends, and because I wasn't the most social person, I wasn't looking for any new friends."

"So, he was harassing you?"

"No. More like determined."

"So when was it that you actually talked to Mr. Hightower, face to face, the night of the incident?" Jeff asks.

This is when her face falls, knowing that she's now going to have to explain one of the worst nights of her life. I wish I could stand next to her, hold her hand for comfort, and it's killing me that I can't.

"I talked to one of my friends." Ellie's eyes flick over to Brody, whose body stiffens, then back over to Jeff. "Then I decided to go look for a place to read on my phone. As I was searching, I started to feel dizzy. That's when Tim found me."

"Were you sick?" Jeff asks.

"I'm not really sure what happened. Anything I drank that night would have been out of my system. I was drinking only water at that point."

"Was it in a bottle, or a cup?" Jeff asks.

"A cup."

"Do you think someone could have slipped something into your cup?" Jeff asks.

"The party was packed, there were bodies everywhere. But yes, I do think I was drugged."

"But you can't be sure by who?"

"No," Ellie says, sounding a little defeated.

"What happened after Tim found you?"

Ellie takes a deep breath, this time turning to look at me. "He grabbed me around the waist then told me he had been looking for me."

"And what happened next? Did he help you sit down somewhere?"

"No." Ellie shook her head. "I don't remember getting up there, but I do know Tim brought me to a room and put me down on a bed. At this point, my body was weak, I couldn't move. But I knew I was scared because I had no control in the situation." Her eyes start to water.

"What happened after Tim put you down on the bed?" Jeff asks. Ellie's eyes flash with panic, and Jeff talks to her in a softer voice. "Take your time. I know this must be very hard for you."

Ellie closes her eyes and takes a deep breath. When she opens them again, I can see the pain in her eyes. Tears threaten to spill, but they don't. She continues with her story. "Tim took off my dress."

"Did you ask him to?"

"No." Ellie shakes her head. "I couldn't talk. So when he took it upon himself to take my clothes off, I couldn't say no."

"Did you want to say no?"

"Yes!" Ellie says, her voice sounding stronger. "Of course I wanted to say no."

"How come?"

"Because, I didn't like Tim that way. I didn't want to have sex with him. I was in a committed relationship with someone I really loved. I would never cheat on them. I didn't want anyone else but them."

"Did Tim know you were dating someone?"

"Yes." She nods her head. "He knew. Almost everyone did. But even if he didn't, I mentioned it on a few different occasions when we had talked. I specifically expressed to him that I was seeing someone," Ellie explains.

"What did Mr. Hightower do after he took off your dress?"

"He started to touch me. He touched my legs, my breasts, kissing every spot he touched as he told me how he had tried to get my attention but my friends were always in the way. But lucky for him, they were too drunk and distracted at the moment."

I may look calm on the outside, but on the inside, I'm a crazed animal. I have to dig my nails into the palm of my hands to keep myself in check. I want to kill him. I want to kill the little creep and bury his body where no one could ever find it.

"And what was going through your mind while he touched you?"

She swallows thickly, and I mouth 'I love you.' I hope she knows how amazing she is. She's so strong. "I wanted him to stop, and I started to panic inside my own head because I couldn't speak. I felt sick, and not because of whatever I was drugged with, but because I was being touched by someone who didn't have the right to." Her voice breaks and my eyes water, but I don't look away from her for a moment.

She goes on to tell the entire courtroom, in excruciating detail, everything he did to her after that and how she felt. Ellie's dad had to force Brody to sit back down at one point. A lot of low cursing came from the others. I can't see them, but I know they are all vibrating and Rain is crying.

"The last thing I remember before I passed out was how I prayed to die because I knew when I woke up and I remembered everything, my life was gonna be ruined," she says, trying to hold back a sob.

"Thank you so much for telling your story, Ellie. That was so brave of you," Jeff says. He turns to the judge. "I have no further questions your honor."

I let out a breath of relief now that Ellie is done talking. My heart hurts, so much. I want to scream, cry, and kill that mother-fucker. She looks like a stoic, stone statue, but I know she's breaking apart on the inside, and I just want to pull her into my arms and tell her everything is going to be okay.

The real test is about to come because this man is going to say some fucked up shit and try to make my woman out to be some-thing she's not. Brody and the guys better watch themselves before they make it worse for her.

"Thank you. Mr. McWilson. Mr. Randell, do you have any questions at this time?"

ELLIE

My heart is pounding so erratically in my chest that I reach up and rub at the spot. My mind feels dizzy, and there's a sick feeling in the pit of my stomach. I just told not only my parents, but the five people who mean the world to me every single detail I remember of that night.

I can clearly hear Rain crying, and I want to hold her. But I can't look at them, I can't because I'm barely holding on by a thread. I know I can take a break, but not yet. I want to get as much of this done as I can and get it out of the way.

You would think the hard part was over, but it's not.

I try to ignore my mother and Rain's light sniffles, and the hushed angry tones coming from the guys as Theo tells them to be quiet before the judge kicks them out. I turn to Tim's lawyer, hating that I can't look at Theo anymore for support at this moment. He helped me more than he will ever know. I love that man so much, and if it wasn't for him, for all of them, I don't think I'd be able to do this.

Maybe that's why this is all happening now. Maybe I needed

my heart to be full and whole again before I was able to rip it to shreds during this process. I needed them to be there to put it back together when all of this is over.

"Miss Tatum, you say my client was always trying to be your friend, did you ever once tell him that you didn't want to be his friend?"

I put a mask on, knowing to only answer questions he can't spin.

"No."

"Why not? If you didn't want him around you, why not tell him that?" he insists.

"I didn't want to be rude."

"But isn't it rude to lead him on? By not telling him you're declining his friendship, he was led to believe you were fine with it. I mean, how else was he supposed to take it?"

I don't say anything.

"And the night of the party, you were all graduating and that included Mr. Hightower, correct? Don't you think he would have wanted to talk to, maybe celebrate with, someone he considered a friend?"

Again, nothing. I'm not going to let him back me into a corner.

"So, when Mr. Hightower found you, is it possible that he saw someone he thought was a friend who looked sick, and that he wanted to make sure you were okay?"

"No, he didn't," I say, my breathing starting to pick up. *Relax, Ellie, don't let them see that they are getting to you.*

"No? Was there anyone else there fighting at the chance to help you? To make sure you didn't fall over? Can't it be assumed that he saw a friend who looked like she had one too many drinks? What kind of friend would just leave someone like that?" Tim's lawyer taunts.

"He wasn't my friend," I state firmly.

"How was he supposed to know that? You never turned him

down. In his mind, you were friends because he was never told differently."

I grit my teeth. I really want to punch this man in the nuts.

"Who was your lover at the time?" he asks, taking me by surprise.

"What does that have to do with anything?" I ask, blood pounding in my ears.

"Is it true that you were dating not only one but three men, as well as a woman? Three men and the very woman who are in this room right now."

"Again, I don't see how that matters," I huff.

"My client had a crush on you. He knew you were open to dating multiple people at one time. Because you never turned him down, he had the hopes that he could be one of those people. You were nice to him, you talked to him, never turned him away. Don't you see how someone might take that as an invitation to pursue a romantic relationship because those are all indications that the other person is interested in them?"

I can't say anything because I will fight back. I will tell him where to go, and how to fucking get there. So, I grit my teeth and let him make me sound like a whore. Because I know what we have, and he does not.

"So, when Mr. Hightower saw the girl he liked not looking so well, he wanted to help her. So he took you upstairs. And when the girl he liked didn't say no to his kiss and his touches, he had no reason to think what he was doing was wrong. Just because you woke up the next day and felt like you cheated on your lovers, doesn't mean what he did was wrong."

"Objection, your honor, he's berating my client," Jeff shouts and the whole courtroom erupts into angry shouts.

Tears fill my eyes, and I will myself not to cry.

"Order!" the judge shouts, banging his gavel. "I will have order in my courtroom."

The room dies down and Tim's lawyer gives me a smug as hell

grin. "I have no more questions, your honor," he says before sitting down.

"There will be a ten minute recess before we resume," the judge states before getting up and walking out a side door.

I get down off the stand and head straight down the aisle, straight out the room, ignoring the calls of my name. I beeline to the bathroom I know is across the hall, pushing the door so hard it crashes against the wall, and run into the first stall. I don't even get a chance to lock the door before I hover over the toilet bowl and heave up everything in my stomach.

My body shakes as it purges itself. I hate him. I hate his lawyer. I hate that the world allows monsters like him to walk free and be represented by men with no morals.

A sob slips free, and I cry, my body shaking, unable to be strong anymore. I thought I could do this, but maybe I can't.

"Shhh," a soft delicate voice says as the person gathers my hair up and out of the way. "Get it all out, baby. I'm here." Rain's voice is broken as she tries to hold back her own sobs.

When everything is out of me, and I have nothing left to purge, I sit on the bathroom floor. She hands me some tissues, and I wipe my mouth, then flush everything.

I just stare at her red rimmed, devastated eyes for a moment before launching myself into her arms. She holds me while I cry. "He said I wanted it. I didn't, Rain, I didn't want anything he did to me."

"I know, baby," she says, rocking me back and forth. "I know. We believe you."

"I didn't cheat on you, I promise," I sob into her chest.

"I know," she cries. "We know that now."

We sit there and cry, holding each other until footsteps outside the stall have me lifting my head from Rain's chest.

"Ellie?" Jax asks, his voice soft.

I turn to Rain, and she gives me a small smile. "Ready to get back out there?" she asks as we both stand up.

"No," I huff. "But we have to."

"You've got this, Ellie. You're so strong, baby. We're here for you, okay?"

I nod and wipe my eyes. I open the stall door to see Jax standing there, looking helpless and concerned.

"Are you okay?" he asks, taking a step toward me. I give him a small smile.

"I will be. It's just a lot to take in." My face falls, tears welling in my eyes again. "I hate that you guys had to hear all of that. I never wanted you to know all the details."

He swallows thickly, his own eyes watering as he pulls me tightly into his arms. "I'm so fucking sorry you had to go through that. We should have been there to protect you. I will hate myself for the rest of my life that we didn't stop him," Jax growls, and I hug him harder.

"Please don't. I don't want you to hate yourself. It won't change anything and only make things worse. Just love me, be here for me, protect me now, that's all that matters."

"I will, baby. I always fucking will," he says into the top of my head before giving me a kiss.

"How's Brody doing?" I ask, pulling back.

"Not so good," he says, giving me a heartbreaking look. "He blames himself. He saw what was happening, and he could have stopped it and for that alone, I don't think he will ever let it go that he didn't intervene."

"It was already too late," I sigh. "Tim already did the damage before Brody showed up. Even if he did stop him, it wouldn't have changed anything. Maybe his friends wouldn't have touched me, but that was nothing compared to what Tim did, the damage he's caused."

"Ellie," Theo's voice echoes through the bathroom. "We have to go back in."

"Coming," I call back, then look from Rain to Jax. "Ready?"

I grab both of their hands, and we meet Chase, Brody, and Theo outside in the hall.

"Ellie," Chase says with urgency as he rushes over to me.

"Fuck, are you okay?" he asks, cupping my face as he looks me over.

"I'm better now. Let's just get this over with, okay?"

"Yeah," he says, nodding his head. "Let's go."

I give Theo a smile, and he looks at me like he's the proudest man in the world. A bubble of emotion takes over me at how loved I really am.

Chapter Thirty

ELLIE

ELLIE

BRODY JOINS US, his face a blank mask, but I can see the storm raging within his hazel eyes.

With all the people who would go to the ends of the Earth for me at my back, I walk back into the courtroom with my head held high. Like Cooper said that day in the food court, 'Hold your head up, don't let them see you break.' And that's exactly what I do.

Looking over at my friends in the back of the room, they all have red rimmed eyes. They look at me with love and worry, and I give them a reassuring smile before taking a seat between Theo and Brody. Brody looks down at me, the emotion in his eyes almost makes me gasp. It's too much to handle right now, so I look away. But I grab his hand, lacing my fingers through his. He grips me tightly but not enough to hurt me.

The judge resumes the hearing, and Tim's asked to take the stand. Tim's lawyer questions him, but I zone him out. I don't want to hear him and his lawyer spewing bullshit and lies. After Tim's lawyer is done, it's Jeff's turn now to question Tim before we break out our smoking gun.

"Mr. Hightower, I would very much like to hear your side of everything. Do you care to tell us?" Tim looks over at me, his eyes cruel and soulless. "Without looking at my client, please."

"Sure, I'd love to tell you what *really* happened," Tim says, plastering a smile on his face like he's some all American boy. *I hate him.*

Brody growls next to me, and I rub my thumb in circles on the palm of his hand to soothe him.

"I went to the same high school as Ellie. We didn't run in the same circles, so I didn't meet her until she was paired up to help me with some schoolwork. She was the smartest kid in our school, and I wanted nothing but the best. She was the best. I was entranced by her right away. Ellie was quiet, but she was nice, kind, and beautiful. I knew she was seeing someone. Actually, more than just one person; she was seeing multiple people at the time. It didn't bother me, I still wanted to get to know her. And the more I did, the harder I fell."

This man is fucking crazy. Sure, I helped him with homework here and there, but I wasn't around him *that* much. He did all the talking, and I just stared awkwardly when it wasn't about school.

"I was hopeful she felt the same way I did. She never mentioned anyone she was dating while we were hanging out. She always smiled and listened to what I had to say. So when it was graduation night, it was my last chance to tell her how I felt. I tried to find her, but she spent the whole night avoiding me. I didn't know why. She was always so sweet, and I told her I would see her at the party. She said she would be there too. When I saw her by herself, looking like she needed to lay down, I was worried."

Something turns in my belly at how genuine he looks, like this monster is actually believing his own lies. My skin crawls, and I grit my teeth, urging myself not to shout out that he's lying.

"When I found a quiet room, I laid her on the bed. I made sure she was okay and went to leave. That's when she called out my name. When I turned around, she looked at me with pleading eyes, asking me to stay with her. How could I not? This was the girl I was crushing hard for. She wanted me, so I stayed."

Angry tears fill in my eyes, but I don't let them fall. We all know it's a lie, every word from his dirty mouth is a lie. He's more disturbed than I thought he was. A part of me wonders what he would have done to my life if I didn't move away with my parents.

"I sat down on the bed next to her and that's when she pulled me down for a kiss. I wasn't gonna say no. So we kissed. Kissing led from one thing to another. Not once did she tell me to stop, or tell me no. I won't deny the fact that we had sex. But it was consensual. She came on to me."

Jax is harshly whispering into Brody's ear from his other side. I can feel Brody vibrating. He's ready to burst. I look over at him, tugging on his hand to get his attention.

"It's okay," I tell him. His eyes hold nothing but pure rage, his nostrils flaring constantly. He knows this is anything but okay. "Don't let him win," I whisper.

"I'm sorry that she regretted what happened the next morning, that she felt guilty for sleeping with me. She felt like she cheated on her lovers, maybe she did, but I didn't force her to," he says with conviction as if it's the absolute truth. "And the only reason why she's claiming these false accusations now is because she wants her old lovers back. She's crying rape so she doesn't have to live with the fact that she cheated on them."

"You fucking bastard!" Brody roars.

"Order!" the judge shouts as Chase and Jax force Brody back into his seat. "I will have order in my courtroom, do you understand me, young man?" he asks Brody. Brody sits back down, forcing his eyes away from Tim and over to the judge. "If you cannot control your temper, you will be removed. You already have a pending assault charge with Mr. Hightower, don't make this worse on yourself, son. Do you understand?"

"Yes," Brody says through gritted teeth.

The judge then tells Jeff to proceed, and I can't help but smile inside like a crazy person because this is it. He might have said a bunch of lies that hurt to hear, but it will make him look like a fucking idiot here in a moment.

"That was a very interesting retelling of your side of the events, Mr. Hightower," Jeff says, grabbing his laptop off the top of his desk and then brings it over to the judge. "Your honor, I have some last minute evidence that was presented to me during the break that I would like to show."

Tim's face falters as he turns to his lawyer who is up on his feet. "Objection. We were not made aware of this!"

"Overruled. I'll allow it if it is relevant to this case," the judge says.

Jeff nods. "It is."

"Then proceed."

Jeff opens the laptop and hooks it up to the smart, flat screen TV to the left of Tim and stands back. The play button hovers over a video and Jeff looks over at Tim. "Now, Mr. Hightower, I'm going to show you something. I'd like you to identify the people in this video for me, please." He presses play, but there's no sound. The video plays and Jeff pauses when you can get a side view of Tim. "Now, could you tell me who this is? And tell the truth please, you're under oath. We also have witnesses ready to testify."

"That's me," Tim says, his eyes filling with rage.

"And who is this?" Jeff asks, pressing play and pausing it on my face.

"Miss Tatum," Tim hisses.

"And you're positive?" Jeff asks.

"Yes." Tim gives him the death glare.

"Thank you." Jeff smiles, then restarts the video from the start, but this time with sound. Tim's voice rings clear through the room.

"*When my guys told me they ran into you at the game, I was disappointed I wasn't with them. To find out you were back in town, going to school with your exes, was a nice surprise. Heard it has been pretty rough for you though. Guess they still see you as the whore you are."*

"*I'm not a whore,"* my voice snaps back.

"*No? Then why did you cheat on them with me?"* He cocks his head to the side.

"*I didn't cheat and you know it. You...you...you raped me."* That word comes out on a hushed sob.

"*Oh sugar, you know you loved it,"* he says back.

"*No, no, I didn't. I didn't want any of it. I was in a loving relationship. I would never have cheated on them. You drugged me. You raped me!"* I shouted a little louder with more strength behind it.

"*Yeah, yeah, I did rape you. You were a fucking tease. Always flirting with me, leading me on then treating me like I was nothing!"*

"*I never flirted with you,"* I insisted. "*I was just trying to be nice."*

"*You're a stupid, selfish whore. You got what you deserved. And you know what? It's all I've thought about. Every time I'm alone, I replay that night. The way you looked up at me with fear in your eyes, unable to move while you just laid there, and I got to take everything I was owed. When I'm with another girl, I pretend it's you. Best fuck of my life."*

"*You're sick!"* I shouted back.

"*Nah, babe, I just know what I want. And now that you're here in front of me, I'm gonna have it again. No one's going to save you, just like they didn't save you last time."*

Jeff pauses and the whole room erupts into chatter. The judge blinks at the screen, dumbfounded by what he just witnessed.

"Looks to me like everything you said before I played this video was a lie, Mr. Hightower. It's clear as day, you just admitted to everything you're being charged with. Actually, you were planning on doing it again that night, weren't you? That if Brody Creed didn't stop you the way he did, then you would have."

"You lying whore!" Tim screams, looking at me with unadulterated malice. He moves to get up, and the bailiff grabs him.

"You're nothing but a waste of space. You deserved what you fucking got!"

"Get him out of my courtroom!" the judge booms.

"Give us a moment, please," Tim's lawyer says, running after Tim.

"Did that really just happen?" I say with disbelief, a crazed laugh slipping out.

"I think it did," Theo chuckles.

"Settle down, please," the judge says, then starts to talk to Jeff.

"We got this in the bag, baby," Rain says over to me, a beaming smile on her face.

I sit there with nervous, giddy energy, waiting to see what the judge will decide to do next.

Everyone chatters among themselves, but my mind is buzzing. A few minutes later, Tim's lawyer comes back into the room without Tim, and goes over to the judge. They have a hushed conversation before the judge nods, the look on his face doesn't look like he's too happy.

"Alright, everyone. Court is postponed for a few days. Within those days, I will look over the evidence and come to a conclusion. The tape that was presented will be looked over by my team to make sure nothing was fabricated. In the meantime, Eleanor Tatum," he looks at me, "I am ordering you to get your daughter, Lilianna Tatum, a DNA test to see if Timothy Hightower is the biological father."

My whole body locks up. No, no, this isn't happening. *What the hell?*

"Your honor, may I say something?" I ask, my voice shaky. I try to ignore the shocked and outraged looks on my guys' faces.

"You may," the judge nods.

"I don't see the need for a DNA test. I was already eight weeks along the night of graduation. There's no way Tim can be the father." *Please listen to me. Please don't make me do this.*

"I understand. But because of the timeline of the events, Mr. Hightower is now claiming the child is his and is

324

demanding his parental rights be instated. The only way to counteract that would be with proof." My heart falls out of my chest. "Court will resume April 20th, and I will make my decision then."

I drop into my seat, my body numb. I know he's not her father, I believe what the doctor said. I was pregnant before...*right?*

What if they read the ultrasound wrong? What if my period was off and messed with the whole timeline? What if Tim really is her father?

Tears stream down my face as the judge gets up and leaves the room. "Ellie, baby, don't. Please don't," Jax says, crouching down in front of me. "He is not her father. We are, okay? We know that already. We are her fathers. He's just grasping at straws. He knows he's done for and is just looking to buy himself any time he can get."

"You're right," I say, wiping my eyes. *I hope he's right.*

"Come on, sweet girl. Let's go home. There's nothing else we can do now but wait," Theo says, holding out his hand.

I take it and follow him out of the aisle.

"How dare you keep our grandchild away from us," Tim's mother says, stepping in front of us. I look up at her with shock. "We are going to make sure we get that little girl and bring her home where she belongs."

My heart starts pounding, and my skin gets clammy. A panic attack is coming. This is all too much.

"Listen here, you wing bat," Val says, coming up behind Tim's mom. "You aren't her grandmother. You're just a mother who gave birth to a fucked up monster who rapes women. No one would allow you to guide any child after the one you raised. Now get your wrinkly, old ass out of my girl's face before we're back here for a whole new reason," Val growls, and I can't help the laugh that bubbles up. *I fucking love her.*

"This isn't over," Tim's mother huffs before turning around and leaving the room with her husband in tow.

"I'm so sorry all of this is happening to you, babe." Val says, pulling me into a hug.

"Don't listen to whatever that nut job says. Lilly isn't Tim's. We all know it, and soon, so will they. God, that whole family is fucked," Lexie says.

We all file out into the main part of the courthouse. I thank my friends for coming and giving me support as they leave. My parents hold me as they cry and say goodbye before taking off to their hotel room. As much as I hate that they had to hear all the details, I'm glad they came.

"It could have been worse," Jeff says as we gather outside the courthouse. "They will look at the video and prove that it wasn't messed with. As for the DNA, they can't fake that. This is just to buy some time when really, in the end, it won't do anything for them."

"I know." I nod, rubbing my hands up and down my arms, trying to get the raised flesh to go down. "So, what happens now?"

"Tomorrow, some of the court appointed medical technicians will come by and take the sample they need and bring it right to the lab. It will take a few days for the results. Then we will come back and get that sick fuck locked up. I'm just sorry they are doing all of this. But it's what I expected. They are currently stalling, but it could have been so much worse. If they found that voicemail, this might have been a lot harder to fight the cheating accusation."

"What voicemail?" Brody asks, coming up next to me.

Fuck. "Ah," I say, biting the inside of my cheek. "The one you left me after graduation night."

His brows furrow in confusion. "What do you mean?" he says. "I didn't send a voice message."

"Umm, yeah, you did. Trust me, you did. I know your voice, it came from your number."

"What did it say?" he asks. *Does he really not remember?*

"It doesn't matter. It's in the past. Let's leave it buried," I tell him. If he doesn't remember, I don't want to be the one to remind him.

"Ellie," he growls. "What did it say?"

"Brody, please just leave it," I ask him with pleading eyes.

His face falls. "I was a monster, wasn't I? I said shit that upset you?" *Oh boy, if he only knew how much that voicemail fucked me up. How the thought of it makes me want to cry.* "Fuck, Ellie, for fuck's sake!" he hisses. "I wanna hear it."

"What?" I ask, my eyes going wide. "No. No, you don't. Trust me."

"Ellie, I need to hear it. I don't like not knowing what I said. Please," he growls.

I still have it. I should have deleted it a long time ago, but instead, I sent it to my email.

"Alright, but not here. Let's go back to my place."

Brody already feels like shit for the part he played in the past and how it's affecting the present. How is he going to feel when he hears the words that crushed my soul?

Chapter Thirty-One

BRODY

MY BODY IS SHAKING with so much rage that not even the tight grip of Jax's hand in mine is calming me down. This whole fucking case is a joke. The judge would be a fucking moron if he can't clearly see how much of a deranged pervert Tim is.

I was like a ticking time bomb the whole time. When Ellie revealed, in detail, everything that happened that night, something inside me died. I walked in on it happening and I did nothing to stop it. I *let* it happen. We got into a fight, and she went off by herself. I left her open to that sick monster.

How does she still want me? How does she still love me after going through that?! She shouldn't even be able to look at me without wanting to kill me.

As she spoke each word, I was torn between staying seated for the good of the case and climbing over that barrier to finish what I started months ago. Only this time, Tim wouldn't be making it out alive. I equally wanted to go over to Ellie, pull her into my arms, and tell her everything will be okay because I'll slay anyone who hurts her again.

I couldn't contain myself anymore when Tim got up there and started spewing all his bullshit and lies. The look on his face portraying that he truly thought what he was said was real. That man is sick and needs to be locked up behind bars where he can't hurt anyone anymore.

Forcing myself to sit back down so I didn't get kicked out was hard, almost impossible, but I didn't want it to look bad for me. My case is going to be settled as soon as Ellie's is done. I can't risk being locked up and being away from the people I love. Not when I just got them back.

"Brody," Jax says, glancing over at me.

"What?" I snap, turning away from the window. He glares at me before turning back to the road he's driving down. "Fuck, sorry." I let out a harsh sigh. "I don't mean to snap at you."

"I know you're on edge, we all are. What we just heard...it wasn't easy for any of us. And I know I can speak for all of us that something inside us broke, hearing what really happened to the girl we love so much." A tear slips down his cheek. "Everything hurts, Brody, but we need to be strong. We need to be there for her because this isn't our pain. This isn't something that happened to us. We can't change the past, no matter how much we wish we could go back and fix it. We need to think about the here and now. And right now, our girl needs us."

"I know." I nod. He said *our girl* and I want so fucking bad to be included in that. "I know...but Tim," I growl. "The lies, fuck, the lies. I just wanna, argh!" I shout, smashing my fist against the dashboard. "And now he wants a fucking DNA test? The man is fucking crazy if he thinks there's even a slight chance that he's Lilly's father. That whole fucking family is crazy if they think they will ever lay eyes on her. She's ours, Jax. She's *our* baby girl, and I will destroy anyone who tries to take her from us." My chest is heaving as I try to catch my breath. I'm so fucking worked up, I just want to scream.

"He's just buying time," Chase says from the back seat. Looking over my shoulder, I see Rain snuggled into Chase. She is staring at the back of Jax's seat and Chase is looking out the window, both with defeated looks on their faces. "She's ours."

"And what if by some freak chance, she's not?" I question.

Chase's head snaps over to me, and if looks could kill, I'd be six feet under.

"It will never matter whose DNA created that little girl. She is, and will always be, *ours*. Fuck off with that shit, Brody, don't even start," he growls in warning.

"I'm not!" I snap back. It's too late for me. That little girl owns my heart now. I will die for her, buy her anything her little heart desires.

"Then why bring it up? You act like you don't deserve them. Hell, none of us do. But get the fuck over yourself and see that the woman you love is hurting. Get over your own fucking pity party and see what's right in front of your face. She doesn't care if you don't deserve her. She doesn't care if you're not Prince Charming. She loves you, Brody, every broken piece. Now, stop hurting her and just fucking love her."

I look away and back out the window. His words sink in. *Am I doing more damage by staying away? Is he right?*

Fuck, I know he's right. For whatever reason, she still loves me, wants me. I don't know if she's forgiven me for all the messed up shit I did, but she's willing to give me another chance.

Why can't I get out of my own fucking head and take it? I should be grabbing that chance and showing her how much she means to me. How she's on my mind every moment of every day. That my heart aches to have her sleeping between me and Jax like she did over Spring break.

Waking up next to her, watching her sleep and seeing how peaceful she was...it ignited something deep inside of me. And the fact that Jax didn't wake up once that night from a nightmare from his past, that he slept like he didn't have a care in the world... it's like she was the missing piece of the puzzle of our hearts.

"What do you think is on that voicemail?" Jax asks, parking the car when we get to Ellie's apartment building.

"I don't know. I honestly don't. I don't remember leaving a voicemail for her. All I remember from that night was me being in a fit of rage, convinced that she cheated on us. I thought she just moved away because of the guilt of what she did." I look to Jax. "Her lawyer said it could have been used against her. Jax, whatever I said in that voicemail...I know it hurt her." Angry tears form in the back of my eyes. "Why can't I stop hurting the people I love? Why am I so fucked up?"

"Because your mom is a raging cunt who doesn't deserve to be anything but gum on the bottom of someone's shoes. And your dad is a raging alcoholic who would rather drink his feelings away than kick the trash that is your mother to the curb. You were dealt a shitty hand, but they don't control who you are now, Brody, so stop letting your past have so much power over your present," Rain says then slides out of the car, slamming the door behind her. Chase follows her, leaving me alone in the car with Jax.

"Brody...whatever it says, please don't let it get to you. Feel mad you said it, regret your words, but don't push us away. Don't let it fuck with all the progress you've made when it comes to Ellie and Lilly. Remember, it's in the *past*, there's nothing you can do to take it back."

"I'll try," I tell him, and we both get out of the car. Ellie and Theo are waiting for us by the front door of the apartment building.

"Are you sure you wanna hear it?" Ellie asks, her eyes full of pain.

"If you had to live with the pain of what I said to you, then I deserve to live with the guilt of it," I tell her.

She sighs in frustration. "Brody, when will you understand that if I'm not letting the past get to me anymore, then you shouldn't either? You keep punishing yourself, but you're only hurting me in the end," she says before going into the building with the others following.

"I heard the voicemail. It's not pretty, man. But if I can say these words after hearing it, and she's willing to still want to be with you after living with those words, then you need to get the fuck over yourself. She loves you, despite everything you hate about yourself. You're only hurting her by staying away, it helps no one. So, get your fucking head out of your ass, and try a different approach to make up for your sins. Love her, protect her, cherish her, but for the love of god, stop hurting her," Theo snaps.

He leaves me standing in the doorway by myself. *I want to.* I *want* to do all that so much, but the words of my mother dance around in the back of my mind.

Alright, Brody, let's go see how much of a monster you truly are.

ELLIE

Why can't he just let this go? It's only going to cause more pain. I haven't listened to that voicemail in years, and hearing it again is just going to hurt more.

I want to throttle Jeff for bringing that up within hearing distance of Brody. I had no idea that Brody didn't remember it.

What if hearing this is the last straw for him? What if it makes him feel so guilty and unworthy that he distances himself from everyone? I can't handle that. I just got them back. Even with the pain that Brody has caused me, I see the man I love every day. When he looks at Jax, or me when he doesn't think I'm looking. How he laughs and smiles more easily now. The way he sticks up for me and protects me. The look in his eyes when I was on my knees for Jax; it was like I was the rarest beauty in the world.

We all move to sit in the living room. Theo stands behind the chair I'm sitting on with his hand on my shoulder in support. I look up at him, and he gives me a sweet smile.

He's been so amazing throughout this whole ordeal. My rock. They all are, but he's been my safe place from the very start.

Chase, Rain, and Jax take a seat on the couch, but Brody sits on the edge of the table in front of me.

"Are you sure?" I asks again.

"Yes," he nods. "If you have to live with the words in that voicemail, then so do I."

Tears start to fill my eyes. "I don't want to. Fuck, Brody." I close my eyes, letting the tears fall. I'm done keeping things to myself, I'm done waiting around. "If I play this, I risk you never coming back to me. I love you, Brody, so much that you keeping yourself away hurts me. You think you're helping, but you're not. I know you don't think you're worth anything, but you are. You're worth so much to me, to Jax, and to your friends. You are none of the words that your parents say. Please, just love me," I cry.

His own eyes well with emotion. "I do love you," he says. "Just play the voicemail."

Stubborn bastard.

I shake my head, letting out a breath, feeling defeated and exhausted after this whole day. I just want to curl up in a ball and cry myself to sleep. "Fine."

Once I find the audio clip in my old saved files, my thumb hovers over the play button. Fuck it, if he wants to hear it, so be it. I press play and his voice rings through the phone.

"Ellie! Ellie, Ellie, Ellie. You must be so fucking proud of yourself, aren't you?" His voice is more of a slur, and I know he was drinking. *"Was he good? Did it feel good? Was he worth it? You had three cocks to keep you satisfied, but that wasn't enough? You had to go fuck the whole damn swim team. It was a lie, wasn't it? The past eight fucking years. You never loved us. You're a heartless, cheating whore, and we're done. We're all fucking done with you. I wish we had never met you. I wish Rain never went up to the quiet girl on the playground and brought you into our lives. I hate you, Ellie, and I will until the day I die. You're dead to me, to all of us. Never speak to us again."* There's a rustling sound and right before the voicemail ends, he says, *"Fucking useless, cheating whore."*

The voicemail ends, and the whole room is quiet. There's a pain in my chest that hurts so much, I can't breathe. You would think I'd be used to hearing it by now with the amount of times I've played it, but it feels like the first time every time.

Brody stares at me, his face fallen and broken while angry tears well in his eyes.

"I'm so sorry," he chokes, falling down to his knees in front of me. I look down at him, a little cry breaking free from my chest. "I didn't mean it. I didn't mean any of those words, please believe me. I'm so fucking sorry, Ellie." He cups my face, and the look in his eye tells me this is his breaking point. I thought this voicemail would push him away, send him running into another world of guilt and self loathing. And he very well may. But not right now.

"I love you, Ellie. You are my whole fucking world. Those words were those of a dumb, dumb boy. A boy who knew nothing. A boy who was told every day of his life he was nothing. That he didn't deserve the love he had, and that it was all a lie. That's not me anymore. I don't think I deserve you, and I don't think I ever will. But fuck, baby, I love you so much and pushing you away hurts my soul. It's the worst pain imaginable. I wanna make it up to you, and I will die trying to be the man you deserve. I'll never drink again. I will do everything in my power to show you every single day just how much you mean to me. I'll be the best damn dad that little girl could ask for. Fuck, please, Ellie, just don't hate me."

"I don't hate you," I sob. "I've *never* hated you. Even after everything, I still love you. Why can't you see that? If I'm willing to put the past where it belongs and start over new, why can't you? I love you, Brody, and not being able to have you like I want is unbearable. You, Jax, Rain, Chase, and Theo, you make me whole. Without one, I'll always be broken."

"Can we put each other back together?" he asks, his eyes wide with desperation. I'm not used to this Brody. So open, so vulnerable. I need to be careful how I answer this because one wrong word and he will never allow this part of him to show again. Do I think we can just jump back into a relationship? No. Out of everyone, we have the most to work on. But I want it to work. I want him, all of him, every fucked up damaged little piece of him.

"Every broken little shattered piece." I give him a tear-filled smile.

"Fuck, Ellie," he growls before crashing his lips to mine. This kiss, it's everything. He pours every ounce of his feelings into this kiss. All of his love and pain. My whole body is humming with energy, like a million little stars are exploding above us.

This kiss is messy with teeth clashing and tongues battling, but it's so fucking right.

Call me crazy, but I swear I can feel that final piece of my soul click back into place. It's not sturdy, both it and my heart need a lot of work. But it's a start.

"Everyday," Brody says, pulling back from the kiss and putting his forehead to mine. Our breathing is erratic as we come down from the high of the kiss. "I will love you, care for you, worship at your feet."

"I don't want you to be anything but you, Brody. I love the real you, the one you've been keeping locked up. Let him back out. I need him."

"I will," he says. "I can't promise you that I won't still be the overbearing, over-protective, alpha-male asshole, but I will treat you like the queen that you are." He gives me a dirty smile, and my heart skips a beat.

"I can't wait." I smile.

Everyone leaves after we order some supper. Brody has me in his lap the rest of the night, his arms wrapped around me tightly. Anytime one of the others tries to have a turn, he lets out this growl that has my lower belly burning and my thighs wet.

I just grin and snuggle into him, loving every moment of it. Jax keeps giving us looks that are pure happiness all night. And anytime I look at Theo, he gives me this cocky *'I told you so'* look.

I knew it wouldn't be easy when it came to Brody. It never

will be. We're both damaged to the core in many different ways. But we love each other despite it, maybe even because of it.

The high of the night is wearing off, and I feel like I've been hit by a bus, run over by a car, and then went a few rounds in the ring with Mike Tyson...in his prime.

"Let me do this," Theo says, grabbing the empty box of pizza I just grabbed from the coffee table.

"It's fine," I say, not letting go. He cocks a brow, and I let out a huff, giving him the box. He goes over to the garbage, then comes back over.

"I love you," he tells me, pulling me to his chest.

"I love you too," I murmur, holding him tightly so I don't fall over.

"Everything will be okay," he says just like he always does. "I just know it."

"I hope so," I say back, my voice breaking. I've cried so much today, and it's made me so exhausted. Not just physically, but my heart and soul feel as if they've taken a beating, and I'm not sure how much more I can take.

The radio is playing in the background and *Don't Dream It's Over* by Crowded House comes on. Theo starts humming along, rocking us back and forth. It's one of my favorite songs, and the universe always seems to play the right songs at the right time.

The song plays as we dance in one spot. I listen to the lyrics as it continues to play. When it gets to the *'don't dream it's over'* part, he starts singing. The next part is about a wall being built between us, and when he sings the lyrics *'we know they won't win'*, I break. I cry into his chest as we dance.

So close, we are so close to being able to put this behind us and move on with our lives. The only thing that keeps me from giving up is my baby girl. She is my reason for living...and them, my lovers, my heart, my everything.

Only a few more days, Ellie. We've got this.

JAX

These past few days have been stressful. We're all trying to hold it together for Ellie, but after hearing what really happened that night, it broke something inside of us. The fact that we were all in the house while that was happening to her and did nothing to stop it will stick with us for the rest of our lives.

Then the ass hat had the nerve to try to stake a claim on our daughter. *Fucking* ridiculous!

When the med tech came over to get Lilly's DNA sample, she was so confused. Ellie hated lying to her, but there was no way she would tell Lilly what was really going on. Instead, she told Lilly she was getting her tested to make sure we weren't sick with the flu that was going around.

We are going back tomorrow for the sentencing, and after that, Brody's hearing will be settled too. I have high hopes that both will end the way we want them to, but I hate all the pain, stress, and worry my girl has to go through because of it.

One thing I'm over the moon about is the fact that Brody finally got his head out of his ass. When I was listening to what he said on that voicemail, I was so mad at him. She went years thinking he meant what he said, living with those words in the back of her mind. I felt sick about it. I hate when people talk for me, and him saying that the rest of us hated her and wanted nothing to do with her wasn't true. At least, not at that particular moment.

But I won't dwell on it, and I won't hold it against him. It's in the past, and he said it during a bad time in his life.

I thought after he heard what he said, he would get up and leave. Go into a fit of self-hatred and self-sabotage, but he surprised me by doing the complete opposite.

Now, I get to be with my two lovers while watching them explore and get to know each other without all the stress.

And when he said he would stop drinking for her, I was so proud of him. I know he hasn't been drinking since I found him the day after he got out of lockup. But I think most of that is his stubbornness to prove that he's not like his dad and that he doesn't have a problem. I see him struggling when we're all out at the club or a party. I see the way he looks at the bottles. We don't keep anything in the house to make it easier on him. Chase and I don't drink unless we're out anyways.

I don't bring it up or point it out like Chase has, but I am proud of him nonetheless. I really wish he would go to a meeting and talk to others who are struggling with the same thing, but I don't want to cause any issues between us. You can't tell someone they have a problem. They need to come to that conclusion on their own. Although, if it ever does get to the point were he becomes like his dad, I *will* say something.

"Jax," Ellie's soft voice pulls me from my inner thoughts.

"Yes, baby," I answer back, kissing the top of her head.

"Can we go to your room?" she asks, tilting her head up to look at me.

"Are you tired?" I ask. She's spending the night at our place tonight, again. Her and Lilly have been staying here the past two nights, and we all love it. It just feels right. I just wish it was under better circumstances. Ellie has missed school since the day of the hearing. She's trying to keep up by watching her lectures online, but I know her mind is elsewhere.

"No. I just want to spend time with you," she says. I look over at Brody who's watching us. He gives me a small smile, nodding his head. We share a room now, so he will be out on the couch for now.

"Thank you," I mouth to Brody.

Chase is snoring, passed out in the chair, and Lilly went to bed a few hours ago, so we have just been watching movies.

"Of course." I kiss her lips. Sliding my arm under her legs and around her back, I stand up, keeping her in my arms.

"Goodnight, Star," Brody says, standing up and placing a kiss on her cheek.

"Night, B." She smiles sweetly at him. His whole face lights up at her use of his nickname and my heart soars.

Brody gives me a kiss. "I love you, pretty boy," he whispers in my ear, sending a shiver down my spine. "Go make our girl feel good and forget about all the bad shit in the world."

I look back at him with lust filled eyes, and smirking at the fact that he called her *our* girl. Because she is, and it's about time he saw that. "I love you too."

"Hey, what about me?" Ellie gives us an adorable pout.

Brody gives her a soft look, so unlike him. "I love you too, baby girl, more than you will ever know." He leans in and captures her lips with his, kissing her sweetly, but also packed with so much love that it causes a small whimper to escapes from her lips.

He pulls back and licks his lips. I know he wants to join us, but he also knows he still has some work to do before he gets to where the others and I are with her.

Carrying her into the bedroom, I place her in the center of the bed. "Want me to go grab you your sleep clothes?" I ask her.

"No." She shakes her head. "I'd rather sleep in your shirt," she says, pulling her top off over her head, revealing her heavy breasts. They're perfect. Stretch marks start from the areolas and go up halfway, making a unique design. She's a work of art.

"Jax, babe, eyes up here," she giggles.

My eyes snap to hers as my face heats from getting caught staring. *Can you blame me?* She is stunning.

She removes her shorts so she's only in her panties, and I feel my cock twitch at the sight of her.

"Umm," I say, shaking my head as I go over to my dresser and grab one of my band tees. "Here." I hold it out to her.

"Put it on the side table. No point in putting it on now when I'm just gonna take it off in a minute." She licks her lips, looking at my now very hard length.

I stand there frozen. I want her; I want her so fucking bad it hurts. I've been thinking about taking her again for years, and since she came back into our lives, it's been something I think all the time.

But I haven't had sex with a girl since her, only messed around. It's been five years. I'm not the same person in the bedroom as I was back then.

Brody and Chase have always been the more dominant ones. When we did things as a group, they were there to guide me, tell me what to do with her. It's just how it was.

We've had sex alone, but I was an awkward teenager back then. Now, I'm used to Brody taking control, telling me what to do and calling me a good boy while I do it. It's how I like it.

"Jax," Ellie says. "Are you okay?"

"Yeah." I nod, then shake my head. "I'm just...I don't know what to do." She gives me a smirk, and cocks a brow.

"From what I saw with Brody, I think you know how sex works," she says, her voice filled with amusement.

I let out a sigh and sit on the bed. "I know how to have sex," I laugh. "It's just, we...me and you, this is new. It's been years and I...I don't know how you want it."

Her face softens. "Jax, you're thinking too much into it. Just be here with me in the moment, make love to me." She gets on her knees and moves to kneel next me. Cupping my face, she brushes her thumb against my cheek, her long blonde hair hanging down over her naked breasts. "Is it because you give control over to Brody?"

I nod. "With him...there is no soft and slow, not really. And that's okay, that's how I like it."

"Jax, can I make love to you?" she asks me. "Can you give me control in this moment, and maybe we can find what works for us?"

"Yes," I breathe. The need to be inside her, to hear her breathy moans as I bring her pleasure is overwhelming.

"I like it hard and fast, I like it sweet and slow. Giving up control was hard for me, but when it's with someone I love and trust, I feel free."

"I feel the same," I say as she brushes her lips against mine.

"How about we find ourselves again, together?" I nod, and she kisses me, slipping her tongue into my mouth. I moan against her soft lips as her hand grasps a handful of my hair, giving it a little tug.

"You're wearing *far* too much clothing," she comments, pulling back from the kiss.

"Allow me to fix that," I chuckle as I move to stand again. Pulling my shirt off, I toss it on the floor. Her eyes are fixated on my body as she slowly takes in my chest.

Scooting closer, her warm soft hands find my chest, and she slowly traces the tips of her fingers over each of my tattoo designs. "You're so sexy," she tells me. Goosebumps cover my whole body as her touch lights a fire inside me. "I wanna trace every single one," she states.

"Okay." My voice comes out husky and rough.

"With my tongue." Her eyes lift to mine as a dirty little smirk takes over her pretty pink lips.

I groan, my cock becoming harder than stone. Ellie may look sweet and innocent, and back in the day, she was...but now? She is strong, confident, and knows what she wants. I'm so honored she allowed me back into her life, and to be someone she loves. I will never take this second chance for granted.

"Want some help?" she asks, looking down at my cock straining against my jeans.

"Please," I choke out. I'll give her soft and sweet, I'll make love to her any time, any day, but having her take control like this? *Hottest thing ever.*

She makes quick work of my pants until they pool around my ankles. I slip my feet out, kicking them to the side and standing there naked, cock pointing right at my girl waiting desperately for her touch.

"Can I be honest with you, Jax?" she asks, wrapping her hand firmly around my cock, giving it a few pumps.

"Always," I moan, my eyes rolling back as she smears the pre-cum over the tip.

"I love to be dominated. I love giving up control, and letting the ones I love bring me pleasure. And everyone, Rain, Chase, Brody, and Theo, they are all very dominant in the bedroom. I fucking love it. But sometimes, I wanna be in control. With you, Jax, I get that piece of me back. So, will you be a good boy and let me ride you until we're both hot, sweaty messes?"

Sweet mother of god, this woman is fucking perfect.

"God, yes," I moan as she takes me into her mouth, swallowing me whole before pulling back.

"Then get your sexy ass on the bed, Jax."

I scramble to do what she says, laying down on my back, my cock aching for her. She moves until she's kneeling over me, her pussy hovering over my cock. "We don't need to have rough sex for anyone to be in control." She lowers herself so that her wet folds meet the underside of my cock. I hiss at the contact, my hips jerking up to meet her. "Lay back, relax, and let me make you feel good."

"I wanna make you feel good too," I say, my breathing is already choppy.

She gives me a wicked grin that sends a jolt of excitement through me. "Oh, trust me, Jax, I'll feel good." Ellie rubs herself against me. "Real good."

Leaning over, Ellie kisses me softly before grabbing my cock. She rubs the tip against her slit, driving me crazy. "So, do you want me, Jax? Do you want me to ride this thick cock?"

"So bad," I whimper, and she takes pity on me as she sits up, and sinks her hot core around me. "Fuck, Ellie," I moan, my hands gripping her hips as she sits there, adjusting to my size.

"Jax," she hisses. "Fuck, all of you, all three of your cocks grew from snakes to fucking anacondas."

I can't help but chuckle. "We're all grown up now, baby."

"And I am not mad about that," she groans as she starts to slide up and down.

She looks like an angel. Her hair fans around her face as she leans over me, bracing herself on my chest. "You're so perfect," I breathe as she picks up the pace.

"So are you," she pants, her breasts swaying with each bounce of her hips. "And so is this cock."

Her pussy is wet, hot, and I'm gonna try my hardest to last long enough for her to use my body for her pleasure. But I don't know if I'm going to be able to. She's intoxicating and addicting, a drug I never want to be rid of.

"Fuck, fuck, fuck," she chants as she rides me faster and faster. She leans back, her hands on my thighs, and this beautiful angel has her head tipping back. "Help me, Jax," she begs. "Move my hips for me."

Gritting my teeth as pleasure courses through my veins, I grab a hold of her ass, getting a good grip before I start to guide her back and forth on my cock.

"Yes, Jax. Yes, like that," she moans. "Fuck, that feels so good."

Sweat lines my brow as I concentrate on keeping this pace, this position, not wanting her to miss any of her pleasure.

"You are so perfect, Ellie," I growl, a familiar tingle taking over.

"Fuck me, Jax, please," she says as she leans back over me, taking up the position from before. "I need to cum, make me cum." Her eyes are wide and frantic, her body has a beautiful glow. Her hair is a mess, and she has never looked so gorgeous.

Wanting to please my girl, I tighten my grip on her hips, and start to thrust up into her with everything I have. "Oh, Jax," she moans. "Don't stop."

Never. I pound up into her like a jackhammer, sweet and slow, and long gone.

She yells my name as her nails dig into my skin, and when I bring my thumb up and over her clit, she explodes. Leaning over, she bites into my pec, screaming out her release as her pussy chokes me, demanding my release too. I follow after her, thrusting into her a few more times before pumping jets of cum deep inside her. "Ellie," I moan, everything feeling right in the world.

We lay like that for a while, just catching our breath. I run my hand up and down her back as she snuggles into me.

"You're perfect too, Jax," she says, her voice sleepy and low. "Can you clean me up? I'm too tired to move. It's okay if I fall asleep, I trust you." I smile, my heart clenching as my eyes water. Kissing the top of her head, I roll her over onto her back when she falls asleep.

"How did it go?" Brody asks after I cleaned Ellie and tucked her in.

"It was amazing." I grin as he pulls me into his arms.

"Was it all sweet and romantic?" He grins.

"Yes," I chuckle. "You know, she makes a sexy little dom."

Brody's brow rises. "Really?" he asks, looking over to our sleeping girl. "Maybe I should recruit her for some sessions."

"Brody," I growl, nipping at his bottom lip.

He chuckles, nipping mine back. "Come on, big boy, let's get some sleep. We have another long day tomorrow."

We both climb into bed, Ellie smushed in between us. With one last kiss to Brody's lips, we fall asleep. I have no nightmares, only dreams of a beautiful blonde who stole my heart at the mere age of ten. She is my world, my heart, my life. And with her and Brody by my side, everything will be okay.

Chapter Thirty-Two

ELLIE

"CAN TODAY BE OVER ALREADY?" I mutter as we sit in the courtroom waiting for the judge.

Tim is already here, and his lawyer is working his ass off to keep Tim's attention away from us. Brody caught his eye the moment we walked in, and Tim earned a middle finger in return. The idea of being in a room with him for any amount of time at any distance makes me feel gross. I could really use a shower to wash this feeling away.

"Soon, sweet girl, soon," Theo says, wrapping an arm around my shoulder, pulling me to his side.

"I hated leaving Lilly this morning," I sigh. "She was so upset she couldn't go to her friend's birthday party. I wish I could be with her and take her mind off of it."

"I know, but her friend got sick, and they had to cancel. I'm sure they will reschedule," Jax says. I look up at him and smile. *My sweet man.*

Last night was amazing. Being with him again for the first time after a long time apart felt right. He gives me a grin that tells me he's thinking about the same thing.

As much as I love giving control to the people I trust while in the bedroom, it was empowering to be the one in control that way. Jax feels most comfortable when someone else is in control, even if it's simple instructions. It didn't make it feel any less sweet and loving.

"I feel like I haven't been spending much time with her lately. With all of this, I just haven't been myself, and I know she can see that." She's been asking me a lot lately why I'm so sad. I hate lying to her, but she's way too young to understand any of this.

"After today, everything will go back to the way it was for the most part," Jax says. "Only this time, life will bring new and happy changes."

"All rise for the honorable Judge Mathews," the bailiff announces as the judge enters the room. We all stand as he takes his seat.

"Thank you, everyone. Welcome back. I'm sure all of you are eager to get this settled, and that's exactly what we will be doing today. I will be giving my verdict, the time for plea deals has passed and my word today will be final," the judge informs us.

I look up at Theo, and he gives me a small smile.

"First, the tape that was presented to the court of Mr. Hightower and Miss Tatum was looked over by our experts, and it has been determined that the video was not tampered with in any way. The video is as is. As for the paternity test that Mr. Hightower requested regarding Lilianna Tatum, I have the results here."

My gut turns, my leg bounces, and my hands start to shake. I trust that I was pregnant before graduation night, but my mind still wondered the last few days with all the 'what ifs' and 'maybes'. *My life hasn't been easy for years, why start now?*

Theo asked me if I was going to get the guys tested at the same time as Tim. I told him no because they didn't ask for it. We've talked about it before, and they don't care who helped make Lilly because she is all of theirs, 100%.

The judge looks over the piece of paper, looking it over before directing this attention to Tim. "Timothy Hightower. Your probability of being the biological father to Lilianna Tatum is 0.00%."

348

"Fuck yes!" Chase shouts. "I knew it."

"Enough!" the judge says, raising a brow at Chase.

"Sorry," Chase says, giving him a grimace.

Zero percent. He's not her father. My guys are. Tears fill my eyes, and I hold back a sob of relief. This isn't over yet. We still have the verdict and Brody's case after.

I look over, and they all have beaming smiles of relief. Rain gives me a watery smile and mouths, 'I love you.' I mouth it back, and turn my attention to the judge again.

"Now, for my verdict. In the case of the state of South Carolina v.s. Timothy Hightower, I Judge Mathews, finds Timothy Hightower guilty on the charges of rape and sexual assault with intent. You are hereby sentenced to twenty years in prison with chance of parole after ten years of time served..."

I don't hear the rest. The judge's words ring loud in my ears. *Guilty.* Twenty years in prison. He's going to jail. He was found guilty. I no longer have to live in fear of him trying this again, on me or anyone else. I'm free. I'm fucking *free*.

All the times I thought for even a moment that maybe I did something wrong, that maybe if I did something different, then everything would have been different.

All these years of trauma. Years of nightmares and pain because of that monster. Now he's going to where he belongs. My hands find my face as I let out a sob of relief.

Everyone who's here for me *whoops* and cheers. My parents, my friends, Chase, and Brody. Jax and Theo hold me while I cry, telling me how amazing I am, how brave I was, and how much they love me.

Is this real? Will I open my eyes and this all have been a dream?

Screaming has my head snapping over to Tim's side. His father is yelling at the lawyer saying that he's going to sue him for failing to do his job. Tim's mother is sitting there crying, repeating, "my baby, my baby," over and over. The whole family is a joke. But the biggest joke is Tim. His eyes lock with mine, and whatever state of shock he was in breaks.

"You!" he roars at me, his eyes filled with pure venom. "You stupid whore. You think you're better than me?" He thumps his chest. "You're nothing! You're just a dirty, used cunt who deserved what you got. You're fucking lucky your stupid boyfriend was there." He lets out this demented laugh. "Because I would have done it again. It was my fucking right!"

"Get him out of my court," the judge booms. A group of cops come rushing in. They grab onto Tim who tries to punch one of them as they drag him out of the courtroom kicking and screaming.

"How could you do this?" his mom asks me, tears streaming down her face.

That's it. I will never again let someone make me second guess what I survived. I stand up and walk over to her. "Your son is a monster. I don't know how you raised him, but by the way you're reacting, like he's not in the wrong, also makes you guilty. You failed at being a parent. You should have raised your son to treat women with respect, not that he was owed what he wanted from them. I'll pray that maybe someday, you will realize what kind of person he is." With that, I turn around and take my seat again. Tim's dad is following in his son's lead and being dragged out of the room in cuffs as his wife follows behind him crying.

"I would like to apologize for the outburst," the judge says. "Mr. Creed, I'm going to do things a little differently. I'm gonna make this simple when it comes to your charges. They are being dismissed. It was clear from the video and how Mr. Hightower reacted that if you did not intervene, then Mr. Hightower would have tried to assault Miss Tatum again. However, I highly recommend you take anger management classes."

"Thank you, sir," Brody says, but I can tell from the look on his face and his grumbling to himself that he's not too happy about the classes. He looks back at his lawyer and nods his head in approval of the judge's decision.

We all file out of the courtroom as happy chatter floats throughout our group of people.

"Fuck yeah, baby!" Chase cheers as he picks me up and spins me around. I burst into laughter. He sets me down, then crashes his lips to mine.

"My turn," Rain says, prying her best friend off of me. "I'm so proud of you, baby," she says with the biggest smile, her green eyes shining bright with love.

"I don't think I could have done this without all of you," I tell them truthfully. I pulled a lot of strength from them all to get me through this time.

"I think you could have," Jax says, standing next to Rain. "You don't realize how amazing you are, Ellie. You're strong and brave. You can handle anything life throws at you."

"Let's hope life fucks off for a while and stops tossing shit at my girl," Brody growls, stepping closer to me. I look up at him, my breath catching at the intense look in his eyes. "You are a fucking warrior goddess, Star. Never let anyone tell you you're less than that. I'm sorry I was a dick."

"You're more like a raging asshole," Chase sings songs.

Brody chuckles. "That too. And I can't promise I won't be stubborn or an ass sometimes."

"All the time," Chase adds.

"Would you, please, fuck right off!?" Brody sneers at his best friend.

"I can fuck something..." Chase gives me a dirty look and I smile, shaking my head.

Brody looks back at me. "But I can promise I will protect you, love you, and I will fucking murder anyone who tries to hurt what's mine. Do you understand me?"

My heart flutters, and my breathing hitches. "Yes." I release my breath before he cups my face and kisses me with so much love my knees give out.

His arm snakes around my waist, holding me up.

"If you are all done sucking her face like a leech, can I please see my best friend?" Val calls from behind.

I giggle against Brody's lips as he pulls back with a growl. He nips my lower lip, giving me a look that tells me there will be more of this later.

Is it a bad time to be turned on? Yes, probably, but I don't care. My rapist is going to be behind bars, leaving me free to live my life with my lovers. I feel like a million pounds has been lifted off my shoulders. For the first time in years, I can really breathe.

"Girl," Val says, pulling me into a tight hug. "You did it!"

"We are so happy," Tabitha says, moving next to Val.

"If he ended up walking free, you know we would have made his life a living hell, right?" Lexie asks.

"Yeah, like tell the whole world what a sick fucker he is. No one would have gotten within ten feet of him." Val nods.

"Thanks, guys. I love you. And thank you for being here for me."

"Where else would we be?" Cooper says, and I give him a hug. "You're not just our best friend, Ellie, you're family. We would go to war for you, always."

My eyes sting at their words. I will never understand how I got so lucky to have amazing friends like them.

"Come on, sweet girl. There's a little lady who is excited to see her mama," Theo says.

"Meet us in two hours," I tell my friends. "At Bill's Diner to celebrate."

We all say goodbye, and they leave. My parents are next in line to tell me how happy they are, how much they love me, and how strong I was. That they are proud to call me their daughter, and how they will always be there for me.

I miss having them close, but I'm so glad they are able to come out here when they can. They were my rock while I was doing my best to be a single mom struggling with PTSD and other things that were brought on by my trauma.

They say goodbye, telling me they wish they could come out and celebrate, but they have a flight to catch soon.

"I gotta go see my dad. It's been awhile, and I just wanna check in on him. I haven't had time to stop by much this past week with court and everything," Brody says as we get out to the cars. "We'll meet you there. Is that okay?"

"Of course." I smile up at him. "See you soon."

Brody gives me a quick kiss before heading over to his car. "I'll go with him," Jax says, placing a kiss on my cheek before following after him.

"What about us?" Chase pouts. "We want kisses!"

"Yeah," Rain agrees, giving me a pout that mirrors Chase's.

"Then come get one," I laugh. They both grin, each giving me a kiss that lets me feel just how much they love me.

"We're gonna head home and take a shower, then we'll meet you guys there too. How about a big sleepover in the living room tonight?" Rain asks.

"Sounds perfect." I smile, and they leave too.

"Ellie," Theo says. "There's something I wanna do real quick. Do you mind if I drop you off at home?"

"Yeah, of course." I smile. "I think I need some time alone with Lilly for a little bit before we go out. I just need her right now."

"You're amazing, sweet girl. Don't ever forget it," he tells me, cupping my face and kissing me softly.

"And so are all of you," I reply, hugging him tightly as I bury my face into his chest.

It's going to take a little while for reality to kick in. *But is life really starting to look up? Will I finally be able to be happy without something in my way?*

Chapter Thirty-Three

THEO

AS I DRIVE to the cemetery, I have the biggest smile on my face. Kind of an odd reaction when you're going to visit your dead wife at her grave. But seeing that monster who has hurt my girl so much get sentenced to twenty years in prison was sweet, sweet justice. Personally, I think sick people like him shouldn't even be worth the time or effort to feed and care for.

I just hope that Ellie can finally have the happiness she deserves without all the obstacles in her way. If there was ever someone who was the most deserving person to be loved and happy, it's her.

Leaving her right now is hard, but with the hearing, I haven't had the time to come and visit in a while. It's been eating at me because it's something I do weekly if I'm able to. And I'm almost *always* able to.

I love that Ellie is so supportive of it. Some might think it's weird that I still visit so often when I've already moved on, but Kristen wasn't just my wife, she was my best friend. We grew up together, and she was always there for me when I needed her. I know she likes that I keep her updated on what's going on in my life as well as our son's.

Also, I never want the memory of her to slip away from

Toby's mind completely. I want him to know everything there is to know about his mother. I will always answer any questions and talk about her when he asks.

When I get to the cemetery, the parking lot is pretty empty. Not surprising for noon on a weekday. Grabbing the bouquet of fresh red roses, I get out of the car and make my way over to her grave.

"Hey, Kristen," I greet her headstone as I sit down in front of it. It's a pretty one with her name, a nice quote from one of her favorite books, and a beautiful photo of her on our wedding day. "Sorry, I haven't been by in a while, but remember the hearing I told you that Ellie had coming up? Well, the verdict was today." Putting my chin on my hand as I lean my elbow on my leg, I look at her photo as if she was right here with me. Letting out a deep breath, I continue. "It was hard on her. My heart broke seeing how much pain she was in, and I wasn't able to do anything for her. But Kris, she was so fucking strong." I smile, my eyes stinging as tears start to form. "She never once complained or wanted to give up. She's a survivor, a warrior. There were times they tried to break her, but they didn't succeed. They didn't know who they were messing with. And in the end, she got her justice."

I sit up, rubbing my hands down my face. "He's going away for a long time, and he won't ever be able to hurt her again." I tell her all about Toby and the things he's learning in school. How Lilly is his whole world and that I'm glad he has a little sister to love and protect. I've already told her how Lilly calls me Dada and I know she's happy that I'm able to be someone so important to a little girl that didn't have that at the time. She's an amazing little girl, and I've grown to love her like my own. Toby, Ellie, and Lilly are my life, my world, and I'd die for them all.

Looking at my phone, I see a text from Ellie asking if every-thing is okay. Shit, it's one pm. I've been here for an hour. Time sometimes gets away from me when I come here.

"Well, I gotta go, love. But next time, I'll bring Toby. I know he misses you and has a lot to tell you himself. We're going out to celebrate this win, because this is something to scream from the rooftops," I tell her, standing up and dusting my dress pants off. A tug of emotion pulls at my heart as I think of my next words. "I want to thank you, Kris. Thank you for always watching over me and Toby, making sure we're happy and safe. But I also want to thank you for sending Ellie into my life. I know I told you back when you asked me to find someone who can love me that I didn't want to, that I didn't think I could find love again, but you were right. You were always right. She makes me happy, so fucking happy, after years of hurting and feeling lost. She filled a part of my heart that was empty for so long. And I have you to thank for that. I love you, Kristen. I always will, and sharing my heart with someone else will never change that, but thank you...for being so fucking amazing by wanting this for me. I miss you." Tears slip free and I have to take a few deep breaths to hold myself together.

Kissing my hand, I place it on her headstone. Thunder crashes in the distance. Looking up, I see big, dark, angry storm clouds heading toward Silver Valley from Spring Meadows.

"Gotta go, love, don't wanna get caught in this rain."

I run back to my car and head home. Hopefully the storm will pass soon.

JAX

"Fucking rain. Of course there's a storm right now, not like we can catch a break or anything," Brody grumbles as the first raindrops hit the windshield of the car as we turn onto his father's street. We stopped at our place to get changed into casual clothes before heading over.

"I'm sure it will pass quickly. After we check on your dad, make sure everything is good, then we can meet everyone at Bill's Diner," I tell him, switching on the windshield wipers.

He feels bad that he hasn't been by to check on his dad in over a week. With the hearing and everything, he's been putting Lilly and Ellie first. I gotta admit, I'm pretty proud of him. I like his dad. Deep down, he's not a bad man, but he let his addiction take over. Instead of taking the help that Brody tried to offer him, he allowed himself to drink his pain away and stay with his horrible witch of a wife.

He should be the one to care for Brody, to be there for him when he needs his dad. To love and support him. Brody shouldn't have to be the parent in this situation, but that's how it's been for a long time now.

Brody turns to me with a smile. "I wanna celebrate. I wanna buy my girls lunch, hell, buy them the whole fucking world, they deserve it. He's gonna be locked up, Jax! That cock-sucking-mother-fucking-sack-of-shit is gonna be behind bars for a long time. And I know this is messed up, but a part of me hopes he drops the fucking soap." He grins.

I can't help the laughter that bubbles up. "I hope he gets what he deserves. And getting a roommate who hates rapists would be the cherry on top," I tell him as we pull up to the gate. I roll down the window, rain drops wetting my skin as I punch in the code.

The gate slides open, and I continue up the drive. When the house comes into view, I get this feeling of unease, like something isn't right. His father's car isn't in the garage, but parked by the front door on the grass.

"What the hell?" Brody asks, leaning forward to get a better look. "I swear, I will kill him if he was out drinking and driving," Brody hisses. "If he wants to stay at home and drink his life away, that's one thing, but fuck if I'll put up with risking someone else's life."

Shutting the engine off, we both get out and run up the steps to the front door, trying to avoid getting wet as much as we can.

Brody unlocks the door, and the moment he opens it, we're hit with a wave of something foul.

"What the fuck is that?" Brody gags, covering his mouth with his hand.

I do the same, the smell of rotting meat filling my nose. Something is wrong, *really* wrong.

"Dad!" Brody yells into the eerily quiet house. "Dad, I'm home!"

"Brody." I start to follow him. "Maybe we should go." The feeling to run, to take the man that I love with all my heart out of this house, is overwhelmingly strong. "Brody." I grab his arm, trying to pull him back, to stop him from going into the living room and seeing whatever is causing that smell.

He ignores me, yanking his arm out of my grasp. "Dad!" he shouts again. We stand in the living room entrance and stop, frozen in our tracks. "Dad..." Brody says with a little more caution as our eyes land on his father face down on the floor.

"Don't," I plead, grabbing his arm again, my hand gripping him tightly. "Please, don't go in there." My voice breaks.

"Let go," he demands, pushing me back. I stumble a few steps and watch him rush over to his dad.

"Dad. God, Dad, look at you," Brody says as he puts his hands under his dad's side. He grunts as he lifts his dad's heavy body, rolling his father onto his back.

I gasp, my eyes going wide as I choke back a sob.

"Dad, come on, wake up." Brody taps his dad's face. "Don't make me carry you up stairs to the shower."

"Brody," I whisper, tears filling my eyes. "Baby, move away from him."

Brody looks up at me in confusion. I know he sees what I see, but I think some part of his mind is blocking it out, refusing to accept reality.

His body is bloated. His skin is a sickening mixture of different colors including green, black, brown, and red. His eyes are wide and vacant. His mouth and nose have blood leaking from them, and there's vomit on the floor.

"Brody," I try again, tears spilling from my eyes. My heart breaks into a million pieces. *Why? Why now when life was just about to be perfect again? What has this man done to deserve all these horrible things to keep happening to him?* "Brody, baby, I don't think..." The words feel wrong on my tongue. "I don't think he's alive."

"What!?" Brody shouts. "Of course he is, he passed out from drinking too much. Come on, Jax, help me carry him to the shower. He just needs to wash off and sober up." *Fuck.* Fuck, fuck, fuck.

"Brody, look at him. Can't you see that this isn't normal?" I try, feeling like my world is crumbling in.

"Help me!" he shouts, ignoring me, trying to pick up his dad's body. "Just help me, please. He just needs to shower, that's all. Come on, Dad, wake up. Show him you just had a little bit too much to drink. Dad?" He shakes his dad, slapping his face. "Wake up. Please, Dad, just wake up."

"Brody," I croak.

"Shut up!" he roars, tears welling in his eyes. "Shut up, okay? He's fine, he's gonna be fine."

Fuck, what do I do? My hands start to shake as I take my phone out of my pocket and call 911.

"911, what's your emergency?" the operator answers.

"H-hi," I stammer. "I need help."

"What's going on?"

"He's dead. I-I think he's dead."

"No!" Brody roars as he drops to his knees, unable to hold his dad's body anymore. "No. No, he's not, he's not."

A sob rips from my chest as I try to answer whatever the operator asked me. All I can do is give her the address. She tells me someone is on their way, and I hang up.

With shaky steps, I go over to my love, my heart. "Brody, come with me," I tell him, leaning over to place my hand on his arm.

"Fuck off!" he yells, bringing his elbow back and nailing me in the nose.

"Fuck," I hiss, my hand shooting up to catch the gush of blood.

I can't get through to him. He's not going to listen to me;

nothing I say will get him to hear me. But maybe *she* will be able to get through to him. I hate to do this, I hate to call her. It should be a happy time. A time to celebrate this win, to laugh, smile, and plan for the future. But he needs me, he needs us and I have to.

Finding Ellie's name in my contacts, I press dial. It rings a few times before she picks up.

"Hey, babe. You guys ready?" she asks, her voice laughing at whatever Theo was saying a moment before. "We're just about to leave."

"Ellie," my voice breaks as I break.

"Jax?" All humor vanishes from her voice. "What's going on? What's wrong?"

"He's dead."

"What?! Who's dead, Jax?" she asks, sounding panicked.

"Brody's dad. Fuck, we just found his body. Baby, he needs you. He won't listen to me."

There's a pause, and for a moment, I think the call ended. "I'm on my way," she says. Her voice cracks with her next word, "Jax?"

"Yeah?"

"I love you. Both of you," she says before hanging up.

I look at Brody, hunched over his dad's body, still trying to wake him up. I fall to my knees, images of my mother, the car, her laying dead on the ground flashing through my mind.

Why do bad things keep happening?

Chapter Thirty-Four

ELLIE

"THEO! She can not wear that to dinner," I laugh as Lilly comes out of the bedroom wearing PJ pants, a tutu, and a swim top.

"Why not? I think she looks adorable. She wants to make a fashion statement," he playfully protests with a grin as my phone rings.

"Please, help her pick something else," I laugh, looking at my phone to see that it's Jax.

"Hey, babe. You guys ready?" I ask, my voice still full of amusement. "We're just about to leave."

"Ellie..." he answers, his voice sounding so broken. My heart sinks, the smile slipping from my face.

"Jax?" I ask, my heart pounding in my chest. "What's going on? What's wrong?"

"He's dead." My stomach drops as my knees start to buckle.

"What?! Who's dead, Jax?" I ask quickly, my voice panicked.

"Brody's dad. Fuck, we just found his body. Baby, he needs you. He won't listen to me," he begs, his voice sounding distraught and helpless.

No! Fuck, no. Not Brody, not his dad. He's just starting to come around. Fuck, this is going to destroy him. "I'm on my

363

way," I answer, my voice cracking. "Jax," I add, needing him to know this.

"Yeah?"

"I love you. Both of you," I tell him and hang up.

"Is this better? I still think she looked fine before," Theo says with a smile as they both come out of the bedroom. "Ellie, what's wrong?" he asks, his smile dropping as he takes in my tear stained eyes.

"Mama? Why you crying?"

"I need to go," I tell him, rushing over to my purse to grab my keys. "Can you watch her?"

"Ellie, go where? What's going on? Who was that on the phone?" he asks, grabbing my shoulders to keep me from running out the door.

I look down at Lilly who's looking up at me with her big, blue eyes that are swirling with concern. She hates when I'm sad.

"It's B-r-o-d-y," I spell, not wanting Lilly to know who I'm talking about. Brody is one of her new favorite people, and I don't want to worry her. "Something happened, and it's not good. I need to get to him."

"Shit, okay." He nods. "But you need to take a moment to breathe and calm down. I don't want you driving like this."

I close my eyes, nodding as I take in a shaky deep breath. It doesn't do much to help. My body's still vibrating with adrenaline, but my mind is a little bit clearer.

"Lilly, baby. Mama has to go out, but Ace and Fire will be over. We're gonna eat at home, okay?"

"Okay," she says.

I look at Theo. "Call them, tell them to come here. I don't want them to see whatever is going on at his dad's place."

He nods, and gives me a quick kiss.

"Be safe," he calls down the hall as I take off running.

My hands shake as I get the key in the ignition. The engine roars to life, and I put it in reverse, peeling out of the driveway.

It's raining as I drive down the highway toward Brody's dad's place. Turning on my windshield wipers, I curse the universe. It's always one thing after the other, *always*. Why can't we catch a damn break?! *Haven't we all suffered enough in our life? Why can't we just be happy, be with the ones we love and just be able to breath for once?*

My mind is racing with so many thoughts, I have to shake my head to be able to concentrate. Frustrated tears fill my eyes, and I angrily blink them away.

I know Brody didn't have the best relationship with his dad, but he did love him. He was the only one who showed him any kind of love, even if it wasn't always the right kind.

I don't know what they walked in on, but I know it's nothing good. Brody is going to blame himself for this, I just know it, and my heart breaks. It aches knowing someone I love, more than life, is hurting immensely right now.

Whatever happened today, it's going to stick with him, eat away at him until there's nothing left.

If we let it.

Jax and I, plus Chase and Rain, won't let him destroy himself. I just got him back. I can't lose him again.

The thought of that makes a sob slip free. "Fuck!" I scream as I slam my hand against the steering wheel.

The rain is coming down hard now. Fat raindrops crash against the windshield. Slowing the car down, I struggle to see the road.

After I get over this hill, I'm going to need to pull over until the worst of this is over.

Pressing my foot on the pedal, I give it a little more gas to help me get up the slippery slope, forcing myself to focus on driving.

We're going be there for him, show him just how much he's loved, that he means the world to all of us. That he is wanted. *We* are his family. He doesn't need anyone else but us. He *will* get through this, we'll make sure of it.

As I reach the top of the hill, I get ready to pull over to safety, but the universe has different plans.

My eyes widen, and I let out an ear piercing scream as a truck appears out of nowhere in my lane and heads straight for me. I yank the steering wheel in an effort to get out of the way.

But is it going to be enough?

To be continued in Secrets Embraced – Silver Valley University Book 3, coming late Fall 2022.

Books By Alisha

EMERALD LAKE PREP – SERIES:

Book One: Second Chances (February 2021)

Book Two: Into The Unknown (May 2021)

Book Three: Shattered Pieces (September 2021)

Book Four: Redemption Found (March 2022)

BLOOD EMPIRE – SERIES:

Book One: Rising Queen (July 2021)

Book Two: Crowned Queen (December 2021)

Book Three: Savage Queen (Coming 2022)

SILVER VALLEY UNIVERSITY – SERIES:

Book One: Hidden Secrets (January 2022)

Book Two: Secrets Revealed (May 2022)

ANGELIC ACADEMY – SERIES:

Book One: Tainted Wings (Summer 2022)

STANDALONES

We Are Worthy- A sweet and steamy omegaverse. (2022)

Thank You

I would love to give a big thank you to anyone who has supported me on this journey. A big thank you to every single person who helped bring Ellie's story to life. Without each one of you, this book would not be possible.

I'm also beyond grateful for Jessica, Jennifer, and Amy. You ladies are more than just my Alphas, you're family now! Thank you for all the time and energy you put into Secrets Revealed and for helping it become the awesome book that it is! I don't think I would have had as much fun writing it without you three! Can't wait to make way more books with you! And a big shout out to Tamara. Thanks for being there for me, and helping me with everything you do, you're the best wifey!

And to Nikki. Thank you for the hours you spend with me, planning and making this series the best is can be. You're amazing, and I'm so lucky to have your help.

Many thanks to my Beta and ARC teams. You all helped me make my book even better, and I look forward to sending you way more work in the future.

And finally, thank you to all my readers. It was an honor to write this book for you. Thank you for giving my new book series a chance.

About the Author

Writer, Alisha Williams, lives in Alberta, Canada, with her husband and her two headstrong kids, and three kitties. When she isn't writing or creating her own gorgeous graphic content, she loves to read books by her favorite authors.

Writing has been a lifelong dream of hers, and this book was made despite the people who prayed for it to fail, but because Alisha is not afraid to go for what she wants, she has proven that dreams do come true.

Wanna see what all her characters look like, hear all the latest gossip about her new books or even get a chance to become a part of one of her teams? Join her readers group on Facebook here - Naughty Queens. Or find her author's page here - Alisha Williams Author

Of course, she also has an Instagram account to show all her cool graphics, videos and more book related goodies - alishawilliamsauthor

Sign up for Alisha's Newsletter

Got TikTok? Follow alishawilliamsauthor

Printed in Great Britain
by Amazon

16133535R00230